After Hours

Also by Lynn Erickson
in Large Print:

In the Cold
Without a Trace

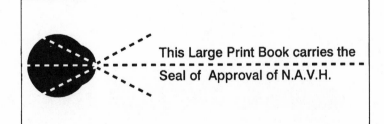

This Large Print Book carries the
Seal of Approval of N.A.V.H.

After Hours

Lynn Erickson

Published in 2004 by arrangement with The Berkley Publishing Group, a division of Penguin Group (USA) Inc.

Wheeler Large Print Softcover.

The text of this Large Print edition is unabridged.
Other aspects of the book may vary from the original edition.

Set in 16 pt. Plantin by Liana M. Walker.

Printed in the United States on permanent paper.

Library of Congress Cataloging-in-Publication Data

Erickson, Lynn.
    After hours / Lynn Erickson.
        p. cm.
    ISBN 1-58724-810-7 (lg. print : sc : alk. paper)
    1. Women environmentalists — Fiction. 2. Murder
victims' families — Fiction. 3. Bodyguards — Fiction.
4. Widows — Fiction. 5. Large type books. I. Title.
PS3555.R45A69 2004
813'.54—dc22   2004057159

This book is dedicated to Tom and Debbie McKibbon, real Colorado ranchers, who helped with all the details, and to Lucas, who lives in the 6th Precinct and put us onto our moonlighting cop.

National Association for Visually Handicapped
serving the partially seeing

As the Founder/CEO of NAVH, the only national health agency solely devoted to those who, although not totally blind, have an eye disease which could lead to serious visual impairment, I am pleased to recognize Thorndike Press* as one of the leading publishers in the large print field.

Founded in 1954 in San Francisco to prepare large print textbooks for partially seeing children, NAVH became the pioneer and standard setting agency in the preparation of large type.

Today, those publishers who meet our standards carry the prestigious "Seal of Approval" indicating high quality large print. We are delighted that Thorndike Press is one of the publishers whose titles meet these standards. We are also pleased to recognize the significant contribution Thorndike Press is making in this important and growing field.

Lorraine H. Marchi, L.H.D.
Founder/CEO
NAVH

* Thorndike Press encompasses the following imprints: Thorndike, Wheeler, Walker and Large Print Press.

ONE

When she walked up to the podium he watched her, and when she began to talk he listened.

Up to now the black-tie affair had been the usual parade of big names giving rah-rah speeches, and fire chiefs with florid Irish faces squeezing out a tear or two. *Hey,* he chided himself, *this is a fund-raiser for the United Firefighters Association. A goddamn worthy cause. Stop being so cynical.*

The scene was a banquet room of the Marriott Marquis Hotel in Manhattan. A sea of white linen and crystal and fine china and men in tuxedos and women in gowns. Lots of skin showing. And legions of firemen, all in uniform, with Medals of Valor on their chests. The press was there, too, reporters and banks of video cameras and microphones thrust forward on poles. It was pleasantly cool in the large room, the air-conditioning unobtrusive but welcome. Outside, the June evening was sultry.

Ex-mayor Guiliani was there. A couple of movie stars, all the movers and shakers. The bigwigs of the NPS, the Nature Preservation Society, were there, because the NPS was sponsoring this fund-raiser for the firefighters.

The cause was so worthy the superintendent of police had provided security free of charge for the event. And that's where he came in: Detective Nick Sinestra, 6th Precinct, moonlighting as a security guard.

He'd volunteered for the duty, something he'd been doing more of lately. When he'd been married to Gwen, he'd rarely worked overtime if he could help it, but that was when he'd had someone to go home to. And tonight was a big deal, a perfect opportunity, what with all the celebrities present.

A perfect opportunity. Yeah.

The woman up at the podium. Portia Carr Wells. Everybody had heard of her, but she rarely stepped into the spotlight as she had tonight.

"Hey, buddy, anything up?" It was Gil Howard, his partner, who'd also volunteered, but in his case, he needed the money. He had three kids to raise.

"Nah, nothing." Nick was posted at one set of double doors of the banquet room. Gil was at the other set. There were six more policemen stationed at various entry points, including the kitchen door and the banks of elevators outside the room.

Gil moved back to his post, and Nick

looked at Portia Wells. She was leaning forward a little to reach the microphone, her hands on either side of the podium. Her voice was soft and melodic, and he realized the entire room was hushed, listening to her.

"As you know," she was saying, "my husband Gary was president of the NPS. And, as you also know, he died last year. I'm only here because he can't be. But I know he'd thank you all for coming, and he'd be proud to raise money for the brave men and women of the United Firefighters."

He watched and he listened. A camera's flash went off just below the podium, and he blinked to banish the white spots from in front of his eyes.

She was a pretty lady. A quiet, understated beauty. Blond-streaked hair falling to her shoulders, light eyes — he couldn't tell what color — and skin very smooth, gold-tinted. She wore a simple black dress in a soft, drapey fabric, a low V of a neck and a — he didn't know what women called it — wraparound at the waist. Not much jewelry. Kind of plain but classy. Yeah, a classy lady.

"We have an ulterior motive, I have to admit," she went on. "We ask that you read the brochure about the NPS on your tables. Maybe you'll be interested in our cause, and maybe you'll donate what you can to us. We are a nonprofit organization, and eighty-six percent of our donations go directly to preserving our natural heritage."

Sure, he thought, *get in your propaganda. Use the forum to push your cause. That's what this fund-raiser is all about, isn't it?*

But, still, he listened because her voice was so lovely, so persuasive, so compelling, as if she were directing her words at him and him alone instead of a room full of 300 people.

She came off as a caring person. A widow, he knew, a widow at thirty-six, when her husband had been killed in a car accident in their home state of Colorado. Her mother was Judith Carr, a once-famous actress who'd dropped out of sight under some sort of a cloud years ago. Her father was former UN ambassador Richard Carr. Because of her parents, Portia had been a darling of the press since her birth.

"Our mission is to preserve the diversity of flora and fauna of the earth by protecting the environment in which they live. As you all probably know, we acquire land if we can, to restrict development on it, but we also work closely with communities, businesses, and people like you. We have protected over twelve million acres in the United States and over eighty million outside of the States." She looked up from the podium and smiled. The glow on her face made her at once young and mischievous and intimately knowing. "But enough statistics. They're boring, aren't they?

"My husband Gary always thought so, and he always tried his best to make the NPS pertinent and . . . well, personal, I guess."

She sobered. "I can't think of a better combination of causes than the Nature Preservation Society and the United Firefighters Association. After all," she paused, her eyes scanning the crowd, and Nick felt her gaze brush him, raising tiny hairs on his arms, "we're both in the business of saving lives. Thank you very much, everybody, and please be generous to our brave firefighters. Thank you."

Applause. The movie star with the craggy face stood, clapping loudly, and then another person rose, then a table full of people, then the men from one firehouse, then the whole room, as if Portia Wells had been a maestro conducting a world-class symphony, one never before heard, or at least one never before played with such finesse.

She smiled again and ducked her head and tried to turn to leave the raised platform, but the master of ceremonies stepped up, took her hand, and held it high in triumph, like a sports champion.

He could see her mouth moving, a flush on her cheeks, an innocent humility. She was the kind of woman who could make a guy feel protective — the most dangerous kind. Yet she'd had the roomful of people in the palm of her hand like a pro.

11

Waiters were moving through the room pouring coffee, refilling wineglasses. The hum of conversation picked up as the emcee finally let Portia return to her table.

Nick watched her walk, saw her slide into the seat next to an elderly man, a slim, erect fellow with fine features and slicked-back white hair and a golf-course tan. Her new boyfriend? Jesus, the man was old enough to be her father. He'd have to find out who the escort was.

And all the time, Nick's eyes roved over the crowd, looking for an odd movement, an out-of-place sound, someone acting suspiciously. He did it unconsciously, automatically, and even though he was looking at Portia Wells, he would be able to pick up a false move anywhere in the room.

So would his partner Gil. He glanced over at Gil, impressive in his rented tux, tall and rangy and very dark-skinned, his hair still in dreadlocks from his last stint as an undercover drug dealer. He wondered if he looked as good as Gil, or if he looked as if he were an imposter in his formal attire.

He moved over toward Gil, motioned with a hand for him to approach. "Who's the guy with Portia Wells?"

Gil squinted. "The old dude?"

"Yeah."

"Don't know. Ask one of the waiters."

Nick waited for a chance, then stopped one

12

of the waiters and asked him.

"I don't have a clue."

"Can you find out for me?"

The waiter shrugged, and Nick reached into his pocket, peeled a twenty off a roll, and palmed it to the man. "Now can you get me the info?"

"Probably," the man replied, pocketing the bill.

"Thanks."

He hoped Gil wouldn't wonder at his uncharacteristic curiosity. Gil knew a lot about Nick; he knew about his failed marriage, he even knew the lurid truth about Gwen. He probably knew Nick better than anyone on earth. But he didn't know one important thing, and Nick didn't plan for him to find out.

The waiter came back. "Aaron Burkhart."

"Thanks, pal."

"Right." The man hurried on, a coffee carafe in his hand.

Aaron Burkhart. Who the hell was he?

He should know who this Burkhart was. Why hadn't the *Star Gazer* coached him on this guy? He could be important. But the tabloid's main focus was on Portia. They'd made that plain enough.

He shook off the small bite of guilt he felt every time he took one of the tabloid's assignments. It was harmless — finding out about celebrities for the well-known magazine. Providing information about where they'd be staying in Manhattan, what they'd be doing, what restaurants they frequented, where they shopped and got their hair done, what they ordered from room service. The kind of headlines and pictures people loved to see: "Famous Actress Boards Flying Saucer with Aliens." Stuff like that.

Police could find out those things easier than journalists. Sometimes all he had to do was call in a tip, and *Star Gazer* paparazzi would rush to the place and get their shots. Quick, easy, and lucrative.

It wasn't as if he were doing any real harm. Celebrities sucked up media coverage, thrived on it. Nick wasn't the first cop on the *Star Gazer* payroll; if he didn't do the job, someone else would.

So tonight his quarry was Portia Wells. Widow, famous daughter of famous parents, proposed president of the NPS, replacing her dead husband. Doer of good deeds, big money raiser for worthy causes. Pretty lady, classy lady.

The guilt gnawed at a place deep inside. He ignored the sensation, the way you ignored a pulled muscle that twinged when you moved a certain way. And you knew exactly what you'd done to pull the muscle, so you deserved the twinge.

He glanced at his watch: 10:30. The party would start to break up soon. So far he didn't have a damn thing to call into the *Star Gazer*. Sometimes that happened, and there wasn't anything to be done about it.

A few people were beginning to leave, passing Nick, nodding at him. He tried to look pleasant, but he'd been standing there for hours, mostly bored, his shiny black shoes too tight, and he was getting impatient.

He craned his neck to keep Portia Wells in sight. She was still sitting with the Burkhart character. People were coming up to her, speaking, shaking her hand. Firemen and their wives, a couple of TV anchormen, an actress, older and rail thin, with too much makeup but famous, very famous.

Nick eyed Gil over the people filing out the doors, held his arm up, and pointed to his watch. *Soon,* Gil mouthed.

His eye caught the movement before his brain registered it. A flurry, a voice raised. He zeroed in on the disruption, was gesturing to Gil and moving even before he knew what was happening. Moving against the crowd, trying to be polite, but shouldering past people.

A man — Nick had an impression of a thin, young man — was bending over Portia, too close, swaying drunkenly, his arm around her. Nick could see she was trying to pull away, and Aaron Burkhart was on his feet, a hand on the man's arm, his face angry.

"Okay," he heard Gil say, "the usual?"

15

"Sure, the usual."

They had the moves down pat, practiced, efficient. Gil on the left, Nick on the right. A heavy hand on the man's shoulder, the other on his elbow, the troublemaker lifted almost off his feet and propelled along by the two cops.

"Now, sir, we don't want any trouble," Gil was saying.

"Let's go quietly." Nick moved swiftly, not letting the guy stop until they were out of the room, into the carpeted lobby by the elevators that led down to the street level.

"I was just . . . I was only *talking* . . ." the man sputtered. "I was only *telling* her . . ."

"Yes, sir, I understand," Nick said. The man stank of liquor.

"What're you two goons, her bodyguards?" the guy asked furiously, slurring his words.

"Can I see some ID, sir," Gil said, shrugging to readjust his tuxedo.

"ID? ID? What for?"

"Can I please see some ID, sir?"

Disgusted, the man pulled out his wallet, thrust it forward. Gil checked out the driver's license; Nick saw his partner flick his eyes over the man, comparing him to the picture. Gil was always thorough.

"Okay, Mr. Wesley, we're not going to do anything about this, but we'll have to ask you to leave right now."

"Why? I was just —"

16

"Because my partner here said so," Nick put in, losing patience.

The man snatched his wallet back and stabbed angrily at the elevator button, missing twice. "You assholes," he said. "Can't even talk to someone."

The elevator came; they watched him step in. When the door slid shut, their glances met, and they grinned, then high-fived each other.

"Never fails," Gil said.

"Well-oiled machinery," Nick countered.

"He was a jerk."

"He was a drunken idiot."

"Can't blame him for wanting to talk to that Wells lady. She's a pretty thing."

"Huh," Nick said.

They went back into the banquet room, which was practically empty. Nick looked for Portia Wells, saw her leaving by a side door with Aaron Burkhart, her friend and protector, or whatever in hell he was. Maybe she was going out to party till the wee hours, maybe she was going to Burkhart's hotel room. Maybe she was just returning to her own hotel. Maybe he could still get that tasty morsel of gossip he was there for.

He'd been a New York City policeman for eighteen years, practically since he was out of college, so he knew how easy it was to tail an unsuspecting person. Burkhart had himself a shiny black limo, its windows tinted so dark you couldn't see who was inside. The car glided up to the curb around the corner from the hotel's main entrance, Ms. Wells and Burkhart got in, and the vehicle glided away, rolling along slowly and sedately in the rush of after-theater traffic.

Nick flashed his badge to a cabdriver. "Follow that limo," he said. Christ, he sounded like a bad movie. "There's a big tip in it for you if you don't lose it."

"No problem," the cabby said.

The limo turned uptown, moving faster as traffic lightened. Not for long, though. The shiny black vehicle turned onto Fifty-fifth Street and stopped in front of the Peninsula Hotel.

Aha, Nick thought.

Portia and Burkhart emerged; he kissed her on the cheek. She tilted her head and smiled fondly, then she turned away from him, nodded graciously at the doorman greeting her, and walked into the hotel.

Nick paid the cabby, tipped him big, and waited outside the hotel for a few minutes. The night was very warm, and he felt sweat begin to dampen his underarms and the stiff collar of his shirt. He felt like a fool in the damn monkey suit, his shoes killing him, standing out there in front of the hotel.

He unclipped the bow tie, stuffing it in a pocket, and undid the top shirt button. Studs held the rest of the shirtfront together; they'd

18

taken him forever to do up. A real pain in the ass.

Moving to the glass doors of the hotel, he straightened his shoulders and put on his cop face. He stopped inside the doors, walked up the thickly carpeted steps to the lobby, and checked out the area. No Portia. Okay.

He pulled out his ID and headed straight for the front desk, where an elegant-looking young man held sway.

"Good evening, sir. May I help you?"

Nick flipped open his ID. The desk clerk studied the ID and the badge, then raised his eyes. "What can I do for you, Officer?"

"Detective."

"Sorry, *Detective*."

"I'm assigned to Portia Wells's security team, and I need to know when she's checking out. Didn't want to bother her tonight, you understand."

"Of course. Mrs. Wells is checking out tomorrow."

Nick thought quickly. "Is she taking that early flight out of LaGuardia?"

"I don't believe so. She's asked for a late checkout."

"Okay, good. Thanks."

"Certainly, Detective."

He left the hotel, thinking. A late checkout. So she had plans for the morning. Maybe something interesting. He'd come back early and keep an eye on her. Tomorrow was

19

Sunday, and he was off, and what the hell else did he have to do anyway?

You never knew, he might pick up some tidbit for *Star Gazer*. Wouldn't it be nice if he could phone the rag sheet Monday morning with a scoop?

He hailed a cab out on Fifth Avenue, not using the doorman at the Peninsula, because he didn't want too many people to remember him. Also, he didn't want to have to tip the guy. He sat in the back of the air-conditioned taxi, heading uptown to where he lived, and thought about the evening.

Portia Carr Wells. He saw her in his mind's eye as she stood at the podium, pretty hair, straight, shiny, not tortured into a weird shape. The soft voice. She obviously believed in her cause: saving the land.

She was from Colorado. Her husband had been a rancher, and now he was dead. A car accident, hit the news big time. Tragic death of young president of the NPS. And now his wife was honoring his public commitments, maybe taking over the presidency herself. Nick had to give her credit. For a woman like her — shy, self-effacing, gentle — being in the public eye must be hard.

Or maybe she wasn't at all what she appeared to be. Maybe her manner was all a carefully erected facade, and she was really a hard, ambitious female.

He wondered about that. He thought about

20

her all the way up to West End Avenue, where he got out of the cab in front of his apartment building.

The hour was late when he let himself in, flicked on the light, and shrugged off his jacket. Late, but he wasn't tired. He picked up the phone and punched in Mia's number. She was a night owl like him.

"It's me. Did I wake you up?"

"No." He heard her yawn. "Excuse me. How was your evening?"

"Routine."

"That's too bad."

"You too tired to get together?"

"Um, no, I guess not."

"Should I come over?"

"Okay."

"The girls asleep?"

"Hours ago."

"Let me get out of this tux, and I'll be right over."

He stripped off the black pleated pants, swore as he undid the studs on the cuffs and shirtfront. Changed into khakis and a polo shirt and left his apartment.

He walked down Broadway, five blocks to Mia Wong's apartment. Mia was divorced, with two daughters, ten and twelve. She was delicate and petite, slim as a reed, with olive skin and slanted black eyes. Beautiful and exotic. She looked fragile, but she wasn't. She was tough and smart and a hellion in bed.

She owned a nail salon on 105th and Broadway, kept six girls busy with customers from ten in the morning till ten at night. And she detested her ex-husband, whom she called "what's his name."

"Hi, honey," she said, opening her door. She leaned into him, and he kissed her soft mouth. She wore shorts and a red T-shirt, bare feet as small as a child's, scarlet polish on her toenails. Long fingernails in matching scarlet, the index nails with inlaid flowers.

"How about a beer?"

"Sounds great."

She got them each a cold one, then settled on the couch next to him, her legs curled up under her.

"So you saw her?" she asked. "I'm dying to know what she was like. What did she wear?"

Mia was the only person on earth who knew about his sideline job with the *Star Gazer.* And she was fascinated by Portia Wells.

"She was pretty."

"*Pretty.* God."

He shrugged, swigged from the long-necked bottle. "She gave a speech. It was very convincing."

"What did she wear? Come on, Nick."

"Black dress."

Mia rolled her eyes.

22

"It had some kind of a waist thing, like, you know, it was pulled across."

"A wraparound?"

"Yeah, like that."

"Did you get anything for the magazine?"

"No, not really. I'm going to go back to her hotel in the morning, tail her. See what happens." He took another swig of beer. "There was this guy bugging her. Gil and I had to escort him out."

"What did the guy want?"

"Who knows?"

"And there were lots of people there?"

"Probably, oh, three hundred."

He set his bottle down and ran his fingers over her cheek, down her neck, trailing across one small breast. She giggled.

"Um," he said. "Nice."

"Let's go to bed," she purred. "It's late."

Her bedroom was dark, fragrant, full of woman smell. She didn't bother to turn the light on. Her window was open; city sounds came in on the warm breeze, and a bar of light from outside striped her bed.

They stood pressed together and kissed. Mia pulled his shirt up and kneaded his bare back. Then she stepped away and pulled her T-shirt over her head. She reached behind her to unhook her bra. She paused, then asked him, "Did she seem like a nice person?"

"Hell, I don't know. Sure, I guess she's

23

okay," he muttered, reaching for his lover.

He drove his own car to the Peninsula Hotel early Sunday morning. A trip that would take an hour on a weekday took only twenty-five minutes. He wanted to be prepared in case he had to follow her somewhere. His vehicle was an '88 Toyota Celica, dusty red, a bit battered, the kind of car you needed in Manhattan, unnoticeable and unattractive to car thieves.

She was probably going to brunch with somebody, perhaps her friend Burkhart. Or someone else, a board member of that society of hers or some rich dude she could hit up for a large, tax-free donation.

A hell of a way to spend a day off. And he was still tired from last night. Tired and annoyed, so that it was easy to hold the guilt at bay. His mind twisting so that it was *her* fault that he was driving down Broadway at this hour.

And Mia, damn her, too. She invariably made him walk home before her girls awoke. His shirt hanging, his belt undone, no socks, he'd walked the five blocks to his apartment. Half asleep before he got in bed. Almost forgetting to set his alarm.

It was a good thing he arrived at the Peninsula early, because shortly after eight, Portia Wells emerged from the hotel and was ushered into a cab by the doorman. *A break-*

fast date, then, not brunch, Nick thought. He'd follow and sit outside some café while she gabbed and had croissants and latte. Boring. Probably futile. His stomach growled.

The cab pulled out onto the almost-empty street. He fired up the Celica and followed, keeping one or two vehicles between him and the taxi. He was irritated. What a wasted morning.

Tailing the cab across town to the West Side, he wondered which trendy bistro she was going to. He drove with the windows down, an elbow resting on the ledge. He could have done this job blindfolded. But her cab never stopped; it continued to the West Side Highway, took the first ramp leading north, and picked up speed.

Forgotten was his boredom and irritation. He swung onto the highway and kept the cab in sight as it sped north. *Well now,* he thought.

TWO

Portia grew increasingly nervous as the cab approached New Rochelle. She hadn't been to visit in five years, although she'd spoken to her mother a few times, always a difficult proposition, worrying whether something she said would set her mother back into depression.

She directed the driver where to exit, winced at the familiarity of her surroundings. She drew in a deep breath as the taxi turned onto Bonair Avenue, drove past the sedately respectable, slightly shabby stone and Tudor houses to the dead end, then continued onto the private drive through the woods to Judith Carr's home. The trees met overhead in a canopy, cutting off daylight. The woods here were thick and green, so very different from arid Colorado. Undergrowth choking on itself, like a jungle. Quiet and dim and brooding in the morning heat.

The house was exactly the same as it had been twenty years before when Judith had moved in. No, not exactly — the trees pressed closer, the bushes were tangled and wild, the rhododendrons an explosion of shiny green.

Portia's father Richard kept in touch with her regularly — thank God she had one relatively normal parent — but he lived in Hilton Head, South Carolina, with his new wife, and he'd always been an intimidating figure, away a lot on diplomatic missions. They weren't terribly close. Lately he'd informed Portia that Judith was on a new medication and was doing better than she had been for years. He'd dropped broad hints that Portia should visit her mother.

He'd even paid for her room at the Peninsula Hotel, which she'd accepted gratefully. The NPS would have offered her a room, but she tried not to use the nonprofit's funds if she could help it. Richard hadn't *ordered* her to see Judith while she was in New York, but his suggestion was implicit.

So here she was. Getting out of the taxi and standing on the gravel of the driveway that swept by the front of Judith's home, looking up at the half-timbered and stone house, the dark, heavy front door, the myriad small-paned windows looking over the damp, green woods.

Instructed to wait, the taxi driver turned off his vehicle, and silence closed in around her. The tick of the cab's cooling engine could be heard, nothing more. There was no breeze, but the trees seemed to breathe, a ponderous suspiring of molecules of air and moisture. A jay screeched from behind her; another answered.

She took a deep breath. Her father had mentioned that Judith had actually started to go out again, incognito, in a big hat and sunglasses. "She's paranoid," Richard Carr had said. "She thinks she'll be followed or stopped for autographs or some sort of nonsense. As if anyone even remembers who she is anymore."

She forced herself to walk up the four flagstone steps to the front stoop, raised her hand to knock, remembered the doorbell, and pressed it instead. She could hear the bell echo inside.

Sometimes her mother got irrationally angry; other times she cried or became unreasonably afraid. Her instability had started many years ago, and she'd suffered a breakdown and been hospitalized. Twenty years ago she'd been able to move into this house that Richard bought for her when they divorced. And now she was apparently much better.

Portia heard footsteps approaching, the door opening. She clutched her purse tightly, forced a smile onto her lips.

"Oh, Portia, honey," came a familiar voice. Anna, her mother's longtime secretary and companion, a woman who'd been wardrobe mistress for Judith in her Broadway days. A slim black woman, her face ageless, her gray hair pulled back severely, her fingers gnarled with arthritis.

"Anna." Portia hugged the woman.

"Let me look at you," Anna said. "It's been too long. How are you?"

"I'm okay. I'm fine."

"You're nervous as a cat, aren't you?"

Portia had never been able to hide anything from Anna. "How is she today?"

Anna took her hand. "She's pretty good. A little ornery, but all in all, she's pretty good. She'll be so glad to see you, sweetheart."

Anna led her into the dim, hushed interior. Nothing was changed; the matching green and brown flowered sofas, every picture and doily and ornate piece of furniture was the same as the day Judith had moved in. Photographs of her as a young ingenue, petite and lovely and smooth-skinned, with her dark curly hair and the aquiline nose that saved her from ordinary prettiness. More photos — of Judith with celebrities, with producers and directors, shots of her onstage in *Our Town* and *The Glass Menagerie* and *Othello*. There was even a photo of the President and First Lady handing her a bouquet of flowers after a smashing opening night. The house was a mausoleum, a shrine to the one time in her life she'd been happy. Before she married Richard Carr and had a baby and fallen into the black pit of depression.

Anna led the way to the sunroom at the end of the house, cheerful, surrounded by windows, furnished casually in bent bamboo chairs and couches with thick green cushions.

Judith sat in one of the chairs. A diminutive figure — Portia was always surprised at her mother's smallness — her faded-flower face made up carefully, her hair dyed dark and worn too long, a white dress draping her tiny body.

"Portia, darling," she said theatrically, rising, holding her arms out.

"Mother." She stepped into Judith's embrace, smelling the achingly familiar scent of Opium.

"You're still so beautiful, my darling," Judith said.

"Thank you. You, too, Mother."

"I guess I'm not bad for an old bird," Judith said.

"And you're feeling well?" Code words for depression.

"I'm quite well, actually." She smiled and put a parchment-skinned hand on Portia's arm. "I'm going out these days. It's wonderful. Anna takes me to the A & P, and we shop. So far no one's bothered me, thank heavens."

"That's great news, Mother."

"Come sit down and tell me all about yourself. Anna and I baked rolls, and there's coffee."

"You didn't fuss?"

"My darling girl, if I can't fuss for my only child, what kind of mother am I?"

The kind, Portia could have said, who sent her daughter a silver tea service for a wedding present but couldn't bring herself to attend the wedding. The kind who knew only the surface of her daughter's life, her marriage and widowhood, but not her battle with hopelessness after three miscarriages killed her dreams of motherhood. The kind who knew Gary had died last year, but had no concept of Portia's awful grief or the fact that Todd Wells, Gary's son from his first marriage, was living with her.

All was superficial with Judith. Her life had become an act; the charade was how she protected herself from the world. But the ploy brought with it a certain cruel self-centeredness.

Portia understood this, but the reality still hurt. Before coming to New York on this trip, she'd talked for hours with her sister-in-law and best friend Lynette, who'd urged her to confide in her mother, saying, "Portia, life's too short. Talk to your mom, tell her about your problems, she might surprise you and be very understanding."

But Lynette couldn't really comprehend a woman like Judith. Portia had never had a mother she could depend on, confide in. A mother who could hold her while she sobbed out her anguish and fear and loneliness. Someone to whom she could describe her hope when she became pregnant and the dashing of that hope. How it felt to be barren. To have nothing left of her husband, not even a child.

How she missed Gary, his grandiose plans, his charm, his ambition. How difficult his son Todd was — a boy whose own mother barely had time for him.

If only Lynette was right. If only she could *talk* to her mother about things that mattered. She'd tell Judith about her belief that Gary's death was not an accident, that he'd been murdered, that the police had thought her crazed with grief, out of her mind, and completed a perfunctory investigation, then closed the case without suspicion of foul play.

All that raced through her head as she faced her mother, and she was bursting with the need to pour out her feelings. She swallowed the lump in her throat and said, "That sounds very nice, Mother."

They sat side by side, Judith dwarfed by the large chair, and Portia told her about the previous night's fund-raiser.

"So Carol was there," Judith said. "How does she look?"

"Too thin and too much makeup."

"She always did wear too much makeup. Even back when we were both . . . younger."

"The fund-raiser was a real success. I'll get the numbers next week, but I expect over a hundred thousand. Did you see it on TV?" *Keep the conversation light; don't venture into anything profound.*

"Yes, it was on the morning news. You looked lovely, Portia."

"You know, Mother, Aaron has asked me to take over the presidency of the NPS."

"Aaron?"

"My friend Aaron Burkhart. I told you about him. He was the Society's president before Gary, and he's still on the board. He's been wonderful to me."

"Wonderful." A pencil-thin, drawn-on eyebrow arched.

"He's been a good friend, Mother."

"And he's asked you to take over as president?"

"Yes. It's quite an honor. But I'm not sure. It's such a commitment." In truth, the commitment terrified her, because all her life she'd tried to stay out of the public eye.

When she was born, her father had already been a well-known ambassador to the United Nations and her mother a beautiful actress. She'd come into the world as a center of attention and only faded slightly from celebrity status when she'd married Gary and moved to his ranch on the Front Range of Colorado.

"Maybe he asked you just to be nice. He

33

probably doesn't really mean it. He expects you to say no," Judith said.

A flush of irritation caught Portia. It was so typical of her mother to denigrate anything she did. But she swallowed that feeling, too, and forced a smile. "I think Aaron is serious."

"Wouldn't a position like that bring a lot of publicity?"

"Probably."

"Well, you're a grown-up, you can make up your own mind."

"Yes, Mother, I'll have to do that."

Anna brought in a black and gold Chinese lacquered tray with a silver coffeepot and a plate of cinnamon buns. Sugar cubes in a silver bowl with silver tongs, cream in a silver pitcher. Linen napkins with embroidered edges and monograms.

She drank a cup of coffee and nibbled on a roll. Anna asked her about the ranch, about her life there, how she was managing without Gary. Caring questions, the kind Lynette would ask, the kind Portia desperately wished her mother would ask.

"The ranch isn't doing so well. You've heard about our drought? It's been going on for years now. So we're running fewer head and making less of a profit. The price of hay is sky-high. Randy is trying to make a go of it, but it's hard," Portia explained.

"Randy?" Judith asked.

"Gary's brother," Anna reminded Judith.

"Yes, of course."

"And I've had Gary's son Todd with me all summer."

"The brat?" Judith asked.

Portia bit her lip. "I said that once, didn't I? Well, Todd can be difficult, it's true. His mother is remarried and, frankly, neither his mother nor his stepfather can handle him living with them."

"How old is Todd now?" Anna asked.

"Fifteen."

"Lord save us from fifteen-year-olds," Judith said. "You were impossible at that age."

No, Mother, I was shy and quiet and only wanted to be like the other girls in school. You were the impossible one. And then you and father got a divorce, and I was sent to France to study, and I had to grow up too fast.

A few more questions, Judith's gaze becoming more distracted, staring off into space. Time to leave.

"I know you have to get back to the city," Anna said; she protected Judith ferociously.

"Yes, I have so much to do before I fly out." She rose gratefully, gathered her purse.

Judith stood. "You barely ate your roll, darling."

"I already had breakfast," Portia lied.

"You'll come again soon?"

"I'll try. I may be traveling a lot more if I accept the presidency."

"I know. I know. You young people are so busy."

"I'll try to come soon, I promise." Her head was pounding with tension. She couldn't wait to leave.

Judith held out her arms, and Portia went to her. She felt her mother's thin arms around her, the scent of perfume, then Judith pushed her away to look at her. "Good-bye, darling," she said.

"Good-bye, Mother." And just before she turned away, she could have sworn she saw tears shining in Judith's eyes. *Tears?*

Anna went with her to the front door. "Please try to come again," she said. "I know she's difficult, but she really does love you."

"I will. Honestly."

"Good-bye, then." Anna reached up and kissed her cheek.

"Good-bye. Thanks for taking such good care of Mother."

Anna opened the door; Portia stepped out, relieved. She'd done it; she was leaving. The yellow cab awaited her in the driveway, like Cinderella's carriage, promising deliverance.

She stopped on the bottom step. There was a strange man leaning against the side of the cab. The driver? No, of course he wasn't the driver. This man wore a red Hawaiian shirt, and he was talking to the driver. Who . . . ?

The man looked up then, saw her, straightened. She saw that he had a camera; he was raising it, snapping pictures.

"Oh no," she heard Anna say from the top step.

The man came toward her, and she froze, not knowing what to do. "Is your mother in there, Ms. Wells? Does Judith Carr live in this house?"

Anna came down the stairs, a frail, elderly woman. But her voice was strong. "Leave here immediately, young man. This is private property."

He paid no attention to her. The cabbie got out and tried to head the man off but got shouldered aside. *Click, whir, click, whir,* went the camera, like a robot gone mad. Portia tried to brush past the man. *Ignore him,* she told herself. *These are small people.* Still, the horror of a lifetime of nosy reporters clutched at her. All the years of evasion and worry, of shame and humiliation came back. *Leave me alone,* she wanted to scream, but she clenched her teeth, knowing a reaction from her would only provide fodder.

"Portia Wells, is Judith Carr in that house? Come on, Portia, you can tell me."

"Please," she said, averting her face as the horrible man thrust the camera at her. She drew back, raising her arm to fend him off, felt her ankle turn in the loose gravel, and she couldn't keep her balance. She fell to one knee, scraping it, and the pain cleared her head.

"Go away," she said, "or I'll call the police." Awkwardly, she stood up, brushing off her knee, her cheeks burning with anger and embarrassment as she walked toward the taxi. She tried with all her willpower not to limp, but the reporter barred her path.

"Come on, Portia, give me something," he wheedled. His breath smelled of stale cigarette smoke.

As if there were not enough freaks in this sideshow, she became cognizant of someone else approaching the group.

"Okay, buddy, it's time to leave," came the new player's voice.

She looked up and saw a strange man walking swiftly toward them. He was slim, had very dark, curly hair, and a grim expression. He wore a white open-collar shirt, sleeves rolled up over muscular forearms, and wrinkled khakis.

The reporter lowered his camera and frowned. "Hey, I —"

The man flashed a billfold at the reporter. "New York Police. Scram."

"What in hell are you doing, asshole?"

The dark-haired man yanked the reporter around to face him. "I *said* it's time to go. Understand?"

"Jesus, yeah, all right."

Slowly, grudgingly, the reporter turned and

walked to where he'd left his car in the shadow of the woods. She spotted another car there, too, just off the driveway under the trees.

The man, the policeman, turned to her and spoke, his expression changing. "You okay?"

"Yes, I am, thank you. I just skinned my knee a little."

He called out to Anna, who was still standing at the bottom of the steps. "It's okay. She's fine."

"Portia . . ." Anna called.

"Go on, Anna. Mother must be upset."

The man was shoving some money at the cabdriver, but before she could intervene, the shaken driver had gotten into the taxi and was pulling away.

"Excuse me, but I have to get back to the city," Portia began.

"Sure, no problem. I'll drive you. I figured you might need some protection after that fiasco."

"Well . . ." Her head was swimming.

"Hey, that's what I'm here for."

Not quite comprehending what he meant, she said, "May I see your ID, please?"

He pulled a worn billfold from his rear pocket, held it out. There was his badge number, a picture of him, his name and rank. "Detective Nick Sinestra, at your service. NYPD, Sixth Precinct, Vice Squad." He grinned.

She compared his face to the picture. He was better looking in person, with curved lines on either side of his mouth, a shadow of whiskers, black, heavy-lidded eyes that tilted very slightly, a touch of the exotic, flared nostrils. He looked as if he'd encountered everything at least once in his life.

And she realized she'd seen him before. Of course. Last night at the fund-raiser, he and a tall black man had come to her rescue when a drunk had accosted her and wouldn't leave. She looked at him again and wondered. Nick Sinestra showing up at her mother's house could not be a coincidence.

"Well, Detective Sinestra, now that you sent the taxi away, I guess you're stuck with me."

"Things could be worse."

"I'll pay you back for the cab."

"Not necessary."

"Certainly it is." She started to reach into her purse for her wallet.

He placed a hand on her arm to stop her. "I'll put it in my expenses, don't worry."

"You're sure?"

"Yeah, I'm sure."

They walked toward his car then, a small red vehicle, definitely not police issue. He held the door open for her, let her slide in. When he was behind the wheel, he leaned over and dug around in the glove compartment, finally taking out a small package of

40

tissues and handing it to her. "For your knee," he said.

"Thank you." She dabbed at her knee as he started the car and pulled onto the driveway. "I feel so dumb. I was just so shocked. I can't figure out how on earth that awful man found me."

"Um."

"For that matter, I can't figure out what a New York City policeman is doing here." She dared a sidelong glance at him; he was staring straight ahead as they drove back down Bonair Avenue.

"I followed you."

"You *what?*"

"I've been assigned to you while you're here. You know, security."

"And no one told me about this?" she demanded.

He shrugged. "Guess not."

"I'm sorry, I don't understand. I've had security following me around?"

"Apparently."

She put a hand to her forehead. Her brow was damp with perspiration. "Why?"

Again he shrugged, draped a wrist over the steering wheel. "Hey, I just follow orders."

"I don't want you to think I'm ungrateful, but I can't believe I wasn't informed about this . . . security."

His gaze switched to her, then back to the road. He said nothing, and she felt the silence mount like a bill that would have to be paid.

"You were at the fund-raiser last night," she finally said. "I recognized you right away."

"Really."

"You and that man, the tall black one with dreadlocks, you got rid of that drunk. That *was* you, wasn't it?"

"Yeah."

She still couldn't quite fathom having security without being told a word. *Crazy.* Still, his being assigned to her wasn't his fault, and his being there last night certainly had helped. "I didn't get a chance to thank you," she said.

"Just doing our job."

"Well, thanks anyway."

He didn't reply, steered onto the Hutchinson River Parkway heading south toward Manhattan. A fine rain began to fall, and he turned on the windshield wipers.

She guessed he wasn't going to say anything more. To him this was all just a job. Maybe he needed the overtime pay. He probably didn't give a damn one way or the other about her — or her mother.

How *had* that reporter known where she was going to be this morning? She hadn't told anyone, not even Aaron. Had the reporter, too, followed her? She supposed he could have. Her being in New York was no secret; the man must have found out where she was staying and tailed her.

Now the press knew where Judith lived. Her mother's paranoid fears would come to fruition, and it was all Portia's fault. Maybe they wouldn't be interested, though. After all, Judith Carr's name was not exactly a household word these days.

At any rate, she'd have to alert Anna. Oh God, what a mess. And what rag sheet did the reporter work for? She'd need to find out.

Well, the damage was done. Anna would keep the media at bay, although perhaps Judith would have to curtail her outings for a while. She'd suggest to Anna that she call the New Rochelle police if things got too bad. Sooner or later, the press would lose interest. They always did. All it took was for some other poor soul with a story to come along. God, she hated the media.

"Do you know who that reporter worked for?" she asked when the silence piled up.

Nick Sinestra was silent for a time. He passed another car, then moved back into the right lane before he answered. "No, I don't."

"Oh."

Another pause. "Sorry."

They were approaching the upper end of Manhattan. She looked out the window at the misty view of ranks of tall brick apartment buildings. On her right was the Hudson

River, with the graceful George Washington Bridge arching over it, leading to New Jersey. The quality of air here was so different from Colorado, dense and humid, the light diffuse instead of diamond bright.

She gazed out her side window at the river, and she was troubled. She was so defenseless against the media, so susceptible to their voracious curiosity. This morning was a precursor to what would happen should she accept the NPS presidency. They'd never leave her alone if she was in public service. They'd ridicule her, call her a celebrity tree hugger, dig up the past, and beat her to death with it. They might even find out about her miscarriages and announce her private torment to the world. She knew she would have to function not only in Colorado but at appearances all over the country, especially in Washington, D.C., at NPS headquarters. The media would hound her till her life was not her own.

There was also her stepson Todd to consider. Was it fair to him to take on such heavy responsibilities, when leaving him with his Aunt Lynette and Uncle Randy was not always a viable alternative?

On the other hand, having the press on her heels might work to her advantage in one way — seeking the truth behind Gary's death. *Maybe.* If her doubts about Gary's death being an accident were "leaked" to the media, the authorities might be forced to re-open the case. She had to weigh the benefits of that against the destruction of her own privacy.

She'd been going around and around in her mind with this decision, chasing her own tail. *Yes, no, yes, no. Gary, Todd, the NPS.*

"I'm staying at the Peninsula Hotel on Fifty-fifth Street," she said.

"I know."

Of course he did. How stupid of her.

"Don't you have Sundays off?" she asked.

"Sometimes. Depends on whether I'm on a case."

"You said you were on the Vice Squad."

"That's right."

"Well, this isn't exactly up your alley, is it?"

"No."

He wasn't much of a conversationalist. The strong, silent type. She wasn't sure how to act with him, shades of awkward high school dances and the feeling of being out of your element, the way she'd felt when she was packed off to France, barely speaking the language.

Perhaps that was why she'd so quickly married Gary. He'd been so easy in his skin, loved to talk no matter the subject. He'd been at home in any situation, impressing men and charming women. A natural leader, charismatic, sure of his path in life.

45

Gary. She missed him so. He'd been the center of her existence for ten years, and then suddenly he was gone. She'd been set adrift, floundering, trying to find her way to shore. Of course, she'd known since the day they'd met at that fund-raiser that her attraction to Gary had been based much more on need than love; she'd always known that, and so had Gary. He'd professed to be fine with their relationship. And she *had* grown to love him. But there was still guilt, and there always would be guilt that she had never been deeply in love. Now he was dead, and she hadn't returned his love fully or even given him a child. Was it guilt alone, then, that was making her even consider the NPS position? Was she doing this all for Gary?

The old car clipped along the highway, its shocks bad, the seams and potholes in the road jarring her spine.

She turned her attention back to Nick . . . a big-city cop. The things he must have seen. He'd dealt with drug pushers and thieves and prostitutes. He had a hard-edged look to him, but he had an air of bemused self-assurance, too, that kept him from scaring the hell out of her.

"Do you live in the city?" she asked for wont of a better subject.

"Uh-huh."

"Are you from New York originally?"

"The Bronx."

46

"I bet you're from one of those families where all the men are policemen."

He laughed. "Nope. I'm the only one."

He had a nice laugh. A nice voice. She glanced at him again and thought, *He looks like one of those men on ancient coins they find on the bottom of the Aegean Sea, an Etruscan or a Minoan or a Greek.* In anyone's book he'd be attractive, masculine.

It was past eleven when he let her off in front of the Peninsula Hotel. She leaned down and said, "Thanks for the ride. And for getting rid of that reporter."

He didn't meet her eyes, mumbled, "Sure, anytime." As soon as she shut the car door, he drove off.

She went up to her room and packed. But all the time she kept replaying the scene in her mind: the reporter, Nick telling him to scram, the ride back to the city. She'd tried to draw him out, but he'd resisted. One moment she thought he was trying to be pleasant, the next he was almost rude.

She was a bit breathless at everything that had happened that morning. Breathless and unsettled and confused. Gary hadn't been gone a year, and she was thinking about another man, a stranger, a New York cop she'd probably never see again.

She sat there on the side of the bed and looked at her scraped knee, and she kept hearing his voice in her head.

He'd been there when she needed help — twice in two days. He wasn't a knight on a white charger, though, she reminded herself. He'd been assigned to her. He was doing his job, that was all.

What about tomorrow — and the next day? And every day after that? There'd be no Nick Sinestra to rescue her. No handsome, tough cop watching over her. She must have been dreaming to think she could take over Gary's position. Had she forgotten the pain of having her life stripped naked in front of nosy strangers?

She had the sudden urge to call Lynette, tell her all about the insane day, about Judith and wonderful old Anna and that sleazy reporter. And Nick Sinestra. *Nick*. She'd confess to her sister-in-law how much she thought about him, and they would make up all sorts of tough-guy cop scenarios, and Lynette would plot how Portia could see him again. Lynette was so good at those things. She was also the only person on earth who knew how lonely Portia was.

She thought about calling Lynette, and then she looked at the time and realized she had to get to the airport.

But there was one matter to take care of first. She picked up the phone and asked for information. She was connected, and the phone was answered quickly. A woman's voice: "Sixth Precinct, Officer Webb."

"Excuse me, I realize it's Sunday, but is your, um, commanding officer in?"

"That would be CO Fitzpatrick. And yes, he's here."

"May I speak to him, please?"

"Yes, ma'am."

"Fitzpatrick," came a gruff voice.

"CO Fitzpatrick, my name is Portia Wells, and I'm in New York for the fireman's fund-raiser that was held last night."

"Uh-huh."

"Well, I just wanted to thank you, or who-ever was responsible, for putting Detective Sinestra on my security duty."

"Sinestra?"

"Yes, Nick Sinestra. He was at the fund-raiser last night, and then today —"

"I'm sorry, what'd you say your name was?"

"Portia Wells."

"Miss Wells, as far as I know, nobody's been assigned to security duty, for you or anyone else. Yes, Detective Sinestra was working that fund-raiser, but beyond that, hell, he's off duty today."

"But . . . he said —"

"I'm sorry, miss, you must have misunder-stood. Hey, did Nick cause any trouble? You have a problem with him?"

"No, no. No trouble. He was very . . . helpful."

She hung up, bewildered. Went over everything he'd said from the moment he appeared that morning. No, she hadn't misunderstood. Then what was going on? Did Nick lie? But why would he?

She checked out of the Peninsula Hotel and caught a cab to the airport for her Denver flight. In the darkness of the tunnel leading out of Manhattan, the answer came to her.

Nick Sinestra hadn't been assigned to her security. No, he'd been spying on her, and he'd followed her to her mother's and called the tabloid that reporter worked for. He'd turned that creep on to her, and then pretended he was assigned to her security.

God! She felt so dumb, so . . . betrayed. Gone were her silly schoolgirl fantasies of thanking him on the phone again, hearing his voice. And would she really have asked him to provide security for her when she was in the city again? *Stupid idiot,* she thought, angry with herself, even angrier with Nick. And hurt.

She put a hand to her forehead, as if hiding her shame.

It occurred to her then, as the cab drove out of the tunnel into the gray drizzle, that Nick must have *some* scruples, chasing the reporter away like he did.

Some, but not many. What a lousy stunt he'd pulled. She detested him all over again, the weasel.

THREE

Every morning for the past three years, Nick and Gil met at a corner market above the 103rd and Broadway subway station. Nick got a blueberry muffin and a large coffee; Gil bought Lifesavers. Gil had quit smoking years ago but had yet to kick the Lifesaver habit.

It was Tuesday morning. Ten past seven and already blazing hot and muggy on the streets.

"Goddamn," Nick said, loosening his tie, juggling the coffee and muffin to find the right change in his pocket. "I need another shower, and I just got out half an hour ago."

"Yeah, it's hot, man." Gil nodded. "And I bet that coffee helps cool you down."

"Huh," Nick said, sipping the brew. Then he saw a stack of *Star Gazer* weeklies bundled, still in string, on the floor between the *New York Times* and *Daily News*. Hot off the press. A photo of Portia and her mother plastered across the cover. Beneath the headline it read, *"Mother Daughter Murderous Reunion."*

He choked and spat the coffee out the

door onto the sidewalk.

"You all right?" Gil patted his back.

"Fine, I'm fine, swallowed the wrong way." Nick coughed and stared down in crawling discomfort at the ludicrous picture, obviously a file photo of a younger but crazed-looking Judith Carr from God knows when and in what situation, and superimposed half over it was the shot of Portia in front of Judith's house the other day, her arms raised as if warding off an attack, hair wild, blouse slipping off a shoulder. In the layout, the women faced each other, so that it appeared as if they were engaged in a violent confrontation, *Very clever, Bern,* he thought. *You bastard.*

He coughed again and followed Gil out and down into the inferno beneath the city. The two men zigzagged a crooked path through the horde of commuters to the end of the platform, where white tiled wall met the black echoing tunnel.

"You sure you're okay?" Gil asked when Nick tossed the untouched muffin into a trash barrel.

"Yeah, yeah, too hot to eat. What is it down here? Hundred, hundred plus?"

"At least," Gil said, rubbernecking up the tracks as if that would make the train come. Thank God the cars were air-conditioned.

Nick wasn't about to tell his partner the truth, especially not now. But that photo. What a rotten stunt to pull just to sell pa-

52

pers. The press had discovered Judith's whereabouts, and they wouldn't let go, not until they had milked the story dry. *Damn.*

He grimaced as the front cars screeched by, blasting them all with a gust of more heat, and the rear cars finally came to a jerky stop, doors cranking open. They both got on, shouldered through the throng to the center of the car, as they wouldn't get off till Christopher Street in the Village.

The cover of the *Star Gazer* stayed in his head till the Forty-second Street station, when he convinced himself the headline story wasn't his fault. With Portia likely to take on the highly visible position of NPS president, the media eventually would have tracked her mother down without his help. *Just a matter of time. Inevitable. Not your fault, Sinestra.*

It was no cooler in the West Village when he and Gil emerged from the station. If anything, this far south in Manhattan, where the Hudson and East Rivers nearly converged, the air seemed even more humid. Both men slung their jackets over shoulders and walked along West Tenth, where the 6th Precinct was located in an unprepossessing, two-story brick building.

"Heat's supposed to last through the weekend," Gil said. "It's what they call a 'weather event.'"

"Who the hell ever thought that one up anyway? A *weather event.*" Nick curled a lip.

The 6th Precinct was one of ten precincts in the Patrol Borough Manhattan South and was responsible for the West Village. The precinct ran from Houston Street in the south to Fourteenth Street in the north. The eastern border was Broadway, and its territory ran all the way west to the Hudson River. If you believed Copstat, an internal police statistical department that kept tabs on crime and conviction statistics citywide, crime had been steadily declining in the 6th for years.

Nick wasn't entirely sure he believed the stats. But he did believe there was a shortage of new recruits in the precinct. Probably not enough excitement for the hotshot youngsters entering the police academy. Regardless, the 6th was understaffed and feeling the pressure. Neither Nick nor Gil had taken vacations in over a year and a half.

Since the official creation of Homeland Security, they'd been saddled with a new problem: Two HS gung ho feds had just been assigned to the 6th. And Nick had been assigned as liaison to them — TG was his unofficial title. A joke on the second floor. TG for *tour guide*. Nick didn't find the joke very funny.

Mike, the on-duty desk sergeant on the first floor, was out front watering the dispirited flowers in their planters when Nick and Gil walked up.

Nick shook his head. "Why bother?" he asked Mike.

"Gotta cheer this place up." Mike tenderly plucked a dead bloom from a scrawny pink petunia plant. "You're just an old cynic, Sinestra. Stop and smell the roses, why don't you?"

"Roses." Gil snorted.

In truth, the precinct looked more like a combination of a prison and a school than it did a station house. Even the official cars and bomb squad were parked out of sight behind the building next to Charles Street. But before the building would get the face-lift it needed — make that desperately needed, Nick mused — they'd remodel the second floor.

"At least Mike tries," Gil said as they passed through metal doors and climbed the narrow steps to the offices that housed the various detective squads.

The Homeland Security suits were already standing around Nick's cubbyhole desk when he tossed his jacket over the vintage swivel chair. Their commanding officer required his detectives to wear suits, but in this upstairs furnace, all jackets were quickly shed.

"Morning, Detective Sinestra," the younger suit said. His name was Richard Jacobson III. Georgetown University grad. Recruited by the NSA, then sacrificed to meet the quota of the new government department. The kid was okay. Hell, he stayed cool and dry all day and never removed his summer-weight suit jacket. Nick figured the heat tolerance came from years of living in D.C., the sultry capital of the universe.

"Yeah, sure, morning." Nick sat and pushed a few files aside, making room to open his mail.

The other HS man was studiously silent. He was older than Rick, maybe thirty-two or -three, had been on his way up in the FBI before being assigned to HS. It was hard for Nick to tell if the guy, Weston Ramsey, liked or resented the new posting. Not that Nick gave a damn either way, but he still had to work with the man, and it helped to know who you took to the streets with. Rick was okay. Wes was a gold-plated asshole.

Affably, Rick said, "What's on the schedule for today?" The kid pulled his city map out of a pocket.

"Uh, NYU and the park."

"Washington Square." Rick smiled.

Wes made a disgruntled sound.

Nick slowly brought his gaze up. "The park is the heart of the precinct. You're responsible for the security of the area, right? Well, it's the core. Unless the weather really sucks, the park's filled with students and tourists and —"

"Transients, bums, and users," Wes cut in.

"Yeah, them, too, *Ramsey*. But they're citizens, pal. And they deserve your protection. What I can't figure out is why you were picked for this job."

"Come on, guys," Rick tried.

"Maybe I wanted a nice apartment over-looking the river," Wes said. "HS comes with a handsome salary and damn good perks. But what you see in this hangover-from-the-sixties, artsy-fartsy precinct is beyond me, Sinestra. But . . ." Wes shrugged. "To each his own."

"Go fu—" Nick caught himself. Playing baby-sitter to these jerks — well, to Wes — wasn't a permanent assignment. And while Nick was doing his *liaising*, he'd gotten a siz-able bump in salary, compliments of the U.S. government.

"So, what time do you want to hit the streets?" Rick checked his watch.

"I've got mail, a few phone messages, a couple files."

"*And,*" Gil interrupted, peeking over the top of the sagging old divider between their desks, "we still got this Internet scam, a new Nigerian thing. We're up to eighteen com-plaints in the Sixth alone. And one of them came in yesterday from a city councilman's mother who's on GVillage.net."

Nick sat back in his creaking chair, pursed his lips, exhaled. "Shit. That means we've got to crack it. How much did they take her for?"

"Over five thousand."

"Oh, man. *Damn.* A councilman's mother?"

"Uh-huh."

Gil's head disappeared.

"Swell," Nick said.

He didn't get out of the building till almost noon after that. Rick was understanding, had spent the morning with his sleeves rolled up, trying to fix the antique window air conditioner that had frozen up when one of the desperately overweight detectives had turned the knob to High. Wes, on the other hand, had gone from looking over Nick and Gil's shoulders, while they frustratingly tried to get a handle on the source of the ISPN on the latest Nigerian scam, to studying Copstat crime reports for Patrol Borough Manhattan South.

Outside, the sun oozed hotly through an oily city haze. Nick walked along West Tenth Street, trying to stay beneath the meager shade of the buildings, feeling as if he couldn't breathe. It was no wonder murder stats climbed on the hottest days. Heat did something to you, made you angry and anxious, your temper on a hair trigger. The last thing he wanted to do was give these suits a tour of the campus and park — the park that was sure to be jammed with tourists, along with the usual suspects. And very little shade to speak of.

Everywhere he walked with the guys, and

they walked because it was actually quicker than dealing with the heavy traffic on Bleecker and Fourteenth and Broadway, Nick began to consider potential terrorist targets. Why not blow up Mama Buddha's restaurant, where movie and stage stars and best-selling authors mingled with tourists? Or the Barnes & Noble? Or a dorm on the NYU campus? Best would be that apartment building over there. Or why not blow yourself up in the middle of Washington Square Park?

Within the 6th was all of the West Village, the length of renowned Bleecker Street, the Forbes Museum — a great target — and Saint Vincent's Hospital. Bombing a hospital would make a profound statement.

Then there were the eight elementary schools and the high school. Oh, and the two other colleges. There were countless symbols of society in lower Manhattan. Why not blow up the *Village Voice* offices?

But Wes didn't see things in the same light. "Who'd bother bombing that crappy old coffeehouse over there?"

"Well," Rick began.

"*Anyone,*" Nick interrupted, "who knew Allen Ginsburg used to read poetry there."

"Humph," Wes said.

"And down the street on MacDougal are two other coffeehouses, icons, buddy. Bob Dylan used to hang at one of them and Jack Kerouac at the other. City'd be devastated if something happened to those sites. Maybe it doesn't mean much to you, *Weston,* but it does to a lot of people."

"Cool down, Sinestra," Wes said, easily striding along the street. "All I meant was a bomber would be more likely to choose the Empire State Building or the UN."

"Oh, yeah?" Nick's fuse was shortening. "That's why they pick cafés and buses in Tel Aviv?"

"They did bomb the university in Jerusalem a couple years ago," Rick put in helpfully.

"Whatever," Nick said.

Later Nick would figure it had been the quick summer rain shower that had been the last straw for him. At the time, he only felt the brief rain shower and then sudden sun beating down on him, steam rising from the damp streets. It was as if he'd stepped from the frying pan into the fire.

"Well, we've seen about all there is to see," Wes was saying as they approached the entrance to the precinct.

"You're joking." Nick ducked through the door that Rick held for them. *God almighty,* he thought, it was even hotter in the precinct than outside.

"I don't joke, Sinestra." Wes followed him up the steps. "We'll find our way around just fine."

Before Nick could reply, Gil strode up, his

black brow damp with sweat, and thrust a file at Nick.

"I'm all jammed up, man. This Nigerian scam . . . Every time I think I'm closing in, it's another false lead. This is bullshit. I'm no computer genius, man."

Nick took the file. "Where's Farley? Maybe the rookie could help us —"

"Farley got reassigned. Uptown."

"He did?"

"Yeah. Wanted to go where the action is."

"And the commander let him? As short-handed as we are?"

"Guess so." Gil lifted his shoulders and dropped them.

"Like I was saying," Wes broke in, "I feel comfortable handling any terrorist threat to the neighborhoods now. I don't believe we'll be needing your assistance any longer."

"Excuse me?" Nick unconsciously brought himself up to his full six-foot height.

"I *said,* thanks for the scenic tour, Sinestra. We'll take it from here now."

"You'll . . . ?" Then Nick laughed sardonically. "Thought you said you didn't joke, *Weston.*" He was aware that Commander Sean Fitzpatrick was standing by the water cooler near the copy room, listening, but Nick didn't give a damn. "You know something, pal, *Weston,* you're so goddamn dumb you wouldn't know a street hustler from a terrorist."

61

"Whoa," Gil began.

"And what's more . . ." Nick said.

Wes puffed up his chest and stuck an index finger out, taking a step toward Nick. "Go on," he said.

"Fuck you, Ramsey." Nick batted the hand aside. "You're nothing but an arrogant little prick."

"Why you —" But before Wes could finish, Nick shoved him. Wes shoved back, and both men threw a punch. Nick sidestepped the blow, and his fist made contact with Wes Ramsey's bottom lip.

The fight ended there. Before Wes could recover to take another swing, there were ten detectives from the squad pulling them apart, and the booming voice of the commanding officer cracking like a whip through the close air. "In my office, Sinestra. *Now.*"

Nick came to as if he'd been doused with water. What the hell had just happened? He was aware of the crowd of detectives around him, and of Gil blowing out a breath, shaking his head. And Wes. Tie askew, bringing a crisp white handkerchief up to his lip. As for himself, he felt his shirt stuck to his skin and sweat popping out on his head.

"Sinestra," the CO repeated. "My office."

"*Shit,*" Nick muttered.

The men parted, making as aisle for him straight to Fitzpatrick's door. He was walking the green mile.

"Close the door," the CO said, and Nick did, hearing the blinds clatter against the glass. "Sit down. We got to talk."

"Yes, sir," Nick said dully.

He knew he was in trouble. Not that fights hadn't broken out among the detectives before, here and at their favorite bar down on Broadway, but this was different. Nick had been assigned as liaison to the Homeland Security men as a breath of fresh air, or so the CO had said last month. And Nick knew he'd been in the dumps for a while, even before his divorce and Gwen's hooking up with her new lover — that *woman. Oh, sweet Jesus.*

Yeah, he knew he was going sour, had been losing his edge, turning his head from too much petty crime and even some department corruption, not giving a damn. He was jaded and growing more cynical and world weary by the day. Last month, on the witness stand, testifying on a drug bust at the high school, a slam-dunk conviction, even the public defender for the dealer had let it go when Nick had blatantly lied under oath. Let the outright lie slide because the PD had a nephew in the high school, and this was the dealer's second bust. Nick had figured if the PD wanted his own client locked up, why not help the cause and stretch the truth?

But Nick mostly felt that way about every aspect of his life. He was down. And instead of reviving his sagging will, the new assignment had only served to bolster his belief that there were more assholes walking the planet than good guys.

Now he'd punched one of them. He looked his CO square in the eye and thought, *Hell, I really don't care.*

"You forced my hand here today, Sinestra," the CO said.

"Sir?"

"Don't play cute with me."

"No, sir."

Sean Fitzpatrick was a big Irishman, an absolute NYPD cliché of a cop. His grandfather had emigrated to the States through Canada and become a cop. And so it went. Fitzpatrick after Fitzpatrick, uncles and cousins, fathers and sons. Nine of them in all. Cops.

"What am I going to do with you?"

Take my badge and gun, I guess.

"Well?"

"I don't know, sir."

"Come on, Detective. You know I should suspend you. I realize it was only a spat. The temperature rose, and so did tempers. Happened before. But these men are our guests. You don't punch your guests, Detective."

"No, sir. It's impolite."

Fitzpatrick raised a sandy brow and let the remark pass. "You're due a vacation. Hell, we're all due. How long has it been?"

A vacation. "Ah, eighteen months. Maybe nineteen? But Gil is due first, sir."

"Gil has his time coming. You let me worry about that."

"Yes, sir, but the Sixth is already short-handed, and —"

"A month."

"Sir?"

"I'll give you a week to clear your cases. Then I don't want to see you till August."

"A . . . month? But —"

"You have six weeks' back time coming. Believe me, Detective, the precinct will get along just fine without you."

"Yes, sir."

"And come back with a better attitude, Sinestra. I mean that."

Nick rose from the chair in front of the CO's desk. *A month.* "Sir," he said, opening the door, "what about them?" He nodded toward the HS men. "Who's going to — ?"

"Not your problem. Now get out of here, get your desk cleared within the week, and don't show your face below Fourteenth Street for a month, Detective, or it will mean your badge."

"Yes, sir," Nick said, closing the door behind him. It was only then that he looked up and saw a dozen pairs of eyes slither away from him. All but one pair, Weston Ramsey's.

Ramsey grinned. Despite the red-blotched handkerchief still held to his lip, the bastard smiled.

Fuck you, Nick thought.

65

FOUR

Portia glanced at the dashboard clock as she drove. It was almost noon. Denver rose on the horizon, and she had half an hour to get into the city, negotiate traffic on I-25's T-Rex construction project. Maneuver through the one-way downtown streets, and park at the Brown Palace Hotel, pay their high rate, because she was running behind schedule for her lunch meeting with Aaron Burkhart, who would already be awaiting her at a table in the Ship's Tavern.

When she finally arrived — the trip had taken forty-five minutes — the host in the dimly lit restaurant led the way, and Aaron rose from his chair to embrace her. "Portia, for a cowgirl you look terrific. I don't know how you do it."

She laughed. *A cowgirl.* "Well, this morning I was covered in hay and dust. But I thought I'd clean up my act for you."

"Something to drink?" he asked as they both sat down across from each other. "Wine? Tea?"

"Iced tea, please. I'm driving back to the

ranch after lunch."

Aaron already had a glass of wine sitting in front of him, and for a moment she debated having one but thought better of it.

"So how is the ranch doing?"

She sighed. "Things are tight. At least I *think* they are. I'm still getting my feet wet. I'm afraid Gary made all the big decisions. Randy —"

"That's Gary's brother?"

"Yes. Randy has always handled the day-to-day operations. As far as that goes, I'm getting comfortable. The banking and keeping the books and things like how many head of cattle we might need to sell because of the drought, well, let's say I'm still learning."

"Surely Randy and his wife . . . Annette, is it?"

"Lynette."

"Right. They must participate in the larger decisions?"

"Um. Sometimes. But Gary was really the brains of the ranch. I'm not saying that Randy can't handle big decisions. He can. It's just that running the spread is a dawn-to-dusk affair. And Lynette has the kids. Three soon-to-be teenagers. She's got her hands full."

He nodded. "And you still have Todd living with you?"

"Oh, yes." She smiled and lifted her brows.

"If I take on the NPS position, that won't change."

"He can't live with his mother?"

"He *could*. But he doesn't want to." Then she had to qualify her statement. "That sounds awful, doesn't it? It's just that Todd's mother has a new family. Todd isn't, well, he isn't comfortable with her new husband or the baby. You know, he feels like an outsider. He's not wild about living on the ranch . . ." Now there was an understatement, she mused. ". . . but he's getting used to it."

"He must miss Gary."

"Yes. We talk about him a lot."

"That's good."

"Yes, it is. For me, too."

Aaron ordered for both of them, hot steak sandwiches and side salads. "There's nothing like Colorado beef," he said.

She excused herself then and went to the ladies' room, finally able to straighten her hair and reapply lipstick. She'd worn a white blouse over a denim skirt and cinched the shirt at the waist with a silver concho belt. Simple. Suitable and quite Western. Her sandals were strictly functional.

Okay, she thought, *back to Aaron.* She knew the small talk was over. Time to discuss the subject he'd flown 2,000 miles to tackle: the presidency of the Nature Preservation Society.

In between bites of steak sandwich, Aaron

got around to the topic. "So, Portia, Gary's been gone almost a year now."

"Ten months. Nearly ten."

"Yes. And the NPS has been functioning reasonably well, considering. You've been a tremendous help, a true heroine, by the way, and the entire board is in your debt."

He was flattering her. She'd lived up to several of Gary's prior commitments, the fund-raiser in New York being one of them. She'd given a few short speeches at dinners and luncheons, but she'd certainly not filled Gary's shoes. Nor was she certain she could or should. Look how upset she'd been with that *Star Gazer* story. She'd been at the grocery store in Castle Rock when she'd seen it at the checkout stand. She had been positive everyone in the store was staring at her, staring and snickering. And all because of that weasel. Nick Sinestra. Nick the traitor. Who'd taken her breath away with his tough cop's demeanor and sexy mouth. Oh, what a fool she'd been.

She focused on Aaron's face and shoved Nick Sinestra's image aside.

"I understand completely your reservations about accepting the position," Aaron was saying. "The job can be extremely time consuming, and there would be areas you'd need to familiarize yourself with before tackling sensitive issues. Nothing you can't grasp. You're very sharp; you know that."

69

"Thank you." *So sharp,* she thought. Nick Sinestra had completely taken her in. *Stop it,* she told herself, *just stop it.*

"I'm quite serious. But I sense a reluctance, and I think we should air everything here and now. We don't want to make a mistake at this juncture. I want more than anything to assure your happiness, you know that."

"Yes, I think I do."

"Good," he said, "good. And I won't lie to you. Having you fill the position will bring media attention."

"I know." Had Aaron seen the *Star Gazer*? But even if he had, he would never say so. He was too . . . reserved, too decent.

"Which," he went on, "will greatly benefit the NPS. Media interest will translate into new interest in the organization, new membership, and our ultimate goal, new money to fund our projects. That's the plus side. But some of the media attention will be unwelcome. And I know how you feel about that."

She listened and she thought how long and hard she'd considered everything he was saying. And she wondered again if he'd seen the tabloid story. She folded her linen napkin neatly on the table, smoothed it open, and refolded it. Finally she looked up into his piercing blue eyes. "Is that all I'll be, really, a figurehead?"

He smiled one of his captivating smiles.

70

"An apt description. And, again, I'll level with you. You'll be a figurehead, but you'll also be so much more. You'll assume all the duties of the position. You'll be a busy woman, a *very* busy woman. And that's why I wanted to fly out here and meet with you face-to-face. We're asking a lot of you, maybe too much. Especially with the ranch. And Todd . . . a teenager. I wasn't certain of his future plans. Now that we've discussed these issues, I want you to know we'll understand completely if you decline the offer. The entire board will understand."

She nodded. "I think I needed to hear that in person, too. It helps with my decision."

"So you've decided to —"

"Oh, no, no, I haven't really made up my mind yet. I need a few more days at least. I hope that's all right?"

"Perfectly fine."

She swallowed. Now that he'd spoken his piece, she had to speak hers. She had to confide in Aaron. How was he going to react? She took a deep breath and plunged in. "There's something I've got to run by you. It's only fair. I've got another motive for considering the position. Now, don't be shocked."

"Not too much shocks me at my age, Portia."

"Well, this might. I believe . . . make

that, I *suspect* Gary's death was not an accident."

"Excuse me?" He stared at her dubiously.

She leaned forward, her forearms on the table, her voice low. "I don't know how much Gary told you about the projects he was working on. But there are some things you don't know."

"I'm listening."

"You know about the developer here in Colorado, Patrick Mahoney. He's the biggest developer of golf courses with all the amenities from Fort Collins down to Colorado Springs. Golf courses, homesites, fancy clubhouses, equestrian centers, you know."

"Mahoney. Yes, I'm familiar with the man."

"Then you already know Gary butted heads with this guy on the Panorama Ranch project. Gary kept saying that we couldn't afford one more high-end, high-maintenance development on the Front Range, and I know the whole board agreed. It's not just the water issues here, though they're bad enough. We've been in an awful drought cycle for years now, not to mention the wildfires. Gary said it was time to take a stand.

"Anyway, that's when he approached the rancher who was going to sell his land to Mahoney."

"Bill Nash, correct?"

"Yes. Nash seemed willing to accept the

offer from the NPS to buy the land to keep as open space."

"Yes, I know Gary was negotiating with the man."

"Well, now that Gary's dead, the project is almost through the approval process, and the land sale is going to be a done deal very soon."

She saw a frown of disbelief creasing Aaron's tan brow. He knew where she was going with her suspicions, and he was thinking that deals involving developers purchasing ranchland were made and broken a thousand times a day across the country. People didn't kill their rivals in these business dealings.

Even if a developer found the right location and acreage, there were water rights, country approval processes to undergo, and fierce local opposition from neighbors, not to mention environmentalists. Anyone and everyone who had the means to hire a lawyer could hold up a development indefinitely.

"It's not like Panorama Ranch is Mahoney's first project," she said. "He knows the drill and has a fleet of lawyers working for him. But I don't think he's come up against the NPS before. And then Gary went to court to get an injunction against the project."

Aaron reflected for a moment, then said, "Portia, I've got to be honest with you. I'm

73

still not hearing enough to understand why you believe Patrick Mahoney might have been involved in Gary's death, simply because Gary was trying to stop his plans."

When Aaron said it that way, her suspicions seemed awfully farfetched.

"Portia? I'm sorry, but . . ."

She looked up earnestly. "It's not just the money involved, which is plenty. It's the things leading up to the accident. Gary met with Mahoney several times. At one point, it seemed as if Mahoney was backing down. And, according to Gary, their meetings were . . . businesslike, even amicable. But then, right before his death, they had a falling out. An argument. Gary was very upset. He said Mahoney actually threatened him. Then there's the place where Gary's car went into the gully. Gary knew that curve. He never, *never* would have driven the speed the police said he had to be going."

Aaron regarded her. "What did the police say? I assume you told them all this."

She rolled her eyes and expelled a breath. "They listened. Undersheriff Whitefeather, that is, who's got jurisdiction. But without proof . . . Colt's a tiny town. With the wildfires and drought, the sheriff's department is understaffed, and Cab — Cab Whitefeather — doesn't have the resources for a full-scale investigation. Besides, the sheriff and the Colorado State Patrol officer

74

on the scene didn't see anything suspicious. Gary was speeding, took the curve too fast, the car flipped . . ."

She felt that miserable burning sensation behind her eyes and had to stop to compose herself. Aaron covered her hand with his.

"I'm sorry," she said, her voice thick.

"No need to apologize."

"Anyway, I've driven that road hundreds of times with Gary. In all conditions. He wasn't speeding. He couldn't have been. I know that as sure as I'm sitting here with you." She shut her eyes for a moment. "Cab Whitefeather must think I'm looking for a scapegoat, trying to blame someone for a senseless accident, but I'm not. Maybe you do, too. Someone, somehow, forced Gary off that road. And there's only one person I can think of with motive."

"Patrick Mahoney."

"Yes." She held Aaron's gaze, trying so hard to make him understand how important this was. "And that's what I want to bring to the media's attention if I take the NPS position." She saw the look of concern on his face. "Don't worry, Aaron. I won't mention Mahoney by name. But I'm hoping the authorities will reopen the investigation into Gary's death. You know how I feel about the media, but this time . . . this time I want to use them to accomplish something good."

"Well," Aaron said, sitting back in his

chair. "I've got to admit, you certainly are full of surprises."

"You think I'm crazy."

"No, no, not at all. It's simply . . . I never once thought of Gary's death as anything but a tragic accident. But if there's anything at all to your suspicions, I'll do whatever I can to help. You know that. The only thing I would advise is to take it slowly. Pick your fights, Portia, the ones you can win. Feel your way carefully. For God's sake, don't get involved with some tabloid."

So he knew. "Such as the *Star Gazer*, right?"

He nodded. "How is your mother taking it?"

"I haven't called. I'm hoping, make that *praying*, Anna kept it from her."

"Of course."

"And that's why you really flew out here, isn't it? To give me an out from all the bad publicity?"

He sighed. "In part."

"Okay," she said, "okay. I have a lot to think over then." And she could have throttled that New York cop if she could have gotten her hands on him. But that was history. Her own stupid mistake.

She shook off the thoughts. "I'll give you my decision by next week, Aaron."

"That's fine. My only concern is that you might be biting off more than you can chew, especially after what you just told me about Gary's accident. But I want to assure you that no matter what you decide, the NPS will pick up the ball again on Patrick Mahoney's development."

"Well, that's a relief to hear. No matter what I believe about Mahoney, the project is too huge, too irresponsible. I'll pull Gary's files and get copies off to you in the morning."

"Good. I don't involve myself in the day-to-day operations at the NPS, you know that. Other than sitting on the board, I'm retired, Portia." He smiled. "But I want to see Gary's work on this. Damn right I do."

Aaron was retired. *Sure,* she thought.

He reassured her one last time about following up on the Mahoney project, whatever her decision on the president's spot. He walked her out to await her car and declined a lift back to the private airport where his plane awaited him. "I'll get a taxi; it's no problem."

"Do you still copilot the jet?" she asked.

"Oh yes. If I ever have to give up my license, I'll sell the Lear in a flash. The fun of owning it is the flying."

"An expensive toy, Aaron."

He laughed ruefully. "That, unfortunately, is quite true."

Her car came down the ramp, and he hugged her. "Send me Gary's files on the

Panorama Ranch. Send them along, and let me worry about it. You take care of your chores at the ranch and look after Todd. Take all the time you need to decide on the NPS."

"Thanks, Aaron. I mean that. You've taken a lot of pressure off me already."

"Then the trip was a success."

She thought about Aaron the whole way back to the Wellspring Ranch. Thought about how grateful she was for all the support. For the first time in months she felt an inner calm. When Gary had died, she'd been so afraid to go it alone. Afraid and depressed and angry at him for leaving her in so much pain and with so many regrets. And the awful guilt. If only she could make it all up to him. If only she had loved him more . . . At least she was caring for Todd. Sure, Todd was there. And as much as she enjoyed his presence — well, *most* of the time — he was not the flesh of her flesh that she longed for, which she should have given to Gary.

The Front Range of the Rockies lifted to her right, the foothills so dry and brown it was frightening. As she drove south along I-25, the endless prairie stretched away into a cloudless blue bowl to her left. There were streamers of dust here and there in the distance, rising from farm tractors moving along country roads as dry and cracked as old cement.

Due south, a haze clung to the slopes of Pikes Peak from fires burning in the Four Corners region between Durango and the Navajo reservation. It was barely July, and already Colorado had suffered ten wildfires. If the drought persisted, there would be many more. She shuddered to think how easily a dry lightning strike or a cigarette carelessly tossed from a car window could ignite a fire close to the Wellspring Ranch. They would be devastated. Already there was barely enough grazing land left for the herd, and the midsummer hay crop would be poor.

Just past Castle Rock, she exited the interstate and drove through the town of Colt, all four blocks of it. Colt was one of those foothill hamlets that serviced the ranchers. There was a small but adequate grocery store, a liquor store, a barber, gas station, seamstress, hardware, co-op feed store, one eight-table restaurant that opened for breakfast at five-thirty in the morning, served lunch till two, and dinner from six till eight-thirty. A mom-and-pop operation. There was a bar.

There were no town police, but there was a sheriff's department annex, where Undersheriff Cab Whitefeather and six deputies worked. When Portia drove by, she waved at a deputy. Everyone in Colt and the surrounding area knew everyone by name. A part of her loved that aspect of living in a small town. Another part of her craved the streets of Manhattan. She'd wondered many times over the last weeks if by taking the NPS position she could not only fulfill Gary's dreams but also have the best of both lives.

But there was the ranch and her seemingly endless obligations to running it, because Gary had left her his half. And there was Todd. He had two years to go till he graduated from high school in Castle Rock. Two of the most important years in his life. He needed stability. He needed a parent at home for him.

The 3,000-acre ranch spread along a rutted county road and ran up into foothill country. Portia lived in the original farmhouse, built in the 1890s, when the Wells's ranch in Nebraska had been wiped out in the Great Blizzard of 1888 and, along with many other Great Plains families, they'd relocated to the foothill country in Colorado. There were still blizzards, but the 14,000-foot peaks of the Continental Divide buffered the Front Range from the slashing wind and killing cold.

The Wellspring Ranch farmhouse was typical of the Victorian era: two-story, white clapboard; tall windows and ceilings; the rooms boxy; a narrow, creaking staircase leading upstairs from the front entry hall. The living and dining rooms were in the front of the house, kitchen and a bedroom, bath and laundry porch in the rear. That bedroom had been used as an office ever since Portia had married Gary. Upstairs were three more bedrooms and two baths. Portia still slept in the master bedroom she'd shared with Gary. Closing the door behind her at night hadn't grown much easier with the passage of time.

Her brother-in-law Randy and his wife Lynette and their three kids lived in their own house, built for them by their parents when Randy married eighteen years ago. Whereas the main house overlooked the wide sweep of the vast prairies from the front, and the kitchen and laundry faced the mountains, Randy and Lynette's home was nestled in a lovely hollow surrounded by mature cottonwood trees. The main ranch road ran past Portia's farmhouse, down to the big barn and corrals, and branched from them, one branch leading to grazing land, the other to Randy's place and beyond to more grazing land, and then BLM — Bureau of Land Management — land beyond that. There were numerous, rutted ranch roads, slimy tracks in wet weather, dusty in dry, and there were numerous gates. Miles of fencing.

She parked near the garage, got out, and noticed Todd peeking out the upstairs window. He was supposed to have been helping his Uncle Randy. But this morning

Todd had complained about coming down with a summer cold and said he'd *try* to help his uncle. Portia knew he'd closeted himself in his bedroom and had been either playing Internet games or surfing sex sites. She also knew he was at this moment deleting files and clearing out the hard drive.

"I'm home, Todd," she called, tossing the car keys and her purse on the hall table. *"Todd?"*

Upstairs, she rapped on his door, got a weak, "Come in," from him. His sick voice.

"How you feeling?" she asked, opening the door and still holding the doorknob.

"Not so great."

"Did you eat lunch?"

"I made a sandwich."

"Um. I don't suppose you've been on the Internet all morning?"

"A little. I guess."

"I bet. Anyway, did your Uncle Randy stop by or phone?"

"He came by. Maybe about eleven. Just after you left."

"And?"

"And he left."

"To do what?"

"I think he said the big tractor was broken down near some gate."

"I see. Did he need your help?"

"He didn't say."

"Well, maybe if you feel up to it, you could

change that latch on the tack room door in the barn. The new one's on the bottom shelf by the bandages."

"Sure." Todd shrugged. He was sitting on the side of the hastily made bed, yesterday's dirty jeans and T-shirt and socks heaped next to the clothes hamper, magazines scattered on the floor, CDs and tapes everywhere, none of them in their cases. The walls were covered with posters of rock stars in concert, favorite movies such as *The Matrix* and *XXX*. Portia knew that the latest Victoria's Secret catalog was under the mattress.

He was a good-looking kid. Just under six feet tall, a handsome blend of both parents. He had Gary's fair coloring and even features and his mother's dark eyes and fine bone structure. Right now his blond hair was cut short, pieces stylishly standing out every which way, a couple of dyed red streaks still showing on a few ends. Maybe he was over the streaked hair stage. Or maybe not. Portia was endlessly glad body piercing was out for now. Hopefully, by the time it came back into fashion, Todd would have outgrown the craze.

She was changing clothes when she heard him bang the front screen door and the rumbling groan of the Subaru's engine as he started it up. Very shortly he'd get his driver's license. For now she allowed him to drive around the ranch, though last month he'd taken the car to a friend's place near Colt. She'd tried to ground him, but he'd threatened to run away, and her attempt at discipline quickly fell apart. If Gary had been there . . . But Gary wasn't, and she was too easily manipulated, too quick to feel she'd overreacted. There was all that guilt mixed in with her actions, too, misplaced guilt that his father had been taken from him and his mother and stepfather were not there for him, either, and somehow this was her cross to bear. Though, intellectually, she knew that was ridiculous.

She tidied up after Todd in the kitchen, wiping her hands on her carpenter jeans. Inexplicably, she could manage to put on an evening dress, do her hair and makeup in the most up-to-date style, then five minutes later she could wear old jeans and T-shirts and scuffed boots, her hair a windblown mess under a baseball cap. She was comfortable in either persona: city fashion plate or country tomboy.

Todd had the Subaru wagon, so she took the pickup truck and drove to where Juan and Hernando were supposed to be working on the hay baler. Aside from Juan and Hernando, the only two full-time ranch hands, there were three part-time workers, all of whom lived in or around Colt.

The chores at the ranch were many. There was roundup and branding. Shots for the cattle, hay to be grown. The herd had to be moved to summer pasture, then moved back to winter pasture. The bull calves had to be castrated and branded. There were always decisions to be made: how many head to sell, how many to breed and, increasingly, how much irrigation water to spread thinly over the needy fields.

There were vet calls for sick cattle and horses to be shod and feed to pick up, hay to cut and bale twice a year. Constant upkeep of fences and gates and the hay barn.

She finally located Randy repairing the gate on the heifers' pen.

Getting down from the truck, she wiped her brow on her forearm and strode up to him. "Hi." She always used her friendliest tone when dealing with Randy.

He made a grunting noise and kept working a new gate post into the ground.

"Need a hand? I could —"

"I got it."

"Um. Well, I found Juan and —"

"You remember to stop by the co-op? Account's a week past due."

"I didn't stop because we need to go over the books first. I thought this afternoon, we could —"

"Do I look like I've got time?"

"Randy, I know you're busy. I'm busy, too. But the bills won't wait."

He made another disgruntled sound, and

she handed him a wood shim. "Maybe at five, five-thirty, I could take a half hour," he said.

"That would be fine. I just don't want to write a check until we've gone over a few expense accounts."

Then she had a notion. "Look, why don't I put some ribs on the grill out back? I've got fresh corn, and I'll do home fries." Randy liked her home fries a lot. "And maybe you and Lynette and the kids could come to the house for dinner. We could write a couple checks while the ribs cook."

"Fine with me. You best clear it with Lynette."

Portia fetched her cell phone from the truck and pressed Randy on the address menu. Dinner was fine with Lynette, but only one of the kids would come along. The other two were spending the night with friends.

"Need me to bring anything?" Lynette asked.

"Dessert, if you want it."

"I'll get some ice cream in town. And maybe we can get Randy to take Paul home early, and we can catch up. I want every last gory detail about that *Star Gazer* story and how that sexy cop screwed you over."

"Oh God," Portia groaned.

"Come on, that was your first close encounter with a man since Gary died. So it turned out bad, but you're learning, right?"

"Oh, sure. Learning. But I don't want to talk about Nick Sinestra. I don't even want to remember him."

"Ha! So I guess that's why you say his name that way."

"I don't say his name *any* way. Now, don't forget dessert."

"Coward."

"Dessert, Lynette," she said, and she clicked off. She turned back to Randy. "Okay, done deal. I'll see you at the farmhouse when you get there."

"Okay. Where's Todd? He still lying around the house?"

She tried not to get defensive. "He's fixing a latch in the barn." *Let's hope he is,* she thought.

"You've got to take a firm hand with that one," Randy muttered, sweat dripping from his brow to form dark droplets on the hard soil at his feet.

"We're doing our best."

"We?"

"Todd and I. We're trying. It's only been ten months, Randy."

Another grunt of disapproval. She drove off, trying not to coat Randy in dust from the oversized tires. *God,* she thought, *some days are just harder than others.* The best being days when she didn't run into Randy at all. She was managing, though, to muddle through. Even before Gary's death, she'd covered for her husband's lapses in managing the ranch and tried to keep the peace between the two entirely disparate brothers. She'd always tried to be a friend to Randy. But he was indifferent to her, always too busy to give her much notice. Not even when she had suffered the miscarriages. Once Portia had tried to break the ice, waylaying him last spring in the co-op parking lot, asking his advice on an issue with Todd. But Randy had shrugged, saying, "Not much you can do about that boy now. Gary should have paid him more mind when he was alive."

She couldn't cry on Lynette's shoulder morning, noon, and night. After all, Lynette had a busy life with Randy and three growing boys. And there were moments when Portia wanted to scream because of loneliness and her fear of making a mistake at the bank or account ledgers. She lay in bed at night and fretted over the drought and the threat of wildfires. Already they'd lost a third of the herd — the BLM grazing lands were too dry this summer to support so many head. She'd lie there in the inky, close blackness and wonder why she even tried. What future was there in this?

But with the new light of day she pushed on, trying so hard to fill her charismatic husband's shoes, craving approval and a life of her own but unable to find either. And since

Gary's death, her relationship with Randy, despite Lynette playing peacemaker, had only gotten worse. Much to everyone's surprise, Gary had left Portia his half of the ranch. Not to Randy, not to Todd, his son. But to her.

At the reading of Gary's will, Randy had blurted out, "Oh, my God, like *she* needs half the ranch!"

If only Randy knew. Portia had little personal savings. Not much was coming from her parents, either. Judith's money had been dwindling for years, and Portia's father long ago remarried and had been dipping into capital ever since. His money, or what was left of it, would go to his present family.

Back at the farmhouse, she defrosted a family-sized package of spareribs and husked ten ears of corn. She put red-skinned potatoes on the stove to boil; Randy liked them boiled, then cut up and fried with onions and green peppers. Then she changed clothes again, into a clean pair of khaki shorts and sandals. Her hair, perfectly coiffed for the lunch with Aaron, was a wreck. She coiled it at the back and clasped it with a tortoiseshell clip.

Todd must have gone by Randy's and taken the dogs with him, because when she saw the two dogs running up the drive, she knew Todd had to be close behind in the car. Thank heavens. She'd been entertaining the idea that he might have slipped off into town.

One day the undersheriff was going to bust him for driving without a license. For now, since Gary's death, Cab Whitefeather gave him some slack. How long that would last was anyone's guess.

The screen door banged, and the dogs made tracks for the water bowl she kept for them on the back porch. "Todd?"

"Yeah, I'm in the living room."

"Get cleaned up. Randy and Lynette are coming over for dinner."

"No way."

"Yeah way."

"Bummer."

"Did you get the latch changed?"

"Yeah. I kept the old one. I think Uncle Randy just replaced it last year. It never worked."

Sometimes she believed there truly was hope for the boy. "Okay, I'll take it back tomorrow. And call Lynette, let her know the dogs are over here, okay?" It was always something.

Dinner was a mild success. Lynette had never been a great cook, and she eagerly accepted any and all invitations. Randy simply liked Portia's home fries. And she got her financial talk with Randy, even kept it on a friendly level. Todd managed to teach Paul, their eleven-year-old, a new video game on the computer without calling his young cousin unmentionable names.

Then there was after dinner. The adults were sitting under the big cottonwood in the backyard, the sun setting, the first cool air of the blistering summer's day flowing down out of the mountains. No one mentioned the lovely evening or the cloudless sky. By now the summer monsoon should have started, precious rain driven up from the Gulf of Mexico every afternoon for the month of July. There was nothing in sight, though, nothing in the near or distant forecast. There was no point in discussing the disastrous weather pattern.

Instead, Portia said, "You know I had lunch with Aaron today?"

"Yeah, sure," Randy said.

"Well, we discussed the president's position with the NPS."

The NPS was not a favorite subject. Randy had more than once told Gary the NPS was a bunch of "rich old tree-hugging farts with too much time and money on their hands."

"Anyway," Portia went on, "you already know I've been offered Gary's position."

Lynette clapped her hands eagerly and said, "Oh, Portia, that's wonderful."

Randy shot his wife a look.

Portia ignored her. "I really don't think I'll have a problem taking it on and upholding my end here at the ranch. But I am con-

91

cerned about Todd. I'm hoping the few times I'll have to be out of town you'll keep an eye on him. And I certainly won't take on any out-of-town engagements until school starts. He'll have his driver's license by then, and —"

"What's your point?" Randy said. "Todd isn't our responsibility. He should be in Denver anyway. With his mother." He gave Lynette another look, as if to say, *You keep out of this.*

Portia sighed. "We've already discussed that. He doesn't get along with his stepfather. He's going to stay here with me."

"When you're here, that is."

"I'm always here. Except for last week, a few days, I'm always right here. But if you can't or won't keep an eye on him, then I'll ask Juan's wife to stay over."

"That might be a better idea," Randy said, and Lynette looked about to cry.

"Fine. Whatever. I just wanted you to be aware of the possibility. I know you aren't, well, enamored of the idea, but the NPS was a big part of Gary's life. I feel as if he'd want me to fight his fights, to finish the projects he was working so hard on. No matter what you think about the NPS, surely you can appreciate the fact that it was Gary's passion. He thought of it as complementing the ranchers and farmers, and he —"

"Look." Randy sat forward in his plastic

chair. "Do what you want. It doesn't matter to me."

Indifference to her, the manner in which he stared at her as if she were useless around here, stung to the core.

She felt her spine stiffen. "Oh, well," she said, summoning her pride. "I just thought I'd let you know. I've decided to accept the offer from Aaron and the board of directors." Not exactly the truth, but she didn't care.

Lynette tried to get Randy to take Paul home, but Randy acted like a jealous child and said, "I'm not going home alone with Paul while you two sit and gossip. No way." And so Lynette left with her husband and son.

Todd hung out in his bedroom, and Portia cleaned up, then sat in the back bedroom that was used as an office and tried to relax. She almost asked Todd if he wanted to watch TV with her, but he was apparently content enough upstairs. Which wasn't always the case. He hated the ranch — well, she thought, not the ranch itself, but the loneliness and isolation. Of course, he hated living in Denver with his stepfather worse.

Finally she picked up the phone and made that call to her mother in New Rochelle. She'd been meaning and meaning to call to see how Judith was holding up, thanks to Nick Sinestra and that *Star Gazer* reporter.

Anna answered, thank God. "Anna, it's

Portia. How are you? . . . And Mom? . . . Really?"

Then Judith got on the line, and much to Portia's surprise, her mother was not nearly as upset by the tabloid's cover story as she'd thought. Judith said, "Oh, goodness, darling, I've had my picture on the front page of more magazines than I can remember. Frankly, I'm a bit curious as to why anyone would even care about me anymore. Wouldn't you think my whereabouts would be old news by now?"

Portia felt a wave of relief wash over her. "Well, I'm glad to hear you aren't too upset."

"Upset that people remember me? No, not at all. I'm just quite surprised."

"Oh, Mom," Portia said. "Of course everyone remembers you."

How could they forget? she mused.

FIVE

Embarrassed and pissed off that he'd lost his cool and punched Weston Ramsey, Nick left work early and caught the subway uptown before rush hour. Despite the air-conditioned subway car, he still felt closed in and over-heated. Who was going to baby-sit the HS guys now? Whoever got the assignment would probably appreciate the bonus salary, but he still felt guilty. No one needed the extra work. No one wanted to traipse around the streets with the naive newcomers who believed they were slumming — Weston, at any rate believed they were too educated, too good to be stuck working out of the old precinct building. Someday, maybe soon, they'd have their own offices. But Homeland Security was too new, still getting its feet wet, sniffing out its territory.

What the hell did *he* care? He was out of the loop now.

A week to clear off his desk and then a month of vacation.

He was going to get off on 103rd. Maybe stop on his way home to see Mia at the nail salon, tell her about the four weeks of freedom coming up. Maybe he'd spend some quality time with her. Her and her two daughters. Rent a house on the Jersey shore, Ocean City, kick back, soaking up rays on the sand. Like that. Temperature was usually ten degrees cooler at the shore, too, plus if you got hot, there was the water. Man, that might be the ticket, a week, ten days at the beach with Mia.

But he didn't get off at 103rd. Instead, he rode the train all the way up to the Bronx, figuring he'd visit the folks, see how they were doing in the heat wave. And he had a lot of cash coming from the *Star Gazer* for the Portia Wells job, so maybe he could persuade his mom to get a new bedroom air conditioner in this awful heat.

Tony and Sophia Sinestra lived in a quiet, mixed ethnic neighborhood three blocks from the subway. The family home was a brick apartment in the middle of the block. Sweating, jacket slung over a shoulder, sleeves rolled up, tie long gone, he strolled slowly by the other homes and thought how little the street had changed in the forty years his parents had lived here.

The houses were mirror images of one another. All brick with wood-framed windows and porches and rails, they each had three sections of poured concrete walks leading to three porch steps. Because they were mirror

96

images, the walks ran side by side, divided by wrought-iron fencing.

The lawns on either side of the walks were merely patches of grass, maybe eight by eight feet square. Funny thing was, everyone owned a gas-powered mower. Except Mrs. Ferrara, who got her exercise pushing an old iron hand mower. On Saturday mornings, all the mowers came out, and the noise was deafening.

If there was a noticeable difference between houses, it was the flowers. Some of the residents had a real touch, others eked by. Mr. Shelley grew roses. His flowers were the envy of the whole neighborhood. Nick's mom had a green thumb, grew lovely delphiniums and even had a purple hydrangea bush next to the porch steps. She grew other flowers, but Nick didn't know their names.

His father, sixty-five now, was due to retire from the textile factory where he'd worked for forty-seven years — an unimaginable feat in Nick's thinking. Nick's grandfather, an immigrant from a tiny Italian village, had worked at the same factory for fifty years and dropped dead of a massive stroke right on the factory floor. No doubt proudly.

Despite the grueling work, the lousy pay, the decades and decades of it, his forefathers maintained a curious and fierce pride, as if they'd just stepped off the boat onto Ellis Island and won the lottery. College? Who needed an education when you could buy a nice house in the Bronx and put food on the table for your family? Hell, Nick's own younger brother worked at the same factory and professed to be perfectly content. He even lived six blocks over. With his wife of fifteen years and their two kids. In a house not unlike this one that Nick now stood in front of.

"Nikko!" His mother beamed when he opened the screen door and stuck his head inside. "You should have called. Come in, come in, your father's in the living room. I'll get you a beer. Oh, I'm so glad to see you. You look wonderful." She held his cheeks in both hands and examined him as if she'd just given birth. Five fingers on each hand, five toes . . .

"You look great, too, Mom. Hey, can you make that a light beer? Gotta watch my figure."

His mother waved a dismissive hand at him, then disappeared into the kitchen. Nick could smell a pork roast cooking. Sure. It was Tuesday night. Could be a hundred degrees in the kitchen, and his mom would still turn on the oven if it was roast night. Spaghetti night was worse in the heat, though. The kitchen so humid and hot you couldn't eat. *They* ate. But Nick rarely could.

He strode into the living room, the familiar dark wood floorboards creaking beneath his shoes until he stood on the faded Persian rug that had been his grandmother's on his mother's side.

"Hi, Pop," he said, draping his suit jacket over the back of the burgundy-flowered couch.

But his father put up a hand. *Just a sec.* He was watching the early evening news. Same news he'd been watching since the advent of TV.

"Um," Nick said, sitting back and taking the beer bottle that his mother handed him.

How did they stand it? The sameness, the monotony, day in and day out, year after year, decade after decade. Same furniture: his pop's dark red faux leather armchair and footstool. Burgundy-flowered couch. Cheap Japanese patterned lamp over there on the ornate, carved end table. Dark green glass lamp on another table by the window. Doilies under everything. And on all the chair arms. Lace doilies, crocheted by his grandmother.

In the corner by the double glass-paned doors leading to the dining room — the house was darn near a shotgun style — was his mother's figurine collection on five shelves in a dark wood cabinet with a glass door. Little ceramic and glass figurines of children and rabbits and cats and birds and flower baskets. His mom's treasures.

Knees splayed, Nick sat sipping the cold beer, the breeze from a floor fan touching him on its sweep, the drone of the news in the background, and from nowhere a notion intruded: What would someone like Portia Wells think of this place, his mother and father?

He stayed for roast pork and carrots and roast potatoes that had cooked with the roast. And his mom's pork gravy, best he'd ever tasted. In spite of the oppressive heat and closeness in the small, overfurnished dining room, he ate well. Even had seconds.

"So, how's work, Pop?" he asked, chewing.

"Not with your mouth full, Nikko." His mother meant business.

Nick swallowed. "Sorry. So, how is work, Pop?"

"Good, good. You remember Joe O'Hurley? Lives two blocks over next to Mr. Kline's grocery? He just got promoted, head of his department."

"Geez," Nick said. "What's he now? Sixty?"

"Sixty-two."

"Same as me," Nick's mom said.

"Seems like a lot of years to work before you get a payoff?"

"Heck, boy, I didn't make department head till I'd been at the plant for, what? Thirty-some years, anyway."

"Um," Nick said. How *could* his father be so goddamn proud? Everyone wanted to better his station in life, didn't he? But not *his* family. They were the epitome of contentment, still living from paycheck to paycheck, paying bills weeks late sometimes, saving for a new fridge for months, thrilled with the new gas barbeque on the back stoop that they'd given each other for Christmas. Christmas because the outdoor grill had been deeply discounted.

"How about you, Nikko?" his mother asked. "You ever going to get some time off? I think it's disgraceful the way they treat you boys."

"Come to mention it, I got a month coming up. Starting end of next week."

"A month," his pop said. "Humph. Isn't that unusual?"

Nick shook his head, swallowed the mouthful of meat. "Not really. You gotta take your vacation days eventually. Mine just piled up."

"A month," his mother said. "You have plans?"

"Not yet. I'm thinking maybe a week or so at the shore."

"Oh, that would be nice."

"Maybe you and Pop could even come down."

"Don't think so," his father said. "My two weeks aren't till October."

"For a weekend, then. And maybe Johnny could come, too, bring the wife and kids." Johnny was his younger brother.

But his father shook his head. "Johnny just

got vacation. Took the kids to the mountains for a weekend."

"That doesn't mean they couldn't drive down to the shore, Pop, even if only for a couple of nights."

"Doubt he will." Nick's father wiped his mouth, folded his napkin, and stood. "Still costs plenty, two days at the beach. They're saving for that bedroom suite Dottie's been eyeing over at Jake's Furniture Warehouse."

"Okay, whatever." Nick sighed and met his mother's eyes. She at least understood. When Nick had gotten the scholarship to CCNY, his mother had been the only supportive member in the family.

His pop had said, "Why'd anyone want to waste four years in school? What you need, boy, is a good job. Paychecks."

Nick hung with his mother in the kitchen while she put the dishes and pots in the dishwasher. It was one of those roll-up-to-the-sink units that they'd saved for. His pop had given it to her as a birthday present. Didn't anyone in the family see what was wrong with that picture? A dishwasher for your birthday?

His mother wiped down the countertops, fastened the dishwasher hose to the faucet, and turned to him. "You ever see Gwen? I think about her a lot. Such a nice girl. What a shame the way things turned out. Whoever would have known?" Wistfully.

"Nah, I don't see her," Nick said. "After the divorce, we just drifted further apart."

"Well, it's a pity. She was so smart and so pretty. I just can't figure out —"

"Forget it, Mom. It's over. She decided she was going to take a different path in life. That's what she called it, *a different path*."

"I wish you'd had children together. Maybe that would have —"

He changed the subject then. "Say, how's that old air conditioner holding up in this heat, Mom?"

"The one in the bedroom?"

"You got another?"

"Well, no. But it's fine."

"Sure it is."

"Nikko."

"Well, damn, Mom, you wouldn't tell me one way or the other. I know that."

"You worry too much. Your father and I do just fine. We're happy, Nikko. Every day we look around at our blessings, and we're grateful. There are a lot of people in the world who have so little, nothing, really. And we have everything we ever wanted."

It was hopeless. "Okay, Mom, sure, whatever. But I got this big raise working with those guys from Homeland Security, and it's not doing me any good." He made no mention of the terrific money he got from the *Star Gazer*. His mom sure didn't need to know about that. "Anyway," he pulled a

103

folded wad of bills out of his trouser pocket, peeled off four one-hundred-dollar bills. "I want you to take this. Get a new air conditioner."

"Nikko." She shook her head. "It works fine. You keep your money."

"Take it, Mom, for me. At least get an air conditioner for the living room."

Nick was sure his father could hear the conversation, could hear it and disapproved. Well, screw him.

"Take it, Mom. Go on. Indulge me."

"Oh, Nikko . . ." But she took it. Of course he knew she'd stuff the bills in that coffee can of hers in the cupboard over the toaster oven. Despite her pride, despite his father's disapproval, she was smart enough to know someday the extra money might come in handy. More than likely, though, the bills would still be there when she died.

Nick took the train back into Manhattan and arrived at his 103rd Street subway stop shortly after nine. He walked up the two flights of steps to street level and broke a sweat for his effort. It was still daylight, fading now, but the temperature hovered up there in the nineties, the humidity murder. People were out on Broadway walking their dogs toward Riverside Park. The dogs wouldn't get much of a walk tonight. Too muggy even for animals, especially in their fur coats.

Restaurant tables on the sidewalks were busy, and people came and went from the neighborhood grocery stores and pharmacies. But no one was moving very fast. The most activity was in front of the movie theater up on Broadway. Nothing like a couple hours in an air-conditioned theater.

Nick's apartment was on West End Avenue in an older building, a walk-up, no doorman. But it was spacious enough and had a view down 107th of the treetops in Central Park. The building was relatively safe, its entrance well lit on the busy street, keys needed to unlock the street door. Everyone thought they were totally secure because an NYPD detective lived on the third floor. He didn't know how true that was, but there hadn't been a robbery in the three years he'd lived there since his divorce.

Ordinarily, he wouldn't bother stopping by Mia's nail salon, which sat on the corner of Broadway and 105th. Even at this late hour, the salon was going to be crowded. It was summer. Sandal weather.

But he was sort of excited. If Nick had it in him to feel excitement anymore. A month off. The idea of renting a small cottage in Ocean City was more and more appealing to him, especially with the sweat collecting at the back of his shirt collar. He felt as if he'd been soaked all day.

He strode up past the pharmacy and liquor

store to Mia's window. Still real busy. A couple women waiting on the cracked, salmon-colored vinyl chairs by the front window, all three elevated pedicure chairs full, the four manicure tables taken.

Mia herself was working. Sometimes she just manned the cash register and phone — unless it was very busy. Tonight the salon was maxed. Maybe he'd call her in the morning?

Ah, screw it. He pushed open the door. The fake bluebird in the wooden cage that hung at the door chirped. He had bought the novelty for her down in Chinatown. All of twelve dollars. Mia loved it.

When she saw him, she smiled and continued filing away on her client's nails, Mia's deft hands working so quickly he could hardly follow the action. The woman's other hand was soaking in a glass bowl of sudsy stuff.

The clients paid Nick little attention. Most of them were women, but there was a big, good-looking black guy getting a pedicure. Nick had to remember to tell Gil that, Gil who assured him only rich white guys, pimps, and fags got pedicures.

The manicurists were Chinese. All ages. They wore brightly colored silk, mandarin-collared jackets, and pretended not to speak English. That way the clients didn't distract them with chitchat. The more clients, the

106

more tips. And Mia had told him her girls cleaned up on tips.

The chair next to Mia was vacated, and Nick scooted it over to Mia's table.

"Hey," he said.

"Hey, yourself. I'm pretty busy. You want to stop by at ten, ten-thirty?" She never missed a stroke with her file.

Tonight she wore an emerald green jacket and her hair piled on top of her head, glitter-coated chopsticks holding it up. That was for the clients. She had a dozen silk jackets like that, all bought from a shop in Chinatown. And she sure looked stunning in them.

"I'm going home, catch the late news, get some sleep," he said. "I just wanted to see if you're interested in a few days down at the shore. The girls, too, of course."

"You got a vacation?"

"Sure did. Whole month."

"Wow."

The woman she was working on gave him the once over. He felt himself squirm a little. This might have been a bad idea, stopping by the salon tonight. What he had to say could have waited till morning.

"The shore, huh? Atlantic City?"

"Nah. Can't stand the place. I was thinking Ocean City. Maybe even that little town, you know, Margate. They got an elephant there, an old wooden relic . . . . Never mind. I just meant any shore will do.

Wildwood, Cape May." He shrugged.

By now quite a few of the women were listening. One client even said, "Wildwood's for kids. Cape May's nice."

Nick gave her a look. "Thanks," he said with no sincerity. He put his focus back on Mia, leaned closer, lowered his voice, and said, "Well? How about it? Say week after next?"

Boy, it was steamy in this cramped place. And the acrid small of nail polish and remover was making his nose itch something awful.

Mia sighed, tapped the woman's hand that was soaking — evidently a secret signal it was time for those nails. "Um, Nick, I'm not so sure that's a good idea."

"What? The shore? Ocean City?"

"No, no. I mean taking a trip like that together."

"The girls are invited. I told you —"

"I heard. And that's very sweet, Nick, really. Most men . . . Well, anyway, the girls have so many summer activities, swimming, gymnastics —"

"They could stay with their dad for a few days."

Mia finally paused and looked him in the eye. "I guess the truth is I like it the way it is between us."

"Huh?"

"You know. Simple. No strings."

"Oh. Sure, well, that's okay. Just thought I'd ask. You know."

He would have been all right with the turndown if her client hadn't glanced at him with that little bullshit smile on her lips.

"You understand, don't you, Nick? You're not mad?"

"Hell, no. Just an idea I had. No big deal." He stood and dragged the chair back to its place. "Well, see you."

"Okay," Mia said.

He nodded. Caught the amused smile on the woman's face again. *Fuck it,* he thought, making his exit. *Hell, fuck them all.* By the time he reached the corner, he'd wrapped his dignity around him like a shroud.

SIX

Nick hated being stuck in the hot, stuffy precinct house and fiddling with the computer. He was lousy at it, too. His forte was the street, mingling with the lowlifes, speaking their lingo, chatting up whores and pimps and petty dealers, getting more out of them than any other cop could. Homeless people, hell, he knew them by name, bookies, numbers runners, bar owners who ran games in their smoky back rooms. All the small fries. He was able to befriend them, coax information from them.

Live and let live was his motto. The sad sacks, the poor prostitutes with kids at home to feed, the strung-out junkies who he'd deliver to detox centers, try to talk them into doing rehab, only to see them on the street again. And again.

He tried not to arrest these losers, his far-flung network of informants. He laid money on them, never too much or they'd OD. Enough for food or another bottle of rotgut. He needed them, because their knowledge of the underbelly of the crime network led him upward to the real criminals. And they needed him; many owed him their lives.

But here he was, parked in front of a computer, his eyes falling out of his head, trying to track down the origin of the Nigerian scam.

The scam always starts with an unsolicited offer from a person writing on behalf of a former government dignitary. Tens of millions of dollars in Nigeria, or some other Third World country, needs to be transferred to a U.S. bank. The victim is promised a big cut if he holds these millions in trust for the so-called dignitaries. Hitch is, he's got to pay various fees up front. The scam continues until the victim wises up or runs out of money.

And the councilman's mother had been stung to the tune of 5,000 big ones. The trouble was, Nick had no idea how to trace the E-mail. Everyone else was out on a case. Out on the streaming streets of the city. *Shit.*

He only had two more days on the job, though. Then the month off. What in the name of God was he going to do for a month?

This was his penance for bad behavior: the phone, the Internet, paperwork. Two more days of it.

A repair man was banging on the window air conditioner. It still didn't work. Nick had a noisy, clattering fan on his desk; mostly it blew his papers around.

At two in the afternoon, after talking to another one of the victims of the Nigerian scam, he pushed back his squeaking chair and put his hands behind his head. He could smell the sweat that dampened his underarms. The trouble with his shirt — and every other shirt he owned — was that it was polyester, so it didn't have to be ironed, but it got clammy when he sweated. Cheap piece of crap. But then, what can you expect when you buy them three for $14.95 at one of the shops on Thirty-fourth Street?

The repairman had stopped banging and was drilling, a high-pitched whine that bored into his brain.

And then, to make his day a perfect ten, Weston Ramsey sauntered in. He wore a pale gray summer-weight suit, a pearl gray shirt, and a blue patterned tie. He also sported a scab on his lip.

"How's it going?" Ramsey asked smugly.

"Oh, just great," Nick muttered.

"Stuck on that latest Nigerian scam? Gil was telling me about it."

"Yeah?"

"I might be able to help."

"Don't you have something really important to do, like saving the world or some crap like that?"

"Okay, Sinestra, truce."

Two days, he told himself. He could handle

Ramsey for two days. "Okay," he said grudgingly. "Truce."

The Homeland Security guy sat down at Nick's computer and started clicking away so fast Nick couldn't follow what he was doing. Ramsey kept up a running commentary while he worked.

"It's really hard to find the origin of these scams. They're usually based overseas, so there are jurisdictional limitations. Oh, here's something interesting, an address in England. Hm."

Gil Howard came in a few minutes later, his dark face shiny with sweat. He shot a look at Wes Ramsey sitting in front of Nick's computer, raised his eyebrows. Nick shrugged.

"Hey, Howard," Ramsey said. "You any better at computers than your partner?"

"Marginally."

"You guys." Ramsey shook his head, clicked some more. "Jesus, this system is slow."

He clicked a few more keys, then hit Print. The printer buzzed and clacked, and a page cranked out.

"There you go. Someplace to start, anyway," Ramsey said.

Gil picked up the printout, studied it. "Thanks," he said.

"Any time."

Nick locked his jaw and said nothing.

He had another job for the *Star Gazer* that evening. There was going to be a free rock concert in Central Park, one of those mega summer events where thousands of half-naked kids jammed the park, drank too much, did drugs, gyrated wildly to the music. There was the usual contingent of uniformed police on duty at the event. Mounted cops, hundreds of men getting paid overtime to protect the public against itself. There were also countless undercover cops there, too.

Free concert. Right.

But his assignment was to shadow the star of the main band, a scrawny, drug-addicted, not-so-young guitarist whose music made young girls scream. The guitarist, Tommy Boy Franz, had just married his fourth young, beautiful, blond wife, and Nick's boss at the tabloid had heard a rumor that Tommy Boy was already stepping out on his future ex with one of the band's light technicians.

The tabloid wanted photos of Tummy Boy and his newest paramour. Up close and personal pictures, the kind that would be splashed on the front page, with startled faces and poor lighting.

He could see it: "Tommy Boy Franz with Illicit Lover. Fourth Mrs. Franz Goes on Killer Rampage."

It so happened that Nick was privy to the

location of the private penthouse apartment where the rock star was staying. The information hadn't been hard to collect. A couple of calls to people he knew — and Nick knew all the right people — and he had the address. Not that he'd let on to the *Star Gazer*. Hell, if he did that, they wouldn't need him.

So he rode the subway to Central Park that evening, had a hot dog piled with German mustard and sauerkraut at one of the sidewalk vendors, and mingled with the crowd as concertgoers gathered for the frenzy. He popped a couple Tums to keep from belching.

It was so damn hot still you sweated just standing around. The heat wave was going to make this scene worse than usual to handle. Tempers flared, kids got crazy. Even the police horses standing patiently were sweating.

The girls, the young tight bodies, wore clothes showing so much skin, bare midriffs, bare legs, bare shoulders, tight shorts, skirts up to their crotches. Jesus, what were kids coming to?

He saw an old buddy from his police academy days. "Kenny," he said, "What in hell are you doing on this duty?"

"Aw, Christ, Nick, I need the overtime. Got another kid coming."

"Another? I didn't know you had the first."

An abashed smile gathered on Kenny's face. "Yeah, I'm just an old family man now."

But his words burst with pride.

Nick moved on, pushing his way through the crowd. Kenny with two kids? Everybody seemed to be happily married. What was wrong with him? With his life? Or maybe there was nothing wrong, and he was just too dumb to realize it.

The music started. So loud, so much bass, he couldn't believe anyone could stand it for long. He hung around at the back of the crowd, trying not to notice the bottles being passed back and forth, or the doobies that were sucked on, inhaled, held. The air was ripe with the pungent odor of pot.

Once he had to hassle a couple that was just too open with their bag of weed. Rolling a joint right under his nose.

"Hey, you kids, I'm a cop. You really want to be doing that right here?" he said.

"You're joking, dude." The boy smirked.

"I'm not joking, *dude*. I'm not going to arrest you this time. Just take that crap and keep it out of sight, asshole."

The boy's eyes got big. The girl grabbed his hand and started pulling him away. In a second they were lost in the crowd, and the *boom boom boom* of music started again, Tommy Boy jumping around on the stage like a frenzied old monkey, screaming out his lyrics, grabbing at his crotch.

Nick positioned himself at the back of the stage at the end of the concert. An old pal he used to work with let him through, and they chatted for a while. "What you doing these days? How's Gwen? Oh. Sorry, didn't know you two were divorced." Like that.

He strolled around, trying not to trip on the snaking wires lying on the ground, looking for the light technician that Tommy Boy was rumored to be screwing. Most of the backstage personnel were men, so spotting her wasn't hard. She was standing there next to one of those big spotlights, a cigarette dangling from her lips. Tall and dark-haired, tough looking but attractive. Long, long legs in tight jeans, a T-shirt that read, Tommy Boy Rocks.

Okay.

He waited there, gabbing, drinking some coffee to which he'd helped himself from a carafe near the band's trailer. Finally the show was over, and the musicians came backstage, soaked with sweat, high as kites. On God knows what.

He waited some more, unobtrusive, patient, until Tommy Boy's limo picked him up, and then he followed in a cab, figuring exactly where the rock star was headed but tailing him to make sure he didn't stop to meet his latest squeeze somewhere else.

Tommy Boy went directly to the apartment building and disappeared inside. Nick paid off his cab and found a nearby doorway in which to wait. He didn't have long; just before one in the morning, she arrived in a taxi, got out. Looked around briefly, furtively, and went into the building.

He waited a while longer, in case the couple decided to go out on the town, then he pulled out his cell phone and made the call. The *Star Gazer* would send a photographer over to stake out the building, and by morning they'd have their dirty little photos.

Hey, what could these celebrities expect if they pulled stunts like this?

He was tired when he finally got home, but there was to be no rest for the weary that night. A blinking light on his answering machine ended his plans for sleep. He almost ignored it, but then he thought, *What if it's Mia? What if she changed her mind?* So he pressed the button and listened to the message.

"Nick, this is Gil. Listen, I hate to bug you so late, but Doug's really jammed up. We're here at the Seventh Precinct, and I remembered that you know some guys down here. Maybe you could make a call or something, pal?"

Oh, shit. Doug was fourteen years old and a problem. He ran with a bad-ass crowd, and Gil was rightfully worried about him. Nick had known the kid since he was a little boy. Doug — in trouble with the law. What in hell had he done?

He called Gil's cell phone, and it rang in

118

his ear too many times before Gil answered.

"Hey, buddy, what's up?"

"Thank the Good Lord," Gil replied. "Doug's in all kinds of shit."

"What'd he do?"

"Underage drinking. They found him in the Delancey Street subway station with a bottle. Him and his goddamn buddies."

"Okay, Gil. I'll be right down."

"Oh, hey, Nick, you don't have to do that. It's late. Maybe you could just —"

"I'll be there in twenty minutes."

He drove his own car, knowing he could park in front of the 7th Precinct house on Pitt Street. Traffic was light this late on a weeknight, and he made the drive in record time. Strode into the concrete bunker that did duty as a precinct house and found Gil sitting dejectedly on a chair in the lobby.

"Thanks, Nick," he said.

"Who's on tonight?"

"Wesley Dominic."

"Okay. Who was the arresting officer?"

"Guy named Vinny Cooper and his partner Rudy Gentile."

"Gentile. I know him. They still here?"

"Cooper went home. Gentile is waiting for the other kids' parents to show." Gil rolled his eyes. "Some of those kids, their folks are more likely to be arrested than they are."

"Come on. We're going to talk to Gentile."

Rudy Gentile was a round-faced, chubby

119

guy who must have been a cherubic looking little boy.

"Hey," he said, "those kids are, what fourteen, fifteen, and they've got a bottle of cheap vodka in a paper bag. All of 'em drunk as hell, one of 'em threw up all over the backseat of our cruiser. Christ, these punks need some goddamn discipline."

Nick knew Gil wanted to punch the guy out; he gave his partner a look. "Come on, Rudy, you can let this kid go. His father here is my partner, man. You don't want a cop's kid to get a record."

"I don't know, Nick."

"Hey, remember the time I helped you nail that guy was robbing old ladies? I'm asking nice, pal."

"The paperwork's done. You know what that means, Nick."

"Undo it."

"Aw, Christ."

"Do I have to beg, Rudy?"

"Yeah, beg."

Nick grinned devilishly and got down on his knees. "I'm begging, man. See? Here I am, begging."

"Get the hell up! What are you, nuts? Okay, the kid gets off. This time. But if I see him or his punk buddies on my turf, he gets the book thrown at him big time."

Outside the stationhouse, Doug pale and scared, Gil read him the riot act.

"You ever do this again, I won't lift a finger. Your mother is half out of her mind. Do you know what you've done to her? And Nick here, has to come out in the middle of the night to get your sorry butt out of jail. Do you *know* what it's like to be in juvenile hall, Doug?"

Doug stood there, head bowed, tall and gawky, smelling of booze and vomit and the indefinable odor of a jail cell.

"Do you hear me, son?"

"Yeah," the kid whispered.

"Okay, Gil," Nick said, putting a restraining hand on his partner's arm.

"Oh, it's not okay, not by a long shot."

"Look at him, Gil. He's a mess. He's sick and hungover and sorry. Aren't you, Doug?"

"Yeah," came the mumbled reply.

"You're grounded, boyo. For the rest of your goddamn life!" Gil raged.

"Hey, take it easy on him," Nick said. "Come on, I'll drive you home."

"I've got my car," Gil said. "Probably got a parking ticket by now."

"That's all right. Doug'll pay it. Won't you, kiddo?"

"Yeah." Doug's voice was choked. Light from the streetlamps shone on tracks of moisture on his cheeks. The poor kid was crying. *Ah, Jesus,* Nick thought.

"Let's go," Gil said to his son.

"See you at work tomorrow." Nick summoned up a smile.

"If I make it. Hey, thanks, Nick. I owe you."

"No prob."

Gil put his hand on the back of Doug's neck and began to propel him toward his car, then he stopped and said, "Hey, you're on vacation in a couple days. Why don't you take the punk with you, keep him out of trouble?"

"Right. Great idea," Nick said.

As he drove back uptown, he thought about what Gil had said. He could take Doug with him, just the two of them, no pressure on the kid from a father figure, some man-to-man talks. Uncle Nick, yeah, that was him.

Except now that Mia wasn't interested in going to the shore with him, he didn't even know if he'd leave the city.

SEVEN

Well, it was done; her hat was officially in the ring. She'd called each member of the board and told them she would accept the presidency of the NPS for the remaining two years of Gary's term. She'd been heartened by their response, heartened and scared to death.

And then she called Aaron to tell him.

"Portia, how good to hear from you."

"Aaron, I've decided to accept the presidency."

There was the slightest hesitation, an infinitesimal pause, and then, "My goodness, that is terrific. Congratulations are definitely in order. Have you told Reenie and the rest?" Reenie was the head of the board.

"Yes, I called them all today."

"I confess, I'm a little surprised."

"You are?"

"I admit I got the feeling you didn't really want to be quite so . . . engaged."

"I know. But I've had time to think, and I decided there were more pros than cons. I want Gary's work to go on."

"Of course you do. So do we all."

"The announcement is in this month's newsletter. It'll be sent in E-mails to every member, and Reenie said she'd send it to the newspapers."

"Well, sounds like you have all bases covered, Portia. But I hope you're not doing this because of the conversation we had in Denver the other day, because of Patrick Mahoney."

"Of course not. He's a part of my decision, yes, but certainly not the whole reason."

"Good, good. I received your fax, Gary's paperwork on the Panorama Ranch, and after reviewing the file, I sent it along to the other board members. If you'll take a little advice from an old man —"

"Aaron."

She heard his chuckle. "At any rate, let the board see what it can do about Mr. Mahoney's plans. You may be too close to the issue."

"You want an objective eye."

"Something like that."

She thought a moment, then said, "All right. But I'd like to be kept up to the minute on everything that's going on."

"You have my promise."

"And, Aaron, I want you to know that I'll do my very best for the Society."

"I know you will, my dear." He paused. "There will be that media coverage, you realize."

"I know that. I'll handle it. If they want to use me as a whipping post, fine, but I'll be using them, too."

"That's my girl," he said.

"Thanks. You know how much I depend on you."

"You have my unswerving loyalty, Portia. You know that."

"Yes, Aaron, I do."

The announcement that Portia Carr Wells was taking on the NPS presidency made a mediocre splash. More than a report on the failure of a new Air Force weapons system but less than a new spate of Mideast terrorism. All three Denver network news programs sent reporters to interview her, and the stories of Gary's death were resurrected, as she'd known they would be. As she'd intended they would be.

There were some questions about her mother Judith, but she fended them off gracefully. No one pressed her on the subject, but she breathed a sigh of relief when the reporters and cameramen left.

That night Todd called to her from the living room while she was working on the computer, trying to balance the ranch account.

"Portia, you're on," he said.

Reluctantly, she left the keyboard and went to see how the nightly news had treated her.

There she was in jeans and a blue short-sleeved shirt, looking suitably folksy but not sloppy. The spot was short, only a few minutes, but the feel was sympathetic. "Portia Wells, widow of conservation activist Gary Wells, has announced she will fill her late husband's shoes, taking on the presidency of the Nature Preservation Society. Ms. Wells, can you tell us what you see as the future role of the NPS?"

Todd was clicking the remote to the other channels, all of which gave her similar coverage.

"You look nice," Todd said, "kind of like you're different but the same, you know?"

"Thanks." Sometimes he could be really sweet; mostly he worked on his relaxed but cocky demeanor.

"It's weird seeing you on TV," he said.

"I may be on a lot now. Will that bother you?"

"Nah," he said. "I think it's kind of cool."

The phone rang then, and Todd went to get it, saying, "Geez, let me guess, it's Aunt Lynette."

He was right. Lynette gushed, "Oh my God, you looked so great on TV! And not even nervous, just, you know, like you do TV every day. I'm so jealous. Where did you get that blue shirt? Have I seen it before?"

They talked for a half hour until Randy could be heard in the background: "Lynette?"

126

"Gotta go; Randy, you know," Lynette said.

"Where are the kids?" Portia asked.

"Oh, Matt's on the computer upstairs, and the other two are tearing up the living room with Randy doing zero to stop them. I'll run by tomorrow sometime, and we can catch up some more. Okay?"

"Okay," Portia said.

She didn't know what she'd do without Lynette. Perish from boredom and loneliness, she supposed. Neighbors and acquaintances always assumed Portia was the alpha female of the relationship when, in truth, Lynette was the tough, outgoing one. Short and a little plump, with reddish brown hair that she fussed with endlessly, Lynette at first glance appeared cute and on the ordinary side. She was the perfect cliché: the girl with the pretty face who needs to lose weight. The fact was, men took to her instantaneously. She had an easygoing, genuine love of males, an acceptance of herself and her place in life, and acceptance of all men, young and old. A man would meet Lynette for the first time, and five minutes later they were best friends, the man confiding things to her that he wouldn't tell a priest in the confessional.

Yet it was Lynette who sometimes appeared dependent on Portia, dragging Portia to clothes shop with her, to the hairdresser in Castle Rock to decide on what color and length to do her hair this month.

"I'm so horrible with myself," Lynette would say. "I always buy the wrong color and let the stylist wreck my hair. If it weren't for you, Portia . . ."

But if it weren't for Lynette, Portia would have gone insane when she'd lost the babies. She had even confessed to Lynette the truth about her marriage to Gary, how she'd loved and adored him but not truly been in love, how she felt she'd forgiven his wandering eye because of her own inability to love him body and soul.

"That is so bogus," Lynette always said. "Do you think every married woman on earth married because she was head over heels in love?"

"*You* did," Portia would say.

"Like hell. I married Randy because the dumb jerk convinced me the Wellspring Ranch was the richest ranch on the Front Range."

"Oh, bull."

"No, it's true. I love him, sure, and our boys, but it's not that I-can't-eat-or-sleep love. Never was. Look at me. I'm fat as an old sow. I'm lucky I even got him. Now *you* . . ."

Lynette's favorite subject: Portia and men, how she could have any man she wanted any time, any place. Which was so far from the truth. Portia simply lacked the openness of Lynette, the fortitude to say what she felt and to act on it. Too reserved. Too afraid of rejection. She knew that was because of her mother and her always-absent father, Portia's misplaced sense of guilt that she'd done or said something to make them reject her.

But she was still young and still a woman, and she went to bed at night so lonely and aching and so afraid she'd never find love again. Then she'd feel guilty for needing so much.

But there was Lynette. "So what if Gary hasn't been dead a year? *You're* not dead. You have every right to want a man, to want sex. What? You think you should become a nun or something?"

And Lynette even thought Portia should contact that policeman when she was in New York again. "Who cares if he called a reporter? He came to your rescue, didn't he? Everyone makes mistakes. My God, I would have told him to pull his car over in Central Park or somewhere and jumped his bones."

When Lynette had said that the other day, Portia couldn't help laughing. "Jump his bones? That's cute, Lynette."

Still, that night and again tonight when she turned in, she wished to God she had the nerve to do just that.

The day following her NPS announcement, she had to go into Colt to pick up some special feed for the cows with calves at the Co-op store. She drove the pickup, a ten-year-old Dodge Ram, a big noisy thing that belched black diesel smoke. She hated driving it, knowing how bad the diesel exhaust was for the environment; she felt like the worst sort of hypocrite. But the ranch couldn't afford a new truck, and she had to get a dozen fifty-pound sacks loaded into its bed.

She parked in the front lot, went into the store. There were shelves piled with tools and halters and horse blankets and medicines equine and bovine, salves and powders and anti-inflammatories, horse shoes, Western shirts and jeans and overalls. She walked by and headed for the counter where she ordered the dozen bags of feed to be charged to the Wellspring Ranch account.

"How are you doing, Portia?" the girl behind the counter asked. "Randy was in the other day, said your irrigation water was almost gone."

"I'm afraid so. Ours and everybody else's, Sally."

"Damn drought," Sally said.

Portia drove the truck around to the back of the building, where the sacks were loaded into the bed.

"Hot, ain't it?" the man loading the feed said.

"Sure is," she replied. Same old ranch talk: the ungodly heat, the drought, water and cattle and horses and the price of hay.

She drove back toward the front of the store, heading for the highway. But a car was in her way, stopped right in the middle of the narrow driveway that led to the front parking lot. She stepped on the stiff brake pedal and stopped to wait for the car to back up.

It didn't back up. Instead, the doors opened, and two men got out and strode toward her. Before she could think, one of them opened the passenger door, slid in beside her, reached over and turned the ignition off, and took her keys. The other man opened her door and stood there, staring at her.

Her first reaction was shock and disbelief. "Hey," she said, and she felt adrenaline shoot through her veins.

"Shut up," the man holding her door said.

She looked from one to the other, anger trying to rise from beneath her fear, falling back. Should she scream? "Get out of my truck," she got out past the lump in her throat. "Get out —"

"Shut up," the one in the passenger seat repeated. She stared at him; he was tall and heavy, with reddish hair and freckles and a double chin.

"I will not." Her voice was quivering. "Give me my keys. I don't know who you are, but all I have to do is yell —"

"I wouldn't yell if I were you," the one

standing next to her said. He was smaller and balding, but his voice was cold and quiet and vicious, and his eyes were like lumps of coal.

"We're here to deliver a message," he said. "Don't screw up Patrick Mahoney's plans."

She drew in her breath. *Mahoney*. A chill settled inside her.

"Don't screw up his plans, you hear?"

Then the other man. "If you do, you'll be in a sea of trouble. Real trouble. And don't even think about talking to the cops."

She wanted to say something, anything, but she knew her voice would fail her.

"One more thing," the balding one said. "Remember what happened to your husband?" He stepped back, slammed the truck door, while his partner got out the other side.

She was paralyzed. With a flick of his hand, the red-haired man tossed her keys into her lap. Then they got into their car, backed up, spun around with a squeal of tires, and drove out of the parking lot onto the highway.

She sat there, her heart hammering and her mouth sucked dry of moisture. Her hands shook. She closed her eyes and opened them. Had that really happened? Had two men accosted her with a threat from Mahoney? Had they really admitted Gary's death was no accident?

My God.

A pickup stopped in front of her, trying to get through. She grabbed at the keys, fumbling, turning on the noisy diesel engine, backing up so the truck could get past. Sitting there, not knowing whether her trembling was due to fear or the truck's vibration.

She finally pulled out onto the highway, wrestling with the steering wheel. Her legs were spasming, her nerves so frayed she had no control of her muscles. Should she go straight to the police? Should she call Aaron and ask him what to do? Should she do what the man said and *not* tell the police?

She didn't remember the drive home. Thoughts ricocheted inside her head. She wouldn't give in to fear, the way Mahoney wanted her to. She'd uncover his schemes and his greed and his complicity in Gary's murder. She'd never bow to coercion. Despite Aaron's words of warning, she'd use her position and whatever small power she had to pull up the rock Mahoney hid under and watch him scurry from the light.

She pounded the steering wheel once. *That bastard. That bastard.* But her limbs still shook.

She bypassed the ranch road to her house and drove straight to Randy and Lynette's. Parking in front, she sat there a second and tried to collect her thoughts. She recalled the smaller man's exact words: *"Remember what happened to your husband?"* Her heart squeezed with fear, then flared with anger.

She got out of the truck and went up to the front door. Probably Randy wasn't even home. She cracked the front door, which was never locked, and called, "Randy? Lynette?"

Her answer was furious barking from their old Border collie.

"Shush, Nellie!" came Lynette's voice.

"Lynette, it's me."

Her sister-in-law appeared at the door, smiling, but when she saw Portia's face, she whistled and said, "What? What's wrong?"

But Portia shook her head. "It's . . . I'm not sure. I've . . . I've got to talk to Randy."

"Portia."

"Look, I promise, as soon as I get this sorted out, I'll call you."

"I can't stand this. Get *what* sorted out?"

"It's . . . I don't know. Can you tell me where Randy is? Please, Lynette, we'll talk later."

Reluctantly, Lynette told her he was irrigating the north hayfield. "Talk to Randy, and then you call. This is unbearable. I hate secrets."

"I'll call, I swear," Portia said.

She drove the dirt track to the field, bumping along, going over and over the quick, ugly encounter with Mahoney's muscle men. Yes, there was Randy's white Ford pickup and his younger dog Charley. He was moving the orange plastic to change the irrigation flow.

Pulling up next to his truck, she climbed down. She was sweating, and the sun was hot, and she was beginning to think this wasn't such a good idea.

"Randy!" she called.

He looked up, his face shaded by the brim of his cowboy hat. "What!" he yelled back.

"Can we talk?"

He appeared to mutter under his breath, then he straightened from his work and strode toward her. Sometimes, if the light caught him just right, he reminded her so much of Gary. Right now she could almost believe Gary was walking across the field toward her.

But Gary had never worn such threadbare jeans or muddy boots or an old plaid shirt with a ripped pocket.

"Yeah, what's up?" he asked, rubbing his dirty hands on the thighs of his jeans.

"I just got back from the Co-op."

"You got that feed?"

"Yes. Listen, Randy, while I was there, these two men stopped me . . . right in the parking lot, and they scared the hell out of me. They warned me not to screw up Patrick Mahoney's plans."

His gaze sharpened. "Two men?"

"Yes." She waved a hand in the air. "Horrible men. One of them said, his exact words,

'Remember what happened to your hus-band?' "

"Oh, for Chrissakes, Portia. I mean, come on."

"Randy, they were serious. Mahoney sent them."

"Oh sure. As if Mahoney has time for crap like that. It was . . . hell, I don't know, a joke."

"It was no joke."

"Look, everybody around here knows you think Gary was murdered. You haven't ex-actly made a secret of it. Someone's pulling your leg."

"It was no joke, Randy!"

He cocked a hip and tilted his head. "Well, if you think these two horrible men are dan-gerous, go to Cab."

She was about to retort that the men told her not to tell the cops, but she stopped her-self. Randy would just mock her. He never took anything she said seriously, not about the ranch's bank balance or a new breed of cow to try, or any damn thing.

"I knew something like this was going to happen. Christ, Portia, you don't belong here. You belong back in New York City, specially now that you're going to be the high and mighty president of the NPS."

"Oh my God," she breathed. "Are you lis-tening to me? This hasn't got a goddamn thing to do with whether or not I'm president or whether or not I can handle living on this ranch. I was *threatened.*"

"That was all bullshit."

"No, it wasn't. And don't you even care that those men practically admitted they killed your brother? *Don't you care?*"

He smirked. "They just said that to get your goat, and it looks like it worked real good."

"Don't you care that Gary was murdered?"

"My brother wasn't murdered. He died in a stupid accident. Took that curve too fast."

She gave up. Randy was the king of denial, and she couldn't get through to him. God knows she'd tried. His defenses were stronger than any weapons she had at her disposal.

She spun away, so mad she was shaking. Then she whirled back around and called, "Oh, by the way, this ranch *is* my home."

She drove the rutted road, furious. Frustrated. Alternating between bravado and abject fear. She'd promised to call Lynette, but if she told Lynette the truth of what had just happened, Lynette would jump all over Randy, and then Randy would be even more irate at Portia and impossible to deal with.

No, she couldn't drag Lynette into this mess. Not yet. She'd tell her some story about trouble she had with a bill or something at the Co-op. Anything.

But without Lynette to confide in, she suddenly felt so alone. She had nobody to help her, nobody to listen, nobody to hold her at night when dreams made her whimper in her sleep. She missed Gary, and she wondered whether Randy was right — she should fold her hand and go back to New York, away from the good and bad memories, away from the problems of the ranch that were draining her. Away from Randy's relentless resentment.

But Gary had loved this land. He had left his half of it to her, and she had to accept the responsibility. She just had to.

There it was again, overpowering her fear: the guilt. Maybe if she'd loved Gary more, borne him children, been a better rancher . . . but she'd failed at all her wifely duties. She had no choice but to stay here and make it work. She had no other options open to her, not if she wanted to look herself in the mirror.

Then, of course, there was Gary's son.

The kitchen counter was a mess, crumbs and splotches of mayonnaise, an apple core. Todd had fixed himself lunch. He was a slob and he was lazy, and he should have been out helping Randy with the irrigation. But he had that way of sliding out of chores, turning on the charm to get away with things. Just like his father. Gary had been able to accomplish everything with his smile and his glib tongue.

Todd was not in evidence, but she knew where to find him. She knocked on his bedroom door, a polite convention she'd decided was fair, and there was a moment of suspended silence, then, "Come in."

"Got a minute, Todd?"

"Sure. I was just E-mailing a friend."

She sat down on his bed, and he turned his desk chair to face her.

"I've got a problem I want to talk over with you. As one adult to another."

He stared at her out of Gary's eyes, belligerence lurking just under the surface.

"I'm going to be very honest with you. You're not a child anymore, and I think you deserve my trust."

"Okay."

"I just had a . . . a confrontation. Some men threatened me at the Co-op. I'm sure they were from Patrick Mahoney."

"That man, the . . . uh, developer?"

"Yes. I'm telling you this because it might be wiser for you to stay with your mother and stepfather at this point. I don't know if those men would really do anything, but I don't want you in any danger."

"What about *you?*"

"I took on the presidency with open eyes. But you didn't. You shouldn't have to suffer because of my decision."

"Suffer?" Todd rolled his eyes. "You know what suffering is? It's living with Raymond."

139

"I'm sure he does his best."

"His *best*." Todd turned sullen. "And he spoils that kid so bad . . ."

"That kid is your brother," she gently reminded him.

"My *half* brother." Derisively.

"Okay, your half brother. He's just a baby."

"I don't hate Oliver, but he's a pain. I *hate* Raymond."

"Todd."

"I do. And I don't want to go live there. But you'll probably make me. You just want to get rid of me, like everybody else. If my father was alive . . ."

There it was again, the old catechism. Everything would be different if his father were still alive.

She tried a new tack. "I thought you liked the city better. You keep saying —"

"I do like the city. But not enough to live with Raymond."

"You're sure?" She wondered if she should put her foot down and make him go back to his mother and Raymond. But she couldn't bring herself to; maybe she needed Todd as much as he needed her. Or maybe her waffling was all about guilt.

"Yeah, I'm sure." He paused, and then he said seriously, so much like his father she felt a pang in her belly, "And, besides, you let me drive the truck and stuff."

She rose from his bed. "Okay then, young

man. Let's go unload the feed. You get to drive. Deal?"

"Deal," he said.

She never called Lynette till the feed was unloaded and stacked. When she did, she lied, said she'd had trouble at the Co-op over their account, but she and Randy sorted it out. Of course, Randy might come home and tell Lynette her stupid sister-in-law thought two men had confronted her, and Lynette would later scold Portia for the lie, but at least it would be Randy who brought the subject up and not Portia.

All afternoon she couldn't get the threat out of her thoughts. What should she do about it? She had no proof but her own word, no witnesses, no idea who the men were. She hadn't even gotten their license plate number. Probably they'd flown into Denver and flown back out again, and there'd be no way to trace them. Or to connect them to Mahoney.

No one could help her, and, oh God, she needed help.

She worked and she thought. And by four o'clock she decided there was one person she could confide in. Cab Whitefeather, the undersheriff.

She told Todd she was going into Colt for an hour or so; she changed from her dusty jeans and T-shirt into clean ones and set out in the elderly dented Subaru wagon. Intellectually she knew the threat about not talking to the police was pure hogwash, that the two men were long gone. But still she checked the rearview mirror too often and parked two blocks from the sheriff's department annex, which was located next to the building that housed the local Douglas County offices. The county seat was actually Castle Rock, but Colt had a resident set of deputies headed by Cab.

She said hi to the deputy on duty and asked if she could see Cab.

He was a tall man, with a narrow, weatherworn face, deep grooves on either side of his mouth, dark hooded eyes, and a hook nose. His hair was white, and he wore it in a ponytail. He was half Ute Indian and had an extended family on the Southern Ute Reservation. His wife had died recently, but he had three grown children who had all gone into law enforcement. He liked to joke that his tribe had too many chiefs.

He was sitting at his desk reading when Portia entered his office. He looked up and smiled, his face creasing with pleasure.

"Howdy, Portia," he said, rising.

"Hi, Cab."

"What can I do for you? You're looking mighty serious. Sit yourself down."

Portia had learned years ago that a lot of rural Westerners affected a certain down-home drawl on purpose. Cab was great at it. Gary had been pretty darn adept at it, too. But when push came to shove, the country bumpkin talk ended.

She sat, and she took a deep breath, not sure how to begin. Cab kept his gaze on her, folded his big-knuckled hands on his desk.

"Something happened today, and I . . . Well, I guess I don't know what to do about it." She rubbed her forehead. "I told Randy, but he didn't take it seriously. You know Randy. If he doesn't want to believe something happened, he just doesn't believe it. End of story."

"Never mind Randy. What's the problem?" Serious mode.

"I was at the Co-op this morning, and as I was leaving, you know the driveway from the back to the front parking lot?"

"Uh-huh."

"There was a car there, and two men got out. One got in the truck and took my keys, and the other, well, he threatened me. He told me not to screw with Patrick Mahoney's plans, and then he said . . . he said, 'Remember what happened to your husband?'"

Cab sat up. He gave a low whistle.

"Randy said it was all bullshit, but it wasn't. And I," she put a hand over her mouth, "I don't know what to do."

"I don't suppose you know the men?"

She shook her head.

"You didn't get their tag number?"

She shook her head again.

"Well." His focus went inward, and he tapped an index finger on his desk. "Well. There's not much I can do, Portia. Even if I wanted to, I wouldn't know who to charge. Mahoney . . . Well now, his name was hearsay. He can deny he had anything to do with it."

"I know. I know. And I really don't expect you to go out and arrest anybody on my say-so. But, I guess . . . I guess I thought you'd have some idea of what I should do."

He frowned. "That's a problem. I wish I could say I'd call out the troops and protect you, but we haven't got any troops here. You know, just the six of us, and we're short-handed at that. I *could* call the sheriff up in Castle Rock, but it'd be a hard sell, I'm afraid."

"I know. I was crazy to bother you with it."

"No, no you weren't. I can put out an alert. I can have the men drive by the ranch a few times a day, look for anyone suspicious." He thought for a minute. "You be careful now. Don't go gallivanting around alone. Take Randy with you. Or Lynette. All else fails, take Gary's son."

"Randy thinks I'm nuts."

"Randy." Cab snorted. "Well, you get yourself some protection then. Hire some."

144

She gave a little laugh. "Think security men would work for food?"

"Um."

She felt like a fool for bothering Cab. He couldn't do anything for her; she was entirely alone facing the threats from Patrick Mahoney. *Remember what happened to your husband?* Would someone run *her* off the road on her way home today?

"You take care now," Cab said as he walked out with her.

"I will. And thanks."

"For what? I can't do a damn thing for you, lady."

She drove home too fast, pushing the Subaru, watching in the rearview mirror for a car to loom up and overtake her. Nothing happened, though, except the tires squealed on the hot asphalt when she turned in under the Wellspring Ranch sign.

She was distracted at home, giving scant thought to dinner, reliving the scene at the Co-op in her mind. Over and over. Every word, the expression on the men's faces. The way the balding one had talked, the way the bigger man had contemptuously tossed her keys to her.

How had they known where she was? Obviously they'd followed her. They must have been waiting at the ranch, waiting and watching, until they'd seen her leave. Shadowing her wouldn't have been hard;

she'd been totally unsuspecting.

She tried to recall their car. When she closed her eyes she could see the doors opening, the two men emerging. A light-colored sedan. White? Gray? She leaned on the kitchen counter with both hands and tried to concentrate. A sedan — like the Taurus owned by Todd's mother in Denver. Something like that. But even if she did remember their car, it was probably back in a rental car fleet somewhere with a hundred others just like it.

She felt so helpless, out of her element. So alone.

She opened the refrigerator and took out salad makings. Picked up a paring knife and found herself staring at it. A weapon?

Gary's shotgun was still in the closet by the front door, but she knew she'd never carry it with her, much less use the damn thing.

A face materialized in her mind's eye. Dark curly hair, flaring nostrils, a wide, curved mouth, a way of moving . . . a strong neck. A certain kind of composure that came from easy authority. A hard silence.

What was she thinking? He was 2,000 miles away and probably didn't even remember her name. But she remembered his.

She set the small knife down and went to the phone. Her court of last appeal. She punched in Aaron's number in Falls Church,

Virginia, hoping he was home. Praying he was home.

His wife Nancy answered. "Oh, hello, Portia. Aaron, yes, he's here. We're just about to go out, but he's got a few minutes."

Aaron came on right away. "Yes, Portia?"

"I'm sorry to bother you, but something came up, and I wanted your . . . well, your advice, I guess."

His deep voice was calm and measured. "Tell me, Portia."

She retold her story. He listened without interruption. When she finished, he cleared his throat, then he said, "This is a very serious matter, my dear. I hate to think of you all alone out there."

"I'm not entirely alone."

"Todd? A fifteen-year-old?"

"What should I do?"

"The police obviously can't do much?"

"No."

"All right. I'm going to handle this, Portia."

She hated the relief that swept over her at his words. What a weakling she was.

"I'm going to call a security firm. Get some men out to protect you. Around the clock. For as long as it takes."

"Aaron, I can't afford —"

"Don't even bring that up. Everything will be taken care of from this end."

"Oh God, I'm sorry to bother you with this."

"It's not a bother. Gary was like a son to me, and you're like a daughter. Not another word."

"Thank you, Aaron."

"You did right to tell me. Thank heavens you did. Now, I've got to make that call, and Nancy and I are expected at a dinner. I'll talk to you soon."

She went limp with relief when she hung the phone up. She wasn't alone, not completely. Aaron was always there for her.

The next morning promptly at eight, two men knocked at her door. Todd opened it, then came into the kitchen where she was finishing breakfast. He had a puzzled expression on his face.

"There're some dudes from a security company here."

"Oh, wow, that was fast. I forgot to tell you. They're here to sort of keep an eye on us."

"Because of what happened?"

"Yes."

She invited them in, offered them coffee. Jerry was not tall but built like a linebacker, his neck bigger than his head. Lev was older, close to fifty, with a bulldog jaw. They both wore city clothes; maybe she should mention they'd look out of place in them.

But maybe they meant to.

"Just pretend we're not around. Go about your life," Lev said. He had an accent, and she imagined him to be some European mercenary. He looked like he could take care of himself.

"Where are you staying?"

"All taken care of."

"Oh."

"We'll take shifts," Jerry said. "One of us will always be around."

"What about food?"

"We'll handle that. Don't worry. We've done this before. Now, if you can give us a list of everyone on the ranch, delivery people, so on."

Todd was watching the men with fascination. When she finished listing everyone she could think of, he spoke up. "So, are you like bodyguards?"

Jerry smiled. "Sort of, yeah."

"Cool."

The men left, and she noted their vehicle, an unmarked blue van.

They'd probably sleep in it, eat in it. Live in it. For how long? Days, weeks? And when would she know she was safe?

"Bodyguards," Todd was saying. "That is so righteous."

"I'm glad you approve," she said. "Now, I guess I better tell your Uncle Randy."

But she didn't call Randy. She stood at the

living room window and watched the rooster tail of dust kicked up by the van until it disappeared behind a hill, and the dust lay on the hot air like a mist, then it slowly drifted to the ground.

What an intolerable situation. *Bodyguards, threats.* And it had only been a few days since she'd made the announcement of her NPS plans.

What would a week bring, a month?

EIGHT

Nick blew his lunch hour on the last day before vacation to run up to midtown and the *Star Gazer* home office. For a crappy tabloid, the weekly seemed to do okay. Maybe better than okay, as its offices were located in Rockefeller Center.

The address was posh, but the office looked as if it had never seen a vacuum. Not only was every desk and file cabinet piled high with clutter, and trash cans were overflowing, but the furniture must have come from a Goodwill store — back in the 1950s.

There was no receptionist. A visitor, such as Nick, either knew where he was headed and who he was looking for, or that visitor was up the creek. Not that anyone at the *Star Gazer* gave a damn.

He had been to the office before to pick up his checks, though he preferred to have them mailed to his West End Avenue apartment. In this instance he figured he'd collect the money in person. You never know, he might just rent a place at the shore and go by himself after all. What else was he going to do?

A couple reporters gabbed on the phone, others sat in front of computer screens, tapping on keyboards. A few more bent over crammed file cabinet drawers.

To no one in particular, Nick said, "Hey, Bern in his cubbyhole back there?"

Bern Radowski was the editor-in-chief. One of the reporters straightened and leaned an elbow on top of a file cabinet. "Who's asking?"

"Name's Nick Sinestra. Now, is Bern back there?" Nick indicated a closed door at the rear of the overcrowded room.

"Sinestra." The man scratched his thick black hair. "Oh, right, the cop. Sure, Bern's in his cage." Then the guy opened a file folder and held up a photo for Nick to see. "Like it? We're thinking it's got more miles to it."

Nick walked closer, cocked his head to eye the photo, and grinned. "You guys run this same photo, what? Every three, four years?"

The reporter shrugged. "More like five. But who's counting?"

The photo was grotesquely familiar: a pig's body sporting the head of a young boy. Nick vaguely recalled the headline from one of the issues years ago: "Astounding Alien Hybrid."

"Where do you guys get this junk anyway?" he asked.

152

"Ah, some farmer in the Florida Panhandle came up with this one. Swore he took the photo himself. Swore in an affidavit it was legit. Hey, we got a team of lawyers clearing the stories for print. Not to worry, Sinestra, they're all the God's honest truth." The reporter snickered.

Nick tapped on Bern's door and went in, found the head man at his desk. "Hey," he said.

"Nick. To what do I owe the pleasure?"

"I was in the neighborhood, thought I'd stop in, collect for the last couple gigs."

"Um, Tommy Boy and the Portia Wells deal. Nice job. Public still gets off on her old lady. Can't believe Judith Carr's been living right under our noses all these years. Who'd of thought?"

"Yeah, who."

"Sorry our man got a little pushy with the lady."

"Um." Nick cringed inwardly. A sudden vivid picture crystallized in his head: her lovely profile as she sat in the passenger seat of his car, long white neck like a swan. His skin burned, and unconsciously he loosened his tie, sitting down across from Bern.

"Sometimes the boys get a bit overzealous when they come across a hot story."

"Shit," Nick said, "you can't run alien abductions every week, right?"

"Hey, we put plenty of good press out

there. Got the Lady Di bodyguard theft scoop, didn't we?"

"If you say so."

"I say so."

"I take it your photographer got his shots of Tommy Boy and the light tech?"

"Excellent shots, by the way. You want to take a look-see?"

"I'll pass."

"Suit yourself. Anyway, nice job."

"My pleasure."

The editor-in-chief rose. "I'll find Martha, see if she can't cut you that check. Take about ten minutes."

"I'll wait."

When Bern left, Nick looked around his office. Place was perhaps twelve by fourteen feet, had a smeared picture window over-looking the plaza ten stories below, the other three walls papered in *Star Gazer* cover story copy from the early days of the tabloid up to the present. The walls were covered with the most bizarre mural Nick had ever laid eyes on. There were shots of a crazed Charles Manson and one of Jeffrey Dahmer, open refrigerator behind him, jars filled with body parts of his victims. There were plenty of shots of Oprah and Liz Taylor and Madonna, Britney Spears and Jennifer Lopez. Dozens of Lady Diana. There was copy of flying saucers and aliens, the ones you saw in *Close Encounters*. There was the pig-boy, the snake-baby, the latest elephant-boy. There was the fattest woman on earth and the skinniest. There was a half-man, half-cucumber, headline "Farmer Found in Field Alive." There were Portia and Judith, behind Bern's desk to the right.

Oh, man, Nick was thinking when Bern came back. He must have noticed Nick's gaze fixed on the Portia Wells copy. "Yep," Bern said, "almost record sales on that one. Sure, Judith Carr's whereabouts was quite a scoop, but Portia's on fire right now. You hear the latest?"

"No."

"The wire had it she's going to accept the NPS president's position."

"Um."

"Yep. After the mother-daughter reunion story couple issues ago, not to mention Gary Wells dying last year, she's great press, all right."

"You'll milk it dry," Nick said.

"You betchum." Bern picked up the phone, punched in a button, said, "Martha back yet? Okay, soon as she's done in the head . . ." He rolled his eyes at Nick. ". . . tell her I need her to cut a check." Bern hung up. "Sorry, should just be a few minutes."

"Um."

"Say, Sinestra." Bern tugged at his gray beard. "You wouldn't have a contact out in Colorado, would you? Someone who could tag around after Portia Wells for a few weeks?"

Nick shook his head. "Sorry."

"Oh, well. Too bad you couldn't take on the job. That woman's hot enough I'd pay a couple grand for some good info."

When Bern said a couple grand, Nick figured he could be squeezed for maybe eight or ten K easy. The proverbial lightbulb switched on in his head. "I might consider doing the job," he said, shrugging. "But it's going to cost you ten K."

"You'll do it?"

"Sure. Got vacation starting tomorrow." Another shrug.

"Well, well, well. This must be my fortuitous day, Sinestra. Tell you what, can't do ten, but I'll go six."

"Sorry. No can do. It's ten or I'll pass."

The phone rang, Bern picked it up. Apparently, it was Martha, the cutter of checks. "Ah, hold on, Martha," Bern said, cupping the receiver with his hand. "Okay, eight, I'll go eight grand," he said to Nick.

Nick smiled and shook his head.

Bern eyed him a second longer, muttered, "Fuck," then spoke to Martha. "Yeah, listen, add another five thou to that check. Five thousand, that's right. Okay, bring it up when you're done." He hung up.

"Five?" Nick said.

"Five now. Five more when I get the goods

156

on the Wells woman."

Nick nodded.

"And you better dig up some really good stuff, Sinestra. Christ, ten K?"

Check in his pocket, Nick grinned all the way back downtown. He came up from the subway on Christopher Street still grinning. The heat and humidity walloped him in the face, and he thought, *Okay, maybe it's hot in the summer in Colorado, too, but isn't it supposed to be a dry heat?*

That same afternoon he finished clearing his desk as best he could and left the precinct with Gil.

"So how you going to kill a month?" Gil asked.

"Well, I was thinking about a trip. A real trip. Been checking airfares on priceline.com, in fact."

"Really?"

"Yeah, really."

"The CO is on my ass to take my time, too," Gil said.

"You should, man. The Sixth isn't going to go to pieces without us, and so far this summer, the streets have been pretty damn subdued."

"Too hot to commit a crime."

"It's usually just the opposite."

"It's usually not this damn hot for so long. Of course, didn't stop Doug from getting into deep shit. I really owe you, Nick. What you did for that kid of mine is above and beyond."

"Hey, don't mention it."

"Like hell."

"You're embarrassing me. I'm a hard-ass, remember?"

"Uh-huh."

They were ducking into the subway when Nick dropped his pocket change into a homeless woman's tin cup.

"She'll only use it for booze or drugs," Gil said, descending the steps.

"Yeah, but I can't stand to see them suffering."

"You're really a sucker."

"Guilty as charged," Nick said.

He was again a sucker when his feet propelled him into Mia's nail salon. But, hell, this was his first night of vacation, and he'd be leaving for Colorado in a day or so.

Mia was at the register. "Hey," he said.

"Nick, hi." She handed a woman her change, then accepted a tip.

"I was just thinking," he began. "You and the girls want to step out tonight?"

"Well . . ."

"Oh, come on, take an evening off. I'm thinking, maybe the Bronx Zoo. You said your girls have never been, and it won't close till nine or so."

"Um."

"Look. I'm out of here for a few weeks," he tried. "I'd like to spend the evening, you know."

"Where are you going? The shore?"

He shook his head. "Come with me, and I'll fill you in."

"Sounds interesting."

"You'll never know unless you do the zoo thing."

The evening went okay. Mia's girls loved the zoo, and so did Mia. Nick could have done without so damn much stink of so damn many varieties of shit. But he survived, and safely back at Mia's, he was glad he'd had the idea. The way she'd acted the other night when he'd asked her to the shore had puzzled him — not to mention humiliated him. But tonight had turned out all right.

The girls disappeared to watch TV, and he and Mia sat with beers in the living room. He broached the subject. "So, what did you mean the other night about liking things the way they are, no strings and all that?"

"You don't have to get upset, Nick. I only —"

"I am not upset."

"That's good." Her tone was doubtful. "I only meant that we have fun the way it is."

"Sex isn't bad either," he added.

She smiled. "That, too. It's just that I'm

not looking for anything more permanent, you know?"

"A trip to the shore hardly means some kind of commitment."

"I know. I'm sorry about how I handled the invitation. Okay?"

"Sure." He drank his beer and shrugged.

"So where are you going? You promised to tell me."

"Oh, yeah. Colorado."

"Colorado? Like out West?"

"Yep."

"But, Nick, why . . . ?" Then she sat up straight. "*Oh*, I got it, Portia Wells has a ranch in Colorado, and the *Star Gazer* is paying you."

He looked innocent.

"That's it. I'm right, aren't I?" She playfully punched his arm.

"Ouch. Hey, you ought to be a detective."

"Salon pays better. But tell me, how are you going to follow her on a ranch? Hide behind cows or something?"

"Ha, ha."

"So, how?"

"Beats me. Feel it out when I get there."

Then her expression grew serious. "Do you think you'll, you know, meet her in person?"

"Doubt it."

"But you might."

"Could happen. But then the gig would be blown, wouldn't it?"

Impatiently, she waved his words off. "If you did meet her, *if*, I'm saying, would you . . . come on to her? I mean, she's so beautiful, and a widow and practically a star."

"What sort of a question is that?" He tried to sound indignant.

"An honest question. Now answer me, wouldn't you at least be tempted to come on to her? Wouldn't you like to sleep with her, Nick?"

He put his bottle down hard on the coffee table. "Jesus, Mia, what's with all this Portia Wells mania? She's just some chick with a famous mother and not even that great looking, either."

"You haven't answered my question."

"Course I wouldn't sleep with the woman," he protested.

"Really," Mia said.

"Besides, she's not even going to know I exist." He picked his beer up again, tilted it to his lips, and knew that given half a chance, he was perfectly capable of sleeping with Portia Wells.

NINE

Nick picked up a rental Camry at Denver International Airport early that afternoon and drove toward downtown. The DJ on the radio station said that by five the temperature would break a 110-year record, but Nick didn't feel all that hot yet. Must be that dry heat.

Downtown coalesced out of a flat plain, and beyond the silhouette of a cluster of skyscrapers, the Rocky Mountains jutted into a flawless sky. He had to admit it, even through his jaded New York City eyes, the sight was really something.

Years ago he'd been to New Orleans for a Super Bowl. He'd driven to Maine and Montreal once with Gwen and followed a perp to Chicago and on to Saint Louis. But Saint Louis was as far west as he'd been. Unlike the intrepid fur traders, who'd set out from the Midwestern city centuries ago, he was too East Coast, had never felt that adventurous streak. As far as seeing the Pacific Ocean and California, well, the Californians he'd run across were all too laid back for his taste. And they walked slow. God, did they walk slow.

Finding his way into the city was a no-brainer. Hell, you could see downtown from the interstate, and there were plenty of signs. Trouble was, the few hotels he ran across looked too pricey, so he turned onto a major street called Colfax Avenue, drove past the gold-domed state Capitol building, up a hill and, as he expected, the area grew a little seedy: pawnshops, used bookstores, lots of liquor stores, a strip joint, shabby hotels, porn shops, couple hookers working the midafternoon bar crowd in front of that Western saloon. And the King Motel. Looked like home to him.

He got checked in to a second-floor room; he always stayed on the second floor or above, figuring a crook would hit the lower floors before doing steps. Then he spent some time studying the city and area maps in the phone book. Found Colt south on Interstate 25, just past Castle Rock. Yeah, Castle Rock, sure, he thought, there was a big golf tournament there every year. Then he drove back into the core of the city and made his way around. There were nice areas of shops and restaurants and fern bars close to the sports complexes: Invesco Mile High Stadium, the Pepsi Center, Coors Field. Closer in was Larimer Square, trendy looking, and LoDo — for Lower Downtown — near

Coors Field, rows of restaurants and brew pubs and loft apartments. Young-looking crowd of residents, plenty of people walking big shaggy dogs.

Everyone in Denver, except for the obvious businessmen, dressed casual. He maybe was too overdressed in khaki trousers and one of his ubiquitous white polyester shirts. Might have to go shopping. *Oh geez.*

It was almost three by the time he drove down Broadway and chucked a left onto Interstate 25 south. Where he immediately got hung up in a massive construction project.

Still, he passed Castle Rock by 3:40 and took the Colt exit shortly thereafter.

Thus far, his journey has been a snap. There weren't that many roads in Colorado, especially not major highways. But now he was in cowboy movie country, middle of nowhere. He sat at the exit stop sign, no one behind him, no one in sight on the road before him. He couldn't even see a goddamn tree, just tumbleweed blowing across the empty road. And he didn't know whether to go left or right. Right, he guessed, because a small black and white sign read, Colt 5 Miles. Not that Portia lived in Colt. Her mailing address was some rural route number, County Road 187, he remembered, wherever in hell that was.

On the way toward Colt he passed only

two ranches, and the rest of the country was flat-out deserted, empty, *dry*. If it weren't for a couple of cows — maybe those were steers, he thought — he might have been on the surface of some distant planet.

Finally, there was Colt, population 253, elevation 5,732 feet. Not only was it dry as hell, but he was sure he couldn't breathe at well over a mile above the East River.

He got directions at the only gas station in town. Three blocks later, he was driving out of Colt, supplied with a liter bottle of Coke. He should have gotten one of those big water bottles. Maybe at the next gas station. If there was one.

There wasn't. But he found County Road 187 and hung a left. To his right was open range. He knew that because there was a sign: Open Range, with a picture of a cow on a road.

Soon the open range became fenced ranchland, seemingly miles of it. He spotted some cattle, though they could have been deer or elk for all he knew at this distance, and a few recently mown hayfields. Those he definitely recognized. Finally, on the horizon, sitting atop a hill, was a farmhouse, white clapboard, Victorian, a few tall trees shading it. Portia's ranch?

He passed the entrance a minute later, logs supporting a rustic sign: Wellspring Ranch, and a dusty farm road snaking up a long rise toward the Victorian structure.

Yeah, Portia's place. Okay.

He was staring so hard at the ranch house, leaning down and twisting his head to the right, that he almost hit the blue van parked below the crest of a hill.

He swerved, braked, and stopped several yards ahead of the van. "What the hell?" he said, his brain already calculating, coming to the conclusion that the van was out of place. It could have been broken down, but there was a man sitting in it. Just sitting. Thick-necked guy.

Nick got out, stretched, and walked back toward the vehicle, his gait easy, nonthreatening. "Hey," he said, smiling, "you from around here? I'm sort of lost."

The man eyed him and leaned out the window. His shirt was soaked through, which told Nick he'd been there quite some time — not enough gas to keep the motor running and the air on.

"Lost, huh? Where you headed?"

Lying was one of Nick's strong points. "Town called Colt?"

"Yeah, well, you're going in the wrong direction. Turn around, go back to the main road, and take a right. It's about five, six miles."

"Isn't that just something," Nick said.

"What?"

"Well, must be my lucky day, running into

you just sitting out here in the middle of no-where."

"A real miracle," the man replied, but his expression read, *Fuck you, pal.*

Nick smiled and shrugged, got back in his car, did a three-point turn, and waved bye-bye as he passed the van. He'd already fig-ured the guy as some sort of security. Either for the ranch or for Portia herself, as there wasn't another ranch or person as far as the eye could see. If the guy was some creep stalking her, he wouldn't be so obvious. Had to be security. Though why right out in the open was a mystery. Maybe the gorilla worked for Clueless Security. Nick had seen enough of them in his time.

He headed back toward Colt, chewing over the problem. Could just be he'd stumbled onto something of interest. Hey, maybe he hadn't been lying to the man after all, and this really was his lucky day.

Colt was four blocks long and a block wide. There was the gas station, a barber shop, a couple hardware type places, a Co-op feed store — a *feed* store! — corner café, seam-stress, a saloon, a Western-style restaurant called Toro's, and a Douglas County office building with an annex that housed the sher-iff's department. If there was some trouble at the Wellspring Ranch, the undersheriff or deputy would most likely know about it.

Nick parked on Main Street, got out into the blistering heat, and walked to the annex. He knew how to chat up cops. But a small-town Western sheriff? This might prove to be a new experience.

The on-duty deputy manning the phone told Nick right out where he could find Cab.

"Cab?"

"Cab Whitefeather, the undersheriff. He'll be at the saloon. Two blocks down on the left. Can't miss it."

Nick strode into the nicely air-conditioned bar having no idea what to expect. Whitefeather had to be a Native American, he guessed. Shit, this place was full of goddamn cowboys and Indians. Cab wasn't hard to spot. Undersheriff Whitefeather sat at the ten-stool bar still in uniform, his white Stetson on the empty stool next to him. He looked to be drinking a Coke. Or an exceedingly tall, straight whiskey.

There were two other men at the bar, crusty old ranch types in denim overalls and stained baseball caps having beers near the back. Couple younger men were shooting pool near the rest rooms. The bartender was a woman. A pro. When Nick settled on the stool next to Whitefeather's Stetson, she tossed a bar napkin in front of him and said, "What's your poison?"

"Beer. What's on tap?" Nick said. He chose a Coors. When in Rome . . .

There was no point in delay, so he took a sip of the beer and pointed toward Whitefeather. "You sheriff of these parts?" he said, tone friendly.

"Undersheriff."

"Right."

"So who's asking? You're not from around here."

"Name's Sinestra, Nick Sinestra. From New York."

"You lost or something, buddy?"

Nick laughed. "Not really." Now for the pack of lies. "I'm due to retire one of these days, and I'm looking for a nice, quiet place."

"New York, huh? Try the Carolinas."

Again Nick laughed. He sort of liked this Whitefeather. "Thought I'd check out the West, actually."

"And you threw a dart, and it hit Colt."

"Something like that."

Whitefeather made a grunting sound. He was maybe in his sixties. Hard to tell, as his face was so weathered. Face, hands, forearms. The brown skin and wrinkles made a sharp contrast to his pure white hair, which he wore pulled back into a short ponytail. He had a large hook nose, wide mouth, and shrewd eyes the color of rich sable.

Whitefeather ordered another Coke, then said, "What you retiring from?"

"Um," Nick said, "NYPD."

169

Whitefeather sat more erect. "No shit? You're a cop?"

"Detective, actually. Vice."

"Well, no shit. Pleased to meet you, Nick." He put out his hand and shook Nick's. He had a grip of iron.

After that they were new best friends. Nick answered a dozen questions about 9/11, where he'd been that morning — uptown at Gwen's divorce lawyer's office — how his Greenwich Village precinct worked, crime stats, retirement packages, the works.

Obviously, Cab Whitefeather was impressed with the big city cop and the humorous stories Nick told him. As for Nick, he really liked the man, his good nature and easy talk. After another beer, the male bonding was complete.

"Hell, I'm just an old hick undersheriff," Whitefeather said. "Wife up and died on me, grandkids drive me nuts half the time, so I hang out in here or watch TV, unless we got a fire going or a couple ranchers arguing over irrigation rights. It's pretty dull, most of the time."

Nick nodded and smiled, then looked up and snapped his fingers. "Say, didn't that Nature Preservation Society guy live around here? The one who was killed recently in a car accident? Hell, all the papers carried the story. Um, what was his name?"

"Wells, Gary Wells."

"Yeah, right, was married to some celeb or something?"

"That would be Portia."

"That's it. Daughter of someone . . ."

"Judith Carr."

"Right, right, the stage star."

"Big stage star," Whitefeather said. "I had a crush on her, you know."

"Hey, you don't say."

"Oh, yeah. She did a Hollywood movie once with John Wayne, and she defended the redskins in it. That's how come I got the crush."

For a minute Nick didn't know what to say, but then he saw the shit-eating grin on the man's face and realized Whitefeather was bullshitting him.

"You had me there for a sec," Nick said.

"Had you pretty good, too."

Nick chuckled. "Yeah, you did." Then, as long as the undersheriff was in the mood to swap stories, he asked, "Say, does Portia Wells still live here?"

Whitefeather nodded. "She's got a ranch a few miles out."

"Wow. You ever see her?"

"As a matter of fact — cop to cop, okay? — she was just in my office complaining about a couple men who threatened her over at the Co-op."

"Really?"

Whitefeather swiveled around toward him

171

and leaned close, lowered his voice. "Portia's got this notion in her head that her husband's accident was no accident, if you get my drift."

"No way."

"Oh, yeah. She's been hinting around ever since last fall that this golf course developer had Gary killed."

"Honest to God?"

"Swear to God. She sat right in front of me and told me the men who threatened her said she'd get the same as her husband if she gave this developer any trouble."

"No shit." *The NPS connection,* Nick thought. Portia announces her acceptance of the position, and some developer gets worried.

Jesus. What was he thinking? Obviously, Cab Whitefeather thought she was wrong, and here Nick was plotting a murder scenario. Still, Portia must believe the story. And that explained the guy in the blue van. *Security, all right.*

"Yeah," Whitefeather was saying, "I felt bad for her, but even if her story of these men harassing her is true, there isn't much I can do. Whole department is only six strong, and half are part-time. And what with the wildfires flaring up every other week, having to put up roadblocks, evacuating folks, providing backup for the firefighters, we get full-out busy, too busy to be watching out for

Portia. I told her to find herself some outside help."

"Security outfit."

"Something like that."

Nick listened, incredulous. The *Star Gazer* was going to go apeshit over this story.

"Well," Whitefeather said, "I don't know about Gary Wells's accident being suspicious. I was on the scene with the Colorado State Patrol, and it sure looked like a rollover to us. Bad curve, nasty gully. Maybe Gary was avoiding a deer. Or Bigfoot." Cab winked. "All I know is Portia thinks otherwise."

"Hell of a thing," Nick said. "I take it you knew Gary Wells?"

"Since he was a boy, he and Randy. That's his brother. Gary got all the looks and brains, too. Hell, even in high school he was the outgoing one, straight A's, football star, the ladies' man. He married his high school sweetheart, in fact."

"Really?"

"First wife. Cheated like mad on her, too. A Bill Clinton type. Women just went for him."

"So Portia is his second wife?"

"Yep. Met her ten, eleven years ago. And it was real love on Gary's part. Everyone could tell."

"Huh. Then he didn't cheat on her?"

"Didn't say that. I think he strayed on her. Just in his nature, plus Portia had those two,

173

or was it three miscarriages?" Whitefeather shrugged. "Anyway, the poor gal has had her share of hurt, that's a fact. And I hate like hell to think there's any truth in her story some men threatened her."

"Seems a shame," Nick said, sobered.

"Yeah, and her being so isolated at the ranch."

"She's all alone?"

"No, she's got Randy and his wife there. They own half the spread. And Todd lives with her."

"Todd?"

"Gary's boy from his first marriage, kid's fifteen and doesn't get on with his stepfather. So when Gary died, Portia just took over."

Nick nodded. *Jesus,* he thought.

"And the ranch is in trouble. The usual stuff. All the ranchers are having problems. They can't get decent hay crops because of the drought, so they're forced to buy hay to feed the cattle, it's really expensive, and they have to sell off their cattle for peanuts. Gotten pretty damn bad. She doesn't complain, but everyone's in the same boat. Loans coming due, no money to pay them. A vicious circle." Cab shook his head.

"And here I thought all ranchers were rich," Nick said.

"Ha!"

It was late by the time he left Colt and drove north toward Denver. He'd only had three beers in as many hours, so he was okay to drive, but his mind was not on the road. He couldn't stop thinking about the stuff the lonely widowed undersheriff had told him, especially about Gary Wells cheating on Portia and the miscarriages. Didn't she have enough problems? Yet she'd been so lovely and gracious at the fund-raiser. And so nice in his car. He cringed inside, but he couldn't avoid the nasty little stabs of guilt.

By the time he parked at the King Motel, he was weary and in a foul mood. It was ten o'clock in Denver, midnight in New York. He'd been in Colorado for nine hours and already had the scoop for the *Star Gazer* and, despite the jet lag, he should be feeling great.

"Yeah, sure," he muttered, emptying his pockets onto the dresser, placing his revolver on the bedside table — habit — reminding himself he hadn't come here to commiserate about Portia Wells's situation. Screw it. Not his problem. First thing in the morning, he'd find a cyber café and research Gary Wells and the projects he was working on for the NPS. Wouldn't take much to learn the name of this golf course developer. More fodder for the *Star Gazer.* He'd have asked Whitefeather, but he hadn't wanted to push his luck. Too much curiosity was a dead giveaway.

He fell into bed telling himself what a terrific detective he was, what a heyday the magazine was going to have with this

175

story — whether or not there was a lick of truth to it. He'd more than earned his ten grand. Damn right. Couple more days of nosing around, and his time would be his own.

By midmorning he had the developer's name: Patrick Mahoney. He was almost ready to phone all the info in to the tabloid. Almost.

He ate lunch in LoDo and found out the Yankees were in town tonight. Things were looking up. The bartender of the sports bar next door to the restaurant had extra tickets. Nick bought one, Club Level. He was really treating himself.

With the afternoon to kill, he drove back down to Colt, drove straight through, hoping Whitefeather didn't see his car. But the cop would only think he was still tooling around, the retirement thing. And what did Nick care, anyway?

The blue van was parked in its place on the narrow county road in front of the Wellspring Ranch. The best security, he thought, was security you didn't notice. Obviously, no one had informed this outfit.

There was a different guy in the van today. Older dude who was picking his nose when Nick passed by the first time. Guy didn't even seem to notice when, five minutes later, Nick came back from the opposite direction.

And it wasn't as if there was traffic. Nick had passed only a single pickup truck in two miles.

He almost drove by a third time just to see if the man noticed, but he figured why waste gas? It also occurred to him that Portia was paying for this shit security, and he ought to do the right thing and tell her — but no way was he going to expose himself. And what business was it of his, anyway?

Driving back toward Colt, he passed an older pickup with a woman driving and what might have been a teenage boy in the passenger seat. Woman could have been Portia, except she'd been wearing a baseball cap, and for the life of him, Nick couldn't see Portia in anything but a gorgeous floppy hat, her beautiful features half hidden like those old-time movie stars.

Back in his motel room, he finally phoned in his information to the *Star Gazer* and, predictably, Bern was as happy as a fly on stink.

"Her husband was murdered, and the same man, this Mahoney, is after her now? My God, Nick, this is terrific! Absolutely astounding. I'll send someone —"

"Look, Bern," Nick interrupted, "I told you this is all Portia's fantasy, and I got it secondhand as it is."

"Like I care?"

"Maybe you should."

"Hey, you getting scruples, Sinestra?

What's up with that?"

"Listen. I don't care what you guys print. Never did care, and I'm not starting now. Only warning you that there's probably no truth whatsoever in the story. I sure as hell wouldn't use the name Patrick Mahoney until my lawyers cleared it. Man's well-known out here. Got the big bucks and powerful friends."

"Yeah, yeah, like I'm worried. Say, you going to hang around there, see what else you can dig up?"

"You got your money's worth."

"Well, sure, but there's more where that came from, and I'm always open to negotiations, you know that."

Nick thought a second, said, "I'll be in touch," and hung up. Fucking Bern was merciless.

By the bottom of the fourth inning, the Yanks were over the Rockies by three runs and had two men on base and no outs. Looked to be Yankees night at Coors Field.

The Club Level seat was great, right between home and first base. And there were waitresses bringing him beer and the best food he'd ever had at a ballpark.

The evening was perfect, temperature in the low seventies, sunset over the Rocky Mountains streaking the sky blue and lavender, the air fresh and clean compared to

178

Manhattan. He could even see stars. In the city.

The Yankees left the two men on, but in the sixth they scored another run. The Rockies were on their third pitcher and had yet to put a man on base. The ballpark was full, an oddity as far as Nick was concerned. Geez, even at the end of the baseball season in New York, you might get three, four thousand fans on a weeknight. But this park must have held thirty thousand fans, and they were all here, and the Rockies were in last place halfway though the season. *Go figure.*

He should have been enjoying the routing of the home team, but instead he felt dispirited, unable to clear his mind of the *Star Gazer* and the reporter who was no doubt already on his way west. What sort of a mess would he make of Portia's already screwed-up life? She had enough troubles. Had lost three babies. How could anyone go through so much torment? And if Whitefeather was right, her asshole husband had been screwing around on her to boot. Did she know that?

He left the ballpark during the seventh inning stretch. His car was at the motel, so he walked along Blake Street to where he caught a free shuttle bus on the Sixteenth Street Mall. Still maybe ten blocks to go to his motel from the end of the bus line. Like he had anything better to do, he thought, his hands in fists in his trouser pockets. Hell, of course he was depressed, he was bored, didn't even have anyone else's life to mess up right now.

He turned onto Colfax Avenue and walked up the hill past the Capitol building, and he thought, *Three miscarriages, Jesus.*

TEN

Todd had just pulled a standard teenage I-hate-you tantrum when the phone rang. Portia grabbed the portable extension, pressed Talk, and heard Todd slam his bedroom door. "Hello?" she said.

On the line was some sort of a staff writer for an environmental magazine she'd never heard of.

"*Earthguard*," he said. "We're out of Phoenix, and I have to fly into Denver early this afternoon for a meeting. I was hoping you'd grant me a short interview."

"Uh, who did you say you were? I'm sorry, but I —"

"Dave Donaldson, staff writer with *Earthguard*."

Earthguard. She'd heard of *Earthwatch*, of course, but . . . "I've got quite a busy schedule," she began, but then she remembered that by accepting the NPS position, she'd set herself up for dozens of these impromptu interviews for dozens of small environmental groups who put out magazines and newsletters and periodicals. Giving interviews was going to become routine, an unavoidable part of her job. Public relations.

He was telling her the thrust of his proposed article. "Due to the drought and the wildfires all over the West, we'd like to profile a few Colorado Front Range ranchers and the struggles they face. I could come to your ranch. You name the time."

He *was* persistent. She closed her eyes, put a hand on her brow, and thought about the day's schedule. "I could see you at four this afternoon."

"That's perfect, and I really appreciate it, Ms. Wells."

"Portia." She told him how to get to the ranch, then hung up, thinking, *Darn, don't I have enough to do?*

Todd. Sometimes she had no idea what set him off. One minute he was watching cartoons on television or playing Dungeons and Dragons type computer games, acting like a kid. The next thing she knew, her women's lingerie catalogs were missing, and he was yelling at her that she treated him like a baby.

He was always reluctant to pitch in around the ranch. His uncle never stopped complaining about how lazy he was, but Portia secretly understood. At fifteen you wanted to get your driver's permit, to be with friends your age to goof off and hang out and test your incipient manhood with talk about how big a girl's boobs were. The last thing you wanted to do was run the baler or give inoculations to cattle. Still, this morning all she'd said was for him to take the Subaru and find Randy, and Todd had come unhinged. He hated Uncle Randy, and he hated her.

She had an eleven o'clock appointment with the loan officer at the Cast Rock bank. It was nearly ten. *Damn.* She went upstairs, didn't even knock on Todd's door, just called out, "I'm on my way to the bank. When I get home, you better have found Randy. You hear me, Todd?"

No reply.

"Fine. Don't answer. Just make peace with your uncle before I get back. Oh, and there's a reporter, some writer for an environmental group, coming by at four. If you're back from helping Randy, try to be civil. Okay?"

She heard a muttered, "Sure, whatever."

"Good." She turned, then pivoted back around. "Look, maybe this weekend we'll go up to the new mall that's opening in Denver. Then I can drop you at your friend Peter's house. Why don't you call him, see if that's all right?"

"Sure."

"Okay, I'm off to the bank."

She dressed quickly in a pair of white slacks and a striped T-shirt. Lots of ranchers went to business meetings in jeans and work shirts, but she dressed halfway decently. For

183

herself. She needed to do that. And the reporter was coming, anyway.

Tyler Silverman was Portia's age and already head of commercial loans at Fidelity Bank of Castle Rock. Gary had always handled this end of the ranch business. Handled the bankers and insurance agents and auctioneers and farm equipment suppliers with his infectious charm and self-assurance. When Gary had died, Portia had made the mistaken assumption that Randy would fill his shoes. Not a chance. Randy had manipulated her into the business end of the ranch within weeks of Gary's death.

"Hell," Randy had said, eyeing Gary's files, "I don't know the difference between a checking and savings account. How am I going to negotiate a loan? Guess I'll have to hire a business manger or something."

Just marvelous, Portia had thought. *We can really afford that.*

Now the ranch loan was coming up for renewal, and they were a month behind in payments on the existing loan. And Tyler Silverman hadn't risen on the banking ladder so swiftly because he was a pushover.

She sat down across from him and put on her best business face, a half smile, eyes meeting his confidently.

"So, Portia, how are you doing?" Tyler began. "I know it's been a rough year. I still can't believe Gary's gone."

They chatted for a few minutes, and then Portia reached in her purse and slid a check across his desk. "Here's last month's loan payment, by the way. I added on the per diem interest and the late fee. The truth is, our early hay crop was terrible, and we're having to buy a lot more than usual. I'm sure you already know how bad the grazing is on the BLM land."

He nodded. "For all the ranches."

Usually Wellspring Ranch grazed at least half the herd on federal BLM land. Each head required fifty acres of grazing land in Colorado. In states even drier, such as Nevada, that acreage could increase tenfold. Each acre used by ranchers to graze their cattle cost around a dollar and a half per month. Which didn't seem like much until you looked at a ranch's books and realized what a struggle it was to make ends meet. After four consecutive drought seasons, Portia was wishing life was merely the usual struggle.

"I need to — *we* need to — renegotiate the loan, Tyler," she said, "and at a better interest rate."

"Now, you understand there's a big difference between a mortgage and a commercial loan's rate of interest?"

"Of course."

"So I'm not certain I can go any lower than the existing rate." Tyler Silverman put on reading glasses and thumbed through the loan file. "Um," he said. "When Gary took out the current loan, I gave him the best rate I could, a quarter percent lower than most of the farm loans I was writing at the time."

He removed his glasses, folded his hands on top of the file. "And I'll level with you, just as I always did with Gary. Now that your herd has been culled by a third, the bank's exposure has risen sharply. In the event of default, God forbid that should happen, but the bank would be hard-pressed to recoup the face value of the loan. Portia, I hope you understand that this is just business, nothing personal, nothing that's your fault. Between the drought and threat of fires, we're rewriting fewer and fewer loans and haven't taken on a new account in almost a year."

"I see," she said. He wasn't telling her anything she didn't already know. He was playing hardball. Now he'd tell her about federal disaster relief funds available at low interest rates to the ranchers, blah, blah, blah. She was often a month behind on payments to the existing loan — Gary had been far later at times — but the loan always got paid. The ranch must have had thirty loans with various banks over the last one hundred years, and every penny had been paid back. What would Gary have said at this point?

Would he have engaged in tough negotiation?

"Well," Portia said, "it sounds like I should do some shopping around." *Oh God,* she thought.

Tyler smiled as if saying, *Fat chance, there's not a bank in Colorado offering new ranch loans.*

"You won't be insulted if I look around?" she asked. "It's just that the ranch has such good credit."

"Of course it does. And we'd be heartbroken to lose you, Portia."

Heartbroken, uh-huh.

"I'll tell you what," he said. "At next week's director's meeting, I'll bring up your request, see if we can't find another eighth of a percent room."

So far, so good, she thought, relieved and proud of herself. "I'd appreciate that." She uncrossed her legs and stood and shook his hand across the desk. "You'll call after the meeting?"

"Of course." He walked her out of his office and to the front doors. "How are Randy and Lynette?" he asked. "The kids?"

"Everyone's fine."

"And Todd is still . . . ?"

"Oh yes, Todd is still at the ranch with me."

"That's good."

"Most of the time it is."

He laughed. "And you're taking over

187

Gary's spot with the NPS?"

"That I am."

"A wonderful organization."

"I think so, too," she was saying, when she saw the blue van parked near her pickup in the parking lot, both men on duty today — her security. And all because of the NPS position she'd accepted. *I must be out of my mind,* she thought, *stark raving mad.*

Todd still wasn't back with the Subaru when she got home. Nor was he back when the writer from *Earthguard* arrived at four, escorted by Lev and Jerry.

"Oh, *oh,*" she said, realizing she hadn't notified them of the visitor. And what must he think, this Dave Donaldson from Phoenix?

She introduced the reporter and apologized to the security men, and they left, presumably going back to their place on the county road near the ranch entrance. She showed Donaldson into the living room and then got him an iced tea, all the while thinking, thinking how to explain the presence of security at the ranch.

Naturally, that was the man's first question. "Can I ask why you have bodyguards?" he said, an eager expression behind thick, horn-rimmed glasses.

He wasn't what she'd expected from an environmental reporter. Having watched Gary give interviews over the years, she'd formed an image of the writers in her mind, stereotyped them as fair-haired activists, a lot of them wearing L.L.Bean or Patagonia brand clothing and Birkenstock sandals, and if they wore glasses, the preferred look was usually small, round, wire-rimmed frames. But Dave Donaldson reminded her more of a city boy, his longish dark hair unkempt, his goatee a little scraggly, glasses heavy and thick-lensed, his skin quite pale for an Arizona resident, almost pasty, short-sleeved shirt and baggy brown summer-weight trousers. He wore tennis shoes, a cheap brand unsuitable for walking outdoors or any distance at all, for that matter. Curiously, she even smelled cigarette smoke clinging to his clothes. In her experience, environmental activists never smoked. But he must have been a reporter, as he carried a notebook and had a camera slung over his shoulder.

She caught herself staring and looked up from his shoes, embarrassed. What had he just said? Oh, the security men. Bodyguards, he'd called them.

"Well," she said, taking a sip of her iced tea, "those men really aren't bodyguards. They're here because of the fire danger, arsonists, you know?" She'd grabbed at the idea, remembering a recent fire near Flagstaff, Arizona, which had been set by an arsonist and had destroyed thousands of aces.

But Donaldson didn't seem to have heard of that fire. *Curious,* she thought, until he explained he'd been out of the state on assignment. "Alaska," he said.

"Oh," she said, "for *Earthguard?*"

"Who else?" He laughed. "Say, can I take some photos? Something nice and homey."

He snapped several pictures of her sitting on the couch, standing next to the bookcase, one holding a picture of Gary, which made her uncomfortable, but Mr. Donaldson insisted. She tried to smile and look gracious, but she was nervous about the whole situation.

He finished with the photographs and went back to asking questions about the security men. "So you must have lots of problems at the ranch?"

"Well, sure," she said. But when she listed a few of the universal ranching problems, he didn't take a single note.

"What about your job with the NPS? You ever come up against resistance from, say, developers?"

She was momentarily taken aback, but then she realized he couldn't possibly be talking about Patrick Mahoney. His question was general and perfectly natural. But how to answer? Was this an opportunity to drop a hint about her suspicions of Mahoney? No, she decided, she needed to wait for the perfect moment and the perfect reporter with a nationally known newspaper or magazine — someone with deep pockets and resources.

Someone hungry for a big story. No, not Dave Donaldson.

Nonetheless, she had to give him an answer.

"Mr. Donaldson, Dave." She smiled. "Developers and environmentalists are oil and water more often than not."

"Can you elaborate?"

"Oh, my." She smiled again and let out a breath. "Let's see. Say someone is planning a development, a housing project, or a mall or something similar, and this person locates the ideal spot and even finds property owners willing to entertain offers. Then he still has to consider the impact of his project on the environment. Whether it's wildlife or forests or marshlands, there's always an impact. Here, in the West, as you know, water is a huge issue."

Now he was scribbling away in his notebook, pushing his big glasses up the bridge of his nose with his free hand, the notebook balanced on his knee. Surely what she'd said wasn't news to an environmental writer? Then again, maybe he was new to the job.

"How long have you been with *Earthguard*?" she asked.

He was still writing. He glanced up for a second, then said, "A year." Then went back to his notebook.

"And you're out of Phoenix?"

"Uh-huh."

"Do I, ah, know your editor? Let's see —"

"She's pretty new, too." He kept writing.

"What is her name?"

"Ah, Sue. Sue James."

"Oh," Portia said.

"So." He looked up. "Any of these developers get rough?"

"Rough?"

"Yeah, sure, pushy. You know, throw their weight around, offer you money, threaten you?"

She felt heat spread on the back of her neck. It was as if he knew about the threat made to her the other day — even about Gary. But that was impossible. He was only searching for a fresh slant on the same hackneyed articles for his little periodical. But what should she say? Truth, lies, half-truths?

"Ms. Wells?"

"Ah, sorry. I was just thinking about your question. Isn't it kind of odd?"

"Hey, can't always write about knocking baby seals on the head, right?"

"I, ah, guess not." *Good Lord,* she thought.

"So?" He waited.

"Well, some developers can pose problems."

"Like?"

"The obvious ones. I think I explained already that they may want to build on pristine lands that are threatened by development. You know, man and progress versus preserving our natural heritage. Fortunately, the NPS has the resources to take firm stands, even, on occasion, to purchase land to protect it for future generations."

"Uh-huh," he said. "Say, didn't your husband have a problem with one particular developer here in Colorado? What was his name?"

This had gone far enough. Clearly, Donaldson had done quite a bit of research and was angling for a whole lot more than some information about struggling Front Range ranchers.

"Gosh, his name is on the tip of my tongue," Donaldson was saying.

"Well," Portia said, "I'm afraid I can't help you."

"I just thought, what with the bodyguards out front and you talking with the NPS, that maybe this guy was giving you some trouble. Maybe he gave your husband some trouble, too."

"Oh gosh," Portia said, the heat spreading up to her face and sweat breaking out on her brow, "I've got to end this interview, I'm, ah, late for another meeting."

"Just a couple more questions."

She stood up abruptly. "I am *really* late. I'll have to ask you to go."

Ushering him to the door was difficult. He was single-minded, bent on getting the name Mahoney from her, as if that was what he was really after. Maybe she was just paranoid. Or maybe not.

"Can I call you again? You know, for follow-up?"

"Ah, sure, I guess so." She didn't know what to tell him.

"You have a cell phone?"

"Ah, no," she lied. Then she thought to ask, "When will the article run in your magazine?"

"Next month."

"Oh, you're monthly?"

"Sure, monthly."

"I see, well, could I have your business card?"

He got a sheepish look on his face and snapped his fingers. "Just gave my last one out today."

"You can mail it to me."

"I'll do that."

"Good-bye then," she said.

"Yeah, I'll be in touch," he said and finally left.

My God, she thought, watching him drive away, his rental car leaving a train of powdery dust hanging in the air until he turned onto the county road and was gone.

She was damp with sweat by the time she went back inside. If this is what she was going to face day in and day out, she wouldn't survive this job another week.

In the downstairs bathroom she splashed

cold water on her face and hung on to the sink, breathing deeply. Her nerves were jangling as it was, and Todd wasn't back with the Subaru. It was almost five. Todd wouldn't still be helping Randy. Or would he?

She picked up the cordless phone in the kitchen and called Randy and Lynette's. Randy was already home, and no, he hadn't seen or heard from Todd all day. He was pissed. "Portia, you got to get control of that kid. Next thing you know, he'll be on drugs. And what you're going to do with him when you're off traipsing around the country is beyond me."

She wasn't about to get in this conversation right now. She would have asked to speak to Lynette, but that would only infuriate Randy. "Look, Randy," she said, "I have to go. I'll have Todd over at your place first thing tomorrow."

"Sure," Randy said and he hung up.

Where was Todd? Obviously not on the ranch, or Randy or one of the hands would have seen the car. That meant Todd had driven into Colt or Castle Rock or, God forbid, Denver. And without even a learner's permit. *Damn, damn, damn.*

She wanted to scream. And she was worried. He could get in an accident. He could so easily reach for a tape to put in the player or do something stupid and take his eyes off

195

the road for a moment and . . . and end up like his father.

By six he was still not home. She fixed dinner, her ear cocked to the sound of tires on the ranch road. She longed to call Lynette, who always had sound advice and calming words, but Randy might answer the phone, and he was the last person she wanted to talk to again.

Dinner went untouched. She fluctuated between, *Certainly Todd has been in an accident,* and, *Certainly someone would have phoned by now if he had been.*

At eight she began phoning his school buddies. But no Todd.

At nine she drove down to the main road and talked to Jerry, who was on duty in the van, guilty that Aaron was paying for this, but she had more pressing problems. She found out that Todd had driven by in the direction of Colt around noon.

"You realize he doesn't have his driver's license?" she said.

Jerry shrugged, and she got back in her truck and drove home. Big help that was.

Waiting for Todd, angry and anxious at the same time, she phoned Phoenix, Arizona, information and asked for the number of *Earthguard.*

"We have no listing of an *Earthguard*," the operator told her. "Perhaps it's in Mesa or Tempe?"

196

Or Scottsdale or Sun City or who knows where, Portia thought. She thanked the woman and hung up and went back to worrying about Todd.

At ten, knowing she was waking the household, she phoned Randy again. Maybe Lynette would answer. But Randy picked up, and he was no more concerned now than he had been earlier. Groggily, he said, "Call the cops, or have those security men go hunt for the kid."

"About the security," she said, realizing she'd never really explained their presence to Randy, "Aaron Burkhart hired them after those men threatened me at the Co-op. I don't want you to think the ranch is paying."

"Whatever. Lynette said something about it."

"Don't you care about anything?" she said.

"Sleep. I care about sleep. Unlike some of us here on the ranch, I gotta get up before five."

"Good night," she said tightly. "Sorry I woke you." She ended the call and stared incredulously at the phone. He was a complete ass. If he was in front of her, she'd shake him till he got it, but then she realized that would do no good; he didn't have any brains to rattle in the first place. How could Lynette live with him?

By eleven Todd still wasn't home. Sleepless, she lay in bed and wondered if she

197

shouldn't contact the police now. But wouldn't they have called her if something was really wrong?

She wondered why she kept struggling here, why she didn't give up and move back to New York. She was no match for this rugged environment, for the high-powered men with whom she was always dealing. And, apparently, she was no parent to Todd. If Gary were here, Gary who had been so fearless, so competent and easy in his skin, Gary would know exactly how to handle everything.

But, damn, she *was* managing. Sometimes better than her husband had. Gary would have let the bank loan go unpaid and unrenewed for months.

Gary. She rolled over, listened for Todd, and she couldn't help remembering how much the women all liked her husband, how often she felt jealous and guilty, sure Gary was straying because she hadn't loved him enough. Or given him children.

Okay, she had Todd now, who was driving her insane tonight. But she truly had come to care for him, and since Gary's death, they'd formed a deep bond. She could almost believe he was her own flesh. Somehow she'd manage to get through the next couple of years until he was off to college. They'd both manage. What she wasn't so sure of was how she'd get through the next years at the ranch and with the NPS. Especially now that she'd been threatened. As Gary had been. She was out of her mind to think she could take on Patrick Mahoney. Men like him played for keeps.

At one in the morning she finally heard the crunch of tires as the Subaru rolled up in front of the garage. Then, a minute later, the furtive snick of the front door opening. She almost got up to yell at him — almost. Instead, she figured she'd wake him early and have it out in the morning.

By two, she felt herself relaxing, sleep overtaking her. Sleep and that too-frequent ache deep in her belly, the need to be with a man. Over a year, she thought, not asleep, not really awake, over a year since she'd made love. She had a wisp of a memory a moment before drifting off: a sultry summer's morning, a car speeding south on the Hutchinson River Parkway, sunlight flickering on a man's face as he drove, then shadow, an aura of danger and mystery to him, her breath too shallow.

ELEVEN

Nick dragged himself up from sleep and found he was in one of those lousy moods where you know something's hanging over your head, nagging at you, but it's ephemeral and unfocused, and you can't get a handle on it.

Until he had coffee in a breakfast place down the street from the motel, and he remembered with absolute clarity what was bugging him.

The *Star Gazer* scoop. Who was Bern sending out to interview Portia? What trumped-up story would the reporter feed her to get an interview? And what loaded, bullshit questions would he ask? He remembered the guy standing at the file cabinet in the *Star Gazer* office, holding up the old photo of the pig's body with the head of a young kid. *Oh, man.*

His stomach turned sour at the thought, and he couldn't finish his greasy eggs. He sat there in the café and thought about Portia. Saw her face, the fine golden texture of her skin, the softness of her streaked hair. He heard the timbre of her voice, and he felt like hell. What was that saying, something he'd heard without remembering when or where or in what context: "Unleashing the dogs of war." Well, that's what he'd done, unleashed the dogs of war on her.

Head down, he walked back to his room, thinking, imagining that sleazy reporter at Portia's throat. He had to do something, he figured, something to mitigate the damage.

He phoned Bern in New York, found out that the reporter had already been to see Portia. *Shit.*

"His name is Donaldson, Dave Donaldson," Bern said. "I still can't believe how fast you dug up that info, Sinestra."

"Um," Nick said.

"You're still on it, right? Could be that stuff about her husband and the developer's the tip of the iceberg, right?"

"Yeah, sure, tip of the iceberg."

"Hey, there a problem?"

"Nope, no problem." Nick frowned. "This Donaldson still in Colorado?"

"Should be."

"Know where he's staying?"

There was a rustling of papers. "Adam's Mark Hotel in Denver. You want to meet with him? Maybe you guys could compare notes."

"Yeah, yeah."

"Keep in touch. I mean that."

201

"Absolutely," Nick said, hanging up.

He called the Adam's Mark and asked for Donaldson's room. Got a sleep-clogged voice. Christ, it was ten in the morning.

"Donaldson?"

"Yeah, who's this?"

"Nick Sinestra. Bern wants us to get together, compare notes."

"Oh, right, you're the cop who turned him on to the story."

"That's me. Can we meet?"

"Uh, sure, I guess so. I'm out of here this afternoon."

"You saw the lady." It wasn't a question.

"Yesterday. She was all uptight, made me leave. Basically, what I got was jackshit."

Nick felt a chill. He knew exactly what kind of stories derived from jackshit.

"I'm coming over to your hotel. Where can we meet?"

"Give me a minute here."

"Come on, Donaldson."

"Okay, there're tables in the lobby. For coffee and stuff. I'll be there."

"How'll I know you?"

"I'll know you, Sinestra. Saw you at the office."

"Half an hour," Nick said.

He grilled Donaldson, trying to find out precisely what the man knew and what Portia had told him.

202

Donaldson drank coffee and chain smoked. He kept pushing his big glasses up on his nose. "I tried my damnedest to get Mahoney's name from her, but she wasn't about to say it. She wouldn't even admit she'd been threatened." He laughed. "Even when I was escorted to her front door by her *bodyguards* when I got there. Jesus, what a crock of shit she handed me."

"What'd she say?"

"She *said* they weren't bodyguards, they were on the lookout for arsonists. Because of fires or some baloney."

"And she didn't say anything about being threatened?"

"Nope. Not a word. Just gave me a lot of mealy-mouthed crap about progress versus preserving our national heritage. The usual junk."

"Basically, you don't have a damn thing."

Donaldson leered. "I noticed that she had nice tits."

A fist of anger tightened in Nick's gut. This asshole was looking at Portia's breasts. One more crack like that, and he'd punch the guy out. "So, what's your story line going to be?"

The reporter shrugged. "I'll describe the ranch, wax poetic about the West, all that stuff. Do a rundown on the NPS — Bern's got the background for me — and talk about the war between developers and nature."

Donaldson leaned forward and stubbed out a cigarette in the dregs of his coffee. "And then I tell how Gary Wells got murdered on a dark, lonely country road and how his pretty young widow is scared for her life, too. Great story."

Nick clenched his teeth. "You going to name names?"

"Hell, yes. Patrick Mahoney, big as life, evil developer, suspect in Wells's murder."

"Whoa there," Nick said. "You can't print that shit. The woman's paranoid. I talked to the sheriff, and even he thinks she's nuts. There was no murder. It was an accident."

"So? If I can get the lawyers to clear it, I use the name."

"Christ, Donaldson. How do you live with yourself?"

"Listen, Mr. High and Mighty Policeman, I entertain the public. I write great copy. I sell magazines."

"Spare me."

He was probably right, Nick thought. The *Star Gazer* would print whatever it wanted. Hell, last week they'd run a story on a two-headed goat boy in Alabama, some farmer swearing he'd seen it, blurry doctored photographs on an inside page. The week before it had been the affair the First Lady was having with her secretary.

He left Donaldson and walked back to the motel, feeling antsy and jittery, those little teeth of guilt gnawing away. Imagining Portia's reaction when she saw the *Star Gazer* staring at her in a grocery store checkout stand, with its lies and insinuations and half-truths. All his fault.

It was sweltering in Denver that morning, must have been at least ninety, the heat shimmering off the sidewalks and streets. The trees dusty, all buildings closed up tight, their air conditioners humming and dripping water onto the pavement.

A dry heat. Sure.

Well, it was too late to stop the story. And why did he care so damn much? He'd worked for the rag sheet for years. He'd never given a rat's ass what they wrote before, so why should he care now?

It sounded as though Portia had been suspicious of Donaldson. Was there any way she could have connected the man to Nick? He was ashamed at his own guilt, but even more that that, he was angry at himself, worried she'd find out he was the prick who'd put the tabloid on to her in the first place. But then he thought, what the hell. He'd never see her again, so what did he care if she found out?

He walked along the sidewalk, the fierce Southwest sun beating down on his shoulders, the air he drew into his lungs hot and dust-dry, sucking moisture from him, and he tried to think of what he should do next. Sit around his motel room with the air conditioner on? Hunt down this Patrick Mahoney? Drive past the Wellspring Ranch, try to get a handle on the security outfit?

He was going to pocket ten thousand bucks. He had a month's vacation and nothing pressing to do. He should be happy. He should be fucking delirious. Besides, Bern had sounded amenable to shelling out more bucks if Nick could come up with some new dirt. "Tip of the iceberg," Bern had said. Could be Portia wasn't crazy, this Mahoney character really was behind the death of Gary Wells.

The guilt evaporated. Nick's brain began to calculate. What if he did uncover a murder plot? What if he pulled a Mark Fuhrman? Okay, this wasn't a Kennedy-connected murder, but there still might be a book deal in it. Big bucks, unimaginable publicity. The whole nine yards. *Yeah.*

Then he did another switch. What was he thinking? One minute he was sinking under the weight of remorse, the next he was scheming again. He was as big an asshole as Donaldson. Bigger. Donaldson wasn't a hypocrite.

In the end, figuring it wouldn't hurt just to take a drive down to Colt, see what was up with the security outfit, he headed toward the interstate. But when he got to the on-ramp of I-25, he abruptly swerved and turned in the opposite direction from Colt. He needed to think, make up his mind: Pursue this assignment or throw in the towel and fly on back to New York?

I-25 ran into another interstate that bisected the Rockies. For no good reason Nick drove toward it, thinking what the hell, might as well see the scenery while he was chewing over his troubles.

He stopped at a minimart before turning onto I-70 and bought a state map, then it was up, up past subdivisions to where the highway disappeared around perilously sharp curves at a 7 percent incline. There were few houses here, fewer exits. The highway kept climbing, semis crawling along the inside lane, for nearly an hour, until the sagebrush and stunted trees gave way to evergreens and aspens, and the Eisenhower Tunnel that pierced the Continental Divide lay ahead.

It was cooler up here; the car's readout showed seventy-six degrees. And still the mountains rose around him, stretching away to the north and south and west. Jagged mountains, not like the tame ones back East. After the tunnel, he descended into a long valley. Stopped for gas and a Coke at a convenience store in a town called Frisco. Then on the road again, watching the scenery slide by, another climb to the top of Vail Pass, then down into the Vail Valley, the idle ski lifts on his left, houses and condos clustered on the slopes wherever he looked. He wondered what the NPS had to say about this runaway development.

Which took him full circle to Portia Wells again. Had she driven this road? What did she think of those monster homes crowded into a narrow, steep defile on that mountainside over there?

He didn't know much about her. Not a damn thing, really. What did she do in her spare time? What did she like to eat? What was truly important to her? All he'd seen, he was beginning to think, was a carefully constructed public facade. He'd seen what she wanted him to see, no more, no less.

He followed I-70 through Eagle and No Name, the Colorado River now running alongside the interstate. The Colorado River, not very wide here, a mountain stream. But didn't it run all the way to California?

Into beautiful Glenwood Canyon, with its vertical rising walls and the railroad track on the other side of the river from the highway, winding along the tortuous curves of the canyon. Gorgeous country. Too bad he didn't have a camera. He'd stop at all those places the other tourists stopped and snap pictures and show them to Mia and her daughters.

Yeah, sure.

Finally the valley widened into Glenwood Springs, with its century-old hotel and natural hot springs pool. Teddy Roosevelt had stayed there, he read when he gassed up. Then a turn south and forty miles along a state highway to Aspen. Sunny and bucolic on this summer's day, great old brick buildings, Victorian style, huge shade trees along Main Street. The ski mountain rising across town, grass-covered now. He tried to imagine it white with snow; it looked steep as hell to him, a nonskier.

Out of Aspen toward Independence Pass, up and up, stuck in a slow-moving line of traffic. Gawking, out-of-state tourists. Of course, he was one of them.

He drove over the Continental Divide again, the road narrow and falling off to one side, thousands of feet down to a silver-glinting river.

His butt was getting tired, but this odyssey had become a challenge to him. Past Stringtown, then the 10,000-foot-high town of Leadville, where the Unsinkable Molly Brown had lived. Dusk fell, and still he drove, the car window open now, mountain air washing over him. Back to the interstate and east toward Denver. A great circle route, he thought. A journey through beautiful country. The Wild West. God's country. And he still hadn't come to a decision, and he still felt like shit.

Darkness was falling by the time he parked at his motel, stiff and tired and in a rotten mood. What the hell had he thought — that he could outrun his feelings?

He carried the bag he'd brought from Burger King into his room, set it down, hungry but too pissed off to eat. Instead he phoned Gil at home, needing to talk to somebody. To connect. But Gil had his own problems.

"He what?" Nick asked.

"The goddamn kid's in trouble again. Thank God not in the Seventh this time. He was picked up for shoplifting. Nudie magazines."

"Ah, Christ, Gil."

"If the juvie judge wants to, he can force Doug to leave the city. What can I do, send him to my sister? She doesn't want him."

"Hey, I'm really sorry. Anything I can do —"

"Sure, two thousand miles away. I swear, he's gonna kill his mother, damn punk kid."

When he hung up he thought, *Hey, everybody's got troubles.* Nick wasn't any worse off than anyone else. Maybe better off, in fact.

He wished he could help Gil out. Dougie, Dougie, poor kid. Damn it, he wasn't a poor kid. He had Gil for a father and Gladys for a mother. He had a brother and a sister, for Chrissakes. Why did kids *do* things like that?

It struck Nick that he could fly the kid out to Colorado and get him away from his buddies, away from home. Take him fishing and hiking, like that. Not that Nick had a clue how to fish or hike. And he wasn't even sure how long he was going to stay here, anyway. But what if he could get the kid out here? Good old Uncle Nick to the rescue.

Nah, he thought, smiling ruefully. *Bad idea.*

He phoned Mia then. What was wrong with him? Was he lonely or something, calling everybody back in the city?

She was still at the salon, closing up.

"Hi, stranger," she said. "Listen, I'm kind of busy here."

"Okay, sure, just checking in."

"How's Colorado?"

"Beautiful. Hot."

"It rained here today."

"Huh."

"Have you seen her?"

"Who?"

"Portia Wells, who else?"

"No, not really. I saw her ranch."

"A *ranch.* My God."

"It's brown grass and cows and a long driveway."

"But a *ranch.*"

"How're the girls?"

"They're good."

"I may be coming back to the city pretty soon."

"What about your vacation?"

"Hasn't been much fun. When I get back, maybe we can go to Coney Island, you know, or Jones Beach?"

"Uh, well, the girls are kind of busy and, you know kids, they want to hang with their friends and not some old fogies like us."

"So? We'll go alone then. Just an overnight."

"I'm kind of tied up, Nick."

"You got to work?"

"I'm kind of tied up," she repeated, and he finally got it.

"There's somebody else," he said flatly.

"Well, no, not *really*. Just a guy, a friend, and —"

"Yeah, a friend. Okay, Mia. Fine, you go out with your *friend*, and I'll be seeing you around."

"Nick —"

"Don't bother," he said angrily.

"I like you, Nick. I want us to keep in touch."

"Oh, okay, sure, we'll stay in touch. I'll send you a fucking postcard."

"Don't be like that."

"What? I'm being immature?"

"Well . . ."

"Bye, Mia." He broke the connection.

What an idiot he was not to realize that she'd met someone else. All that horseshit about not wanting to leave the city, the girls' activities. Excuses. Jesus, she'd dumped him. After two years, she'd dumped him. The bitch.

He didn't know how he felt. His pride was

hurt, his ego wounded. He hadn't been in love with Mia, but they'd been good together. Now what? He was alone, no one to call, no one to hang around with, floating, abandoned, in a huge and empty ocean. And yet, under the hurt, there was a sneaking relief. No Mia, no emotional responsibility. It was a sort of freedom.

He watched TV and ate his cold burger and fries. The local news here was a joke: car accidents and traffic jams because of that giant highway project, cutely named T-Rex. That was about it. What did cops do here, anyway?

He was tired, but he couldn't sleep. The air conditioner hummed soothingly, but that didn't help. He was too pissed off at Mia, too worried about Dougie, and too goddamn tense about the story Donaldson was going to write.

He could see the headline: "Beautiful Widow Takes on Husband's Murderer." Or maybe "Widow Seeks Revenge for Husband's Murder." Something like that. Something to grab the public's attention, get them to buy the rag sheet.

He went over the conversation with Cab Whitefeather in his mind. The three miscarriages, her husband too fond of the ladies. The accident. So she was without a husband, without children of her own. Her crazy mother's whereabouts leaked to the press. A struggle with wildfires and drought and money troubles and selling off her cattle cheap.

And maybe real danger to her from some asshole developer.

She'd told Cab two men had threatened her at a Co-op. He'd seen the place in Colt when he'd driven through the town. Had she really been threatened? Or was her imagination running away with her?

He remembered her at the fund-raiser, so warm yet in control, the audience held in thrall by her words. And when he'd driven her into the city from New Rochelle, that had not been a nutty, paranoid female.

All her problems. Dead husband's kid, the ranch, her batty mother, the NPS. Christ, the woman was a saint. And here he'd been digging a deeper grave for her, loosing those frigging dogs of war onto her.

He rolled over, the covers tangled around his legs. He was sweating, even though the room was cooling down. Sweating and wide awake and edgy as hell. He sat up and flicked the bedside light on. What a son of a bitch he was. For money. For a lousy ten K. He put his face in his hands and scrubbed his fingers through his hair until it stood up in tufts.

Next thing he knew, he was tugging on his pants and shirt, snatching up the car keys. His brain was working overtime. If Portia was really in some kind of danger, he might have made her situation worse by putting Donaldson on to her. *If* someone had seen Donaldson on the ranch. *If* the security she'd hired was as lousy as Nick suspected.

He stood in the parking lot with his brow creased. What was he doing? Sodium lights overhead hissed and laid a lurid brightness on everything, and he was aware of cars rushing by on the street, going fast at this hour. What was he thinking? That he'd drive to the ranch and confess all?

He almost climbed back up the stairs to his room, his hand on the gummy wood rail. But he swore under his breath and strode to the Camry.

"Idiot," he muttered. Nevertheless, he pulled out onto the street, joining the fast-paced traffic, feeling that cop's sixth sense that something wasn't right.

The trip didn't take that long at night, his headlights piercing the darkness like two tunnels. The stars were incredible here, in the clear, dry air, but he didn't take the time to enjoy them. He drove, his foot heavy on the gas pedal. Turned off at the exit for Colt, slid though the sleeping town, took the county road. His headlights found the blue van parked near the ranch entrance, swept over it, illuminated nothing but the vehicle's empty interior. *Huh,* he thought.

A tingle moved up his spine. He turned

onto the long drive, passed under the Well-spring Ranch sign, came over a rise, saw a glow in the distance. A weird, yellow orange, sickly glow where there should be only darkness.

"Sweet Jesus," he whispered, stomping on the accelerator.

TWELVE

She woke to a noise, a peculiar roar, and for a second she thought, *Why did Todd start up the tractor?* But then she saw the light flicker against the windows, and her heart contracted.

She lunged out of bed and ran to the window. Flames shot up in malignant blossoms, orange and yellow and red, staining the night sky.

The barn!

She gasped, and her breath stopped in her throat, and later she would think an eternity passed before she grabbed the phone by the bed and pressed 911. Her hand was shaking, and it seemed endlessly long again before there was a reply.

"A fire! Wellspring Ranch, County Road One eighty-seven, five miles south of Colt!"

"Yes, ma'am, I have that. Are there any injuries?"

"No . . . I'm not sure. I have to go now. Wellspring Ranch!"

Then she was running down the stairs, across the living room, slamming open the

217

front door. Her feet were bare, and she wore a tank top and pajama bottoms, but she didn't stop. She ran.

The flames licked upward, and as she got closer, her heart beating a terrible cadence, she could hear the crackling of burning wood under the roar.

My god, the barn. What's in there? Nothing alive, no, no cattle, the horse with the foot abscess turned out yesterday. But the hay. Half of the barn was filled with the early hay crop.

The heat hit her like a blow, and she couldn't go any closer. She slopped, panting. She heard the panicked whinnies of horses, and she remembered the half dozen in the pen near the barn.

Dogs barked frantically. Randy's dogs, black and white bodies streaking toward her. Then Randy, yelling something to her she couldn't hear. And over it all, the noise and flames sucking all the air from the world.

Todd raced up wearing only pajama bottoms. His eyes were wide, his mouth open, red flickering on his face like watered-down blood. She was deaf, she couldn't breathe, her eyes stung. Smoke burned her nostrils and lungs.

Lynette appeared with the three kids. Everyone was screaming, but you couldn't hear over the freight-train roar. Portia got to Randy and grabbed his arm, said into his ear, "The horses in the pen!"

He nodded, took off for the gate, gesturing his dogs to follow. He'd open the gate, get the dogs to herd the frantic beasts out. They could run free for now.

The security men Jerry and Lev were there, standing back, Lev talking on a cell phone. They seemed stunned, their faces blank. Maybe Lev was reporting to Aaron. Oh God, she couldn't think about that now.

Thick black smoke billowed up from the roof, and in the jaundiced light bits and pieces of hay could be seen floating upward, carried on superheated air.

Where were the fire trucks? But they couldn't have gotten here by now; it'd only been a few minutes. The barn was a loss. No one could save it in any case, not even if the tanker trucks drove up this very second.

Randy was back. Out of the corner of her eye, she could see the shadowed forms of horses galloping off into the night.

The hay. Some tools. Oh God, was the baler in there, or had Randy parked it by his house? The tack — saddles and bridles and blankets. Had the barn cats escaped?

And then — she'd always swear it was like the trailer for that movie *Backdraft*, the character materializing as if by magic — a person came out of the barn, through the big open doors, emerging from that inferno, a misshapen form, staggering, under some kind of burden. Who? Oh dear God, had someone been in the barn?

She put her hand up to her mouth, too dazed to move. Then Randy was dragging at the figure, and they staggered together. Todd was helping, too, and she could make out a man, and he'd been carrying saddles, big heavy Western saddles, and the three of them got beyond the fire's reach and dropped their burdens, and the strange man fell to his knees, head hanging, trying to breathe.

Then she did move, going up to them, tugging at Todd's arm. "Are you all right?" she yelled, drowned out by the fire. Todd nodded, his face blackened.

She saw Randy grabbing a hose connected to the water pump, pushing the handle up. Was he crazy? Was he going to try to put the fire out with a *hose?*

But, no, he turned the spray onto the man on the ground. Who was it? Juan . . . Hernando? But they wouldn't be here at night. They'd be —

The man ran a hand over his face, and the water mixed with soot turned his skin glistening black in the firelight. There was something familiar about that face, even running with water, sooty, grimacing. . . .

She stepped closer, buffeted by the unholy heat, and she looked at him. *Nick? Nick Sinestra? Here? Now?* A vast confusion held her. *Nick Sinestra. Here?*

Then her brain clicked on again, and her first thought was that *he'd* set the fire. *The bastard. He'd set the fire!*

He was standing and yelling something at Randy, and she caught some of his words: ". . . back in. Wet me down and . . ."

He half turned, ready to return into the mouth of hell. For what? For whom? If he set the fire, why . . . ?

She ran to him and snatched at his arm, shook her head vehemently. *No no!* No blood on her hands. Not even his.

By then surely he could see it was no use. The roof blazed, shooting fire thirty, forty feet into the air. The barn doors were a ravening yaw of flame. Every board stood out in sharp relief, red-hot. The fire seemed to burn even hotter, and they all stepped back, Randy still holding the hose.

She heard something above the fire's din, turned her head. Lights, sirens, three fire trucks, two of them tankers. An ambulance.

Some of the firefighters hooked up their hoses to one of the tankers, training them on the barn, moving everyone back, while other men from another truck put out several small fires that had ignited downwind in the field.

Portia looked back at the barn, and she knew it was past saving. The flames wavered and expanded and expanded and collapsed upon themselves finally in an explosion of smoke and sparks and tatters of straw floating over everything like a blizzard of blackened snow. The barn caved in upon itself, a pile of smoking, flaming wreckage, hissing back at the streams of water the firemen aimed at it.

By the time the firefighters had doused the pile of wreckage, and the noise had stopped, and the only light was from the fire trucks, Portia was sitting on the ground, an arm around Todd, shell-shocked, disbelieving.

More tankers appeared, and men clambered over the site, searching for hot spots, roaming the field and still finding flare-ups. Lynette was crying, holding her children tightly, and her tears made furrows through the soot on her face.

Cab Whitefeather drove up just before five in the morning.

"You okay?" he asked Portia.

"Yes," she said dully.

"Well, no one's hurt, that's good. And the horses?"

"They're out there somewhere." She waved her hand.

"It's a pisser, ain't it? Got the call from dispatch, but I was over at the Aikens place. They got a wildfire up on their north section."

"Oh God," she said.

Cab nodded. "Hope to contain it, but who knows." He stared at the ruins, then pivoted. "I see that New York cop's here."

222

Her head snapped up. "You know him?"

"Met him, that's all."

"What in hell is he doing here?"

"Told me he was looking for a place to retire."

She stared uncomprehendingly at Cab, then shook her head, pushed herself to her feet, and strode over to where Nick was talking to a fireman. The ground was hot and wet, and her bare feet were tender. There was a burn on her arm.

"You," she said, standing before him.

He turned to her, his face drawn and blackened, very still, dark eyes leveled on her. "Ms. Wells," he said, nodding.

"How in God's name did *you* get here?"

"It's a long story."

"Can you make it short?"

"I saw the flames." He shrugged. There were holes burned in his white shirt, an angry red patch on his neck.

"What are you *doing* here?"

He ran a hand through his hair, and she could see the singed ends. But he said nothing, as if he wasn't even sure himself why he was there.

"Did you burn down my barn?" she asked angrily.

He stared at her for a moment longer. Then he gave a short laugh. "Just about got myself fried in there. Why would I — ?"

"I don't believe in coincidences."

"My being here is no coincidence."

"Well, *did* you set the fire?"

"Hell, no."

She gazed up at his face, searching for answers, but she got nothing from his expression. He was right about one thing: if he'd set the fire, it was highly unlikely he would have run into the inferno to save what little he could — then tried to go back in a second time.

That still didn't answer what he was doing here. She started to say something, but he cut her off.

"Look, make me some coffee. I'll explain everything," he said. "And maybe you have something for this burn."

"Coffee?" she asked, incredulous. "My barn burned down, and you want coffee?"

"And a Danish, if you got one."

She became cognizant of the scene then: an overpowering sodden stench, water running over the ground, fat hoses snaking everywhere, men combing the pile of charred timber in the quickening light. Todd sitting dejectedly on the ground. Lynette sniffing, and Randy standing in the shadows glowering. Everyone shaken, sooty, hair singed, clothes ruined. She herself practically undressed, her face no doubt as black as everyone else's.

Then Randy walked over. *Oh God,* she thought. "So who the hell are you?" He stood chest to chest with Nick, taller and heavier across the shoulders.

"Friend of Portia's."

She swiveled her head. *A friend?*

"You just tell me what you're doing on my ranch at this hour," Randy said.

"Saw the flames. Thought I could help."

"Just happened by?"

"Yeah, just happened by."

"Randy," she tried.

"Is this guy really a friend of yours?"

"He's a . . . yes, I know him."

Randy narrowed his eyes. "You sure he wasn't just happening to *leave* at that hour?"

"Hey, wait a minute, pal," Nick said.

"You butt out of this." Then, to Portia, "It's your goddamn fault. You and your threats, and that reporter. This is all your fault!"

"I thought that *threat* was a big joke," she retorted. "You said —"

"You shouldn't have had that reporter here. You pissed someone off, that's for goddamn sure." He swept an arm at the smoldering rubble.

Lynette, the kids following her, tried to take Randy's arm, but he shook her off. She burst into tears again.

"Randy," Portia tried, "for God's sake."

"It *is* your fault. You don't belong here, never have, never will. By the time you're done, there won't even be a ranch! Why couldn't you leave well enough alone! Just had to take that fancy spot with the NPS, you did, and now look, look what you're —"

"Randy!" Lynette cried.

And Nick stepped up to the plate. "I think that's probably enough for tonight," he said. "We've all had a bad time."

"*Bad time.*" Randy snorted.

"Take it easy, pal. Everyone's upset."

"I told you to butt out," Randy said.

"Sure, fine. Just about got roasted saving your frigging saddles . . ."

And then as if there weren't enough pandemonium, Jerry and Lev approached. Lev put a hand on Nick's shoulder, and Nick slowly and deliberately removed it, his dark eyes fixed on the security man. "Don't touch, buddy, okay?"

Lev hesitated, then just stood there, but Jerry got in Randy's face. Randy not giving an inch, saying, "And where the hell were you two, anyway?"

"Just what are you getting at?" Jerry began.

"You know goddamn good and well what I'm getting at."

Randy slashed a hand through the air, seemed about to say something else, but Cab strode up, and said, "Whoa there, son, let's all cool down now." Cab waited a minute to see if Randy was getting the message, then he said, "I'm going to need statements from everyone. You can do them now, or call them in, if that suits."

"Jesus," Randy said, chest heaving, kicking at the soaking mess on the ground.

Portia could barely think. No way could she make a statement right now. *Nick.* She glanced at him. *And what would his statement be? Oh God,* she thought, *this isn't happening.*

Cab put away his notepad when no one was forthcoming, and then he eyed Randy, whose shoulders slumped.

"Come on, Randy," Cab said, "I'll get you and Lynette and the little ones on home. Come on."

Beaten, Randy followed him.

But, apparently, Nick wasn't quite through. He eyed Lev and Jerry and said, "So, where *were* you boys?"

"Nick," Portia said. This was absolutely none of his business.

He ignored her. "Didn't see a thing, huh?"

Lev took a step toward him, but Jerry got in between them, saying. "Come on, let's split. We'll give our statements to the sheriff. Come on, Lev." Then Jerry paused. "You all right, Ms. Wells?"

She was not all right. But she couldn't deal with them now. She just nodded.

"We'll be at the entrance if you need us," Jerry said, and they left.

After a minute, his eyes still on the security men, Nick glanced in Randy's direction. "So who's he?"

"Randy."

"Oh, the brother."

"My husband's brother."

"That your house?" He gestured with his head.

"Yes."

"You got that coffee?"

"I can't *believe* you. I can't . . ." She put a hand to her forehead.

"Come on. No use standing around here anymore."

What should she do? Order him off the ranch? Take the hand he held out? Laugh hysterically? Cry?

She did none of those things. She called to Todd and told him to come home. She started walking toward the house, picking her way across the ground, her bare feet smarting. If Nick followed, so be it. Right now it didn't seem to matter one way or the other.

In the kitchen, she started a pot of coffee, then excused herself to go upstairs to grab a shirt to put on. She splashed water on her face, saw the paleness beneath the soot. Ruined a towel drying her skin. She'd have loved a shower, her state of undress and filth ludicrous, but she went downstairs and dutifully poured coffee into mugs, pushed sugar toward Nick.

He was tilted back in one of the kitchen chairs, his legs stretched out in front of him, head back, eyes closed. Todd leaned against the sink, slowly and methodically eating a banana.

"Todd, go get yourself cleaned up. And throw those pajamas out."

"Okay." He seemed a zombie, not arguing.

"Have you met Detective Sinestra?"

"Nick." He spoke with closed eyes.

"Yeah, hi, Nick."

"Go on now," she said.

She sat across from Nick and watched as he opened his eyes and reached for the coffee. "Thanks," he said. "Nice kid. Is he your stepson?"

"How'd you know? Did Cab tell you? Or do you have some other method of gathering intelligence, Detective Sinestra?"

He ignored her and drank his coffee. He looked weary under the soot, and his clothes smelled like smoke; she supposed hers did, too.

Such an ordinary scene: the big country kitchen with its honey-colored pine floor and the old-fashioned glass-fronted cabinets. The pine trestle table and rush-seated chairs. The striped café curtains on the two windows that looked out at the foothills, the tarnished copper pots and pans hanging over the stove, a glass pitcher of daisies she'd picked yesterday on the table.

But nothing was ordinary about this dawn, about this man who sat drinking her coffee, reeking of her burned barn.

"Why are you here?" she asked quietly. "Really."

"It's a long story."

She leaned forward, elbows on the table. "Look, I know what you did. I called your CO, Fitzpatrick, before I left New York, and I know about the shitty stunt you pulled. Pretending to be my security." She twisted her mouth.

"Yeah, well . . ."

"I know you sicced that reporter on my mother. And now that I think about it, I bet you turned Donaldson onto me, too. You did, didn't you?"

His black eyes stared at her from his soot-covered face, his gaze clear and sharp. Dirty as he was, weary and used up, ugly red welts on his neck and arms, he still looked good. Sexy. Dangerous.

Well, he certainly was dangerous.

"You did. Admit it."

"Okay."

"You son of a bitch," she said evenly.

"Opinion's divided on that one."

"Okay, Detective Sinestra, you listen to me. I was threatened by a couple of men. I think I know who sent them, and I have to assume he's keeping an eye on me, and if so, he's aware of that bad joke of a reporter." She leaned back, almost too tired to be angry. "He knows I talked to a reporter, and he warned me, so . . ." She closed her eyes, feeling the knowledge flood her, the evil of it. "Now he's followed through on his warning. Which makes *you* ultimately responsible for the fire."

"Yeah," she heard him say, and she opened her eyes to see his gaze still on her. Direct, unapologetic, a cop look. "Yeah," he repeated, "I know about the threat. From Undersheriff Whitefeather."

"Cab," she said tiredly.

"Yeah, Cab. And as far as me being responsible for the fire, you got that right."

THIRTEEN

Todd returned after a shower just as Nick was ready to confess all. *Saved by the bell,* he thought, *for the moment.*

"Should I make some eggs or something?" the boy ventured. His voice quavered, and his eyes were red. He stood in the middle of the room, hands jammed into the pockets of his oversized shorts. He still looked shell-shocked.

Nick glanced at Portia, and he could see she was surprised, searching for the right thing to say. And she went to the boy and put her arm around his bowed shoulders. "That's a really good idea. You can do scrambled, can't you?" she asked tenderly, the way you'd talk to a small child, but Todd didn't seem to notice. Or to mind.

"Yeah, scrambled. I can do that."

Then she fixed her attention on Nick. "You need a shower."

"Look," he began, "I can get cleaned up later. First —"

"Please, just be quiet, and I'll show you the bathroom. I don't think I could carry on an intelligent conversation right now anyway."

She'd washed her face clean, but her arms and shoulders were still sooty. She'd put on a man's shirt over the tank top. She looked pale. But beautiful. Her feet were still bare.

"Come on," she urged, pushing her hair back behind an ear, and he gave up protesting.

He followed her out of the kitchen into the front of the house, where they climbed a creaking wooden staircase. On the second floor there appeared to be three bedrooms and a couple of baths. She checked Todd's bathroom, shook her head, then led him into her own bathroom.

"There's the tub and shower, towels are over there, and I'll find something of Gary's for you to wear." She gave him a once-over. "Yes, they'll fit," she said, and she disappeared.

He closed the door all the way and caught himself in the mirror on the inside of the door. *Christ,* he was covered in soot and grime, eyes red-rimmed and swollen, hadn't realized quite how bad he looked. His hair was singed in front and left a smudge on his hand when he touched it. There was a red burn welt on his neck, which he had no idea how he'd gotten.

Okay. He looked like shit. To be expected; he'd just been in an inferno. He stripped naked and, not knowing what to do with the sodden clothes, he bundled them and dropped the heap next to the sink. When he straightened, he noticed all the feminine stuff surrounding him: lacy underwear drying near the window on a towel rack, top of the toilet lined with lotions, oils, and perfume, a lipstick and compact open on the sink, hair blower and clips and fuzzy rollers in a basket underneath. *Oh, man.*

The shower was in the tub; obviously it had been installed later than the heavy, claw-footed tub itself. The curtain rod was a half oval, the curtain pulled back, awaiting him.

He stepped in, pulled the curtain shut, making sure the whole thing was inside the tub. He turned on the water, then switched the flow to the showerhead; one of those large round foreign jobs that worked so great you could stay under the waterfall all day.

Soap. He guessed he'd use hers. What else was he going to use? And the shampoo. But once he'd opened the bottle, taken a sniff, he opted for soap in his hair. It was that or stink like a goddamn pimp.

He could have stayed in there a lot longer, his muscles finally relaxing, the razor-sharp edges in his brain flattening. But he figured Portia had to clean up, too, and the kid was making eggs, and they had to have a talk, and, hell, the barn had just burned to the ground.

He reluctantly turned off the water and

groped for a towel, found it, and dried off a little before stepping out onto the bath mat. Gwen would have been proud of him, he thought fleetingly, and on the heels of the notion, he got a mental image of Gwen's lover stepping gingerly out onto a bath mat, Gwen holding the towel for her. *Jesus.*

Then he spotted the pile of clothes next to the sink — men's clothes. How . . . ? Well, obviously Portia had come in and placed them there while he'd been in the shower. What if he had picked that moment to open the curtain? But he hadn't and, of course, she'd have heard the water running and known it was safe to leave the clothes. Sure. Still, it would have been interesting if he'd stood there butt naked, Portia half dressed, her small breasts so distinctly outlined in that flimsy top. . . . He felt as if a tornado was swirling through his head.

Get off it, Sinestra, he thought, carefully hanging the towel and eyeing Gary Wells's clothes. Man was dead. Why had she kept them?

The jeans were a size too big, a little baggy but okay. The white T-shirt was fine, men's large. The shirt she'd left, a light cotton, long-sleeved, plaid shirt, would probably have fit, but it was too hot to wear it. He put back on his own socks, which were damp but had not been ruined — his shoes were on the porch — and picked up his bundle of clothing, figuring he'd leave the reeking mess at the motel or somewhere. Right now he desperately needed to get out of that steaming hot room, where Portia's dainty white underwear hung drying, and everything smelled of exotic flowers, too sweet, cloying. His brain was swelling against his skull.

She passed him on the steps, said, "Find everything all right?" Then she was upstairs, closing her bedroom door, presumably heading to the same shower he'd just vacated. He tried not to picture her raising her arms to peel off that top, her small, slim hands moving to slide the PJ bottoms down her hips. Her pale flesh would make a startling contrast to her sun-gilded limbs, cream against liquid gold. She'd step in the shower, take up the soap, the same soap he'd used, and glide it along her arms and breasts and down to her thighs, in between her legs.

He was in the kitchen, and the kid, Todd, was saying something to him. "Huh?" Nick mumbled.

"I said, you want me to throw those away? Your clothes?"

"Oh, right, these. Nah, I'll dump them in the car. Be right back. Those eggs any good?" Nick nodded at the iron skillet on the stove.

"They're okay I guess."

"Well, dish them up, I'll be back in a sec."

The eggs were sort of rubbery, but who

cared? Right now food was mere sustenance, fuel to keep them going.

Todd was attempting to eat, too, but his hands were shaking. Nick took a mouthful of eggs and toast and heard the water running through the pipes behind the kitchen sink — Portia's bathroom would be right above the kitchen. He tried to shut off the images of her in the shower, sheets of water sluicing off her skin, her arms raised to wash her hair. . . .

"You okay?" he asked Todd, noting the eggs still on the boy's plate.

"I'm not very hungry."

"Adrenaline'll do that."

"Why did you go in the barn?"

Nick put his fork down. "Good question. I don't know. Saw the flames, thought maybe somebody was inside. You know, in trouble."

Todd got a faraway look in his eyes. "I never . . . I never saw anything like that. It was so . . . big."

"Yeah." Nick drank some coffee. "Well, nobody got hurt, so it could have been worse."

"Our house could have burned down," Todd said solemnly.

"But it didn't."

"Uncle Randy is really mad. He thinks it's Portia's fault."

"I heard."

"Is it?"

"No," Nick said, flinching inside.

"But if she hadn't done that NPS thing . . ."

"Listen, Todd, Portia is not the one at fault here. Your uncle was just upset."

"Was it an accident then?"

"Don't know. Nobody knows yet. There'll be an investigation, and they'll find out."

"Did you ever investigate a fire?"

Nick smiled. "Nah. That's part of the fire marshal's job. They got arson investigators, like their own detective squad."

"So what do you do then?"

"NYPD. Vice."

The boy frowned.

"You know, drugs." Nick bent close and said in a low voice, "prostitution."

"Wow."

"Internet fraud."

"Cool."

The boy was trying to act grown-up, but Nick could tell he was very shaken.

"It was really scary," Todd said, his eyes downcast. "And then when you came out of the barn and all, like out of a ball of flame . . ."

"It was a dumb move on my part."

"You saved my saddle from when I was a kid."

"Did I?"

"Uh-huh. My dad got it for me because I was too little for a regular saddle. And I had a pony."

"Your dad must've been a great guy."

"Yeah." Todd played with his fork, mashing the eggs on his plate. "The fire was worse than in the movies." He shook his head. "It was so *hot*."

"Yeah."

"You know, it's like different when you see something in real life."

"I believe the word is 'immediate,'" Nick said.

"Immediate. Yeah, I guess that's it."

"You done there?"

The kid looked at his plate, at the cold, mutilated eggs, at butter congealed on the toast. He grimaced. "I'm done."

"Let's clean up, help Portia out a little bit."

Todd cleared the table while Nick rinsed and put the dishes in the dishwasher.

"I don't have a dishwasher," he said.

"You don't?"

"Lot of people don't in New York. Dishwashers overload the sewer system. You know, millions of people turning them on at the same time."

"I've never been to New York. Seattle once and L.A. But I'd love to see New York."

"I have an extra bedroom."

"Portia wouldn't let me."

"Why not?"

Todd hunched his shoulders. "I don't know. She worries too much."

"Women do that."

"Yeah."

Nick was going to put a glass in the top rack when he hit it against the faucet and it shattered.

"Shit," he said involuntarily, then, "sorry."

Todd gave him a look. "Like I don't know the word."

"What are we going to do?"

Todd was gingerly taking the pieces out of the sink. He put them in the trash can, covering them up. "She'll never know. Run the water to get rid of the little pieces."

"You've done this before."

"Lots of times."

"Must've gone to the same cooking school I did."

Todd grinned and raised a fist. Nick clicked his knuckles against the kid's just as Portia walked into the kitchen.

"What?" she asked, looking from one to the other.

Nick shrugged.

Todd said, "Nothing." Then, "I better go see if Uncle Randy wants me to do anything," and he left.

"You did the dishes," she said. "Thanks."

"No problem."

She wore shorts and a T-shirt. He couldn't help noticing she had a bra on now. She seemed more in control, her hair still wet, her skin freshly scrubbed. But more distant somehow, less showing physically and emo- tionally. She was just as beautiful without makeup as she had been all dressed up at the fund-raiser. Just as lovely as she had been in his car the next day. She looked young and pretty and innocent. And he'd screwed her over, got her barn burned down. For money.

"Sit down," she said, holding up a tube of some sort of ointment.

"What?"

"For those burns."

Her touch on his neck sent shock waves rippling through him. He closed his eyes, let her smooth on the ointment. And then she started on his arms. He breathed shallowly, goose bumps rising on his skin.

"There," she finally said, "is that better?"

"Uh . . . yeah, better. Thanks." Then, "Want some eggs? We saved you some," he said too quickly.

She took a plate from the cupboard and dished eggs on it, slid it into the microwave. Put a piece of bread in the toaster. She moved around the kitchen with unselfcons- cious grace, and he felt another pang.

"Coffee?" he asked.

She glanced at him in surprise, almost as if she'd forgotten he was there. "Coffee . . . I guess so."

He poured her a mug. She took it absently and sipped. The microwave beeped, the toast popped up. She set her plate on the table, the coffee mug next to it, sat, picked up her fork, then placed it down, her head bowed.

He was standing, arms folded, leaning back against the counter. Studying her. What he wanted to do was walk over and put a hand on her shoulder, stroke her damp hair, tell her everything would be all right. Even though it wasn't all right. Not by a long shot.

Finally, she looked up at him, and he could see her eyes glistening.

"Portia," he began.

"We can't afford to rebuild the barn," she said in a voice that slashed his heart. "And we can't afford to buy more hay. And . . ."

He moved then, sliding out a chair and sitting close to her. He touched her hand where it rested on the table. "Don't worry about that right now."

"I have to worry about it. I just applied for renewal of our loan at the bank."

"You have insurance?"

"Yes, but if I file, our rates will go up and . . ." She put a hand to her forehead and closed her eyes.

"I'll pay for your barn," he said, surprising himself.

She opened her eyes and stared at him. "You?"

"Yeah, me."

"How could you possibly afford that?"

"I can, trust me."

"Trust you?"

It was time to level with her. "I can build you another barn. I owe you that much."

She said nothing, merely watched him, waiting. He saw that her eyes were green. Funny, he hadn't noticed that before.

"Look . . ." He hesitated, fighting that natural urge to gloss over the truth. "I have another job. I moonlight for the *Star Gazer*, and I get paid well. Least I can do is pay for your barn."

Still, she didn't say anything. He looked down, hating the pain etched in her face. "But you already figured that one. Yeah, I followed you in New York. Followed you to your mother's. And they sent me here to see what I could dig up. That guy, Donaldson? He works for the *Star Gazer*, too."

"Do you feel better now?" she asked calmly.

"No."

"Then why tell me all this?"

"Listen, Portia, I feel like shit. Your mother, Donaldson, the barn."

She searched his expression. "You don't think the fire was an accident."

"Hell, no."

"I don't either."

"You have any idea who did it?"

"Yes, but I don't think I should tell you."

"Patrick Mahoney," he said.

"How did you . . . ?"

"I'm a cop."

"So you are."

"I swear, I'm going to find out who set fire to your barn."

"Don't you have to go back to work?"

"Got a month off."

"Oh."

"I'm going to find out who did this to you. Nail the guy. Whether it's Mahoney or somebody else."

Her mouth twisted, and he could see she didn't believe a word he said. Her distrust was a dagger in his gut.

"I'll track him down. And I'll pay for your barn."

She shook her head slowly, and a tear ran down her cheek. She brushed it away.

"Let me do this, Portia."

"Why?" A whisper.

"I told you."

Her gaze held his. But in the end, she didn't say no. He figured she was desperate. "Those security guys?"

"Uh-huh?"

"Pretty damn useless. They let the arsonist onto the ranch in the first place. I don't know who hired them, but they're a joke. You want decent security, I could find out who's good in the area. These bozos are a waste of money."

"Aaron hired them. I trust him. He

knows what he's doing."

Aaron. The old guy she was with at the fund-raiser.

"Aaron who?" he asked innocently.

"Aaron Burkhart. A very good friend of mine."

Friend, "Oh yeah, wasn't he at that fund-raiser?"

"Yes, he was."

"Well, your pal Aaron doesn't know squat about security."

She set her jaw. "I trust him completely."

"Okay, fine." He wished he had the nerve to ask her if he could stay right there at the ranch. He didn't know Burkhart, but he sure didn't like the man's choice of watchdogs. He'd feel better if he could stick around and keep an eye on her. On Todd. On things. But it'd be a cold day in hell, Portia Wells letting him stay in her house.

So he'd have to go back to Denver and worry. Start sticking his detective's nose into things and hope for the best.

"Now, look, if you don't do anything about your bodyguards, at least don't give anyone a reason to come after you again. Don't be seen talking to cops or even your friend, Cab Whitefeather. Especially don't be talking to the press."

"Okay."

"Good. And don't go anywhere by yourself. If somebody was going to confront you, they wouldn't want witnesses. Don't be alone."

"I'm not sure I —"

"Portia, listen, I'm taking this seriously. I think you should, too. Real seriously." He felt a surge of protectiveness for this woman, which he'd never felt before, not for Gwen and certainly not for tough little Mia.

"You really think . . . ?"

"Yeah, I do. First a threat, then the fire. Right after you announced you'd take on the NPS gig. Like we say in police work, it's not smart to ignore coincidences."

"Oh God." She sighed and put a hand over her mouth.

"You'll be okay. Take a few precautions, you'll be fine. And I'm not far. Staying at the King Motel in Denver. Here, let me leave you my cell phone number."

"You can really find out who burned my barn?"

"You bet your ass."

"But I don't understand why you'd do this." She studied him with wide green eyes.

"I told you, I got you into this. Hell, I'm lousy at explaining why I do things. I feel responsible, I guess." He turned his attention away from her, drummed his fingers on the table. "Guess I'm trying to apologize. Trying to fix what I screwed up."

"You're right. You're lousy at apologies. Don't bother. I'd just like to know what you find out. Maybe I can help. Maybe —"

"It's a deal. You got my number. Call if anything comes up. Anything. I'll be in touch with Cab, okay?"

"Um."

"Don't worry, Portia. You hear?"

"I hear you."

But all he could see as he drove north toward Denver in the bright blaze of a Colorado summer morning was the veiled look of distrust on her face. He hated what he'd done, hated himself for putting her through hell. And for what?

The sere brown prairie skimmed past, the sky sapphire blue from horizon to horizon, the sun a glaring sphere in the hot blue sky.

Money, he thought. *It always comes down to the same thing.* He'd screwed the pretty lady over for money.

FOURTEEN

Shopping made Nick tense. Malls were the worst; they made him ooze sweat. At home, he did all his Christmas and birthday shopping ten feet inside the doors of Bloomingdale's. The whole first floor was nothing but aisle after aisle of cosmetics. He'd walk into the department store, hands clammy, select the first expensive bottle of perfume he spotted, whip out his credit card, tell the saleslady to wrap it. Thing was, he was buying the Bloomie's wrapping paper. Who cared about the product? A gift could always be exchanged.

But this was Denver, and he was a stranger in a strange land as far as shopping went, and he desperately needed some casual, maybe even Western attire: jeans, couple shirts, he figured. He'd keep Gary Wells's jeans, hell yes, but they sagged down his hips.

On the way back and forth from Colt, he'd seen this mega mall from the interstate just off County Line Road. Place called Park Meadows. Okay, so it wasn't Thirty-fourth

Street, and there wouldn't be racks of cheap polyester shirts and pants for $9.95. This was Denver, Colorado. And he just left Portia, so he should be concentrating on her, on her problems, on Patrick Mahoney or whatever lowlife had burned her barn. He should be putting his whole mind on this case, like he always did on the job. But here he was, sweating bullets over buying some items of clothing in a mall. *Get a grip, Sinestra.*

He steeled himself and took the exit, threaded his way through the rows of parking, found a spot, marked it in his head so he'd find it again, and walked across the flaming-hot asphalt into the mall.

More sweat popped on his brow. There were women with strollers everywhere, clusters of gangly teens, young lovers window shopping, holding hands, screaming kids, men sitting on benches next to gargantuan potted plants, looking as uncomfortable as Nick felt.

A Levi's store. Thank God. He knew he'd pay more for jeans here than in that department store right down there, but who cared? And he'd buy a couple shirts while he was at it. A couple because he'd need them; he'd told Portia he was going to track down the arsonists, and he meant to do just that. Which was going to take time.

Two pairs of 501s, and two short-sleeved solid-color shirts later, he left the mall over a hundred dollars poorer and dripping as if he'd sprung a leak. Even the ninety-five-plus-degree heat out in the parking lot was a pure breath of fresh air after the mall.

When he got back to his motel, there was a message from Bern Radowski. "Hey, Nick, give me a ring. Anything new with the Wells woman? I have a spot tomorrow I could put in a little something interesting."

Oh yeah, Nick thought. *There's plenty new with the Wells woman.* But he'd rot before he'd tell Bern another thing about Portia.

There was no way he'd catch a couple hours' sleep, so he took yet another shower and changed into his new duds, wishing he had a casual belt to go with the jeans, but what the heck? Didn't really need a belt.

Gary Wells's clothes were lying in a heap on the bed. Should he throw them away? Geez, the man was dead. She couldn't have saved them as keepsakes. Could she?

Then he had a brainstorm. He'd return them to her. Perfect excuse to see her again. Like she really wanted to see him. Couldn't blame her, either. He could hardly stand to look himself in the mirror, for chrissakes. Nothing he could do was going to make it up to her. He realized that. Regardless, he was going to try to patch a few of the holes he'd torn in the fabric of her life.

Starting now.

He stuffed his pockets with his keys, loose

change, wad of bills, and his NYPD identification and headed back out into the scorching heat. He was a man on a mission.

Ordinarily, being a New Yorker and used to walking a lot, he would have hoofed it to Cherokee Street, where the Denver Police Administration building was located, but in this blazing heat, he figured he'd drive the mile or so. Besides, his gun was locked in the glove box, and he really wasn't comfortable leaving the Camry at the motel.

He found a spot right on Cherokee Street, parked, and killed the engine in front of a bail bonds shop. There was a whole row of them. His favorite sign read: Mary Ellen's City Bail Bonds. He grinned. Bet old Mary Ellen was a gem.

The Police Administration building sat on one side of a large, modern courtyard separating administration from the Pre-Arraignment Detention Facility. *Right,* Nick thought, *detention facility. A jail was a jail by any name in his book.*

Inside the blessedly cool administration building, he strode up to the desk sergeant and showed his ID, said he was vacationing, and asked if there was someone who could give him the tour. The sergeant was pleasant enough, that brotherly cop bond, and phoned upstairs to Vice. While he spoke to a Chuck DeLucca, Nick spied the bold-lettered sign above his desk: No Picture ID, No Entry.

And behind that was a security screen apparatus that looked state-of-the-art new. But then, after 9/11, a lot of procedures had tightened.

About five minutes passed before vice cop Chuck DeLucca emerged from a bank of elevators and greeted Nick. "Hey," DeLucca said, "you're NYPD? Vice?"

"That's me. Nick Sinestra." He showed DeLucca his ID, then they went through security together. "Call me Nick, okay?"

"Sure. And it's Chuck. Short for Chuck. Parents had no imagination."

"You sure giving me the tour is no imposition?" Nick said, as Chuck punched Four on the elevator.

"Imposition? Whole job is an imposition, Nick. No, seriously, I'd love to. Working this damn car insurance scam for months, and any break I get is a good break."

"I hear that." Nick smiled.

Of course he was not there for the tour. He was there to network. But Chuck here didn't need to know that little detail.

Up on the fourth floor, Chuck introduced him to his partner, Leddy Heckshore. Whereas Chuck was lean and narrow, a ferretlike face, Leddy had maybe been hitting the jelly doughnuts too hard. Together, they looked like Laurel and Hardy. Nick would have bet anything the guys tagged them just that behind their backs — probably to their faces, too.

252

Vice was a rabbit warren of desks in cubbyhole dividers leading to the captain's office in the rear. The smells were achingly reassuring to Nick: stale cigarette smoke — despite the No Smoking Facility signs — sweat and adrenaline and copy paper and heated electronics, leather and steel, carbon and Outers Gun Oil.

Desktops and accessories could have been beamed from the 6th Precinct to Denver. The coffee stains and smears of Liquid Paper, ancient computers stuck with memo notes so faded you could no longer read them, Styrofoam cups, pizza boxes, individual coffee mugs, most of them sporting favorite teams, Avalanche, Rockies, Broncos, Cubs. Sitting on top of one monitor was a human skull, no doubt real. Someone had stuck a stogie in its mouth. Jackets and shoulder holsters, guns neatly sheathed, adorned chair backs.

"Just like home," Nick said reverently.

Both Chuck and Leddy nodded. Could have been a church service.

Nick sat and chatted with a pod of Vice detectives. Shop talk. He was basking in joy. They took him to lunch at a nearby diner. More shop talk and a lot of snickering and laughter. Outside the diner's window, a black-and-white pulled a pickup full of teenagers over and made a righteous bust — glove box full of crack cocaine. Nick watched the action going down while eating a BLT and felt a true pang of nostalgia for the Village and Gil. Tonight he'd phone Gil, see how Dougie was doing. Damn right.

Back in administration, as he'd hoped, Chuck and Leddy offered to meet him in LoDo after work. "Say, you know the Yankees are in town? Playing at Coors Field tonight. Game four or five of a series, I think. We could catch it on the big screen at this brew pub. You up for it, Nick?"

"It's a date," Nick said.

"We got a pool going on the game. Few slots still open. Two bucks a slot."

"I'll take them."

He met the guys at the brew pub at six and had tilted a couple longnecks by seven. The game was on the big screen, the Rockies over New York by two in the top of the third. It was time to pump his friends.

"Hey, you guys hear about that barn fire down near Colt, on some ranch?"

"Fire? Nah. But you want fire, welcome to Colorado. We've had four years of drought, and we still got six, no, make that seven wildfires burning all over the state."

Nick nodded. "Funny it's not smoky. You know?"

"Was the other day. Will be again soon as we get an upslope wind. Burns the hell out of your eyes. And people with asthma and lung disease, well, it gets bad."

"I bet. So I guess a barn fire is no big deal right now."

Leddy shrugged, ate a mouthful of fried onion rings, his second order.

"Thing is," Nick went on, "the fire was on the Wellspring Ranch. Wasn't that . . . ?"

"Yeah, Gary Wells," Chuck said. "His widow, Portia, runs it now. You know her old lady was Judith Carr?"

"Not *was*," Nick said, "*is*. Saw in some tabloid just the other week that Judith Carr is living outside of New York."

"Yeah," Leddy chimed in. "I saw that, too. *Star Gazer*, I think it was. Wife buys it."

"Gary Wells," Nick said, screwing up his forehead. "Wasn't he like this environmentalist or something?"

"Head of the NPS. Died last year in a car crash," Chuck put in.

"Right, right." Reflectively. "And there was some question about the accident being an accident?"

Leddy's mouth was packed with onion rings, so he shook his head and swallowed. "Nah, it was an accident. Least that's the way I remember it. It was front-page news out here."

"You know," Chuck said, his attention fixed on the big screen, "his wife is taking over his position. The announcement was all over the TV just the other day." He swiveled and looked at Nick. "You say her barn burned down? When?"

"I heard it happened last night. Actually, make that real early this morning. Hey, you don't suppose some antinature group torched the place or something?"

"Now there's an inductive leap," Chuck said. "But I'm sure there are plenty of folks who'd like to see her dry up and blow away."

"How's that?" Nick asked.

"Well, see, the NPS has a habit of getting in the face of developers in these parts. You know, putting a stop to some pretty big projects, in fact."

"Really. So — and let me get this straight — Portia Wells is slipping on her husband's shoes, he's already been killed in a crash, and now her barn burns? Sounds kinda weird to me. I mean, maybe Wells stepped on some big shot's toes once too often. You know? Now, here comes his wife, carrying his banner . . ."

He let the boys chew over his budding hypothesis, then said, "For argument's sake, who'd have motive?"

Leddy laughed. "That's a no-brainer. Mahoney."

Nick lifted a brow.

"Patrick Mahoney. Man's an icon for Colorado development. Does ritzy projects, golf courses, starter castle homes, equestrian centers. Builds playgrounds for the rich and famous."

Chuck shook his head. "What the hell do you know about equestrian centers, Leddy? You wouldn't know a horse from a donkey."

"Fuck you, pard. I can read, and I got eyes. Which is more than I can say for you."

"Boys, boys," Nick said, smiling, "you're digressing."

"Digressing," Chuck said. "You really talk like that out East?"

"Every day."

"Well, fuck my visiting *you*, buddy."

It took a bit of finesse to steer them back to the subject. After a minute of baseball chat, Nick said, "So this Mahoney character, you two really think someone like that would give Gary Wells a second glance? I mean, sounds like Mahoney could buy and sell a Gary Wells type a hundred times over. Why even dick with him?"

"Wells had friends. In the state legislature, in every damn county up and down the Front Range. He had clout," Chuck said.

"Yeah, and the NPS has bucks. Wells had them behind him." Leddy sopped up the last of the ketchup on his plate with an onion ring.

Chuck said, "Gary Wells was no slouch. He'd take on Mahoney any day."

"How's that?" Nick said.

"Wells was a mover and shaker. Had himself somewhat of a reputation." Chuck met Leddy's gaze, then shrugged. "Hell, and this is between us cops, okay?"

"Sure." Nick nodded.

"Well, me and Leddy were on this bust one night, oh, around three, four years back, at one of the pricey hotels in town here, an escort service bust, and who do we find at the orgy?"

"Let me guess," Nick said, "Gary Wells?"

"You got it. Wells and two chicks butt-ass naked in a bedroom. You shoulda seen the other bedroom in the suite," Leddy said.

"You arrest Wells?"

"Nope," Chuck said. "We were breaking up the escort deal. But we told the guys next time it was them. We meant it."

Nick pursed his lips and grimaced. *Jesus,* he thought, *why would anyone need more than Portia?* But he knew that power and sex drive went hand in hand with some men, and they just couldn't keep their flies zipped. Still, cheating on Portia . . . He couldn't feature it. Had she known or even suspected? Sat home on the ranch alone, desperate for a baby, and pictured her husband banging a couple hookers in a fancy hotel room?

Other than some bits and pieces about Mahoney, he didn't learn too much more from the vice cops that night. First off, he'd probed enough. Secondly, the Yankees staged a great comeback in the eighth, and then the Rockies met the challenge in the top of the ninth, and you couldn't hear

258

yourself think in the joint.

The Denver cops went home to their wives by ten, and Nick walked back uptown toward his motel, where he'd left the Camry, gun still hopefully safe in the glove box. No way was he going to risk a DUI.

He mulled over the info. You had Gary Wells on the one hand, charismatic, a mover and shaker, good-looking, intelligent, an environmentalist who, apparently, wasn't afraid to mix it up with a man like Patrick Mahoney. Maybe Wells had pushed this Mahoney too far, was going to cost him a bundle by blocking a project. So Mahoney takes care of the problem.

Mahoney . . . Chuck had told Nick the man had been the focus of a state attorney general's probe into illegal campaign contributions not too long ago. "You know," Chuck had said, "Mahoney was greasing the palms of county officials, taking them on these golf outings to places like Cancun, filling their campaign war chests. The man was sleazy, all right."

Nick had pointed out that, really, Mahoney's antics sounded pretty much like business as usual. Hell, most stuff got done because palms were greased. "A little oil in the machinery makes it run better, right?" Nick had said.

But cops here in the West had different issues facing them day in and day out. Not the least of which centered on the extremes of the climate. Winter blizzards that caused sixty-car pileups or just plain shut the city down. Spring tornadoes and golf ball–sized hail that took out office windows and a million car hoods and windshields, summer drought and wildfires that swept the perimeter of the city, or the other side of that coin, torrential rains and killer flash floods. Cops in the West wore a lot of different hats. Nick found their job all very interesting but, if the truth were known, he preferred his own turf, the gritty action on the streets, feeling that twitch on his skin that something was not quite kosher. Like when he'd driven to the ranch last night, sensing the world had tipped a little off its axis.

He stopped at a McDonald's on Colfax Avenue, then trudged up the hill past the Capitol building to his motel. Finally he was tired. Really tired. Damn, he hadn't slept in nearly forty hours. Maybe, he decided, he'd wait till tomorrow to phone Gil.

His message light was blinking on his phone in the room, and for a moment he thought: *Portia, Portia's in trouble,* but it was only Bern again, wanting to know if Nick was still on the job. "Call me, man, even if you've got nothing new, phone in." *Yeah, right,* Nick mused.

He clicked on the TV and stripped down to his jockey shorts, turning the air-conditioning to high. Not that it worked all that great. The digital clock blinked 10:45 p.m. Was it too late to check up on Portia? Or maybe he shouldn't disturb her. Maybe those security boys were on their toes after the fire.

His cell phone was on the charger, so he dragged the motel phone over, found her number on a slip of paper in his wallet, and dialed. No way could he sleep until he was sure she was okay.

She answered on the third ring, her tone sleepy but with a decided edge. No one appreciated late-night phone calls.

"Oh, Nick, it's you," she said, and he thought he could hear her settling down into a chair, or was that the rustle of sheets?

"Hey, did I wake you? Sorry if I —"

"I was ready to go to bed, yes." Irritated now.

"Listen," he said, "I was wondering if I could come by tomorrow, drop off Gary's clothes and maybe talk to Randy and his wife a minute."

"Why?"

"I just have a couple questions to ask them."

"You're serious. You really have taken this on? What is this, a crusade? A guilt trip?"

"Guilt trip, absolutely."

She sighed, but he was certain the sound was full of relief. His heart banged once against his rib cage, then settled. "I guess you can come by," she finally said. "Make it around noon, okay?"

"You bet. Noon."

"Now can I get some sleep?"

"Sure," he said, trying desperately not to picture Portia in her bed. "See you tomorrow."

"Night."

"Night," he said, and he placed the receiver gently in its cradle, as if not to disturb her further. He reached up to the burn on his neck. Felt the phantom touch of her fingers when she'd put medicine on it.

He switched off the lamp and stretched out then, channel surfing. But his mind was on Portia. He badly needed her cooperation if he was to get anywhere on this case. Whatever the case really was. Arson, for one. Maybe murder. She'd trusted him in New York, before she'd learned the truth. And he dared to think her feelings had exceeded trust; she'd been interested. Cops knew when a woman was interested. Happened all the time. He'd seen her looking at him that way in his car on the drive from her mother's back to the city.

Yeah. She'd gotten that secret thrill a woman got from a man in a dangerous profession, a man carrying a gun. At the time, he'd had to brush the knowledge aside. Had no other choice. But now . . . And what would she think if she knew he'd legally brought his service revolver on the plane with him to Denver? Would she be pissed? Or would the knowledge spark that thrill in her again? *Dream on, Sinestra.*

He rolled over, punched his pillow, and felt regret chew at his gut. Not that he'd ever really have a chance with a classy lady like Portia, but still, he could fantasize.

Thing was, thing he had to focus on, was her safety. He'd put her in jeopardy. He owed her. And this was a tab he intended to pay in full.

He rolled over again, thought he'd never get to sleep now, and that was his last thought.

FIFTEEN

"You look nice," Todd said, and she flushed with embarrassment. "How come?"

"The man from Farmers Insurance is coming. I thought I better dress decently."

She could have gone on to say she was expecting Nick Sinestra at noon, and that was more likely the cause for her clean jeans and white linen safari shirt. After all, what did an insurance adjustor care about how she looked? She could have given Todd an honest answer, but she was too busy trying to convince herself she really wasn't concerned with what Nick thought.

The insurance man arrived on time, and he brought an arson specialist with him. "Mrs. Wells, this is Fred Wygard, out of Denver," her local man told her.

She'd known they'd investigate the fire, and she knew they'd find that it had been deliberately set. They'd discover accelerant had been used, and the fire would go down as arson with the resulting delay in getting the insurance money. But there was no way around that.

"So you think the fire was suspicious?" she ventured.

"We don't know yet. An investigation is routine in a case like this."

Should she tell them she suspected who did it? Should she throw out Patrick Mahoney's name? But she couldn't. She had no proof. And they'd talk to Cab Whitefeather anyway. Maybe he'd decide to tell them. Better Cab than her. If Mahoney thought she'd opened her mouth, he could easily go after her again. Burn down the entire ranch? Run her off an isolated dark road?

Randy arrived, shook hands with the men and, ignoring her, led them to the still-smoking rubble that until yesterday morning had been their barn. She tagged along, feeling unwanted, while the arson investigator went to work and Randy talked with the insurance adjustor. She wondered if her resentful brother-in-law would blurt out his own theory that she was at fault for the fire, but even Randy wouldn't be that dumb. He knew as well as she did that an investigation would hold up the insurance check. Maybe indefinitely.

The men were still talking, still ignoring the *little lady,* when her cell phone rang. She stepped away and answered. It was Lynette, tired from yesterday's ordeal but in better spirits. "I'm so sorry for how Randy behaved last night . . . well, the night before. Damn.

The *morning* before. Anyway, he didn't mean the things he said."

"Really," Portia said.

"See, I knew you wouldn't believe me. But, honest, Portia, he felt bad all day."

"Um."

"Oh, you can't talk?"

"That's right, I'm here with Randy and the insurance men."

"Darn. I wanted to hear the whole scoop on your cop."

Portia put a few more feet between her and the men. "He is *not* my cop," she whispered.

"Then how did he end up at the barn? I mean, I just thought, well, that he'd been up at your house or something."

"It's a long story."

"So leave the insurance guys with Randy and tell me. I'm dying to hear all about it."

Portia thought a second. "Hold on," she said to Lynette. Then she called out to the men, "If you need me, I'll be up at the house." They barely even acknowledged her. A man's world. *Screw it,* she thought.

It took forever to explain Nick's presence at the ranch to Lynette, and then she looked at the clock — almost noon. "Listen," she said, "he's due here any minute. I need to make some lunch, and —"

"Your cop's coming today?"

"Don't get so excited. He's coming because

he wants to talk to you and Randy. Well, Randy."

"Talk to us? But . . . why?"

"Lynette, he's a policeman. He says he's going to find out who burned the barn. He's investigating, I guess."

"But why us?"

"Because, silly, it was your barn, too."

"Oh. *Oh*. So when will he be here?"

"Soon. I'll feed him, then bring him over at, say, oneish?"

"Oh my God, I better get this place straightened up," she said, and she clicked off.

Nick drove up just as Portia was making chicken salad sandwiches. She'd put cheerful yellow and white striped placemats on the kitchen table, and a pinch of curry powder in the chicken salad, her secret gourmet touch.

Ridiculous, how she was fussing for the man. How she'd counted on his visit, how she'd washed her hair and put on mascara and lipstick so that even Todd had noticed.

He was a stranger, and worse, a man who'd betrayed her to a ravenous tabloid. He'd followed her and spied on her and lied to her. And yet she was full of anticipation.

Why had he called late last night to ask if she was all right? Why should he care how she was? And, come to think of it, why on earth had he really been on the ranch at three in the morning, conveniently in the right spot to see the barn burn?

He knocked on the screen door, and she went to let him in. He looked much better today, rested, in clean clothes. Jeans that were much too new and a blue short-sleeved shirt that still had store folds in it.

"Hey," he said.

"Hi."

He stepped inside. "Phew, hot out there."

"Yes, it is."

"But it's a dry heat," he said, a hint of a smile curling up one corner of his mouth, making him look young and a bit mischievous, like one of the Greek gods who was playing a trick on Zeus, she thought fleetingly. Then she caught herself. The poor pathetic widow, drooling over the sexy cop, the same self-serving bastard who'd caused her nothing but heartache. *You're an idiot, Portia.*

"You know, your security guys should at least have called when they saw me drive in," he was saying.

"They probably remembered you from yesterday."

"They're bozos."

"You're not going to start that again, are you?"

"Okay, forget about it." He shrugged. "Hey, I was going to bring the clothes you lent me, but I didn't have time to have them washed."

She waved a hand. "Oh, don't worry about that."

"Did I catch you in the middle of something?"

"Just making lunch."

"Lunch."

"You're welcome to stay. Chicken salad sandwiches."

"You're sure?"

"Yes, for goodness' sake. It's only lunch."

"I'm not real good at eating regular meals. Usually grab something on the street."

"Sounds unhealthy."

"Probably."

"Well, come on. Todd is somewhere with Hernando, and he'll show up when he's done with his chores. And right now Randy's busy with the insurance adjustor. We're supposed to stop by his house around one or so."

They ate the sandwiches with tall glasses of iced tea.

"This is good," Nick said.

His apparent want of home-cooked food piqued her curiosity. "You, um, don't cook for yourself?"

"Not much."

"Too busy?"

"Too lazy." He swallowed and drank some iced tea.

"I'm assuming you aren't married?"

"Divorced." He looked at her over the second half of his sandwich. "No children."

Had she seen regret in his eyes as he'd said that? Or was she projecting her own feelings onto him?

They finished lunch well before one. She stacked the dishes in the sink and suggested they sit on the porch where the breeze could reach them.

He seemed edgy. Was it her? Or was it the fire and his guilt? She had a hundred questions she wanted to ask, but she felt that would be too pushy. He didn't seem the kind of man who'd discuss why he and his wife were divorced or why he'd become a cop or what he was really doing out here on the ranch.

She didn't quite trust him, and she knew she wouldn't trust any answers he gave her anyway. He was a New York cop, and they had absolutely nothing in common. She wondered again what he was still doing here.

"This Aaron Burkhart," he said abruptly, surprising her. "Who exactly is he?"

"Aaron was a very close friend of Gary's. And me, too. He used to be president of the NPS, and I suppose you'd say he was Gary's mentor."

"Where's he from?"

"He lives in Falls Church, Virginia. With his wife Nancy. Why the curiosity about Aaron?"

"Don't know. Trying to cover all bases. He seems to be very involved in your life."

"He's my *friend*." Was Nick insinuating what she thought he was? "He's been wonderful to us, to me. He's helped me so much since Gary died. I really don't know what I'd have done without him."

Nick frowned, apparently thinking.

"There is nothing, absolutely nothing improper between us, if that's what you're getting at."

"I didn't mean anything. Sorry."

But he wasn't sorry. She could tell.

"What did Burkhart do before the NPS?"

"He was CEO of a big investment house. Real estate investment trusts, things like that. Now he'll tell you he's retired, but he still sits on the board of the NPS, and he's really quite active in it."

"So he's not hurting."

"Of course not."

"Okay, just trying to feel the situation out."

"Why?"

"I told you."

She stood and went to lean on the porch railing. A hot, dry breeze touched her damp skin. "Well, Aaron had nothing to do with the barn burning, if that's what you're thinking."

"Maybe not."

"Of course not!"

"He did hire your security boys. Incompetent ones."

"What do you mean? That Aaron deliber-

271

ately hired men who are incompetent?"

Nick shrugged.

She turned, leaning her back against the rail now, facing him. "You're insulting a very good friend of mine, and I don't like it."

"Cops ask uncomfortable questions sometimes."

"You're not on duty. You're not in New York. This isn't your Sixth Precinct."

"You're right." He looked at her, his dark eyes revealing nothing. There were tiny dots of sweat on his upper lip. "So . . . let's try another subject."

"Like what?"

"Like Mahoney."

"Patrick Mahoney is a big developer on the Front Range. But you know that already."

He nodded, his gaze heavily on her.

"He's been very successful, and his developments are very high end."

"Like how high?"

"Oh, houses going for a half million and up. Greens fees, clubhouse fees. But this new development, Panorama Ranch, was just too big. It still *is* too big. Too much impact."

"Where's it located?"

"North of here. In the foothills. The land belongs to an old ranching family."

"And they want to sell? Or is Mahoney pushing?"

"The ranch was up for sale, and Mahoney had started negotiations, but the owner, Bill

Nash, was working with Gary, too. Now, for all practical purposes, since Gary's death, the project has just about received all of its county and state approvals."

"So it's too late to stop the project?"

"It's never too late to stop it."

"Okay. Let's back up a little here. Before your husband's death, the NPS made this rancher, this Bill Nash, an offer to buy his land?"

She folded her arms on her chest. "Yes, Gary made an offer on behalf of the NPS."

"How much?"

She wondered if she should tell him. After all, this was private NPS business. "It was eight figures. Beyond that, I really don't think I should give out any specifics."

"So we're talking big money."

"Yes."

"Was Bill Nash playing both ends, I mean, was he trying to get Mahoney and Gary to outbid each other?"

"No, not really. I believe he was talking to his tax lawyer and his accountant and trying to make up his mind. Then Gary died, and everything stopped for a time, but now, as soon as all the approvals are in place for Mahoney's project, I assume the sale will go through."

"How did Gary get along with Mahoney?"

"Oh." She unfolded her arms. "They were . . . um, I suppose you'd say they were adversaries who respected each other. At first. Then, just before Gary died, something happened between them. Gary never told me exactly what, but he was upset, and he said Mahoney threatened him."

"What kind of threat?"

She raised her shoulders and lowered them. "I don't know. I assumed it was a legal threat, you know, 'I'll see you in court over this.' But then, after Gary died, I remembered what he said, how upset he was, and I thought maybe the threat was physical."

"You told Cab about Gary being threatened by Mahoney?"

"Sure. Over and over. But he didn't seem to take it seriously."

"I do."

"Thank you," she said with irony.

"Hey, I take it very seriously. People have killed for a lot less."

"Do you think . . . ?"

"Don't know yet."

She turned and glanced down at the railing. The white paint was chipped; the whole house needed painting, but she couldn't afford the expense. Then she became aware that Nick had gotten up from the chair and was standing next to her.

"Sorry about all the questions. I'm still getting a feel for everything."

"Ask away. I guess."

He was leaning on the rail with both

hands. Strong hands with long fingers. She inadvertently imagined those fingers curled around a gun.

"Have you ever shot anyone?" she asked out of the blue.

"Once. Hit his arm. I'm a lousy shot."

"Was he trying to kill you?"

"Nah, he was firing at my partner."

"Did he hit your partner?"

"Nope. I winged him first."

"Do you like your job?"

"Which one?" he asked pointedly.

"Your real job. Being a cop."

"Like it? Used to. You know, when I thought I could make a difference, then it seemed important. But there's a lot of bullshit."

He sounded so disillusioned. "There is in any job."

"Yeah, guess so."

Their shoulders almost touched. She could actually feel the warmth emanating from his body. She wondered if he was as aware of their closeness as she was.

"Let me give Randy a call," she said, "tell him we're coming over." And she moved away from him to the door, finding herself drawing a deep breath for the first time since he'd stood next to her.

She asked him again on the drive to Randy's, bouncing on the dirt road in the old pickup: "Why are you really doing this? I just don't understand. What do you hope to accomplish?"

"Hey, I told you. Can we leave it at that?"

"I don't even know why I'm talking to you after what you did."

"Guess you got a big heart."

She gave a short laugh. "Wouldn't you rather be in New York than out here on a ranch?"

He hesitated. "Not at the moment."

"I don't understand you one bit."

"I don't understand myself. Don't worry about it." He paused; then, as they pulled up in front of Randy's house, he said, "That fire was a warning. Clear as a bell. You and Todd and Randy's family could be in serious danger. When I had that chat with Cab Whitefeather, he admitted he doesn't have the personnel to cover you. Unless there's hard evidence someone's out to get you. Well, now there's evidence."

"So you think I should talk to Cab again?"

He looked at her, straight on. "If you go to the sheriff, either in Colt or in, what's the county seat called?"

"Castle Rock."

"Right. You go there, the bad guys find out, you're in even more danger."

"Oh, great. I can't win for losing." She felt the weight of despair descend on her again.

"Okay, now listen, don't get like that. I'm going to figure this out."

"Maybe I should forget about the NPS. It isn't fair of me to put Todd and Randy's family in jeopardy. I'm just being stubborn."

"You could do that."

"But then what would I be? A loser, a quitter."

"There's no cowardice in taking a safer path. Like the song says, you gotta know when to hold 'em, know when to fold 'em."

She studied him. "What would you do if you were me?"

"Hell, I'd quit."

"Liar."

Randy and Lynette's house was a modern split-level built in a stand of cottonwoods, with a fishing pond at the bottom of a long sloping hill behind the house.

"This is the new house," she explained. "Todd and I live in the original one. Well, it's been renovated some. Gary and Randy's great grandfather was a Nebraska rancher who got wiped out in the Blizzard of 1888, so he moved here, where he figured the land was more protected. Not that we don't have blizzards sometimes."

"Must be something, a blizzard out here."

"Oh, it's something, all right."

Randy and Lynette and the boys were just finishing lunch. The boys ran outside with the dogs, banging the back screen door, while Lynette dried her hands on the dish towel and Portia introduced her to Nick.

"So you're the big city cop," Lynette gushed, two spots of red on her cheeks. "I think that is so wonderful, so brave. And they never pay you men enough for what you do. I read all sorts of horror stories about what you go through." She still held Nick's hand in hers, and Portia could have sworn there was a flush crawling up Nick's neck.

Another conquest for Lynette. How did she do it? And Portia reluctantly wondered if Nick would ever look at her like that, his expression boyishly shy.

"Maybe," Nick was saying, "you ought to call someone, like the mayor, tell him I need a raise."

"You tell me where and when, and you bet I will," Lynette said.

Randy was shaking his head at his wife when they all settled in the living room. He knew the effect she had on people, and he never seemed to mind. As for herself, she was nervous, wondering how Randy was going to react to a barrage of questions from Nick. Yesterday morning, at the fire, the two had almost come to blows. But then everyone had been overwrought. She mostly prayed Randy wouldn't start in with his snide remarks about her. Nick shouldn't have to witness the family dissension, the ugliness.

"So you're a cop," Randy began.

"That's about it."

"Lynette tells me you met Portia when

278

she was in New York?"

"Right again."

"Huh," Randy said, obviously still trying to figure out how Nick had been on hand at the fire.

But Nick put his mind at rest. "Hey, I need to tell you how bad I feel about the other morning. I coulda handled the introductions a lot better."

"Oh, well." Randy squirmed, but Lynette patted him on the arm, as if to say, *Go on, it won't kill you to apologize.* "I guess we were all a little hot." Randy actually laughed. "No pun intended. But, really, I shouldn't have jumped to conclusions. I still can't figure how you got there, though."

Nick had the answers for everything. "It's like this, Randy," he said in a friendly tone. "Portia told me about some trouble she was having and some of her suspicions, and I got to worrying. Couldn't sleep. So I drove on down from Denver."

"A good thing, too," Lynette said. "Is that what you call a hunch?"

"Some guys do, yeah," Nick said. "But me? I get this twitch." He grinned.

Lynette knew all about Nick and the *Star Gazer* and the miserable stunt he'd pulled. She even knew he'd put that reporter Donaldson onto Porita. But Lynette kept her counsel. And Nick, he just outright lied.

Randy seemed to buy the twitch story. "So

279

you're hanging around to help Portia or something? I mean, because of these . . . ah, threats she got?"

"That's about the sum of it."

"Huh. Well, what can I do to help? Lynette said you got some questions?"

Nick paused a second. "Just a few. To start, is there any reason to think someone deliberately burned the barn?"

Randy smiled thinly. "You mean all that stuff I was yelling at the fire? Oh yeah, I know you heard. I was a mess. And, I got to admit, Portia and I don't always see eye to eye. But the stuff I said was a lot of crap."

"So you think it was an accident?"

Randy crossed one leg over the other, held his knee with his fingers interlaced. "Probably. Though I wouldn't put it past some of those city slicker tree huggers. You know what they'd like? They'd like cattle banned from all public grazing land. Out and out banned. They're pretty uppity on the subject. Call cattle 'range maggots.' "

Portia had heard Randy's opinions often enough. She knew the pros and cons, and she knew ranchers would defend to the death the right to graze their herds cheaply on public land. The NPS had a policy of promoting what they called holistic ranching, a new concept of working with nature, predators, societal values, and the economy to provide healthier beef and rangeland. Holistic ranching had been Gary's crusade, and she wanted to continue his fight. She'd love to talk to Nick about the subject. But not now. Now he was questioning Randy.

"Uh-huh, but you can't name any specific group or individual as the arsonist?"

"Hell, no."

"Anyone else come to mind?"

"God, I don't know. I can't believe anyone around here would set a fire deliberate like that. Lynette?"

Lynette sat comfortably next to her man, hands folded in her lap. "No rancher would ever do such a thing. If someone set the fire, it was a stranger, I can promise you that."

"What would the motive be for burning your barn?" Nick asked.

Randy shrugged. "You tell me. Put us out of business?"

"Do you think it could have anything to do with your brother being head of the NPS? Or Portia taking over?"

Randy looked blank. "Like what? You mean that threat she supposedly got?"

"So you put no credence in her story about being threatened?"

Randy's eyes switched from Nick to Portia and back. "I guess she heard what she heard. I wasn't there."

Portia almost rose to her feet, ready to leave, but she made herself sit there, and Nick changed his tack then. "You know, I've

281

never been on a ranch before. This is a beautiful place you got."

"You should see it when there's no drought," Randy said. "In the spring. Green all the way up to the foothills."

"I hear the drought's bad."

"Four years' worth. A real bitch. Gary, well, Gary was always going off on how the West was so dry, wasn't enough water for all the development. He always said the day would come when we'd see the bad results of so much growth. Well, I hate to admit he was right, but goddamn, here we are. Not enough water. And there're a million green lawns and gardens in those fancy subdivisions around Denver."

"Ranching must be a tough way to earn a living."

"It's tough. Damn, it's tough. And I always resented my brother, you know, for being off politicking all the time, while I got stuck doing all the hard work." Randy shook his head. "But now that he's gone, and we got this drought, I guess I can see what he wanted for us. I mean all of us."

Portia could hardly believe her ears. Randy had never said anything like this. He'd never even approached such reasonable thought. Was he trying to impress Nick? Was he simply responding to Nick's interest?

"Yeah, you know," Randy was reflecting, "I can see what Gary meant. All that building around Denver, especially south toward us. Did you know Douglas County is one of the fastest-growing counties in the country? Or maybe it *is* the fastest, I'm not sure. Ranchers keep selling out. Hell, why not? You can barely make a living. So you sell, get cash money, and retire."

"What did Gary think about selling the ranch?"

"Good Lord, he never considered it. Been in the family for over a hundred years."

"What about you?"

Randy appeared shocked. "I'd never sell. This land is my life."

This was yet another side of Randy that Portia had never glimpsed. Maybe he was like this with other people and only prickly with her. Then again, he'd been a jerk around Gary, too. Always.

"The truth is," Randy went on, "my brother and me, well, I guess we had that thing called sibling rivalry, you know? The way brothers do."

"Yeah, I have a brother. We fought like demons," Nick said.

"So, you know what I mean. And now that Gary's dead . . . Could be it's a little easier for me to say he was right about some things. I always made fun of his environmental stuff, but I can see his point. Like this drought. I mean, drought is normal, but when you got so many people living on the land, well, then drought's a catastrophe. And fire. It's good for the land. Except when people live in its path. Like us, for instance."

"Sure," Nick said.

Portia felt as if she'd entered the *Twilight Zone*, was witness to an alien entity inhabiting her brother-in-law's body.

What had come over Randy? Even Lynette was staring at him with wide eyes. The only explanation Portia could come up with was Randy finally missed his brother, and this spouting off of Gary's ideals was a sort of guilt trip.

Lynette was smiling at her husband now, reaching over and covering his hand with hers. "You never told me how you felt," she said. "I'm so proud of you. I wish Gary was here. He'd be so happy."

"Yeah," Randy said wistfully. "Gary."

Portia could barely believe her ears. Had she misjudged him all these years, seen him as the lesser of the brothers because she'd been looking at him through Gary's eyes? How petty of her.

She subconsciously tilted her head, as if trying to view him at a new angle. And that was when she recalled his words, "I guess she heard what she heard," and she straightened again. That was not the new and improved Randy. That was Mr. King of Denial. So much for the rehabilitation of Randy.

She and Nick left shortly after that. In the

truck, she said, "Well, *you* certainly got on Randy's good side."

"I take it you and your brother-in-law don't get along?"

"Oh, we get along," she said. "It's just a question of *how* we get along."

"He wanted to talk."

"Apparently."

"He seems like an okay guy. Between a rock and a hard place."

She was silent.

"What?"

"Oh, well," she said, "you might as well know. . . . The man you just talked to wasn't the real Randy. Not the Randy I know. I don't believe he's finally seeing Gary's point of view. That is just *not* Randy."

"Huh. And what about his wife?"

"Lynette? She's a sweetheart. Well, you can see that for yourself. She had you going."

"Hey," he protested.

"I saw you blush."

"You're nuts."

"Whatever you say." She shot him a smile. "Anyway, did you learn anything from Randy? I mean, besides his obvious opinion that I've got mental problems?"

"I'm getting a picture. Every detail helps." He hesitated, braced himself against the dashboard as the truck hit a pothole. "Tell me about Gary's accident."

"Accident. You don't believe me either."

She was surprised at how disappointed she felt.

"It's just a word. Tell me how he died."

She drew in a ragged breath. "There's a sharp curve on the county road south of Colt. There's a deep gully on one side. His car went off. Going too fast, they said."

"You don't buy that."

"No. He'd been driving that road ever since he was a teenager."

"What was Gary like?"

"Gary." She turned into her drive, wrestling with the steering wheel. "Gary was wonderful. Very blond. Like Randy, but better looking. Charming. Persuasive. He could get anybody to do anything he wanted. He could get them to *want* to do it for him. He was exciting to be around. He had such energy." She pulled to a stop in front of her house and sat there, her hands still on the wheel, the diesel engine still rumbling, dust sifting through the open windows.

"How'd you meet?"

She turned to look at Nick. His face showed nothing. Why was the asking these questions? "Are my answers going to help you find out who set that fire?"

"They might."

She studied him. "I met Gary at a fundraiser my dad took me to. To save the coral reefs off Florida. I'd never heard anyone speak so persuasively. I was introduced, we talked. He'd just been divorced, and we . . . we hit it off. We got married . . ." She thought. ". . . eleven years ago." She didn't like talking about Gary with this man, practically a stranger. She felt a little guilty, as if talking about him with Nick tarnished his memory.

"And you moved here," Nick urged.

"Yes, I moved here. I loved it. Traveling with Gary, then coming home to the quietness of the ranch. It was perfect." Well, not quite perfect, but Nick didn't need to know that. Carefully, she said, "We had a good marriage. People said things, and I know Gary . . . liked women, but we had a *good* marriage. We went through —" She almost blurted out that she'd had three miscarriages, but she stopped. ". . . a lot together."

"Then he died," Nick said quietly.

"Yes, he died. And I had to take over for him, the bill paying, the taxes, the banking. Randy does the everyday running."

"Must have been hard."

"Sure, it was hard, but I've done pretty well. Until this." She gestured down the drive toward the pile of blackened wood. The stink of it stung her nose. "It's too coincidental. The threat to me, then this. And before he died, *right* before, Gary was being threatened, too."

"Can you show me the spot Gary's car went off?"

She shuddered. "No. I can't. I never drive that way anymore."

"I understand."

"Look . . ." She lifted her gaze to him. "Gary never would have driven so fast around that curve. I told you that."

"Yeah, you told me."

"You don't believe me?"

"Reserving judgment till I have all the facts." He opened the truck door and got out.

"You sound like a lawyer."

"Yeah, right."

She opened her own door and slid out, walked around the front of the truck. The sun beat down. She could hear rap music coming from Todd's room upstairs. "What will you do now?" she asked.

"I got some ideas."

"What ideas?"

"Tell you when I have answers."

She tried to smile. "Now you really sound like a lawyer."

"Portia, I . . . let's just say I'm going to pursue some leads. I'll keep you informed."

"Promise?" She shaded her eyes with a hand.

He walked to his rental car, opened the door, whistled at the heat inside. Before sliding in, he looked at her and said, "Call your pal Aaron and ask him to do something about those security guys."

"Oh, for goodness' sake," she said.

"I'll be in touch," he said, getting in his car, turning it on, and backing out of his spot.

Her hand still shading her eyes, she watched as he headed down the long ranch road toward the highway, until all she could see was the rooster tail of dust dispersing slowly in the hot afternoon sun.

SIXTEEN

Nick stopped at the sheriff's department annex in Colt and learned Cab was out on a fire line some ten miles south of town.

"The Aikens place," the dispatcher told him. She rose and led him to a county map pinned to the wall. "You're here," she said, pointing, "and this is the Aikenses. Take the first right out of town, here." She drew her finger along the map, "And go around three, maybe four miles down County Road One thirteen, then just look over to your left, you'll see the fire. Follow the road, turn right after the old drive-in theater. That's the Aikens ranch."

"I won't be bothering Cab?"

"Nope. Cab's there just keeping order. The hot shot firefighters are on it."

The dispatcher was right. About four miles out of Colt, Nick could see the line of smoke and epicenter of the fire glowing over a distant ridge. The sight was spellbinding. Blue sky above, a distinct line of hazy yellow against the blue, then the rising smoke in a tall, billowing cloud of pristine white, a fire cloud, he would learn later. Created from condensing water droplets above the fire. A single, bizarre cloud in the hot blue sky.

Even with the air conditioner blasting, he could smell the sweetly pungent odor of burning sage and juniper. He'd been here less than a week, and already his thoughts turned to rain.

The route through the Aikens place spread ran along a badly rutted track abutting the lower fence line, and then turned sharply up a gradually sloping field littered with a herd of bunched up cattle. Hell, Nick had never seen cows that weren't eating or shitting. Must be the fire.

He drove carefully, not wanting to bottom out the rental car, and thought about his conversation with Randy, how little he'd learned for his efforts. But mostly he thought about Portia. Pictured her so vividly she might have been sitting in the passenger seat. He could smell her scent and see the fine blond hairs that ran up to her hairline at the back of her neck. He could even see the shape of her brow and the curve of her eyelashes. She'd worn mascara today. For the insurance investigator? And why hadn't he noticed how green her eyes were before the other day? Green with gold flecks in them, the same gold as her skin tone. The effect was a pure physical pang in his heart.

"Goddamn it," he said.

They'd discussed Gary's accident. Sure. That was why he needed to talk to Cab. But she'd also said some off-the-subject stuff about her husband that had surprised Nick. Maybe not what she'd said, he realized, but rather the way she'd said it. As if everything in their relationship had not been all that rosy. The notion swamped him with relief until he realized only a loser would take pleasure in someone else's problems. The man was dead. Hadn't Nick's mom always told him never to speak ill of the dead? Thing was, in Nick's judgment, Portia was still hung up on the guy. Why else would she have taken on the NPS position? Placed herself in jeopardy? Far as Nick could see, she was lighting her own private eternal flame for Gary Wells. Not that it was any of Nick's business, but the image of Portia toting around that torch royally pissed him off.

He drove around a rocky escarpment, crossed a dry gully on a shaky old wooden bridge, and saw in the distance a hodgepodge of vehicles parked every which way in a high meadow below the fire. There were fire engines, pickup trucks, vans, a few low-slung cars like his, an ambulance, couple cop cars.

The air was thick with smoke now, but he could make out the firefighters working along the ridge. Looked to be digging a fire line. That they could labor wearing all that garb in this oppressive heat was downright amazing. The men — and probably women up there, too — deserved medals.

He got out and strode past a modern-day chuck wagon: a small, metal-sided truck that opened into a full-blown cooking unit. Couple women were offering coffee and sodas and bottled water, along with sandwiches and burgers to the firefighters who were on break. Behind the chuck wagon, Nick could see a few brightly colored tents. Housing, he figured. How could these people do this work day in and day out, flying from fire to fire, state to state, month after dry month?

Cab Whitefeather was talking to an EMT when Nick found him.

"Well, you sure do get around," Cab said, staring at Nick. "You looking at this property for your retirement? Bet you could pick it up cheap."

Nick had known Whitefeather was going to be suspicious of him, and he had his lines all figured. Just like on the witness stand when the public defender prepped him. Sprinkle enough truth into your story to make it convincing.

"Well," Nick said, holding the undersheriff's gaze despite the urge to rub his smoke-filled eyes, "I *am* looking at retirement, but the truth is, I was on Portia Wells's security team while she was in New York for a fund-raiser — firemen's fund-raiser, in fact — and we sorta met."

"Oh," Cab said, "*oh*. And you figured to maybe bump into the pretty widow out here?"

"Not sure if I planned that far. Always wanted to see Colorado, had vacation time coming." He lifted his shoulders, dropped them. "But I guess I got real interested when I saw that half-ass security outfit parked on her road."

"Um," Cab said. Then, "If you don't mind me asking, what *were* you doing there when the barn went up?"

"I was worried about the lady, couldn't sleep, so I drove on down. Call it a premonition."

"You that good, huh?"

Nick laughed. "Sometimes. Yeah, sometimes I get it right." This time he did rub his eyes. "Helluva thing, this fire."

"Sure is." Cab glanced up at the burning ridge. "Damn," he said.

"How'd it start?"

"Dry lightning strike. Which is a lot easier to figure than Portia's barn."

"The inspector got a handle on the source?"

"Uh-huh. Just spoke to him today, and it looks like an accelerant was used."

"Definitely arson."

"Oh, yeah. Question is, who? Now, if I was to ask Portia, she'd tell me it was that developer. But as far as Randy's thoughts . . . Now, him I don't know."

"How's that?"

"Randy? He's kinda hard to read. Talks big but doesn't follow through. Always been in his older brother's shadow. Sort of trying to play catch-up all his life. A good guy basically, but I can't say I know him. He tends to put his head in the sand about a lot of stuff. Handles the ranch okay, but he's out of his element in anything else. This arson . . ."

Cab took off his Stetson, mopped his brow, then settled the big white hat back on his head. "Randy won't want to admit someone would burn down his barn."

"Um," Nick said. "So why would someone torch it? I mean, we know Portia's opinion, but maybe you have other ideas."

"Not me. Near as I figure, Portia taking on that NPS job got someone pretty riled."

"That someone being Patrick Mahoney?"

"Didn't say that."

"But you're thinking it."

"You an evidence man?"

"Always."

"And there ain't going to be any trail leading back to a man like Mahoney. You can put that in the bank, son. But worse, you just watch the insurance company hold up a check for the barn."

"Because it was arson."

"Uh-huh. Like maybe Portia or Randy set

295

the fire. They got to be cleared of wrong-doing first."

"You could clear them."

"Sure could."

"Will you?"

"Most likely."

"But it will take time."

"Yep, it will."

All the more reason for Nick to pay for the new barn. His fault, no matter which way he looked at it.

"So tell me about Gary Wells's accident," Nick said. "You were on the scene."

"I was wondering when you'd get around to asking," Cab said.

The site where Wells had died was only a few miles from the Aikens ranch. Nick followed Cab's directions and wondered why Wells had been on this particular road. Not that it mattered now. But Nick just wondered.

He saw the set of curves leading up a sloping hill exactly as Cab had described: a long, straight stretch of road, irrigation ditch running beside it on the left, a ranch on the right, and then the hill where the road climbed sharply in a set of switchbacks. Wells had gone off into a gully on the third switchback, the one with the 20 mph sign. "There's a pull-off on your right," Cab had said, "big drop on the left. Wells rolled maybe three, four times. Didn't stand a chance."

Evidently, Nick thought, as he turned into the pull-off, the undersheriff and state highway patrolmen figured Wells had either been going way too fast into the curve or an animal — a deer or elk, or maybe a loose cow — had darted in front of the car, and he'd jerked the steering wheel too abruptly, caught a tire on the loose, gravelly edge, and gone over.

Cab had said Wells must have been going awfully fast to roll so many times. "How fast?" Nick had asked, and Cab had said, "forty, fifty miles per hour."

On foot, Nick crossed the road, looked down into the deep-sided gully, and thought, *Impossible*. Only a maniac would have approached this curve at those speeds. Wells, from all Nick had gathered, was a lot of things, but not a maniac. And there'd been no alcohol or drugs found in his blood.

Nick stood on the dusty roadside staring down into the ravine, hands in his jeans pockets, thinking, seeing the car careen over the edge, maybe strike that boulder down there, flatten the sage and juniper, flip, and flip again and again, until it came to rest at the bottom, probably still rocking, maybe the engine still running, a tape or radio playing, Gary Wells still in his seat belt, neck broken.

Nick stared up as a hawk wheeled overhead in the azure sky, then he blew out a long, whistling breath, and said, "Phew. What a way to die."

He walked the road a few yards up the hill and then back down again, trying to picture the scene from Portia's eyes: a vehicle following Gary, headlights coming up fast in Gary's mirrors, blinding him, following so close Gary had speeded up. Maybe the vehicle had even given him a few adrenaline-producing bumps from behind, then pulled alongside, steering directly into Wells's car, nudging him, causing him to panic and speed up even more. Then the final bump, which had sent Gary's car over the edge.

Sweat was staining the back of Nick's shirt, dampening the collar. But he still stood on the empty road and played the scene over in his mind, wondering if there'd been skid marks, if the cops had even looked for marks, and if they had, had they taken photographs and measurements? And what about Wells's vehicle? It would have been sold for scrap metal months ago. Even so, maybe the state patrolmen or Cab Whitefeather had noted inexplicable scratches on the paint or even paint from another vehicle.

Nick walked back to the rental car, picked up his cell phone, and called Cab's dispatcher, asking to be patched through to Cab.

"Car was totaled," Cab said. "Hell, there could have been a hundred dents, and no

298

one would have noticed. As for paint, you got to be kidding. No one was looking for paint from another vehicle. You been watching too much TV, that CSI show. This is real life."

Nick had to smile. "But what about Portia's claim her husband was forced off the road?"

"Portia didn't start that talk till Gary was ice cold and the car a heap of tin. But I'll tell you what. Stop back in Colt, and I'll have a copy of the accident report waiting for you. Okay?"

"Hey, thanks."

"Say," Cab said, "you want to meet later at the saloon in Colt for a Coke?"

Nick thought. "Can't. Need to get back to Denver and check out Mahoney's office this afternoon. I'll take a rain check, though."

"Rain check. Now that's a funny idea from where I'm standing."

Rain, yeah. "I bet."

He was ready to click off when Cab said, "That'd be on Larimer Street in downtown."

"Huh?" Nick said.

"Mahoney's office. It's on Larimer," Cab said, and it was Cab who switched off.

There was another message from Bern awaiting Nick at his motel, the tone irritated now. Thank God he'd never given the editor his cell phone number, or he wouldn't have a moment's peace. He put Bern and the *Star Gazer* out of his mind and went to take a shower.

It was after four by the time Nick parked in Larimer Square, an upscale commercial area of downtown Denver.

Mahoney's place of business, a small but well-appointed storefront office in the heart of the square, was located between a bakery-café and a kitchenware store. Nick knew the office belonged to Mahoney, because inside the picture window sat a scaled architect's model of the Panorama Ranch.

Here goes, he thought, opening the door. You could have filled the Library of Congress with what he didn't know about golf course developments.

A shapely, nicely dressed redhead greeted him. "Hi there, come on in and please feel free to look around." She readily stuck out her hand. No wedding ring. "I'm Cheri Morris, head of sales."

He shook her hand. "Nick, Nick Sinestra."

"A New Yorker," she said cheerfully.

"Accent shows, huh?"

She laughed. And so it went.

If he expected a hard sales pitch, he was mistaken. Cheri was very sweet, not overly talkative but artful, filling in any gaps in their conversation. He gave her the same pitch he'd given Cab Whitefeather: NYPD, looking to retire. Of course, she had no idea what his net worth was, but she had to assume he'd inherited. Cops, even detective grade, could not afford 250 grand for a building lot. And that wasn't even a lot with fairway frontage.

Cheri talked while they both stood over the model, exclaiming over the undulating beauty of the setting, the clubhouse and various amenities — that equestrian center — the large residential lots, private roads, security and gatehouse, the layout of the thirty-six holes. Nick almost said he thought a golf course was eighteen holes, but then he figured it: two golf courses? *Jesus.*

"So, do you golf, Nick?"

"Not as good as Tiger Woods," he said, and he smiled, shrugging.

She showed him color brochures of the property, brochures that must have cost a fortune to print up, a year's salary for him, anyway.

"So where, exactly, is the Panorama Ranch? I'm pretty new to Colorado."

"Of course. Well, let's see. Do you know where Castle Rock is?"

"South of here."

"Yes. And the ranch is to the west of Castle Rock. It's in what we call foothill country. It's so lovely," she said.

"So it's a real ranch?"

"That's right. A beautiful piece of —"

"And it's being built right now?" he cut in,

unable to bear another glowing review of the property.

"The development is almost through the approval process."

"Which is?"

"Oh, my, there's a lot involved in platting a new community. Hmm, let's see, there are water issues, sewer." She screwed up her nose. "There are environmental concerns, road usage issues —"

"Environmental issues, huh? Such as?"

"Goodness. My. Things like setting aside wildlife protection zones, providing open space and nature trail design, rules about golf course drainage into particular wetlands due to chemical fertilizers."

"Guess that could be a problem, the approvals?"

"Well, it certainly could be, but Mr. Mahoney is very knowledgeable in these areas and so terribly concerned himself for preserving the natural beauty of his projects, and, really, the process is nearly complete."

"Is it."

"Oh, yes. Both golf courses will be opening in two years. That's very quick for this area, you know. And we expect build-out to be completed in eight to ten years."

"Build-out?"

"There are nine hundred home sites."

"Whoa."

"Oh, that's not in the least excessive,

Mr. . . . Nick. Most projects with so much available acreage would build out with twelve to fifteen hundred sites. The wonderful thing is that you can select your lot right now at a pre-construction ten percent discount, and the lot comes with a lifetime owner's club membership, valued today at fifty-five thousand dollars."

"Uh-huh," he said. This was getting over his head.

"Best of all, Nick, you can hold your lot for as little as eighteen thousand dollars in our escrow account, *and* the account pays five and a half percent interest."

"Very nice," he said, nodding. "So, for argument's sake, let's say something goes wrong with the approvals? Like maybe somebody finds spotted owls on the property?"

"Spotted . . . ?"

"Owls. Happened in the Northwest years ago. Environmental group halted a big logging project because a couple owls were found in a tree."

"Oh. Well, I don't think that owls are a concern here."

"That was just an example, Cheri."

"Oh. Sure. I see." She smiled winningly.

"Say," he said. "This Mr. Mahoney around? Maybe he could answer a couple questions."

"Of course. He was on a conference call in his office, but let me see if he's free now."

She turned toward the rear of the building.

And Nick lightly touched her sleeve. "Hey, and I'm not coming on to you, I swear, but could I buy you a coffee or cocktail or something after work?" He glanced at his watch. "It's almost five."

She hesitated. He gave her an innocent smile. She sighed and said, "Sure, why not? Maybe right next door. Now, I'll go see if Patrick is free."

"Thanks, Cheri," he said.

Patrick Mahoney was a fine-looking man in his forties. He was tall and handsome and had a closely cropped blond mustache and goatee. He held himself erect. His handshake was strong and felt genuine, as was his smile. Under other circumstances, Nick would have said the man was immediately likable. It was easy to see why he'd gone so far in life. Style and charm. Of course, he was Irish and Nick, being Italian, began sniffing out the blarney.

"Sit, sit," Mahoney said, gesturing to a leather chair in front of his desk. "Can I get you something to drink? Coffee, tea, wine, water?"

"I'm fine, but thanks."

Mahoney sat down. "So, Cheri tells me you're worried about owls?" Mahoney indulged himself in a good laugh. "Well, let me assure you, Nick, no spotted owls on the Panorama Ranch."

"That's a relief to know," Nick said with heavy sarcasm. "But there's got to be other environmental issues. I read about problems every day out here, and before I invest, I want all the info I can get."

"Don't blame you a bit. But I can assure you all that is behind us now."

"All that?"

"Environmental concerns. We've already jumped through those hoops, Nick."

"So you're all set to start building?"

"Absolutely."

"Like when?"

"Oh, a worst-case scenario would be as late as this October but, in reality, I believe all the permits will be in place by the end of August."

"I see. Well," Nick said, "I think you've answered my questions." He stood.

"I hope Cheri mentioned the preconstruction discount on our lots, Nick." Mahoney also rose.

"She did."

"And the lifetime club membership?"

"Uh-huh."

"Good, good. And, Nick, I don't want you to think I'm giving you the hard sales pitch here, but the Panorama Ranch is going to be one of the most beautiful communities in the Western United States. If you like, Cheri can drive you down to the property tomorrow or whenever your time allows, and give you the grand tour. But I warn you, once you see the beauty of the land, you'll be hooked."

"Sounds like a plan," Nick said. "I'll talk to Cheri about it."

Mahoney's phone rang, and Nick waved at him to take the call. Mahoney waved back, smiled. Nick escaped. If anyone used the word *beautiful* around him again, he'd puke.

Good to her word, Cheri switched off her computer, turned off lights, indicated to Mahoney through his open door that she was leaving, and she joined Nick out front.

"Next door all right, or you want to go somewhere else?" he asked.

"Oh, I love the atmosphere next door. And we could get that outside table right there. If you want to sit outside, that is?"

"Outside's good."

They sat in the heat beneath a green market umbrella and ordered two glasses of house Merlot and a plate of nachos and cheese. Nick had the wine and switched to a beer. Cheri had a second wine. He chatted her up, feeling kind of bad, because she was an okay woman, a little lonely and on the rebound from a four-year relationship. Or so she said.

After an hour, he steered the conversation back to the Panorama Ranch. "You know," he said, "something sticks in my mind about your project, something to do with that Nature Preservation Society outfit and your Patrick Mahoney, but for the life of me, I can't remember what it is." He stared at her expectantly.

"Oh," she said, sobering.

He pushed a bit harder. "Yeah. And wasn't that environmentalist Gary Wells somehow involved?"

Then she sighed. "Poor man. I just couldn't believe it when I heard."

"Heard what?"

"Oh, didn't you know? He died last year in an auto accident. Such a waste."

"I guess I did read that. Right, right here in Colorado."

"Yes," she said.

"And there was something between Wells and Patrick Mahoney?" Nick prompted.

"Oh, well, yes, I suppose it's all water under the bridge now, but, yes, Gary Wells tried to block the Panorama development."

"Really."

She nodded. "That was in the very beginning. The rancher who owns the land was dealing with Patrick and with Gary Wells at the same time. The NPS buys up ranch land, you see, and turns it all into open space. It was a mess."

"Huh. So what happened?"

"Oh, goodness, let's see. As I recall, Patrick came to some sort of agreement with Gary Wells and the NPS. And at that point, the rancher signed the intent to sell to Patrick as soon as all the approvals are in place."

"Which is soon."

"Yes, a month or so."

"Huh," Nick said, thinking. Then, "I wonder what sort of compromise an environmentalist like Wells can make with a developer?"

"Oh, goodness," Cheri said. "I believe there is a bald eagle protection zone set aside now at the ranch, and of course the hiking and nature trails and the open space. Oh, and the wetland zone."

"Makes sense." But what made more sense to Nick's cynical mind was that money would have been involved. A lot of money changing hands. Gary Wells and the NPS were no doubt aboveboard, but Nick had just seen too much corruption.

He couldn't help saying, "Geez, I wonder if the NPS is on Mahoney's Christmas list?"

"Excuse me?"

"You know, I wonder if your Mr. Mahoney makes donations to organizations like the NPS?"

"Oh. Oh, golly. I suppose you'd have to ask Patrick about that."

Maybe he would.

The thing that stuck in his mind was how close the Panorama Ranch was to getting its approvals. That hadn't happened overnight. From what he'd gleaned from Portia, her husband and Mahoney had gotten along for a spell, then had a falling out, resulting in a threat from Mahoney. Could it have been over money? And if so, there was one person who was quite likely to know the details: Gary's good friend and mentor, Aaron Burkhart.

She changed the subject to more general topics, but Nick barely heard. He was still too busy sorting this information in his head. But nothing seemed to fit. In the beginning, Mahoney and Wells butted heads over purchasing this ranch land. Then suddenly they came to some sort of a compromise. Could money have changed hands? Maybe. But then something turned sour, there was a disagreement, Mahoney threatened Gary Wells, and Wells died.

Like that.

Something else occurred to Nick. If Aaron Burkhart was really so buddy-buddy with Gary Wells and Portia, then how come Burkhart hadn't stepped up to the plate when Wells died, put a halt once and for all to the Panorama Ranch project? What had Burkhart been doing for the past year, anyway? Other than hiring the security outfit from hell to watch over Portia.

Nick was missing something, a big chunk of an ever-widening conundrum. He sat for another hour talking to Cheri before they parted, and he still couldn't make any sense of the whole deal.

Back at his motel, he kept running the facts through his head. Portia believed Mahoney was responsible for her husband's death. She was now taking on Gary's cause, and she was in somebody's crosshairs. Mahoney again? Everything kept pointing to the developer.

But Nick still couldn't fit Burkhart into the picture. The man had money, clout, reputation, and the connections. Why *hadn't* he crushed Mahoney's project? Gone after Mahoney with a vengeance? Instead, knowing, at least believing Portia might be in danger, Burkhart hired the idiot security outfit to protect her. Just didn't add up, no matter how many times Nick tried to make it work. And what was even more puzzling, for God's sake, was that Burkhart had offered Portia the NPS position in the first place. Putting her in the very danger he was now paying to protect her against.

Nick sat on the edge of his bed, frowning. Maybe, just maybe, given the facts, Burkhart had never been serious about the NPS offer to Portia. Maybe he'd only offered as a gesture, never expected her to accept, and now he couldn't admit that to her.

Nick's cell phone was on the charger, so he picked up the motel's phone, dragging it over to sit on his lap. He dialed Portia's number, got her on the third ring. He asked her exactly that: "Was Burkhart serious when he offered you the president's position?"

She was silent for a long moment, and then she said, "That's not a very nice question, Nick, but I assume you have a reason for asking."

"Yeah, I do."

"Of course Aaron was serious," she said, but he heard it, a slight hesitation, doubt in her tone.

Well now. "All right," he said. Then he asked if everything was okay, and he told her to be careful. He told her he was driving down in the a.m., they said good night, and he hung up. She'd answered his question, and he'd heard the uncertainly in her reply, which gave him yet one more oddly shaped piece to this crazy puzzle.

SEVENTEEN

Nick phoned Gil at seven in the morning mountain time, figuring it was nine on the East Coast and his partner would be at his desk.

"How's the Wild Wild West?" Gil asked.

"Pretty friggin' wild," he replied. And then he had to tell Gil exactly what he was doing in Colorado, had to describe the barn burning and the threats to Gary Wells and Portia. Mahoney, Burkhart, the whole story. He left out the *Star Gazer* connection; Gil didn't need to know about that.

"Holy shit," Gil said. "Arson, murder? Man, that's some vacation you're on."

"I have a big favor to ask, partner."

"Hey, I owe you. You know that."

"Get that Homeland Security guy Rick to look up the last eighteen months of bank records for the Nature Preservation Society, that nonprofit headquartered in Washington, D. C., one we just did the security gig for at that fund-raiser. And also the bank records for Mahoney Enterprises out of Denver. Ditto for the Wellspring Ranch in Colt, Colorado. Gary Wells, deceased, Portia Wells, Randy and Lynette Wells. Got all that?"

"Yup."

"If he gives you any grief, tell him . . . Shit, tell him I suspect the NPS is one of those charities that siphons money off to Al Qaeda."

"Jesus, Sinestra."

"Think he'll do it?"

"I'll be my persuasive best. Hey, he loves to play on the computer, doesn't he?"

"And keep Wes out of it if you can."

"What, your best friend?"

"Yeah, that's him."

"I'll do my best."

"Oh, and income tax returns for the last year on all of them, as long as he's at it."

"In for a penny —"

"How's Dougie doing?"

"Sullen and obnoxious."

"Poor kid," Nick mused.

"Poor kid? He's a spoiled brat. He's ruining our lives. He tortures his mother. *Poor kid.*"

"Sorry. But don't you remember, Gil? Don't you remember how it felt to be fourteen?"

"I try not to."

"My point, pal."

Someone had left the gate to the horses' pasture open. The dozen horses had, of course, crowded together and escaped, galloping up the ranch road wildly, as if celebrating their long-lost freedom. Never mind that inside the fence they had twenty acres of irrigated fields to graze in and nothing but dirt road and fences outside of their pasture.

Portia, Todd, Randy, Juan, and the dogs finally got the horses rounded up and herded back into their field, whereupon the animals turned once more into docile cow ponies, lowering their heads to graze the minute the gate was chained shut.

They had to keep one mare out of the herd, because her leg had been badly cut in the melee. They'd need to call the vet to come stitch her up, another three hundred dollars or so in vet bills.

"Who left the goddamn gate open?" Randy asked for the tenth time.

"I don't know." She was hot and soaked in sweat, and her mouth was gritty with the dust kicked up by the horses. The two Border collies lay panting next to the gate, heads outstretched between their front paws.

"Todd?" Randy said. "Damn it, did you leave this gate open?"

"No. You think I'm that dumb?" Todd replied. He was holding the cut mare, whose leg was wet with blood.

"Who rode last?" Randy demanded. "Who used a horse last?"

"I think Hernando put the horse he used

314

away yesterday afternoon," Todd said.

"He knows better than to leave the gate open!"

"You asked, Uncle Randy."

"I'll call Hernando," Portia put in. "Maybe he saw somebody around —"

"Why in hell didn't your bodyguards see this imaginary person of yours?"

"I don't know, Randy. I'll ask them, too. I'll tell them to be on the lookout."

Randy stomped away, muttering.

"I'll call Dr. Coffman," she said to his back. In answer, he flapped a hand. "I guess that's a yes," she said to Todd.

"I did *not* leave that gate open," the boy said.

"I know. I know."

They put the mare in a small pen with a makeshift bandage wrapped around her leg. Normally the horse would have awaited the vet in a stall in the barn, but there was no barn. The area still smelled of smoke and wet, burned wood. Portia tried not to look at the site. Soon she and Randy would have to think about getting the mess removed — more money they didn't have.

She'd saved that afternoon to clean house. Change the beds, wash the sheets, dust the never-ending dust off every surface, vacuum upstairs and down, scrub the bathrooms. She was on her knees washing out the tub in Todd's bathroom when she heard a knock on the screen door downstairs.

"Just a minute," she called, pulling off her rubber gloves, pushing her hair back with a wrist.

"Portia?" she heard. *Nick*.

She descended the stairs, feet bare, in shorts and a sleeveless blouse, still sweaty from the morning's roundup.

"Got a minute?" he asked as she let him in.

"Actually I don't. I've been housecleaning. And this morning the horses got out because someone left the gate open, and the vet just left an hour ago. He had to put stitches in one of the horse's legs, because she got cut when they got out. And Randy's madder than hell about it."

"Someone left the gate open?"

"Well, unless one of the horses sprouted fingers and turned into Houdini."

"You got any ideas who did it?"

She sat on the couch, knees splayed, hands hanging between them. "No."

"Could it have been an accident? You know, someone being careless?"

"There's a rule on ranches: close all gates carefully. Oh, and another rule: leave all gates the way you found them."

"So the gate being open, it was deliberate?"

She looked up at him. "I don't know."

"Great." He stood there in her living room, in his brand-new Levi's and another store-creased shirt, this time coral, and he frowned. "You get threatened by two men. Your barn burns. Now your gate is opened, and a horse gets injured."

"Oh, I forgot to mention, I've been getting phone calls in the middle of the night," she said.

"From who?"

"They hang up. Caller ID is blocked. So I just turn the phone off at night."

"Christ, Portia, why didn't you tell me?" He put a hand on the back of his neck and massaged it.

"Well, I . . . At first, a couple nights ago, I guess, I thought it was just wrong numbers or Todd's school buddies playing pranks. But I talked to Todd, and it isn't his friends." She shrugged. "Last night it happened twice before I just unplugged it."

"And you tried Caller ID?"

"Yes, I *told* you, there's a block on their number."

"Okay, okay," he said. "Did you tell the guys out in the van?"

"I . . . no, not yet."

"I see. And I suppose they didn't notice anything out of the ordinary when the horses got loose? Sort of like the fire, huh?"

"What do you want me to do? Go down there and tell them how to do their job?"

"No," he said, "I will."

The next thing she knew, Nick was

speeding down the ranch road in the Camry. *Oh God*, she thought, picturing the confrontation. *Would he just read them the riot act? Or maybe they'd exchange punches.* She had another awful thought: *Were any of them carrying a weapon?*

He was back in fifteen minutes. "What happened?"

"Nothing much," he said tightly.

"*Something* must have happened."

"I fired them."

"You . . . what?"

"Goddamn it, I fired them. They said I didn't have the authority. I said I'd have you drive down to do it."

"And?"

He shrugged. "They left."

"Just like that?"

"Sure."

"You're not telling me everything."

"I'm telling you all you need to know."

He was infuriating. "Well, don't you think you should have consulted me first? My God."

"Yeah, I should have. Sorry."

"You're sorry an awful lot."

"Don't I know it."

Then, before she could sort out her feelings, he said, "I think it's time you leave here, for a while, anyway."

She couldn't believe her ears. "And go where?"

"I don't know. Somewhere. To be safe."

"I can't just *go* somewhere. There's Todd. And I have responsibilities."

Nick began to pace. "I don't like this at all."

She followed his movements. "Do you think I do?"

"Someone's after you. I got some ideas. But I need time, and I'm afraid you're in danger. The more I dig, the more they'll go after you."

"Why wouldn't they turn on you?"

"You're the weak link. I mean, what can they do to me?"

"By *they*, I take it you mean Mahoney and his hired hands?"

"I'm not sure it's Mahoney. He's only one possibility. I know what you think, but —"

"Have you found out anything new?"

"Not really. I was almost talked into buying a lot at the Panorama Ranch," he said dryly. "Big discount if you buy now."

"He's awfully sure of himself, isn't he?"

"Yeah, he's a sure-of-himself kind of guy."

"Is that what you came out here to tell me?"

"Well, no."

"Then . . ."

"I wanted to make sure you were okay. And I wanted . . ." He stopped pacing and looked at her. "I wanted to discuss the barn."

Oh God, here it is. "I can't —" she began.

He held up a hand. "Now, just listen."

"Nick, please, I'm too tired to argue about it. I can't accept your money."

"Not my money. The *Star Gazer*'s money."

"It doesn't matter, I can't —"

The back screen door slammed, and she heard Todd in the kitchen.

"Portia, I'm starved. What are we — ?" He appeared in the living room doorway. "Oh. Hello."

"Hey, Todd," Nick said.

"Can you fix yourself a snack? I have to finish the upstairs," she said.

Todd was looking at her and Nick questioningly. Interested. She flushed.

"There's a box of cookies in the cupboard," she said, standing up. "And —"

"Tell you what," Nick said. "I'm taking both of you to dinner."

Surprised, she began to make excuses. "No, really, I have a million things to do."

"Do them tomorrow." Nick glanced at Todd. "Anyplace good to eat around here?"

"Toro's," Todd said promptly. "In Colt. Wicked burritos."

"They serve meat at this Toro's?" Nick asked doubtfully.

"Steak, prime rib. Dad used to get the barbecued ribs."

"Okay, Toro's."

"Nick, really —"

"Oh, come on, Portia," Todd said.

She looked from one to the other. "I guess I'm outvoted."

"Yeah," Todd said.

She showered while Nick waited downstairs with Todd. *Thank God for the boy,* she thought, rinsing shampoo from her hair. He was a kind of safe buffer. He'd interrupted what was in the process of becoming an awkward conversation. And he seemed to get on well with Nick.

No children, Nick had said. Yet he was easy with Todd, and he seemed to genuinely like him. No children. Just like her.

She wondered if Nick had ever wanted children. She put her hand on her bare belly. So empty. She'd been pregnant three times; once she'd even gotten to her fourth month, and her stomach had begun to swell a little. Each time she'd been so wondrously happy. Each time her happiness had been dashed in a haze of cramps and blood and Gary rushing her to the hospital. A habitual aborter was what the doctor called her.

Enough. No sense dwelling on the subject. She didn't even have a man to father her children, so what on earth was she thinking about it for?

She was nervous getting dressed. She could hear their voices downstairs, indistinct but animated. What where they talking about? Male things, sports? Or maybe they were

321

talking about the ranch . . . or her.

She put on a pair of white slacks and a pink checked blouse. A pair of sandals. She wished she had time just once in her life for a manicure; her nails were a mess. Ranch work did that to you. She blow-dried her hair and brushed it out. She needed a trim. Then she decided she looked too prim and proper for the occasion. Casual was better. She changed her blouse to a blue denim sleeveless one. Pulled her hair up behind an ear on one side and fastened it with a clip.

When she got downstairs, Todd had gone to take a shower, and Nick sat on the couch looking at a book: *Tom Horn and the Wyoming Range War.*

"Interesting," he said. "I had no idea."

"Gary collected books about the history of ranching."

"Have you read this?" He held up the book.

"Yes."

"This Tom Horn was quite a character."

"Did you see the movie about him? Steve McQueen starred in it."

"I'm not a big movie buff."

She stared at him, her head on one side. "What to you like to do in your spare time?"

He set the book carefully on the coffee table. "You mean, like hobbies?"

"Sure."

"Don't have many." He gazed into the

middle distance. "Gwen and I — my ex — we used to go jogging in the park every weekend, and she dragged me to every museum in the city. But now . . ." He shrugged.

"How long have you been divorced?"

"Around three years."

She could see how uncomfortable the subject made him. Gwen. What had gone wrong between them? Had it been a passionate union, with emotions boiling over? Nick had a side he hid from her. She sensed that. But she wasn't sure what that side was. Or had their marriage been merely convenient, loveless? Maybe they'd simply fallen out of love. *Gwen*. She wondered if Gwen was beautiful.

"No ladies beating down your door?" she asked lightly.

But he looked away, his expression going stiff. "Not a one," he said.

He drove them in his car. She sat next to him, Todd in the back. He'd turned off the radio, but not before she recognized the Denver station that played oldies from the '50s and '60s. Great old songs.

Toro's was very Western. Wagon wheel chandeliers, a bare wooden floor, cowboy paraphernalia on the walls, photos of old-time movie cowboys: Tom Mix, Gene Autry, Roy Rogers, John Wayne. There was a jukebox. An open grill where steaks sizzled. A salad bar. Gary used to bring her here all the time.

She noticed Nick taking in the decor. "Not exactly subtle," she said.

"Not exactly. But I like it."

They were led to a corner table by a waitress in tight jeans and a tank top. She wore a Stetson — all the waitresses did. Her name was Mindy, and she'd known Gary and Portia for years.

"Haven't been here for a while," Mindy ventured.

"No, I've been busy."

"We all heard about the fire. I'm real sorry."

"Thanks."

When she handed them menus and left, Todd leaned forward and said to Nick in a low voice, "She's really cute, isn't she?"

"Not bad," Nick said.

"She thinks I'm a kid, though."

"You *are* a kid," Portia said.

"I hate it when women are like that," Todd said.

"Yeah, me too," Nick replied.

They ordered. Burritos for Todd, a T-bone for Nick, barbecued chicken for Portia. Nick got a beer, Portia a glass of wine.

The salad bar was next; Todd heaped his plate high and spooned lots of salad dressing on it. Portia told Nick to try the pickled mushrooms, which were a house specialty.

Seated again, she smiled at Todd, who was attacking his plate. "This is nice," she said to

324

Nick. "I honestly had no idea what to fix for dinner. Thanks."

"You work too hard," he said, his attention on her.

"There's a lot to do."

"Why do you stay on the ranch? I mean . . . now that your husband . . ."

"I love it. And Lynette's my best friend in the world. And Todd needs a secure home."

Todd rolled his eyes. "A secure home," he mimicked. "In Hicksville."

"Come on, kid. It's a pretty cool place to grow up," Nick said.

"But you, like, live in New York City. That's way cooler."

"Not always."

"Have you been to, you know, Ground Zero?"

She saw a shadow cross Nick's features. "Yeah, I've been there. Knew a couple men who were killed."

"Oh." Todd was silent for a minute, and then he said, "I'd like to see that place. Portia went, didn't you?"

"Yes."

"Do you carry a gun?"

"Sure."

"You have it with you?"

"Not right here on me now, but it's close by."

"Like in the car?"

"None of your business, kid."

"My dad let me shoot his shotgun. I know how to load it and all."

"Good for you," Nick said, and Todd wisely dropped the subject.

Their food came. Plain, tasty fare. Nick had a baked potato with his steak, piled with sour cream and butter. He ate with gusto.

Portia was relieved that Todd was there to keep up the conversation. A little guilty about it, because she was using a young boy as an intermediary. But it gave her time to study Nick, to listen to him, to gauge his reactions. While he was guarded with her, he was open and natural with Todd.

She ate her dinner, and she watched, and she wished she could talk to Nick Sinestra in the easy way Todd could.

"There was this prostitute," Nick was saying, and he shot a glance at Portia as if to ask: *Is it okay for Todd to hear this?*

Well, she didn't believe in censorship, and Todd needed exposure to the real world, so she didn't object.

"She was real beautiful, and she had lots of business. Trouble was, she stole her customers' wallets. Now, I don't believe in hassling working girls, they have to make a living, but stealing." Nick shook his head. "So one of the guys in the precinct posed as a john, and when she pulled her stunt, he arrested her. Only thing was, *she* was really a *he*."

"No way," Todd said.

"Oh yeah."

"What about drugs? I see all this stuff on TV. Is it true?"

"Some. Hey, there are kids your age in the projects make so much selling crack they don't know what to do with the cash. They're too young to buy cars. Can't even drive yet."

"Wow."

"They buy gold chains."

"Do you arrest them?"

"We don't have much of that in my precinct. But, sure, if kids are caught, they get sent to juvie hall."

"I'd really like to go to New York," Todd said wistfully. "I bet it's real exciting."

"It is that."

"Maybe I'll apply to college there. You know, Columbia or NYU or something. Where did you go?"

Nick gave a short laugh. "I went to CCNY, that's City College of New York. On scholarship. Couldn't afford the big-name schools."

"Did you like it?"

Nick thought. "I worked my ass off, excuse my language. Lived at home, had two jobs, had no time to study, but I got through. Mostly I remember being tired all the time."

Portia ate a piece of chicken and realized she was learning more about Nick than she had in any of their conversations. She studied him and tried to imagine the young boy who went to college on scholarship, who worked and lived at home and was tired all the time, and suddenly she was ashamed of her own privileged years at Sarah Lawrence.

A glimmering of understanding came to her then, an answer to the question of why Nick had betrayed her to the *Star Gazer*. On some level, conscious or unconscious, he wanted to strike back at celebrities, those who had it easy, who had money. Yes, it made sense to her now. She watched and listened as he told Todd another cop story, and she recalled everything he'd done, but her memory was shaded differently, like those movies that started with old-fashioned, sepia-toned photographs, which then morphed into full color and motion.

Todd and Nick ordered dessert, hot fudge sundaes; Portia opted for coffee. She wondered if Nick noticed how quiet she was, but he seemed comfortable enough talking to Todd.

When he put his spoon down, he turned to her. "I want to say something. I hate to spoil dinner and all, but I think you need to consider this."

"Go on," she said.

"Todd . . . ?"

"I'm not a little kid," he said.

"Okay." Nick leaned forward, elbows on the table. In the background the jukebox played "Don't Let Your Babies Grow up to Be Cowboys." "I think I should stay at your house," Nick said.

"Oh, I'm not so sure —"

He held up a hand. "Just listen. I'd feel a lot better if I'm there. You said you won't leave, okay, so you stay, but you need to have some real security. The phone calls, the things that are happening? You need protection."

She sighed. "You're being obsessive."

"No, careful. Doing what I'm trained to do. Why not take advantage of me?"

"I *had* security men."

"What you had was a couple jerks making money taking naps in their van."

She was torn. Part of her felt frightened and alone and in need of help. The other part craved independence and a tough facade.

"Portia, listen to me," he said in a low, urgent voice.

She gave in. Gave in because it was easier, and she didn't have the mental energy to fight him and, deep down inside, she was scared. "All right," she said. "Fine. You can stay in the guest room."

He leaned back and fastened his gaze on her like a dark lantern. "Good," he said.

Todd looked from one of them to the other. He didn't say a word, for which she was grateful. She'd explain it all to him later;

329

he deserved to know about the mounting danger. Maybe she should try again to convince him to go back to his mother's.

"I've got to check out of my motel," Nick said. "I'll do it soon as I drop you at the ranch. Won't take long."

"Can we come along?" Todd asked. *Words from the mouths of babes.*

Nick switched his eyes to her, questioning.

She didn't know why she said it; somehow the words formed and emerged. "We can all go."

"Cool," Todd said.

The sun was low behind the mountains to the west. The peaks cast long shadows, fingers reaching out toward the high plains. Nick drove north on the interstate, got off on Colfax Avenue, and pulled into the parking lot of a dingy motel. She waited in the car while he went into his room and gathered his belongings. Five minutes was all it took. One small bag.

He checked out at the office and returned to the car, stuffing a receipt into his jeans pocket.

"The bozo charged me for another night," he groused. "Said it was after checkout time."

"Well, it is," she said mildly.

"Yeah, like he can't rent that room tonight."

She grew increasingly uneasy as he drove

330

back to the ranch. Nick Sinestra in her house. She'd see him in the morning. Was he grouchy? Did he get up early or sleep late? Would he disrupt her routine? Would he follow her around as she went about her daily activities? Would he leave whiskers in the sink when he shaved? He had dark whiskers, a perpetual five o'clock shadow. Gary had been so blond — he hadn't really had to shave every day. What would it be like having Nick there?

And then she thought, *Oh, gosh, what will Lynette say about Nick staying at my house?* Portia wasn't sure, but she guessed Lynette would think it was a good idea. *At least it wouldn't hurt,* she'd say. *You need someone to look over you.*

Todd disappeared into his room when they got home. She was tempted to ask him to stick around, but she couldn't depend on a fifteen-year-old to continuously provide relief. She showed Nick the guest room, down the hall from hers, across from Todd's.

"You can share the bathroom with Todd. I even cleaned it up today."

"I'm not fussy," he said.

"And I'm not Martha Stewart."

He smiled, and his whole countenance was changed. "Good thing, too."

The guest room had a maple dresser and matching night tables, a double bed with a brass headboard. A quilt on the bed. A simple room, small, with a dormer window that looked out toward the foothills. Lace curtains on the window.

"Nice," he said. "Better than a motel."

"Do you . . . I mean . . . what do you have for breakfast?"

"Breakfast?"

"You know, the meal you eat in the morning?"

"Usually grab coffee and a muffin near my subway stop."

"Don't you ever eat regular meals?"

"Nah."

"Well, we do. We try to, anyway."

"I'll try to adjust," he said dryly.

He'd set his bag down on a rocking chair. He opened it and took out a shoulder holster and a gun.

She gulped, her heart seizing. "Do you . . . have to . . . ?"

"You need to know I have this in the house," he said soberly. "Does it bother you?"

"Yes," she whispered.

"Sorry." But again he wasn't sorry. He was matter-of-fact. Guns were a part of his life, and he was bringing that part to her, to her home.

She left him then, unsettled, not tired yet. Downstairs, she thought of calling Lynette, but it was too late. And Nick might come down and hear her talking about him. No, she'd phone Lynette tomorrow morning.

She turned on a Denver news channel and tried to concentrate on it. She thought of Aaron; she should tell him Nick had let Jerry and Lev go and was staying with her himself. She was intensely aware of this stranger in her house, upstairs. Unpacking perhaps. Using the bathroom. She heard the creak of the old floorboards in the upstairs hallway. Would she be this sensitive to his presence the entire time he was here? And how long would *that* be?

She should be comforted by Nick in her house, but she wasn't. She was on edge, second-guessing her easy acquiescence. Too easy.

He came downstairs, stood there, looking as ill at ease as she was.

"I'm just watching the news," she said.

He sat down in the leather armchair. Gary's chair. How bizarre, a stranger in her husband's favorite chair, in her home, in her life.

"This Mahoney," he began, "he's slick. But I can't get a handle on a motive for him to go after your husband. He's too smart to get caught in something over the top like murder. Too obvious."

"Who else could have done it?" she asked.

"You can't think of anyone else with motive? Someone your husband pissed off?"

She shook her head. "Don't you believe me?"

He hesitated, then he put a hand out, palm up. "Look, I believe your feelings. There *is* a certain logic to your feelings. But that's not evidence. That's not proof."

She felt a sudden spurt of angry frustration. No one listened to her. No one. "Mahoney did it," she said tightly. "Mahoney murdered my husband."

EIGHTEEN

Lynette was her usual no-nonsense self. "Hey, that's great. You're killing two birds with one stone. You've got a live-in cop *and* a romantic possibility."

"Lynette!"

"I'm just calling it the way I see it."

"It was easier to say yes, that's all. I didn't feel like arguing."

"That's good. You're learning." Portia could hear water running, the clink of dishes as Lynette cleaned up after breakfast. "Where is he now?" Lynette asked.

"In the office. He said he was expecting some faxes."

"Let's get together tonight. Dinner," Lynette said. "I'm dying to talk to this guy some more."

"You hate to cook."

"So what? My curiosity is overcoming my aversion to cooking. I'll make that chicken thing."

"You don't have to —"

"You're not getting out of it. I want to see Nick again. More up close and personal."

Thank God for Lynette, even if she was nosy. "Where's Randy?"

"I think he went down to the barn site. He's talking about calling a trucker to cart the mess away."

"Oh."

"I know. It costs money."

"Doesn't everything?"

When Portia hung up, she sat for a minute musing. Why couldn't she be as open as Lynette? Wear her feelings on her sleeve, elicit a blush from Nick as easily as Lynette had done? Well, if she were incapable of such easy warmth, at least she'd learned one thing by Nick's response to her friend: he was not the tough guy he made himself out to be. That toughness was a shield. Inside, he was as vulnerable and in need of love and affection as everyone else. But he seemed incapable of showing that need to her, and she wondered just what it would take to get him to blush from ear to ear and smile at her like he'd done with Lynette.

She finally went into the room that had been Gary's office. She needed to do some work on the computer, but Nick was still there, on the second phone line, standing over the fax machine while page after page piled up in the tray.

"You need to use the office?" he asked, moving so that he blocked her view of the faxes. Deliberately?

"No, I'll do it later."

"Be done soon."

She went to finish cleaning up the kitchen, saw out of the window that Randy was trudging around the wreckage of the barn. His hands were in his back pockets, elbows stuck out behind him, his shoulders hunched. He kicked at a blackened beam.

She left the dishes in the sink and walked out the back door. Randy saw her coming, turned to face her.

"What a mess," he said as she approached. He sounded really down.

"Lynette says you've got someone in mind to haul it away?"

"Yeah. Huey Gleason, you know, Eric's son."

"Uh-huh." Randy still blamed her, and she guessed it was her fault. Hers and Nick's.

"I'm worried, goddamn it." He waved a hand at the pile. "This is gonna cost us. The insurance will never cover it."

"I know."

"Damn drought. We're gonna have to sell some more cattle."

Should she tell him about Nick's offer to rebuild the barn? But no, there was no point. She'd told Nick she wouldn't accept his offer. And, most likely, neither would Randy.

"We'll work it out somehow," she said.

"Easier said than done."

She left him tramping around the rubble,

head sunk between his shoulders, and started back toward the house. She hadn't said anything to him about Mahoney being to blame for the fire. She was sure he'd pooh-pooh her suspicions, anyway.

She was positive Mahoney had the barn burned. She also knew Nick wasn't as certain as she was, but then he didn't know the background of the situation as well as she did. He hadn't seen Gary's distress, his sleepless nights. All over Mahoney.

Who else would have sent such a loud and clear message?

She walked slowly, feeling the morning sun press heavily on her head and bare arms, and she tried to think. Who else had it in for her? No one. Well, Randy would love her gone, especially since Gary had left her half the ranch. But Randy would never sabotage his own property. There *was* no one else. It was Mahoney.

She noticed Nick watching her through the office window. What did he see when he looked at her? An almost middle-aged woman, frantically busy, unsure of where she was headed? How did she appear to him in her jeans and T-shirts? Or in practically nothing on the night of the fire?

She'd been wakeful last night, too aware of him down the hall. Did he sleep in pajamas? His body would be spare. He used to go jogging with his ex-wife, he'd said. She imagined him running, a sweatband on his forehead, his legs scissoring, his arms and shoulders glistening. And his ex-wife — Gwen, he'd called her. But she couldn't picture Gwen.

When she got in the house, she heard the fax machine, still spitting out pages. She went to the office again, stood in the doorway. "What on earth are all those?" She nodded at the printouts.

"Nothing much." He turned the pile of faxes facedown.

"If this has something to do with me, I want to know."

"Guy in New York is sending me some records is all."

"What records?"

"Technical stuff."

"Nick, I think you owe me the information."

"It's nothing, I'm telling you. Boring. About Mahoney Enterprises."

"You know what?" she said, "I don't like being treated like a child." She was on the verge of telling him to pack up his clothes and his faxes and go back to the King Motel, but she stopped herself, took a deep breath.

"Look, I'll show you this stuff when I've had a chance —" he began.

The other phone line rang. She moved to the desk, checked the Caller ID. Her mother. It was only her mother. She snatched up the phone and turned her back to Nick.

"Mother?"

"Portia, darling, oh, I'm so glad I caught you in."

There was a harried tone in Judith's voice. Portia felt her heart squeeze.

"I don't know . . ." Judith said, then Portia heard her draw in a sobbing breath. "Oh, I swore I wouldn't break down like this. I told myself . . . and Anna warned me, but . . ."

"What is it, Mother?" Her head began to pound. She knew. She knew what was coming. Another reporter had gotten to her.

"They've been calling me. People. Oh God, I've tried to . . . but it's been such a shock. And I was feeling so much better . . . going out." She drew in another long breath. "Now I can't set a foot out, can't answer the phone. I feel as if I'm going to pieces."

"I'm so sorry, Mother." Her fingers were white, clutching the receiver. She could hear the fax machine, still spewing out paper. And Nick . . . listening to the conversation.

"I know what happened. Anna told me. I know it wasn't your fault. I know . . ." Silence on the phone, ticking.

"Mother?"

"I . . . I'm here. Oh, it's terrible."

"Mother, did you call the doctor?"

"Anna called. There's not much he can do. He wants me to come in to see him."

"Oh, Mother," she said sadly.

"I was better, and then this had to happen." A sob. "You know how hard . . . I get so anxious."

"Tell me what I can do to help." She tried to keep her voice calm.

"Oh, Portia, I think . . . I better put Anna on. She'll tell you. I can't talk anymore."

"Portia, honey," Anna said a moment later.

"How bad is she?"

"It comes and goes."

"I feel awful. It's all my fault."

"Now, just stop that. What's done is done. But you can do something to help."

"Anything, Anna, you know that."

"Well, that late-night show, *After Dark*? They called and asked a million questions. Damn nosy people. Of course, I didn't let them speak to your mother. They asked personal questions, you wouldn't believe how they went on."

"Yes, I would."

"Well, Judith and I had a good talk. She was plenty upset, but she decided that if she went on the show, talked right to that dreadful man, you know, the host, maybe the press would stop hounding her. Just up and go on TV and show those people . . . You get the idea."

"Mother would go on television?" Portia was astounded. "She actually said that?"

"She sure did, but then she got frightened, and she decided she was afraid to go on

341

alone. It was too much for her. So she wants you to go on with her."

"What?"

"The two of you together."

"Anna . . . I . . . I'm not sure what to say."

"Just say yes."

"And you think she's okay to do this?"

"If you're there."

"When is this happening?"

"Sunday night."

"*This* Sunday? You mean, in three days?"

"That's it."

"Oh, my God."

"Will you do it?"

"I'll do it, of course."

"I knew you would. I told her as much."

When Portia put the phone down, she just stared at it, saying nothing, thinking, weighing her options, figuring out —

"What?" Nick asked.

"My mother."

"I got that."

"She's going on *After Dark*, and I have to go on with her."

"Christ."

"In three days."

"Why in hell — ?"

"To get the press off her back. She's a wreck."

He scrubbed the back of a hand against his whiskers. "Okay, all right," he said. "I'll go

342

with you. Take you and your mother to do the show."

Her initial reaction was to tell him no, but something inside told her to accept his offer, not to be stupidly stubborn. She needed help with Judith; why make things even harder?

He was waiting, looking at her with a kind of expectancy. "Okay?" he asked.

"Okay," she replied. And again she thought, *Am I too easy?*

Nick really needed to study the records Rick Jacobson from Homeland Security had just faxed, but Portia was on the move. After all his harping on how lousy her security had been, he could hardly let her traipse around by herself now.

So he tagged along while she and Todd took off in the Subaru to run errands. She stopped at the vet's, then Todd reminded her he wanted to get his learner's permit for his driver's license, but first it was the grocery store, where Nick followed her up and down the aisles feeling useless, but it was too damn hot to wait outside. Then he helped her load the grocery bags into the car. He was aware of her bare arms, the smooth golden skin, and the glow of perspiration on the V at her chest. He tried not to notice her at all but, goddamn, he was only human.

Next it was the Douglas County Division of Motor Vehicles, where Todd went through

343

the nerve-racking ordeal of getting his permit — nerve-racking for the kid. Nick just suppressed a grin.

Back home it was more of Portia's chores. He was worn out by three in the afternoon, dragging his sorry ass around the ranch after her. Holding the horse while she rebandaged the cut on its leg. The creature lifted its head and rolled its eyes so the whites showed while Portia crouched, trying to wind the gauze around its leg.

"Tell her it's okay," Portia directed him. "Pat her nose. Scratch her ears."

He tried, but he didn't have the touch. The big animal scared the crap out of him. And there was Portia under its feet.

After that she had to fill a water tank and feed a corral full of last year's crop of calves.

"How many cows do you have?" he asked.

"They're not all cows. Cows are female. But all in all we have four hundred head."

"That's a lot."

"Not so many." She pushed the pump handle down to stop the water, dusted off her hands. "We used to have five hundred, but with the drought . . ."

"How many do you sell each year?"

"About eighty percent of the calf crop. We keep twenty percent to replace old cows."

"Where's the bull?"

"We actually have three. They're out on BLM land with the rest of the herd."

"So it's been tough the last few years?" he asked, following her to the next chore.

"Yes, it has. You can take one year of drought, maybe two, but when it goes on so long . . . I don't know what's going to happen. It's hard. We've done our best, really pared down. Randy figured out a feeding program so that we could run the four hundred head for only twenty percent more overhead than it used to cost us to run two hundred. That's feeding every day."

"Randy, huh?"

"I know, he's rough around the edges, but he's a good rancher." She paused to push her hair back, and he noted how white the underside of her arm was. "And, by the way, we're invited to Randy and Lynette's for dinner tonight."

He stepped over the hose. "That's neighborly."

"Lynette's curious about you."

They ate on the deck behind Randy and Lynette's house, shaded by cottonwood trees. Lynette stared at Nick unabashedly this time and asked a lot of questions. She would have made him uncomfortable again, except for her obvious good humor, her warmth, and her infectious laugh.

"Divorced," Lynette said, giving Portia a knowing glance.

Portia only shook her head; there was obvi-

345

ously no way to stop her friend.

"Jesus, Lynette, let the guy breathe," Randy said.

Their boys were on the lawn, playing softball with Todd. The little ones had to be helped a lot, but Todd was good-natured about it. Nick thought of Gil and Doug, how great it would be for Doug to live in a place like this. With kids like this.

"I went to New York once," Lynette was saying. Her cheeks were pink, and the hair at the nape of her neck was damp and curling. "I loved it. But I could never live there."

"It isn't easy," Nick said.

"Where is it easy?" Randy asked sourly.

Later that night he finally had a chance to study the faxes. Portia was working in the office, so he went up to his room where he'd put the stack of papers in a dresser drawer. He settled himself on the bed, turned on the lamp on the night table, and started looking through this stuff. He wasn't great at the paper trail thing, but he was good enough to get the gist. After a half-hour or better, his eyes getting tired, he finally got to the NPS nonprofit tax returns. Included was a long list of donations over $10,000. All properly itemized. He scanned the list, running a finger down the columns. After a minute he whistled, his finger stopping on one name. Mahoney Enterprises, $100,000. Holy shit.

Mahoney's head saleslady, Cheri, had mentioned that Wells and Mahoney had come to a compromise. Was this what she'd meant? A whopping big donation to convince the NPS to back off?

And yet Wells had some kind of argument with Mahoney, who had subsequently threatened him, according to Portia. Why the change of heart? Had Wells struck a deal with Mahoney, a sweetheart deal, a kickback or something, and then changed his mind?

Nick tried to figure the dead man's motives. Had Wells felt guilty about taking the money? Had he come to the realization that the donation could be construed as a bribe? Had he suddenly been afraid the public would find out?

So he'd reneged on the deal with Mahoney. No wonder the developer was pissed.

Now, with Wells out of the picture, the development was on a fast track. Reservations were being taken on home site lots. An escrow account was all neatly in place. Yeah, Mahoney knew his project was set for the approvals. And with, say, 900 lots for sale, at a minimum of 250 grand per lot, some going as high as a million, Mahoney stood to rake in the big bucks. Motive for murdering Wells? Damn right it was.

Then, when Portia announced she'd take on the NPS presidency and presumably continue her husband's fight, there were suddenly threats, a fire, phone calls. Could be Mahoney was investing in the future, making sure in advance that the lady kept her nose out of his business. Made sense to Nick.

Course, then, Nick could be wrong.

And where did Aaron Burkhart enter the picture? Surely he must have known about the donation. Why hadn't *he* made certain the money was returned to Mahoney? Or, better yet, why not keep the money and order Gary to back off? Hell, it was only one golf development, and a hundred big ones could buy a lot of goodwill.

Burkhart. A cipher. Nick just couldn't get a handle on his actions. If he was the intelligent, great old man Portia made him out to be, his behavior was suspect. If he was Gary's mentor — a father figure, Portia had said — Burkhart should have seen the writing on the wall and either persuaded Gary to back off or found a way to placate Mahoney.

Nick put the papers down and tried to concentrate. He could hear noises from Todd's room, a computer game running. Portia was downstairs in the office. He could see her at the desk, her slender fingers tapping on the keyboard. She worked so hard trying to make the ranch succeed in her husband's memory. Even though her husband had screwed around on her and, it seemed, screwed around on the NPS.

She must have loved him very much. That bothered Nick. He told himself he was bothered because Gary was not the paragon she thought. But he knew, he knew on a deeper level, he was freaking jealous of the man. Of a *dead* man.

He heard footsteps on the staircase. Portia going to bed. He wanted to step outside his room and say something to her, a word of comfort maybe. He wanted to touch her, to feel the skin that he had only feasted his eyes on. He wanted to put his arms around her and kiss away the lines of care on her face.

He forced his attention back to the papers in his lap. Heard her bathroom door close, water groaning through the pipes. What did she think about, alone as she was? How did she find the strength to go on? Admiration for her swelled in him.

He managed to block the sound of running water from his thoughts and picked up a new set of papers: copies of statements from Portia's personal checking account. Feeling like a shit heel. Nothing there, the minimum balance barely kept up. Then Randy and Lynette's account. Equally uninteresting. There was a joint ranch account, obviously used to pay bills. A few large deposits entered at wide intervals, most likely proceeds from the sale of cattle, then a lot of checks following quickly.

He looked at the next set of faxes. A

money market account called Wellspring Ranch, Randy's Social Security number on it. At a Colorado Springs bank. Geez, Portia had told him the ranch was in trouble, yet in this account there were periodic deposits of $3,000 to $8,000. No deposits of $10,000 or over, which would have to be reported to the IRS. Over $60,000 in the last twelve months. Where did the money come from? He shuffled through the papers and rechecked Randy and Lynette's personal income tax statement. Yes, the deposits from the money market account showed up there, under "gifts." Gifts? From who?

Follow the money. And he needed more information. He'd love to ask Portia about that account, but he didn't dare. She'd be so mad he'd accessed their bank records and tax returns she'd kick him off the ranch. And rightfully so. But why did Randy have an account in Colorado Springs, when all the others were in nearby Castle Rock? Was Lynette aware of the account?

He'd sure like to know where those deposits came from.

He thought about knocking on Portia's door, asking if she knew about this particular account. Maybe she was already asleep, though. He tried not to imagine her in her bed alone, the sheets rustling, her window open. Did she miss having a man in her bed? Did she miss Gary?

Restless, he wandered downstairs, turned the kitchen light on, and sat at the table, put his head in his hands. Trying not to think of Portia upstairs in bed. Had she been alone since her husband died? He got himself a glass of water, drank it, drummed his fingers on the table.

What was Randy up to? A nice fat account, yet the ranch was barely able to pay its bills. Was Randy deliberately hiding cash from Portia to make the ranch appear to be a losing proposition so she'd give up her half?

He stayed there in the dimness, a ceiling light casting a circle of brightness on him. The kitchen window over the sink was open, and he could hear a cacophony of crickets and the unfamiliar cry of a night bird, the lowing of a cow from afar. Alien sounds to him, accustomed as he was to the city noise. Calmness and peace. But the quiet night was deceptive. There could be someone out there watching. This old house was a sieve as far as security was concerned.

He had two tasks now. Find out more about Mahoney. Find out a lot more about Randy Wells and his finances. Trace the deposits in that account. And, he remembered, they were leaving for New York. New York with Portia again, and this time was going to be entirely different. He thought about Bern at the *Star Gazer* — Bern, whose many calls Nick had totally ignored for almost a week now — thought about how angry the man was going to be when he found out after the fact that Nick had been in the city with not only Portia Wells, but her mother, too. Nothing to be done about that, though. And most likely Nick was through with the rag sheet, anyway.

A reformed man. *Right.*

He was thinking about the wasted time in the city, thinking about how that time would be better spent here in Colorado digging deeper into Mahoney Enterprises, not to mention Randy's bank account, when an idea came to him. Maybe his time back East wouldn't be completely squandered. He could always take a short side trip down to Washington and pay good old Aaron Burkhart a visit, get some answers in a face-to-face.

Yeah, he thought, why not?

He finally got up from the table, his mind settled now, padded around the house making sure the doors and windows were locked. Not that any two-bit burglar couldn't open any one of them with a penknife or credit card.

Then he turned the light off and made his way up the stairs, trying not to let the boards creak. He passed Portia's closed door, and he halted for a moment; then he shook himself mentally and moved on down the shadowed hall.

NINETEEN

She awoke just before 5 a.m. mentally ticking off everything she needed to accomplish before flying to New York. And how long would she be gone? Two days, three? Plus she needed to make a reservation at the Peninsula Hotel again. Corporate or AAA discount, something. She could stay out in New Rochelle with her mother and Anna, but two days there was more than she could handle. Maybe her mother would pay for the room?

Todd was taken care of. Lynette was going to keep an eye on him. And Juan's wife Maria was coming to clean the house. She could also watch over Todd.

Bills? Were there any that couldn't wait till, say, Tuesday?

She was still clicking off her mental list when her bedside phone rang. Probably a hang-up again. It must be. For most people five in the morning was the middle of the night. Could the caller possibly be a reporter? Since the fire, she'd had several requests for interviews, all of which she'd put off. But, really, no reporter would phone at this hour.

Then again, it could be an emergency, her mother, someone. She answered. But it was Randy, and he needed her up in the heifers' field. Now. "There's a dead calf in the water tank," he said. "And it isn't an accident, I can tell you *that*."

She used the bathroom and tugged on jeans and a T-shirt, didn't even brush her teeth or comb her hair. Her pulse was pounding in her ears. Another act of sabotage. Another warning: leave Mahoney alone.

Nick was already up and dressed and in the kitchen having coffee. There was no time to think how nice it was to have someone in her house, someone with whom to share a pot of coffee before the sun even streaked across the prairies.

"The phone call?" he said, his brow creasing the instant he saw her.

She took a breath and nodded. "Dead calf in the water. Randy's up at the tank waiting."

"I'll drive," he said, and she didn't even argue when he snatched up the truck keys from the counter. Then he paused. "Todd?"

"He'll sleep till at least eight." She held up her cell phone. "I'll call him if we're not back."

Randy was furious. In the half-light of dawn, he was already pacing the ground around the carcass, which he'd dragged from the water tank.

"You call Whitefeather?" Nick said, standing over the animal.

"Matter of fact, I did."

"Huh. Guess it didn't occur to you to leave everything as it was?"

"What?"

"This is a crime scene. Ground's muddy from the water tank. You'd have to think there were footprints, tire tracks."

Randy stopped and looked around, circling in his spot. He took off his hat and mopped his brow with a shirtsleeve. "I never thought, I mean, I just reacted. I mean, it wasn't even light yet, and I stopped to check the tank for the week. . . . Cab'll never be able to figure out all these tracks now, will he? Oh, Jesus."

Portia gave Nick a look. "It's okay, Randy, I would have done the same. Now what do we do about the water? I wonder if it's —"

"Damn body must have been in the water for days," Randy said. "We've got to drain the tank and clean it out. What a mess." Then he looked at her. "Portia, I'm not trying to be a hard-ass here, but *goddamn*, woman, you gotta reconsider this NPS business. We lost the barn, and now this."

She was nodding, biting her lower lip, trying not to glance at the poor animal in the quickening light, when Cab drove up in his official Chevy Blazer. He checked over the scene, then stood staring at the dead calf, hands on his hips. "I don't suppose anyone heard a vehicle last couple of nights?"

Portia and Randy shook their heads.

Nick said, "Would anyone hear a truck coming up here? I mean, is there another access road to this field that doesn't lead past the houses?"

"There's a dirt track up that way," Randy said, pointing. "It's on BLM land, but we got a gate leading to it over that rise there."

"This for sure one of your calves?" Cab asked.

Portia answered. "You can make out our brand." She indicated the animal, then looked away.

"And it was grazing in this field?" asked Cab.

"Yeah," Randy said, "we were gonna move the stock next week."

Even before Cab could tell them there wasn't much he could glean from the crime scene now, Portia knew whoever had done this was going to get away with it. Like the barn and phone calls. Like Gary's murder. Nick could try to protect her. He could protect Todd and the house, but he couldn't be everywhere at once.

"Oh, God," she whispered, shaking her head.

Cab asked her a few questions, while Nick took Randy aside and spoke to him. She wondered about that, wondered if there wasn't something she needed to hear. But Cab was taking notes, asking her stupid questions that weren't going to help at all. Then he said, "If it was me, Portia, I'd stick to ranching. Someone is not real happy about you and the NPS."

"So *I'm* to blame again." She felt her stomach sink. Did everyone want her to quit?

"No one is assigning blame here. But it could take a long time before we find out who's sabotaging the ranch. And I gotta tell you, we may never know. It's not like someone knocking over a liquor store with surveillance cameras recording everything."

"No fooling." She sighed. Then, "Sorry, Cab. I'm just so frustrated. It's been, what? A week since I announced my decision about the NPS? And look what I've gotten for it. What *we've* gotten."

She stood there, still curious as to what Nick and Randy were discussing, and she remembered all her high-and-mighty intentions of setting the media on Patrick Mahoney, hoping to summon up interest in Gary's untimely death, hoping to bring Mahoney to his knees and make him pay. What a laugh. She was terrified to give another interview. Look what had happened when she'd given the last one. Their barn had been torched. Mahoney had won the battle. Soon he'd win the war.

"You men help me wrap this here carcass

in my tarp, and I'll haul it to the vet, get him to run some tests, see what killed the animal," Cab was saying.

"Then I got to pay to have a dead animal examined? Hell I will," Randy said hotly.

"Sheriff has to ascertain how the animal died," Nick put in.

Randy grumbled under his breath. "You can see it was shot, for chrissakes," he said to Cab.

"Well," Cab said, "might be a bullet in it, might not. If there is, we got to have it in case we can ever make a match."

Randy muttered some choice words.

On the ride back to the house, she said to Nick, "What were you and Randy talking about?"

"When?" he said.

"Don't play games."

"Okay. Okay." He let out a breath. "I was asking him about this bank account."

"What?"

"The faxes I got? Some of them were bank records."

"You told me. Mahoney Enterprises —"

"And the Wellspring Ranch," he said, keeping his eyes on her face.

"*Our* bank accounts?"

"Knew you'd be pissed."

"You blame me?"

"Nope, not a bit."

She went into the kitchen to clean up, but

she was still seething. The nerve of him, sticking his nose into her bank accounts. Was that legal, for God's sake? She mopped the floor and watered the flowerpots on the porch and put a load of laundry in, so she'd have something to wear in New York, and then she returned to the office, where Nick was going over the faxes again.

She stood in the doorway, folded her arms, and said, "All right. I guess I understand why you accessed our records. I don't like it, but what's done is done. Now, will you tell me what you were talking to Randy about?"

He looked up and regarded her for so long she squirmed. Then he said, "You aware of a bank account in Colorado Springs in Randy's name?"

"An account in Colorado Springs?"

He showed her the records. She wasn't about to admit she was miffed at Lynette for not letting on that they had over $60,000 lying around collecting interest down in Colorado Springs. She did say, "Well, I'm not shocked or anything. Lynette has a lot of family here, and I'm sure the money comes from them. Grandparents or something."

"Um," he said. "That's about what Randy told me."

"You don't believe him?"

"Right now, I don't know what to believe," he said. "But one thing's for sure, I need to see Aaron Burkhart."

"Aaron? But — ?"

He held up a hand. "Don't go getting all defensive again. I'm just talking about catching a shuttle flight down to Washington while we're in New York, asking him a couple questions."

"I still don't —"

"Portia, this is routine. Burkhart's well aware of the trouble you're having. Hell, he hired the security men, didn't he?"

"Yes."

"So he'll be happy to help get to the bottom of this, right?"

"Well . . ."

"Trust me, he'll be okay with it."

"Trust you, huh?"

"Yeah."

She was about to tell him she didn't trust herself anymore, much less him, when Todd interrupted them. "I just talked to Raymond, and he's buying me a ticket to go to New York with you guys," he said.

"Ah, Raymond?" Nick looked confused.

"My stepdad. I told him I was going to have to spend a week with them in Denver, and he came up with the offer so quick it was pathetic."

Portia was too shocked to speak. Finally, she swallowed and said, "Todd . . . You called Raymond and weaseled a ticket out of him and didn't even *ask* me?"

"Uh-huh. And I'm going. Don't tell me

I'm not going, because I *am* going."

She shook her head in disbelief. No way could she afford two rooms. And no way could she stick Judith and Anna with a teenager on his first trip to the big city. *No way.*

"Look, Todd," she said. "This just isn't the right time. You have to understand that this trip isn't for pleasure, it's —"

But Nick cut her off. "I got an idea."

"Now, Nick," she began, "I really think —"

"What if Todd stays with me? I got a spare room."

"*You're* going to Washington, remember? To see Aaron? And I'm going to be so busy with Mother, I can't possibly —"

Nick snapped his fingers and then reached for his cell phone. "Gil," he said.

"Gil?" Todd said.

"My partner. He's got three kids. What's one more? And Dougie is near your age. Gil owes me."

"This is so awesome," Todd said, grinning. Then Nick was on the phone with his partner Gil, and everything was set — before she could put a stop to it. Though how she'd planned to do that, she had no idea.

"A conspiracy," she groaned, leaving the room, her head reeling. First it was Nick moving into her house, into her life, and then her mother calling and desperately needing her, while out here someone was trying to scare her out of her wits, and now Todd was

361

going to New York? She felt as if she'd fallen down the rabbit hole.

Somehow everything got done before they took off for the airport on Saturday morning in Nick's rental car. And somehow she'd gotten herself and Todd packed and spent an hour with Lynette. Though she hadn't had the nerve to ask about the bank account.

Randy had even sat down with her for a few minutes and gone over the papers for the loan renewal, which Tyler Silverman at the Castle Rock bank had sent down for them to review. At the quarter percent interest rate reduction Portia had held out for. And somehow she had gotten to sleep on Friday night with Nick still down the hall in the spare bedroom. Only a few feet away.

She sat on the plane in the aisle seat while Nick and Todd talked about New York, and she wondered how she could keep juggling so many disparate facets of her life before she came apart, a thousand pieces of her flying every which way. And no one could put her back together again.

And there was still Patrick Mahoney to deal with. When she got home from New York, nothing was going to have changed. Maybe even now he was planning his next nasty trick.

She had a thought then. She even nudged Nick's arm, getting his attention. "Maybe on that show, *After Dark*, I'll announce to the whole nation what Mahoney's been up to and ask for an all-out investigation."

"Huh. Bad idea," Nick said. Then he half-turned toward her and lowered his voice, his hand coming to rest on her knee. "I'm gonna get your bad guy for you, Portia. Takes the rest of my life, I'll get the jerk, whoever it is."

"You sound awfully sure of yourself."

"I am."

"I wish I could be as certain," she breathed.

"Let me do the worrying," he said. "I'll take care of it, all of it. Okay?"

"Okay," she said, wanting desperately to believe him, wishing, in the secret recesses of her mind, that he'd said, "I'll take care of you."

They landed at Newark right on time, and Gil was waiting in front of arrivals to pick them up. He'd even brought his son Doug along. Portia watched the initial exchange of greetings. How would Todd react to his first African-American friend? But the boys didn't seem to notice skin color. Doug said, "Hey, welcome to the Big Apple, man." And Todd shook his hand. "This is like so cool," he said. "I mean, Denver is major boring."

Nick introduced Portia to Gil, and then he asked Doug, "You been behaving, kiddo?"

"Sure, man," Doug said.

Then Gil put a big hand on both boys'

shoulders and pulled them close. "One thing, kids, and I'm only going to tell you guys this once, okay? Either of you give me any trouble, and you'll both wish you were dead. You got that?"

Nick grinned.

Doug looked past his father's chest at Todd and said, "He's packing a gun, bro."

Portia rolled her eyes, took a deep breath, and wondered just how she'd gotten here.

TWENTY

The pace of life always seemed to speed up the minute she arrived in New York. Though it was a weekend, everyone still drove too fast, honked their horns too often, darted across streets too quickly despite the color of the traffic lights. The July heat didn't appear to slow anyone up, either.

Gil drove them to the Peninsula Hotel, where Portia got checked into her room, AAA discount. Then it was up to Nick's neighborhood, where his car was parked. Todd was stunned into a breathless silence, his neck craned from the backseat to view all the tall buildings, Doug babbling away with a running commentary on *his* city, some of his facts so far off base it was ludicrous. No one corrected him. The boys were having too good a time.

When Gil dropped them at Nick's car, she thanked him profusely for taking Todd under his wing.

"No prob," Gil said. "I actually got vacation right now."

"You do?" Nick said. "Didn't tell me about it."

"Hey, you were off in the Wild West having a gay old time. I figured you'd worry about who was covering our beat."

"So, who *is* covering?"

"Freddo and what's his face."

Nick leaned down to Gil's window. "Ah, no, man," he said.

She and Nick took off for New Rochelle, while Gil and the boys headed home to Yonkers. After that, according to Doug, the whole family was going to show Todd Ground Zero and then have dinner in Chinatown.

No such sightseeing for Portia, though. She heard Anna approaching the front door to let them in, and she steeled herself. This was a really bad idea, she thought, a sense of panic seizing her — a late-night television interview with her mother? Absolutely crazy. And what was Nick going to think of *the* Judith Carr? *Oh God.*

As if reading her mind, he touched her elbow and said, "It'll be okay."

Anna pulled open the door, and Portia whispered, "Easy for you to say."

Somehow Nick's impression of the house and Anna and especially her mother mattered far too much. Why should she care what he thought? He already knew how eccentric Judith was.

Judith was sitting on a velvet settee in the dimly lit room with its dark, heavy furniture, having afternoon tea. She didn't rise to greet them; the matriarch rarely rose to greet anyone. People came to her. Portia leaned down, exchanged air kisses on both cheeks with her mother, then straightened to make the introductions.

"So you're *that* policeman," Judith said, surprising Portia for a moment. Of course she had told her mother how the press had gotten onto her whereabouts, and Judith might have been a bit *off,* but she wasn't stupid.

"Sit down next to me, Mr. Sinestra. Or is it Detective Sinestra?" Judith patted the red-and-gold velvet seat next to her.

"Nick. Call me Nick," he said, sitting as instructed. Portia and Anna exchanged glances.

"I should be furious with you, Nick," Judith said. Then, "Don't just stand there, Anna, my goodness, woman, Portia and Detective — that is, Nick would like tea."

"I'll get it, Mother," Portia said, appalled. Anna was a friend and companion, not the parlor maid. But Anna waved Portia off and poured the tea. Anna would set Judith straight in private.

"I'm a wreck about this television appearance tomorrow night," Judith said abruptly. "I haven't been onstage for years. And this is all your fault, young man."

"Um," Nick said, studiously dropping sugar

cubes into his tea.

"Nick is going to drive us there, Mother," Portia tried. "And it will be over before you know it."

"But what ever will I wear?"

Not black on black lace with your big black hat and big black sunglasses, Portia thought. *Oh, God, please not that getup.*

"I have the outfit all picked out," Anna said.

"Well, what if I don't approve?" Judith sat up.

"You'll approve," Anna said.

Nick must have been ready to either burst out laughing or run for cover. Portia tried without success to read his expression. He was still methodically stirring sugar into the lukewarm tea.

Judith, diminutive, her features faded and creased like old walnuts, was considering Anna's decision about her attire, when she suddenly swiveled toward Nick again. "Are you seeing my daughter? Are you her lover?" she asked. "Is that why you're here, why you're escorting us to the studio?"

"Judith," Anna admonished.

"Mother," Portia choked.

"Well," Nick said, utterly caught off guard, "I . . . ah, guess you'd say we're friends."

"Friends can be lovers," Judith stated. "You haven't answered my question. I think I'm entitled to know. Portia is my daughter, after all, my only child."

Child? "Mother, please," Portia said, so embarrassed she could barely breathe.

"Well," Nick said again. He cast Portia a quick look, and something in his expression made her heart pound. *Lovers.* But he turned back to Judith and was saying, "Nothing like that. We're just friends."

Anna tried to save the situation. "So, what time should we be ready tomorrow? The studio called and wants us there at eight. Makeup, all that." Anna was the old pro at backstage preparations, and of course she was going along. She would never allow Judith to make a public appearance without her in the wings.

"Guess I'll pick you up at quarter of seven then," Nick said. "Okay?"

"Will that be enough time?" Judith looked to Anna for guidance.

"He can always use his siren," Anna said.

Then Judith, satisfied everything was properly planned out, leveled her attention on Portia. "You're staying for dinner, of course."

Mercifully, Nick saved the moment. "Gosh, Judith," he said. "We got to stop by my folks' place in . . ." He checked his watch. ". . . an hour. Then I'm dropping Portia at her hotel."

"Just where is your family from?" Judith wanted to know.

"The Bronx."

369

"A nice neighborhood?"

"Sure, I guess so." He shrugged.

"Well, then, I suppose that's all right."

The sultry summer heat outside never felt so heavenly to Portia. Nick held the passenger door for her, and she slid into the scorching interior and was filled with relief, as if she'd just been set free from prison.

He got in on the driver's side, turned on the engine, and twisted the air conditioner knob up to high.

"Now you know why I always get a hotel room," she said, fanning her face with an old newspaper from the backseat. "I can't *believe* I agreed to come here and do this. With everything else that's going on in my life, this is just too . . . too stressful."

"You'll get through."

"You sound awfully sure of that."

He started to turn the car around in the shaded drive. His arm still resting on the back of her seat, his head close to hers as he backed the car up, he said, "I have yet to see anything you *can't* handle." And there it was again, that fluttering in her belly and the thumping of her heart against her rib cage. If he touched her, even an inadvertent brush of his hand on her shoulder, she would lean into him and kiss him.

"So where to?" he was asking. "Back to the city?"

"Oh, I thought we were stopping by your

family's place. It's on the way."

"What?" He stomped on the brakes. "That was just an excuse."

"Quid pro quo. You got to see the awful truth about my family, about my mother, now I want to meet your parents. Will they be home?"

"Hey, look, I don't think —"

"Will they be home?" she repeated. "Maybe we should use the cell phone to call first?"

"Hey, now, I never said —"

"What's the number? I'll dial while you drive, and you can pull over and talk to them."

"You really gonna make me do this?"

"Absolutely. The phone number?" she said.

She tried not to examine her true motives for this rather desperate impulse to meet his family, to see where, exactly, he came from. But she knew, not quite on a conscious level yet, she just knew this visit would answer her questions as to who he really was and what made him tick. She listened while he spoke to his mother, and she tried to imagine the woman who'd borne this man. She would be a strong woman, simple and down to earth. Somehow Portia was positive of that. But his father . . . She couldn't form a mental image.

His mother was exactly as she had expected; his father turned out to be standoffish. Whereas his mother, Sophia, was genuinely hospitable, taking Portia aside to show her "Nikko's pictures from when he was a little boy" and her own much-treasured figurine collection, kept safe and dust free in a lovely old display case, Nick's father, Anthony, was quiet and aloof. He almost seemed irritated that he had to turn off the TV to socialize.

They stayed for dinner. The heat in the brick row house was oppressive, but when Sophia brought a fan into the tiny dining room, Anthony grumbled so much, Nick intervened.

"If Mom's hot, Pop, let her have a fan, okay?"

Anthony mumbled something else. Then, for all to hear, he said, "Nikko always wants something more than he has. It's never good enough for him."

Nick, who'd barely eaten a bite of the stew his mother had prepared, put his fork down and glared at his father. "What's wrong with wanting to better yourself, Pop? You always got to put me down."

"Put you down? Hell, boy, I spend half my time at the factory telling the guys my son's a cop. A detective, I tell them. He's got a college education. You call that putting you down?"

Portia looked across the table at Nick and realized he'd been stunned into silence.

Sophia had reached out and was stroking Nick's arm, as if to say, *See? He's so proud of you.*

And finally Nick spoke. "How come you never told me that before?"

Anthony shrugged. "Because it doesn't change anything. You could be chief of police, and it wouldn't be good enough."

"Oh, man," Nick sighed. "Just can't win around you, Pop."

"Who said it was a contest?" his father countered.

They were still talking, more like arguing, when Portia helped Sophia clear the table. In the kitchen, Sophia said, "I'm sorry about those two. They're always at it. Always have been. But Nikko's father really is very proud of him, brags about his son every chance he gets."

"I guess it's a father-son thing," Portia said. "Nick's the oldest?"

Sophia was rolling an old dishwasher over to the sink. "Yes, he's the oldest." She lowered her voice. "And the one I worry about most. Ever since Gwen —"

"His ex-wife?"

"Yes, well, ever since she left him —" Sophia stopped cold. "You know about Gwen?"

"Not really."

"Well . . . I better let Nikko explain."

"Um," Portia said, scraping plates, burning

with curiosity now. Then there was no steering the conversation back to Nick's former marriage, because Sophia wanted to hear all about Judith Carr.

She said, "I was just dating Tony, you know, when he took me to see your mother on Broadway. Can you imagine? *He* took *me?* It was so romantic. We rode the train down to Forty-second Street and went to dinner at the Backstage Café and went to the theater. It was when your mother was playing Ophelia. She was so beautiful."

"Well, I wasn't even a notion in her head then, but I've seen all the playbills and photos, even a film clip. She was really lovely, wasn't she?"

It was dark when they left an hour later, Nick tight-lipped, his shirt damp with perspiration. She, too, was perspiring, had been all evening.

"Damn," he said. "You know, I've only offered about a million times to buy them an air conditioner for the living room, but Pop won't hear of it. Can you believe that guy?"

"He's just set in his ways."

"Yeah. That and a lot more."

"He really is proud of you, you know. It was written all over his face."

Nick made a disgruntled noise.

"Well, he is."

"He shoulda told me that maybe twenty years ago then."

"He probably should have," she agreed. "Your mother is a sweetheart, though."

He nodded slowly. "She drive you nuts with questions about Judith?"

"Actually," she said, "I enjoyed all the questions. It made me remember better days with my mother."

"Glad to hear it."

"You're still mad I made you take me to meet them, aren't you?"

"Nah."

"Liar."

"Yeah," he said. "I'm lying."

Nick might have had a lousy time, but she certainly hadn't. Except for the heat. Still, it had been an illuminating visit; she now had a better idea of what made Nick so hard-core, why he was often sarcastic, and why he could do that vile work for the *Star Gazer.* He was ashamed of his background, angry deep inside, and willing to do just about anything to improve his station in life.

What he needed, she decided, turning to study his profile in the flickering of city lights, was some tender loving care, someone to hold him and tell him his family was okay, that they were good, strong, hard-working, honest people — tell him he was okay.

"What happened with your marriage?" she asked.

"Huh?"

"Your mother said something —"

"Ah no."

"She didn't tell me anything, I just got the impression something awful happened."

"Nothing happened. We got a divorce."

"You are such a bad liar."

"Huh," he said.

"So what happened? Did Gwen find someone else?"

"You could say that."

"Tell me."

"No."

"Just, no?"

"Uh-huh. Now change of subject. When I drop you at your hotel, I want you to go straight up to your room. Lock the door. Gil will be by first thing in the morning to pick you up, do some sightseeing with the boys."

"But I —"

"No buts, lady. I got to fly down early to D.C. and have that chat with Burkhart, and I don't want you traipsing all over Manhattan by yourself. You stick with Gil and the boys till I get back. Then I'll pick you up and we'll get your mother and Anna and do that TV gig. Okay?"

He was rounding the corner, the Peninsula Hotel ahead on the right. "Okay?" he repeated.

"Okay." She wasn't foolish. If Mahoney could get to her in Colorado, he could just as easily get to her in New York. "But are you sure you really need to question Aaron?" she said.

He stopped in front of the hotel, gave the doorman a wave through the windshield. "I'm sure," he said.

"Are you . . . I mean, do you think you're getting closer to solving this case?"

"Yeah, getting closer," he said.

There was a long moment of silence between them, and she almost spoke her heart, almost said out loud that as crazy as it seemed, she didn't want him to solve the case. Because then she'd never see him again. But she couldn't possibly tell him that.

Instead, she took a breath, opened her door, and said, "Well, good night."

He met her glance, and she could have sworn she saw a hint of regret in his eyes. "Night," he said, and she closed the car door, feeling herself sink inside as she walked up the steps and into the hotel.

TWENTY-ONE

Nick managed a standby seat on the 7:15 a.m. shuttle out of LaGuardia to Dulles International, the closest airport to Falls Church, Virginia. He even finagled a discount on the ticket after flashing his NYPD ID and saying he was on a case. After all, in theory, he *was* on a case.

No discount on the rental car. Though the manager at Alamo gave him an hourly rate as opposed to a full-day charge. He guessed he could have caught a taxi, but figuring the round trip, plus tips, a cab was going to be more expensive.

Burkhart was expecting him. While Portia had been checking in to the hotel yesterday, Nick had phoned, introduced himself, and been given directions to the man's home. It was almost ten when Nick pulled into the circular drive and killed the motor.

Nice joint. A tall, sprawling Georgian house surrounded by well-manicured lawns and gardens. Stately trees shaded the house on the south side, and on the western end of the place there looked to be a swimming pool behind that fancy stone wall.

A maid answered the door and led Nick through a marble-floored foyer to a sunny Carolina room, pleasantly air-conditioned.

She'd just brought him a cup of coffee when Aaron Burkhart showed. Nick had forgotten how tall the man was from the one time he'd seen him at the fund-raiser in New York. Tall with a full head of white hair, a handsome, angular face, and a flawless summer tan. Burkhart was obviously going to golf today, either that or he just liked pastel golf shirts and Madras slacks.

"Detective Sinestra," Burkhart said, shaking Nick's hand. He had a strong, solid hand-shake. "Sit back down and drink your coffee. Did Franny offer you rolls or toast?"

Nick sat and nodded. "Coffee's fine; I ate on the plane." He hadn't, but he didn't want to waste time discussing breakfast.

Burkhart took the chair across from him, and Franny appeared with a glass of a thick, brownish drink. "My special concoction of wheat germ, flaxseed oil," Burkhart explained. "Would you care to try some?"

"Thanks, I'll pass." Nick smiled.

"So, Detective," Burkhart began, "you're a friend of Portia's, helping with some problems she's been having in Colorado?"

"That's about it. I was on her security in New York back in late June, and I ran into her again in Colorado. I was on vacation.

Still am, so I offered to look into this threat she'd gotten. Then, of course, her barn was burned down."

"Dreadful, dreadful. And I understand you let the security outfit go."

"Uh-huh."

Burkhart shook his head in disgust. "I should have looked further into the company before I hired them. I phoned a friend who knows a lot more about that sort of business, and he gave me their name. He assured me they were tops. Apparently, he was quite mistaken."

"Uh-huh."

"Well, I'm in your debt for dismissing them."

"My pleasure," Nick said.

"So, then, how is Portia? You said she's in the city, doing *After Dark* with her mother tonight?"

"That's right. A command performance."

"Judith Carr," Burkhart reflected. "My God, she was stunning. But then, so is Portia."

"Yeah," Nick agreed.

"You know her father, Richard? Former ambassador to the UN?"

"Never had the pleasure."

"Well, you haven't missed much. He's got a young family down on Hilton Head Island, I believe it is, and Portia was, for the most part, set aside."

"Interesting," Nick said.

"Now then, detective, tell me what I can do to help Portia out. I feel partially responsible for the trouble she's having. If I hadn't offered her the NPS position, I don't think any of this would be happening."

Nick held his gaze. "Tell me," he said. "Were you serious about the offer, or was it just a gesture?"

"Oh, quite serious. But after I met with Portia in Denver and learned she still had Todd living with her, I wondered if she weren't biting off more than she should. And, of course, running the ranch."

"Did she tell you about her suspicions concerning this Patrick Mahoney?"

"She did."

"And?"

Burkhart took a drink of his health concoction. He swallowed, then said, "And I had no idea what to think. We were all of the belief Gary was killed in an accident."

"You still believe that?"

"You want my honest opinion?"

"Absolutely."

"Yes. I'm afraid Portia is searching for meaning in the senseless, *meaningless* death of her husband."

"Um," Nick said, taking a long sip of his coffee. He lifted his eyes to Burkhart. "And how would you explain the sabotage, the threat she got? You must have an opinion on that, too."

"I really can't explain it. Not everyone is enamored of the NPS, and there are certainly a number of radical, progrowth groups out there, but to burn down her barn?" He shook his head. "That's really taking your beliefs a little too far, especially in a drought year, when the whole damn ranch could have been lost."

"How about Mahoney? Portia's positive he's behind all her problems, not to mention her husband's death."

"Frankly, Detective, I can't see it. If you knew the background of Gary's relationship with Mahoney, you might agree with me."

"So, let's hear it."

"Understand," Burkhart said, "that Gary was a highly intelligent man, and very determined, but he was a touch naive when it came to the politicking required to run the NPS. He was learning, God rest his soul, but we can all falter at first, especially when we're learning the ropes.

"Gary met Patrick Mahoney, oh, I'd say around two years ago, when Mahoney began to negotiate with a rancher —"

"Nash. Bill Nash."

"That's correct, Nash. At any rate, Gary and Mahoney were at odds from day one. Rather than work with the man through negotiations, Gary jumped to the conclusion that the only course of action was for the

NPS to purchase the land itself and halt the development entirely."

"Isn't that what the NPS does?"

"Not necessarily. We purchase only as a last resort, when a development is so detrimental to the environment there's no other course of action."

"The Panorama Ranch isn't detrimental then? That what you're saying?"

Burkhart laughed gently. "Patrick Mahoney has planned and developed many projects, and he knows the process as well as any developer in the country. He knows how to negotiate, when and where to concede a point, when it's time to press forward."

"On stuff like wetland protection zones, like that?"

"Sure, that's a part of the negotiation process, the give and take. You can't always put a stop to progress and development. Nor should you. But you can demand certain concessions to preserve the environment."

"Uh-huh. And Gary demanded too much?"

"Yes, at first, but Mahoney is an old hand, and pretty damn savvy when it comes to making things work. At any rate, he made a donation to the NPS, a rather large donation."

A hundred grand, Nick thought, wondering at Burkhart's game. *Why admit it?*

"Gary wasn't certain how to handle the donation," Burkhart was saying, "more to the point, how to handle the implications of it."

"It could have been seen as a bribe or payoff," Nick put in.

"Exactly. The reality is that lots of developers donate large sums of money to environmental groups such as the NPS."

"But doesn't that mean the environmental group has to grant concessions? You can't bite the hand that feeds you."

"Donations smooth the path to negotiations."

Spoken like a politician, Nick mused. "So how *did* Gary handle the money?"

"He handled it with inexperience. He was so worried the donation would be misconstrued that he filed an affidavit with the court with a motion for a temporary restraining order against the development. Most, *most* unfortunate. If I would have known —"

"You didn't know?"

"Detective, I founded the NPS but, for all practical purposes, I'm retired. I sit on the board, but I'm not active in the day-to-day decisions."

"And you golf."

Burkhart smiled. "Yes. In about an hour from now, in fact."

"Okay," Nick said. "What you told me so far sounds like Mahoney would have been damn glad to see Gary Wells disappear — for good."

"Oh, I agree, absolutely. And Mahoney flew to Washington and sat right where you're sitting and let me have all four barrels."

"But you're retired." Nick smiled.

"In that instance, I felt I should step in and smooth the ruffled feathers. It was an excellent learning process for Gary, too."

"So you smoothed Mahoney's feathers?"

"Yes, yes. I explained to him Gary had only panicked at the size of the donation and the implications, and that we would all come to an agreement about specific environmental concerns at the proposed project."

"And the affidavit Gary filed?"

"I assured Mahoney that it would be dropped within the week. He left for Colorado that same evening in a much better mood."

"And Gary Wells?"

"I never got to speak to Gary." Burkhart set his glass down and sat back in the chair, clasped his hands together, and solemnly met Nick's gaze. "Mahoney was here on a Wednesday. Gary died that Saturday night."

"Um," Nick said.

"So you see why it's so difficult for me to believe Portia? There was no reason for Mahoney to harm Gary. No reason whatsoever."

"And you still think the threat she got and her barn being burned, couple other incidents at the ranch, are being done by some right-wing nutcase group?"

He nodded. "Or left-wing, Detective. Portia is also a rancher."

"You're aware these men who stopped her at the feed store used Mahoney's name? Said leave Mahoney alone? How do you explain that?"

"I thought about it, of course. But I honestly believe she was so distraught when those men approached her, she could have heard just about anything. You need to understand, Detective, on some level, conscious or unconscious, Portia *wants* to assign blame for Gary's death. And I believe she wanted to hear the name Mahoney." He leaned forward. "And, Detective, Nick, you also need to know how dearly I love her. Nancy and I consider Portia family. But this . . . her accusations . . . I simply can't go along with it. I'm sorry. But you wanted my opinion; now you've got it."

"Huh," Nick said. "You think she should give up the NPS presidency? Concentrate on the ranch?"

"If Portia were sitting here, I'd tell her to follow her heart. I'd also have to tell her that Todd's well-being and certainly hers are far more important than the position with the NPS. If giving it up would help end the sabotage, then, yes, I'd have to urge her to reconsider."

"Okay," Nick said. He placed his hands on his knees, pushed himself up, and shook Burkhart's hand again. "Thanks for your time."

"I hope I've been of help."

"Oh, you have," Nick said.

He had the drive back to Dulles International and then the shuttle flight to New York to sort out his thoughts. He believed one thing: Aaron Burkhart was full of shit. He bought his story up to the point where Mahoney came for the tête-à-tête at Burkhart's. But as for Mahoney leaving pacified, not a chance. You put two powerful men like Burkhart and Mahoney in the same room and at odds, and what you got was an explosion. The more plausible scenario was Mahoney flying here, mad as hell, swearing to bust Burkhart and the NPS for taking the donation, probably by informing the media, who'd call it bribe money, graft, whatever. Mahoney wouldn't give a damn about the publicity. Hell, he was already accused of shenanigans by the state attorney general of Colorado and hadn't missed a beat, as far as Nick could see. Some media bullshit? Water off a duck's back.

But Burkhart. Mr. East Coast Bigshot. To have the press accuse the NPS of accepting bribe money would have been devastating. Would have destroyed Burkhart's reputation along with his credibility.

Nick stared out the plane's window at the hazy, hot Maryland sky, and he figured he'd gotten the scene at Burkhart's pretty much right: Mahoney spitting mad, threatening — Burkhart sweating bullets.

So had Mahoney flown back to Colorado and hired thugs to do Wells, or had Burkhart seen only one way out for himself and his precious NPS: get rid of the loose cannon, Gary Wells?

Thing was, if Nick's thinking was on target, one of them had done Wells. But which one? And how the hell to prove it?

The plane crossed the southeastern corner of Pennsylvania and flew over the Delaware River into New Jersey. Nick was forgetting another fly in this gummy ointment: the brother. The not-so-bright, jealous brother who had $60,000 sitting in a Colorado Springs bank. Where had the money really come from? Lynette's family? Or could either Mahoney or Burkhart have approached Randy, implored him to talk sense into his brother, maybe even paid him for his services? Paid him, ultimately, to kill his own flesh and blood? Truth was, almost all murder was committed by a family member. And Randy would have counted on inheriting the entire ranch. Maybe he still thought he could inherit — if Portia was out of the picture.

The plane was on approach to LaGuardia,

and Nick was still mulling over the Randy-as-suspect hypothesis. The scenario would explain Portia's version of Randy's attitude toward her. And, of course, she'd vowed to get to the bottom of the murder of her husband. If Randy was the killer, then he had to be worried. So worried he might have paid two goons to get in her face at the co-op in an attempt to scare her enough so she'd back off with her accusations, shut her mouth. Randy could have told the thugs to use Mahoney's name — really put the fear of God in her. But she hadn't backed down, and the warnings had continued.

Nick's thoughts skidded to a halt. He was pushing the facts and suppositions to the limit simply because Randy and Lynette had a bank account of their own. And Randy as the killer seemed pretty farfetched in the light of the sabotage at the ranch. Why would Randy cut off his nose to spite his face? There had to have been other tactics he could have devised to frighten Portia, get her to drop her search for Gary's murderer.

He deplaned with a major headache pounding against his skull. He had three men with enough motive to kill. But the murder was almost a year old now, and the odds of solving it diminished with each passing day. Not that he'd tell Portia *that* grim detail.

After he picked up his car in the day parking at the airport, he tried her cell phone, but the message service was active. Either her phone was switched off, or she wasn't taking calls.

She'd be back from touring with Gil and the kids, he figured, so he drove to her hotel. After talking to Burkhart he had a few questions only she could answer. Then he needed to run by the precinct, see if he could coerce Rick Jacobson into doing him one last favor.

Yeah, Nick thought, as he double-parked in front of the Peninsula Hotel, *this is one tough case to solve.* But he wasn't dead in the water quite yet.

Portia was in her room. Obviously she'd just showered and changed into fresh clothes, though most likely not what she'd wear to the TV interview tonight.

"I tried your cell phone," he said at her door.

"I was in the shower. Sorry, come in, I want to hear how your talk with Aaron went."

She was dressed in a sleeveless white top with a pointed collar, summer-weight denim jeans, and high-heeled black sandals. Really high-heeled. She was as tall as Nick in them. She'd blown her hair dry, and it hung in a silken curtain. She even had on makeup and perfume. Standing in the hotel room alone with her, not even able to touch her, was torture. He had the fleeting thought he'd rather have his fingernails ripped out than have to keep his hands off her.

"You and the guys have a good day?" he asked, his hands in his trouser pockets.

"We had a wonderful day. Gil's great with the boys. If my mother hadn't phoned, well, actually she had *Anna* phone at least three times, it would have been a perfect day."

"Your mother okay?"

"Oh, she's a nervous wreck, but surviving."

He didn't need to say this was his doing. They both knew it. The ultimate irony was that the TV studio was located in Rockefeller Center, right across the plaza from the *Star Gazer.*

"So, Aaron? Tell me how it went."

"Went fine," he said.

"*Nick.* Stop shutting me out. What did you learn?"

He studied her for a moment, then walked to the window, holding aside the drape and gazing down at the street. "I'll fill you in, okay, but first answer something for me."

"Sure. If I can."

Damn, she'd stepped close to him. He moved aside. "The temporary restraining order Gary was trying to get against the Panorama Ranch, did he ever mention dropping it? Like right before he died?"

She rapped a knuckle against her teeth, thinking. "I don't believe so."

"Okay. Now think hard, did Aaron phone Gary the week he died? Or maybe Gary mentioned phoning Aaron?"

"I . . . You know, Aaron might have talked to him."

"That week?"

"Oh, boy, I'm not sure. You see, they talked a lot, and I can't be certain they did the week before Gary died. I think they did, but . . ." She shrugged. "Is it terribly important, I mean, if they talked?"

"Could be."

"Tell me why."

"Has to do with the injunction. Burkhart says he had a visit from Mahoney the Wednesday before Gary died. He assured Mahoney he'd speak to Gary and get him to drop the motion he'd filed. They were going to negotiate as opposed to bringing in the lawyers, I guess. But Burkhart claims he never got a chance to speak to Gary."

"Oh," she said, "*oh,* I see where you're going with this. You think Gary was killed simply because Aaron hadn't gotten hold of him? My God."

"Maybe," he said. He wasn't about to tell her that he was considering her pal Burkhart as a suspect, a lying bastard who'd been facing disgrace and ruin because his protégé wouldn't back down on his stance against the Panorama Ranch development. Nor was Nick going to let on about his newest hypothesis — that maybe her brother-in-law had seen an opportunity to get rid of his nemesis and had snatched it. All of which brought Nick around to remembering he wanted to run down to the Village and talk to Jacobson about digging deeper into the deposits in Randy's bank account.

Nick checked his watch. "Look," he said, "I got to go by the precinct before we take off for New Rochelle to pick up your mother. It's four o'clock now. I'll be back here to get you at, say —"

"I'll go with you right now," she said. "I'll throw my outfit in a bag, and I'll just change at the studio."

"You really want to go to the precinct?"

"Yes, I want to go. I want to see where you work. I'm allowed, aren't I?"

"Well, sure, I guess," he said, absolutely bewildered. Why on earth should she care about where he worked?

The sad petunias in front of the 6th Precinct were just as wilted and spindly as ever when Nick opened the door for her.

"Someone should feed and water those poor flowers," Portia said.

"Don't say anything to the sergeant inside, okay? He really tries."

The squad room upstairs was so hot and humid you could barely breathe, and Nick found himself apologizing. He found himself apologizing for the whole building, in fact.

"I think it's great," she whispered, following him through the maze of desks, "it's just like in the movies."

"Huh," he said.

He had to introduce her to all the guys, every last one of them. They acted as if they'd never seen a woman before, especially a beautiful woman. But Portia took the attention in stride and graciously shook hands and smiled and laughed and brushed aside the jokes aimed at Nick.

The worst was Ramsey. Good old Weston Ramsey. While Nick took Rick Jacobson aside and made his request, Wes came on to Portia with a vengeance. Of course Wes recognized her. He would, Nick thought, watching him, his jaw locked, while he spoke to Rick. He almost wished Portia would notice the fading cut on Wes's lip and ask about it. Yeah.

"How long you think it'll take to get the deposit records on this account?" Nick asked Rick.

"If I'm lucky, a few days."

"That long?"

"Hey, I know the whole world thinks we can go into their private records at will now, but it doesn't quite work like that. I'll get the records, but give me a little time, okay?"

Nick was still glaring at Wes, who'd managed to get Portia away from the crowd and was leaning close to her, his demeanor enough to make Nick want to puke.

"Okay?" Rick repeated, noting Nick's preoccupation.

"Ah, yeah, okay. And thanks, buddy. I really owe you now."

"Don't mention it." Rick nudged his arm. "She's really pretty, Nick. You two an item? Is that what you've been doing in Colorado?"

An item. He only wished. "Nah," he said. "Just helping the lady out with a problem."

"Well, if you need more help . . ."

"I'll let you know."

Much to Nick's amazement, not only was Wes chatting Portia up, but he was in the process of asking her for a date when Nick strode over.

"You must have some free time while you're in New York," Wes was saying. "I'd love to show you the sights, or maybe we could have dinner?"

Portia seemed ready to reply, but then she noticed Nick. "Oh, here you are," she said, casting him a winning smile. "Weston and I were just talking." Then she turned back to Wes. "Thank you for the invitation," she said, "but Nick just takes up every free minute I get."

Then, shocking Nick into speechlessness, she folded her arm into his and tilted her head toward his shoulder. "All done?" she said, giving him another smile, her perfume making him dizzy.

"Ah, sure, all done," he answered, and his knees turned to jelly.

TWENTY-TWO

"I didn't get a chance to tell you," Portia said in the car on the way to New Rochelle, "but I spoke to Randy, and we've had more problems."

"Ah, no," Nick said.

"We had a fence cut, and some steers wandered onto the main road. One of them was hit by a pickup truck."

"Oh, geez. Anyone hurt?"

"Luckily, the driver was okay, but Randy is really done in by it all. He begged me to quit the NPS and, how did he put it? Oh, right, he wants me to drop my vendetta against Patrick Mahoney."

"Huh," Nick said.

"He even . . . Maybe I shouldn't tell you this," she said. Then, "Oh, what the heck, he even cried on the phone. Nick, he was *sobbing*. I don't know what to do. Do you think . . . should I give up?"

He frowned. "You fight, is what you do. Fuck giving up."

She let out a sigh. "Is that a French word?"

"Nah. Pure American. Learned it on the streets." He gave her a sidelong glance at a red light. Then he cleared his throat. "What you did back at the precinct, you know, in front of the guys? Well, just wanted to thank you. You know?" *Shut up, Sinestra,* he thought, and thank God the light turned green.

By the time he and Portia picked up Judith and Anna, got back to Rockefeller Center and parked, it was almost eight. Anna and Portia were fine with being a few minutes behind schedule, but Judith seemed on the brink of a panic attack.

"I can't possibly be dressed and through makeup by eleven," she breathed, a hand on her breast.

"Mother," Portia said, "this isn't the stage. I'm sure there's more than enough time, and we'll just be bored to tears waiting."

Anna was sitting in the back with Portia, and she opened her purse and took out a pill bottle, shook one into her hand, and tapped Judith on the shoulder. "Take this."

"I will not."

"You take this or we turn around and go home and no one will ever invite you to go on the air again. Of course, no one will ever remember you again, either. Certainly not your fans."

"I don't have fans. Not any longer."

"If you say so."

"Oh, give me that darn pill then," Judith said. "I don't feel like listening to your blather for the next six months."

Nick caught the little grin on Anna's lips in his rearview mirror. Portia innocently stared out the car window.

At 11:20 p.m., Mike Graham, the host of *After Hours*, introduced Judith Carr and her daughter, the new president of the Nature Preservation Society, Portia Carr Wells.

Nick had a seat in the second row, and when the applause sign blinked, he clapped and cheered along with the rest of the studio audience.

In Nick's opinion, both mother and daughter looked stunning. Judith was wearing a beige silk suit with a ruffled white blouse peeking out of the neckline, and Portia wore a moss green matching pants and tunic top that clung and formed itself to her body in the bright lighting.

Mike Graham didn't waste a moment of airtime, launching right into what Nick considered a thinly veiled attack. "So, ladies, the last time our viewers saw you was on a cover of a tabloid. What was the headline?"

Another camera zoomed in on the ghastly, faked photos of Judith and Portia and the caption, "Mother Daughter Murderous Reunion."

Mike didn't let either of them reply; he forged right ahead. "But you must have made up, because you're sitting here together. You're not going to have a catfight or anything?"

The audience laughed appropriately, and Portia waited for a moment before saying, "Gosh, Mike, I didn't know you read the tabloids. But to answer your question, Mother and I promise to behave on your show." More laughter.

Mike laughed, too. "Well, seriously, how did you feel when you saw your photos splashed all over the newsstands and grocery store checkouts? Here Judith Carr hasn't been seen in public in what, twenty years? And then suddenly she's the big story."

Portia started to say something, but Mike had to go to a commercial break. When they were back on the air, Mike was talking again, regaling the viewers with a capsulized history of Judith's stage career. Finally Portia said something pleasant and witty, and then Mike was talking again. He finished with, "So, Judith, you must have something to say?"

Judith sat up straight, leaned forward, and met his gaze. "Young man," she said, "I haven't been able to get a word in edgewise. You certainly do like to hear yourself talk."

The audience pealed with laughter, as did Mike Graham. Portia stared at her mother and smiled, but Judith, the consummate actress, kept her icy glare riveted on Mike, milking her triumphant moment.

The interview ended a few minutes later, when the cameras swung to the next guest, a female rock star, who held a cordless microphone and began to sing, the studio band accompanying her. Nick met Judith, Portia, and Anna, who'd waited backstage, and they were shown a private exit.

"You did terrific, Judith," Nick said. "I mean, you literally stole the show."

"Of course," Judith said, matter-of-factly, "I stole shows for a living. And did it pretty darn well, didn't I, Anna?"

"You always were the best," Anna said.

Nick was ready to drive them to New Rochelle, but Judith insisted she was going in a taxi. "I won't have you driving out there and back another time today. But first we're going to Sardi's, aren't we? My gosh, I haven't been to Sardi's in ages."

"I bet no one goes to Sardi's after the theater anymore," Anna said.

"Well, *I* do," Judith stated. "Now, Nick, where did you park your car?"

Judith treated everyone to a late-night supper at the wonderful old New York gathering spot of the stars. A lot of the patrons recognized her and stopped by their table to shake her hand and tell her how lovely she looked and how nice it was to see her out and about. Judith flushed with delight. Anna shook her head. Portia looked relieved. And Nick just silently played escort to the three women.

Good to her word, Judith hired a taxi to take her and Anna back to New Rochelle. Before stepping into the cab, she put a crepe-thin, cool hand on Nick's wrist. "You're a handsome young man," she said, "and even though you pulled that rotten stunt, if you'd like to stop by the house sometime, feel free to do so." She turned to Anna. "We'd like to have him, wouldn't we, Anna?"

"Thanks," Nick said. "Maybe I'll just take you up on that."

He watched as Judith and Portia embraced and kissed the air around each other's cheeks. They'd never be warm, phoning each other every day or anything close to that, but maybe, he thought, Portia might come to the city more often now — if she didn't get herself killed over this NPS job, that was. But if someday, in the future, when and if her life was back on track, she did come to New York, maybe she'd let him see her. Or not. Maybe he was dreaming.

It was one in the morning by the time he pulled up in front of the Peninsula Hotel. They'd both had a couple glasses of champagne, and he was loose enough to say, "I'll come up, make sure you got the door locked."

"I'll be fine, honestly," she said. "I'll go

401

straight up. You've had a long enough day. My God."

"It's no problem," he said.

"Okay," she said, awfully easily.

They rode the elevator, talking about the TV interview and how well Judith had managed. Then Portia laughed and said, "My mother actually owes you for turning that awful rag sheet on to her. Who would have thought?"

He laughed, mocking himself. "Yeah, who would of thought?"

"Are you going to keep working for them?"

He shrugged. "Bern — he's the editor — anyway, Bern's so pissed at me he wouldn't hire me to follow a dog around right now."

The doors slid open on her floor, and they stepped out. "You didn't answer my question."

"I guess . . . Maybe it's too easy to get people hurt. Innocent people."

"People like me?"

He inadvertently put his hand at the small of her back, and he could have sworn he felt her tremble as they walked down the hall. "People like you, sure," he said. "And, hey, I'm still on your case, no time to track the stars for Bern, anyway."

She was carrying the bag with her jeans and shirt, fumbling now in her purse for the room key. She stopped for a moment and met his gaze. "You really are a weasel, you know."

"A weasel, huh?"

"That was what I thought when I found out what you pulled. But now . . . Let's just say you're turning out to be a somewhat likable weasel."

He smiled. Maybe it was the champagne, or more likely it was the way the soft lighting turned her hair and eyes so golden; at any rate, he reached up and touched her silk-smooth cheek with the back of his hand.

And she leaned into it.

The next thing he knew, his hands were all over her, and she'd dropped her bag of clothes, and her arms were wrapped around his neck. They sagged together into the wall, their mouths meeting in a desperate search.

Nick finally found the presence of mind to unlock the hotel door and, still clinging to each other, they made their way inside.

"Oh, my bag of clothes," she whispered against his lips, so he had to open the door and snatch up the bag. By the time he'd shut the door again and dropped the bag to the floor, she'd kicked off her shoes and was pulling her top over her head.

"Here, let me," he said, and his hands were on her everywhere.

He couldn't believe the strength of his feelings. He couldn't believe this was happening. Portia. Portia, here and now, in his arms, her firm breasts pressed to him, her silken arms around his neck, her mouth to his.

He backed her toward the bed — or was she steering him? And then she was sitting naked on the bedspread, her lovely slim fingers undoing his belt while he nearly tore the buttons off his shirt trying to get rid of it. She looked up at him and smiled, and kissed his belly, and an explosion of sensation ripped through his limbs.

"Oh, Jesus," he gasped.

When they were both unclothed, she stretched out on the bed and pulled the covers aside, and then she reached for him.

That was when he froze. "Ah, man," he said, "are you, you know, protected? I don't have anything with me."

But she laughed. "Oh, Nick," she whispered, and she held her arms out, "if I get pregnant, I'd be the happiest woman alive. I . . . I've had three miscarriages, and —" But her voice broke, and she turned her face away for a moment. "I'm sorry, it's just that I haven't been . . . with anyone since Gary. I guess I'm nervous. Are you . . . ? I mean, have you been with anyone else? Since your divorce?"

He sat on the bed next to her and ran his fingers through her hair, gently pushing it aside. "There was someone. But it's over."

"Because of . . . me?"

He smiled. "No. Because we didn't really like each other enough." He kissed her shoulder, his hand moving along her hip. He could feel the tremor of her flesh against his fingers, and he moved to stretch out against her, his mouth trailing down her arm. She was so warm and smelled of some exotic lotion that made his head swim.

She kissed the back of his neck and breathed into his ear. "What really happened with your marriage?"

"Not now," he got out.

"Nick?" She kissed him again on his neck. "Tell me."

"She, Gwen . . ." *Oh, hell,* he thought. "She left me for a woman."

"That's the big secret?"

"You don't think that's big enough?"

"It wasn't your fault."

"How do you know it wasn't me?"

"I know, Nick, I know," she said, "you're so different from . . . Gary. You're . . . I think you're the most honest man I've ever known. What happened with your marriage, it wasn't your fault." They were still close, so very close, skin to skin, but he sensed she was hesitant now. Then she said, "I need to tell you something."

"Later." He could feel every inch of her against his length. God, he wanted her so bad. "Later," he repeated, and he moved his lips to her brow, her eyelids.

"Let me say this," she whispered, "while I still have the nerve. I . . . I was never madly in love with my husband, I . . . He had other

405

women. It was my fault, Nick, if I . . ."

He pulled back from her, stared at her in the dimness. He couldn't believe his ears. "Portia," he said, his voice hoarse, "my God, you sound like a battered woman, blaming yourself because your husband beat you up. Are you crazy? Your husband ran around because it was in his nature. Had nothing to do with you, nothing. Never does. Damn, for an intelligent woman, you should know that."

"But, Nick, I . . . if I'd loved him more, if —"

"Shut up," he said tenderly, "you were *not* at fault."

"How can you *know* that?"

"Because I do. Trust me."

"God, how I want to believe you."

"Believe it," he breathed, and after a moment she sighed, almost a purring sound, and she put her hands on the sides of his head and moved him to her breasts. He was lost.

He opened one eye, found the digital clock, saw it was blinking 4:08 a.m., and he heard water running in the bathroom, what sounded like a glass being set down on the marble vanity.

She slid quietly back into bed a minute later. "You okay?" he whispered.

"I've been better. The champagne . . . I

just drank a gallon of water, and my head's pounding."

"Sorry. Maybe I should go?"

When she didn't say anything, he felt a pang in his chest. *Damn.* "I'll go," he said.

"You don't have to," she said, but there was no conviction in her voice.

He sat up, scrubbed a hand across his jaw, and swung his feet to the carpet. "I better take off. Told Gil I'd drive over early in the morning."

"Oh," she said.

He was tugging on his pants when he stopped cold and found her in the dimness. "You okay with what happened between us?" He couldn't believe he was asking.

"Of course I'm okay. I just hope you don't think I . . . do this sort of thing . . . as a habit. You know?"

He was still just standing there, his pants half on. "Hey, I know you don't. And neither do I."

"Oh, listen to us, would you?" She laughed lightly, the sound a little false. "What happened last night just happened. We're both adults."

"Right," he said.

Somehow he got his clothes on and found the door. Should he go back, kiss her? On the brow or something? But that seemed like a stupid idea. Instead, he turned the doorknob and said, "You'll need to hook the chain when I go, okay?"

"Okay," came her voice from the darkness.

"And I'll be by with Gil and the kids in a few hours."

"Okay," he heard her repeat.

"Get some sleep."

"I'll try. You, too."

He mumbled something, then pulled open the door and made an escape. He was halfway down the hall when he stopped, listening, till he heard her lock up, and then he moved on to the elevators, punching the Down button. He'd just had the most astounding night, and he felt like something the dog had dragged in. How had he let that happen between them?

The elevator came, and he stepped on, pushing the Lobby button. And he thought, more to the point, how had *she* let it happen?

TWENTY-THREE

The Denver-bound plane was taxiing onto the runway before Portia had a chance to really consider the state of affairs. The morning had been a scramble of plans and packing and phone calls, and she hadn't had a moment to herself.

What had she done?

She'd slept with Nick. My God, how had that happened? Right now he was sitting two rows behind her on the aisle, and she kept wanting to turn around to look at him. The man who'd kissed her last night, who'd whispered to her and caressed her and made exquisite love to her. The man who'd asked her this morning if she was okay with what happened between them.

Okay? She was not the least bit okay, and she was full of joy, all at the same time, a jumble of unfamiliar emotions clamoring in her head.

Todd was seated next her, and across the aisle were Gil and his son Doug.

How had *that* happened?

Todd had confided in her when they all

got to the hotel for the drive to the airport. "Dougie snuck out last night, and I had to make up an excuse this morning. I was kind of pissed."

"I bet."

"So his dad's really mad, and I figured it's just as well I'm leaving, because I think his mom and dad blame me, too."

"Oh, Todd."

"I tried to stop him." Sullen.

"It's not your fault." That must have been when the idea had come to her, and she'd taken Gil aside and told him he and Doug should come out to Colorado to stay on the ranch for a while. "To get your heads on straight."

"Cool," Todd had said.

Gil had stared at her for a minute. "You sure?"

She hadn't been at all sure about anything that morning, but she'd nodded her head. Wondering if she hadn't latched onto the idea to provide a buffer between her and Nick. Lynette would call her a coward.

There had been a flurry of phone calls, excited boys' voices, Nick gazing at her searchingly.

"It'll be good for Todd," she said, evading his look.

And now the plane was taking off, curving on a long, lazy circle and heading west, back to Denver, back to the ranch. Back to Randy

410

and Patrick Mahoney and all the problems, large and small, that she had to face.

What would she tell Lynette? And when she did confess, what reason would she give? Loneliness, fear, attraction? Of all the men to pick, Nick Sinestra was the last . . . the last sort of person . . .

But she *liked* him. More than liked. There had been something between them from the beginning — a spark, an interest. She hadn't recognized the attraction for a while, because she'd never felt that giddy sense of longing with Gary. And she'd suspected that her inability to bear children was her punishment for not loving her husband enough. A fitting punishment. And yet last night . . . last night, Nick had almost convinced her how wrong she'd been. He'd compared her anguish to the guilt a battered woman suffered. Could Nick be right? Could she have been so very wrong all these years? God, she prayed he was right. If only she had time to examine what he'd said. But right now she was too tired, too emotionally unstable. Later, though, yes, later she'd think over his words. Absolutely.

She sat there on the plane, hearing the steady drone of the engines, feeling the vibration, and she closed her eyes, and suddenly Nick's hands were on her. She smelled his scent, heard his voice. She put her hand up and unconsciously touched her cheek where

411

it was tender from whisker burn.

What *had* she done?

"Can I take Doug riding?"

Todd's voice intruded, and she opened her eyes. "Just start him off on Tansy or Noodle."

"Okay."

"Maybe you can both help Uncle Randy."

"Yeah."

Gil leaned toward her across the aisle. "I've never been on a ranch in my life. Neither has Doug."

"Well, then, it's about time."

"Ever see the movie *City Slickers*?"

"Of course. It'll be just like that, except there's no Jack Palance."

"I used to be on mounted patrol in Central Park," he said. "So I've been around horses."

"Oh good, then you can be our head wrangler."

"Wrangler," Gil said, tasting the word.

They were back at the ranch by four in the afternoon. Nick stood in the middle of the living room, his bag at his feet, while Portia showed Gil the office, where he could sleep, and Todd took Doug up to his room.

It had all happened too fast for him. A night of loving and then doubts. From sultry metropolis to hot, dry Colorado ranch.

Roll with the punches, he told himself. But the blows kept coming, and he couldn't duck every one. What he wanted was to get Portia alone, sit down, talk. But she was busy making up the daybed in the office for Gil, asking what the boys wanted for dinner.

The phone rang, and she answered, and he could see her face fall.

"Okay, Randy," she said. "Yes, I understand. Can we talk about it tomorrow? I have houseguests."

He saw her listening, her shoulders hunched. What was that prick Randy laying on her now?

He felt his fists clench, and he tried to relax them. He wasn't here to make love to Portia. He wasn't here for the rehabilitation of Doug. He was here to find out who had killed Gary Wells, who had burned the barn, who was threatening Portia. If he couldn't hold her and love her, then he'd damn well make her life as safe as he could.

The boys took off, Todd driving the Dodge pickup down the lane toward Randy's, Doug pretty impressed by Todd's ease with the heavy truck. Gil sat on the front porch, feet propped up on the railing, staring out toward the foothills, watching the truck's rooster tail of dust slowly sag to the ground.

"Holy shit, Sinestra," he said. "Home, home on the goddamn range."

"Yeah."

"How many acres have they got?"

"Oh, I think around three thousand."

413

Gil whistled. Then he cocked his head. "What's up? You're too damn quiet. And you keep *looking* at her."

"None of your friggin' business," he replied.

"Oh, so it's like that."

"Listen, Gil, I like the lady. She needs help, okay? I'm going to take care of her problems. Which is one reason you're here."

"What's the other reason?"

"Hell if I know."

Gil gave a short laugh. "So what's your next step? I take it you have a plan."

"Going into Colt."

"Colt."

"Town we drove through on the way here."

"I saw the sign. But only because I didn't blink."

"I'm going to go see the undersheriff there, guy by the name of Cab Whitefeather."

Gil was shaking his head. "Whitefeather. Don't tell me, he's Native American."

"You got it. You stay here, keep an eye on Portia and the kids. Keep your ears open, see what goes on. Feel things out."

"Man, I got to tell you, I'm out of my element."

"Crime is crime."

Driving into Colt, Nick turned over in his mind what he'd learned: Randy, Aaron Burkhart, Patrick Mahoney. Motive and means. Which one was guilty? His head

414

ached. And while he tried to concentrate, images of Portia slipped unbidden into his head. The lovely, smooth texture of her skin, her hair like spun silk in his fingers, her mouth, her voice.

Damn it all.

Cab was in his office. He stood to shake Nick's hand. "Saw the ladies on *After Dark* last night. Everyone in the whole town watched."

"They both did good," Nick said.

"They sure did. Isn't that Mike Graham an asshole?"

"He is that."

Cab sat down. "You're not here for a review of that TV show, are you."

He told Cab about his visit to Burkhart, tried to make the man come across clearly.

When he finished, Cab was staring down at his interlaced fingers. "So you suspect Burkhart?"

"Something's not right with him. Call it cop's instinct. I think Gary got in too deep, and Burkhart couldn't convince him to get out. I'm missing something, though."

"Like why in hell Burkhart would ask Portia to be president of the NPS if he really wanted a yes-man in the position?"

"Yeah."

Cab leaned forward. "The trouble with Burkhart as a suspect is that he's not a rancher. Not local. Whoever's been sabotaging the ranch has to be someone from around here."

"He could've hired someone local."

"Risky. Too many people would know."

"Yeah, that crossed my mind, too." Nick frowned, rubbed his scratchy cheek with the back of a hand. "Another thing's been bugging me. Randy Wells. Could he have hated his brother enough to off him?"

"Randy?" Cab looked up and pursed his lips. "Don't think so. Randy's kinda passive. He might contemplate a lot of stuff, might shoot off his mouth, but he don't have the guts to act on it. Randy — he's a follower."

Nick left with the same questions milling around in his head. He drove back to the ranch, planning to sit down with Gil and lay all the evidence out for him. Maybe Gil could provide an objective viewpoint.

But when he got back, he found Gil pacing the living room, cursing.

"She took off," Gil said. "When the boys got home with the truck, she took it and left. Hell, I didn't even realize it till the kids told me."

"Oh Christ," Nick said.

She knew she shouldn't have left the ranch alone. Nick would be having a fit, and she'd have to make sure he didn't blame Gil. But she had to get away, if only for grocery shopping in the Castle Rock Safeway.

416

She pushed the cart up and down the aisles, trying to concentrate on what she needed to feed a houseful of hungry males. Cereal for breakfast. Fruit for the cereal. Milk, coffee, tomato sauce and ground beef, salad. Some nice looking peaches and grapes and corn on the cob and a ten-pound bag of potatoes. Up and down the aisles, a familiar, calming routine. Trying to put Nick out of her mind. As if she could.

They'd have to talk eventually. One-on-one. Some difficult questions. Or would they slide into that special closeness again, without words?

Making love had probably been a terrible mistake, but she didn't regret it. Not a bit. One night — and it had been worth a year of guilt and mourning and loneliness.

Sugar, fresh tomatoes, two cartons of orange juice, a bag of chocolate chip cookies for the boys. Was that everything? Maybe she should buy some ice cream. But no, it would be soup by the time she got home in this heat. If they wanted ice cream, they'd have to drive into Colt later, get it at the minimart.

Nick, Nick. He must care, a little at least. He *must*. If he knew how much last night meant to her, would the intensity of her feelings scare him? A man whose wife had wounded his ego like that — he had to be pretty darn sensitive right about now.

She went through the checkout, paid for

the groceries, pushed her full cart across the blistering-hot parking lot to the truck, where she transferred the bags to the cab, because the sun was too fierce to put them in the bed of the pickup.

She turned toward the ranch, into the setting sun. A clear sapphire sky, the sun casting long shadows this evening. She drove the bumping, recalcitrant pickup, and her mind ricocheted between Nick and his promise to find out who was threatening her, onto the NPS presidency, Todd, the ranch. Maybe she should give up the idea, move back to New York with Todd, give Randy free rein with the ranch. He'd never accept her. Forget about proving Patrick Mahoney was a murderer.

What should she do? What was the *right* thing to do, not the easy thing? For Todd, for herself, for the NPS, for Gary's memory.

Everything seemed to be conspiring to draw her back to New York: her mother, her own survival. And Nick.

Oh God, she couldn't think that. One fleeting night of sex shouldn't determine the direction of her life.

She steered the truck off the interstate at the Colt exit, her mind sifting and weighing. Dinner when she got home. An easy one, burgers on the grill, corn, a salad. She'd forgotten hamburger rolls. Did she have buns in the freezer? The boys were no doubt starved

418

by now. And that ice cream . . .

The truck seemed particularly hard to handle, its big wheels tugging at her arms. Maybe the power steering was going, another expense.

Nick. She couldn't run from him. She owed him honesty, at the very least. She needed to confess that she'd lied this morning, that making love to him had been wonderful and crazy and it hadn't just happened. She'd wanted to make love to him since the instant they'd met. Yes, she had to tell him that.

Damn this truck. She'd have Hernando check the steering fluid, maybe that's all it was. There was a definite pull to the right.

Her cell phone rang in her purse. She fumbled with one hand and got it out, keeping her eyes on the road. Clicked it on, guessing who it was.

"Hello?"

"Where the hell are you?"

"On my way home."

"I've been trying you for the last hour, for chrissakes."

"I had my phone switched off. I'll be there in a few minutes," she said. "I was at the grocery store. I'm —"

The truck jerked to the right, and she dropped the phone to wrestle with the wheel. She heard Nick's voice, but she couldn't pick the handset up. Adrenaline swamped her, and she stamped on the brake as hard as she could, yanked the wheel to the left, overcorrecting, heard a muffled bang, and the truck swerved out of control, a tire off the pavement, a sickening lurch. She cried out, heard Nick yelling, his voice tinny over the phone, then the world turned over and she was flung sideways into the window and everything went black.

She awoke in foggy confusion. It was nearly dark. Lights flashed from police vehicles, an ambulance was there, its light bar flashing, too. She tried to orient herself, put a hand up, tried to come to a sitting position.

"Easy there," she heard Nick saying. How . . . ?

His face swam into her vision.

"Nick?" She could barely whisper. Her head hurt so terribly she felt herself curling inward.

"You're going to be fine. Ambulance is here."

"What . . . ? I can't remember . . ."

"Your truck rolled over, you hit your head."

"Oh . . . the truck . . ."

"Don't worry about it."

She tried to sit up again, felt a wave of nausea. Two ambulance attendants approached with a gurney.

"They're going to take you to the hospital

now, Portia," Nick was explaining.

"The hospital," she repeated. Her last memory surfaced, the wheel jerking out of her hands.

"Okay?" Nick said.

Something had been wrong with the steering, yes. The truck . . .

"Portia?"

"Wait, wait," she breathed.

"Hold on, fellas," she heard Cab Whitefeather say.

"Portia, let's get you in the ambulance," Nick urged.

"Am I bleeding?" she asked. Things were coming back to her. She saw she was on the ground on the side of the road, and Nick held her in his arms.

"No. Just a couple bruises. But you've got a concussion."

"I'm all right."

"Hell you are," Nick growled.

Cab squatted down next her. "Portia?"

"Oh, Cab, what a mess I've made of everything."

"Might not be your fault."

"What?" Nick asked quickly.

"Truck acting weird on you?" Cab asked.

"Yes, it was . . . pulling . . ."

"Looks like the front tires were slashed. You run over anything?"

She tried to shake her head, but it hurt too much. "No."

She heard Nick swear.

"I'm okay," she lied. "I want to go home."

"You're going to the hospital," Nick said.

"No. I'm all right now. It's nothing."

"Portia —"

"Please, Nick, just take me home." She struggled to sit up, felt the tender spot on her temple.

"Take her home," she heard Cab say.

Thank God; she didn't have the energy to argue anymore.

"She's a grown woman. She can decide."

"Thanks," she said to Cab.

She looked up at Nick, focused a little, and saw how worried he was. She reached for his hand and squeezed it. "I'm fine, really."

He helped her to his car, got her seated, pulled the seat belt across and fastened it with such infinite care, she almost smiled.

He went around to the driver's side and got in. Cab leaned down and said, "You take good care of her, you hear?"

"Yeah, don't worry."

"I'll get the truck towed in, and we'll take a closer look at the tires. Might even call in the CBI."

"The what?" Portia asked, still a little fuzzy.

"Colorado Bureau of Investigation. Evidence, stuff like that."

"Oh." She couldn't believe it, but she kept remembering the steering wheel jerking like a live creature in her hands. Someone had slashed her tires? Another warning? But no. Evidently, the warnings were over. My God, this time they'd almost killed her.

Nick drove her home. He kept asking if she was okay, watching her as if she'd vanish or something.

"Keep your eyes on the road, for goodness' sake," she said.

"That was a really dumb move, going off alone."

"I know. I just —"

"Will you listen now?"

"Yes," she whispered.

He was turning under the Wellspring Ranch sign when she remembered. "Oh no, oh gosh."

"What?" he asked, alarmed.

"The groceries. All the groceries . . . in the truck."

"Jesus, Portia," he muttered.

Lynette was at the house when they got there. She'd fed Gil and the boys, organized everyone, made sure they didn't barrage Portia with questions.

"Thank the Lord you're okay," Lynette said, hugging her.

"I'm fine. Please don't make a fuss."

Lynette stood back, hands on her hips. "Oh, okay, we'll just ignore the fact that you almost got killed."

Portia looked at her friend. "I'm so sorry

to have caused —"

"Enough with the martyr act. And don't worry about the boys. They can manage. I've got to go home to my kids now."

"Thanks, Lynette. I'll never be able to —"

"Oh, shush. You'd do the same. Nick, you take care of her."

"Damn straight I will."

Another hug, and Lynette was gone.

"That's some woman," Gil said. Chalk up one more to the list of Lynette's conquests.

"You have like the biggest bruise on your head," Todd said. He looked a little scared and a little relieved.

She put her hand up to the sore spot. "I bet. I must look awful."

"You look okay," the boy said doubtfully.

She was very glad she hadn't gone to the hospital; Todd would have been so upset. She went to him and hugged him. "I'll be fine."

He squirmed out of her embrace, and she knew he was embarrassed in front of his new friend Doug.

"I'm putting Portia to bed now, guys," Nick said. "Keep it down, will you?"

She realized she was exhausted, and her head still hurt. Was it just that morning she'd been in a New York hotel room, waking to Nick's body beside her?

"The EMT said you had to be watched," Nick told her as they went upstairs.

"Excuse me?"

"When a person has a concussion, they need to be under observation for twenty-four hours. Something about possible complications."

She faced him in the hall. "Nick —"

"Twenty-four hours, that's what he said. And since you wouldn't go to the hospital —"

"Oh, for pity's sake. I'm just going to sleep. I'll be fine in the morning."

"You need to be watched."

"Can I brush my teeth without you?"

His eyes held hers. "You scared the shit out of me, Portia."

She looked down. She had to talk to him. She had to. But not now. She was tired, her head jangled too much. Tomorrow.

She pulled on her favorite long T-shirt to sleep in. Nick hovered, but she was so weary she didn't even mind. She climbed in bed and laid her head back. "Oh, that feels good."

He pulled the rocking chair close and sat down. "You feel okay? The guy told me if you start getting nauseous or dizzy, it might mean —"

"I'm okay. Stop fussing." She looked at him. "Are you going to sit up all night?"

"Yeah."

"You're crazy."

"Like a fox."

She closed her eyes, snuggled into her pillow. She was secretly glad he was there watching over her. She loved him being there, and she'd tell him . . . tomorrow.

Portia woke up and glanced at the clock: 3:35. In the pale moonlight that spilled through her window, she could see Nick slumped in the rocking chair, his head on one shoulder. She studied him for a moment, his dark hair and brows, his mouth and shadowed cheeks. A hand in his lap. Watching over her. A swelling of love gathered in her chest.

She reached out and touched his knee. "Nick."

He came awake fast, startled. "Huh?"

"Nick, it's just me."

"You okay? Sick?"

"I'm all right. I just . . . I woke up . . . Why don't you get in bed? You look so uncomfortable."

After a moment, he rose and slid gingerly into her bed, back propped against the pillow next her. On top of the covers, his clothes still on. "Go to sleep," he said.

"You, too."

"Don't worry about me."

"Okay," she said, and she sighed and slept again.

TWENTY-FOUR

He couldn't believe how stubborn she was. Up in the morning, showered, dressed in shorts and a tank top, insisting on going downstairs to fix breakfast. He thought she looked pale, but he couldn't stop her, and she seemed okay. Except for the big bruise on her temple and a couple others on her shoulder and thigh.

She caught him staring at the bruises. "Ugly, aren't they?"

He switched his gaze away. "They'll fade."

She pulled out cereal boxes, put coffee on, while he sat at the kitchen table feeling like a fifth wheel, still in the rumpled clothes he'd slept in. Not that he'd slept much.

"Why don't you go clean up?" she asked.

"Later. Can I help you, you know, do the dishes or something?"

"Lynette left everything shipshape. Honestly. I can handle this. The boys aren't even up yet."

He rubbed a hand over his face, let his eyes rest on her as she bent over to get something out of a cupboard. Her hair was still damp, pulled back into a clip. One strand had fallen loose, and she pushed it behind her ear. He'd stayed in bed next to her for hours, dozed a little, but mostly he'd watched her. Studied the rise and fall of her breathing, the rounded shape of her hip under the light cover. So many times in those hours he'd wanted to reach over and rest his hand on her bare skin.

His mind shied away from the moment last night when he'd heard her cry out and drop the cell phone, the moment he'd thought she'd been taken from him.

"You should still see a doctor," he tried.

"I don't think so."

"You have a headache? You feel sick?"

"Will you stop?" She turned around and rested her back against the counter. "But I do appreciate your concern. Really I do."

Concern.

"And . . . and thanks for staying with me last night."

"Portia, Jesus, you don't have to thank me."

"You look sleepy."

"Yeah."

"Go on, Nick. Go take a nap."

"Later."

She sighed. "You're laying a real guilt trip on me."

"Okay, so we're even."

She filled two mugs with coffee and sat

down next to him. He could smell her — shampoo and body lotion and her own heady scent. His gut clenched.

She stirred sugar into her coffee. "I wanted to say . . . I wanted you to know that . . . the other night. It was special for me." Her gaze was downcast, her voice soft, intimate. "You know, I was going to tell you yesterday, but there was so much going on. And then the accident . . ."

He put a hand out and tilted her chin toward him. "Me, too," he said.

Her eyes were wide and green, her throat tanned. A graceful line that he longed to trace with a finger. Her mouth was there, so close, pink lips slightly parted. He leaned forward, drawn by a force too strong to resist.

"Oh," he heard her say, then he was kissing her, reaching out to pull her close, crushing her mouth against his, tasting her. Her arms went around his neck, and he could feel her hands on his back.

She tasted sweet and warm, like honey. One hand rose to stroke his hair. They clung together there, in her kitchen, on a sunny morning, blackbirds chattering in a tree outside the open window.

Finally they drew apart and sat there, gazes mingled. He could see her quick breathing. His own heart hammered in his chest.

Then there were feet thumping down the stairs, and the boys crowded into the kitchen.

Portia stood, too fast, her leg bumping the table, sloshing coffee from her mug.

"I'm starved," Todd said.

"All I've got is cereal," Portia said. "The groceries were in the truck."

"That's okay."

Gil appeared a few minutes later. He poured himself coffee and sat at the table. He looked at Portia, then swiveled his glance to Nick. "Everything okay?" he asked.

"Yeah, fine," Nick said.

"We're going riding after breakfast, Dad," Doug said. "Right?"

"That okay?" Gil asked.

"Yes, Todd can show you where everything is. He knows the horses."

"Did you two punks realize I'm the chief wrangler?" Gil said.

"Chief wrangler?" Doug cocked his head.

"Uh-huh, Portia gave me the job."

"Your dad said he used to be a mounted cop, so . . ." Portia said.

"He was," Doug said. "He's always telling stories about his horse. She was named Martha."

Martha. An amused look gathered on Nick's face.

"Yeah, well, she was a gray, you know, sorta like Martha Washington. I know, it's a stretch," Gil said.

"She bucked him off once." Doug grinned broadly.

"I was a rookie," Gil protested.

"Now I'm the rookie," Doug said.

"I think I should put Doug on El Diablo," Todd said.

"El Diablo?"

Nick saw Portia hide a smile.

"Don't worry, he's a pussycat." Todd shrugged.

"El Diablo?"

Gil took the boys out to ride after he'd seen to it that they cleaned up after themselves. Nick went upstairs and showered and thought about what he had to do that day. Another visit to Mahoney was definitely in order. He'd push the guy this time.

He wondered as the water sluiced over him if he hadn't solved this case yet because subconsciously he needed a reason to be near Portia as long as possible. He was even glad he'd worked for the *Star Gazer*, sleazy as the job was. Without it, he never would have met her.

Downstairs again, the house quiet, everyone gone. Portia doing a load of laundry. A clock on the wall ticking patiently.

"Oh," she said, coming from the laundry room. She halted, appeared shy, and he wanted to kiss her again and never stop.

"We can't . . . I mean," she took a deep breath, "we can't do that anymore. The boys . . ."

"Sure, I know." But their eyes met and held.

The phone rang then, and she answered it.

431

He saw her tense up, then put the phone down. "A hang-up?"

"Yes." Her tone was somber.

Maybe it was a good thing, that call. It shook him up, made him recall why he was there. He sat her at the kitchen table and gave her a rundown on his plans.

"Okay, so, this afternoon Gil will be around. I'm going to talk to Mahoney again. Now that I have Burkhart's take on things, I need to push the guy."

"He's not going to confess to you."

"Hell, no. But there are ways around a confession. That's what I do."

"Sorry." She waved hand. "How dumb of me."

"No running off alone?"

"No." She smiled. "I've learned my lesson." Then she put a hand on his arm. "I've been thinking about that bank account you found. Randy and Lynette's? Lynette and I never discuss money, but I remembered Gary telling me, oh, years ago, that Lynette wanted to start a savings account for the boys. You know, college."

"And?"

"Well, I think Gary made a remark about Randy, something like Randy would never be that organized or responsible, but obviously Lynette must have talked him into it, and the money would come from her family, anyway." She shrugged.

"Um," he said, thinking. She was too nice, too good, to recognize deception in others. A college fund? With what he'd seen of Randy, that explanation was not too likely.

"And when you asked me if Gary talked to Aaron right before the accident?"

"Yeah?"

"I've been going over and over that week in my head, and —" Her voice broke.

"Hey, you don't have to —"

"Yes, I do." She looked up and put a brave smile on her lips. "I think Gary did talk to Aaron. He was in the office on the phone, and when he came out, he was upset. I remember because I asked him who that was, but he blew me off, which was so unlike Gary. I guess I was miffed, and that's why I remember."

"It coulda been Mahoney he was talking to."

"I suppose it could have, but I had the impression it was Aaron. Don't ask me why; I really don't know."

"Could you have heard Gary say his name on the phone?"

"Honestly, Nick, I just don't remember."

"If it was Aaron, why do you think a call from him would have upset Gary?"

"Oh, Aaron has this way . . . this way of micromanaging things. Sometimes he can be a little overpowering."

"I get the picture."

433

"Does any of this help?"

"It might."

As soon as Gil brought the hot, dusty boys back for lunch, Nick got ready to leave for Denver.

"Don't let her go off by herself," Nick told the three of them.

"I need to pick the truck up this afternoon," she said. "Cab called. He had new tires put on it."

"I'll give you a ride when I get back," Nick said.

"Maybe Randy can take me," she suggested.

"No, wait till I get back."

"I have to pick it up before five."

"I'll be back," Nick said.

Her head still throbbed, and the bruises were tender to the touch, but other than that, she felt all right. She tried to act cheerful in front of the boys, but in reality she was anxious and worried. Nick was going for Mahoney's throat — she knew that. She heard the resolve in his voice and seen the hard glint in his eye. If he got proof of the developer's guilt, it would all be worth it. But if he didn't succeed, then she was in even more danger.

Someone had tried to kill her last night. She had to keep reminding herself of that. What if she hadn't been wearing her seat belt?

She didn't always wear it, especially if she was running around the ranch or just going into Colt. . . . *My God,* she suddenly thought, the boys had taken the truck right before she'd driven to Castle Rock, what if . . .

But no. Most likely the tires had been tampered with while she'd been in the grocery store. Still, what if she hadn't been alone? Did they care how many were injured or killed? Was she putting everyone she knew in jeopardy?

She was keenly aware of Gil keeping a constant eye on her. The boys, too. He'd obviously enlisted their help. Six pairs of eyes followed her every move. It would have been funny — if it weren't so terribly serious.

She told Gil she had to go to Randy's with a stack of bills and the checkbook, their monthly meeting on finances. "He wanted me to come by after lunch," she said.

"How about I drive you there, wait for you, drive you home?"

"That's silly. I'll just be sitting with Randy writing out checks. It's such a waste of your time."

"I think that's what I'm here for," Gil said dryly.

"I feel like a . . . troublemaker."

"Nah, think of yourself more like a damsel in distress."

"How embarrassing."

Gil sobered. "No, not at all. Nick just

wants to play it safe."

"How about a compromise?" she suggested. "You drive me to Randy's, then you take the boys to fish in the pond below Randy's house. Everything you need is in the garage. I'll call you on your cell when I'm done, and you can pick me up."

Gil thought a minute. "Okay. Deal."

This time Nick strode into Mahoney's front office with a curt nod at the redheaded Cheri.

"He in?" he asked.

"Well yes . . ."

"No calls, okay?"

"I . . ."

He walked past her and pushed open the door to Mahoney's private office. The man was in his shirtsleeves, a pale blue silk tie loosened at the collar; he was on the phone.

"Listen, I'm going to have to call you back," he said. "Something just came up." He put the phone down and fixed a questioning gaze on Nick. "Mr. Sinestra, isn't it? May I ask — ?"

Nick pulled his wallet out and opened it to show Mahoney his badge. He saw the man's eyes flick over it, then rise to Nick's face. "Is this official?"

"You got that right."

Mahoney sat up straight, his blond brows pulled together. "And I suppose your visit the other day had nothing to do with purchasing a homesite?"

"Right again."

"What's going on here?" Angry. A flush under the close-cropped blond beard.

"I'm investigating a murder. I got a couple questions."

"A murder?"

"Gary Wells."

"Wells? That was an accident. What in hell are you talking about?"

Nick sat down uninvited. He leaned forward. "We can do this the easy way or the hard way."

"I don't know what this is all about, but maybe I better call my attorney."

"Sure, go ahead," Nick bluffed. "You'll still have to answer my questions sooner or later."

Mahoney chewed that over for a moment. "I don't have a thing to hide. Wells was killed in an unfortunate accident."

"Yeah, yeah. But with him out of the picture, your Panorama Ranch is a go."

"It would be going forward with or without him. He couldn't stop it."

"That's not what Aaron Burkhart said."

"Aaron Burkhart?"

"Know the man?"

"Slightly."

"He says you flew to Washington and confronted him about the injunction Wells was bringing against you."

"I may have." He lifted his shoulders, dropped them.

"Burkhart told me everything was hunky-dory when you split. You were going to negotiate away all your problems. The injunction was history."

Mahoney looked down at his fingernails, his mouth working. Nick waited a beat, then he asked, "That right?"

"Aaron said that, did he?"

"Oh yeah."

"Look, this was business. A lot of money was involved. I went to see Aaron, yes, and I admit I was damn mad. So was he, as a matter of fact. We talked and ironed a few things out, and I thought everything was settled. At least I was under that impression."

"And suddenly Wells was dead."

"It was an *accident.*"

"Pretty convenient accident."

Mahoney threw his hands up. "Oh, for God's sake, go see Aaron. He's the one who said he could talk Gary out of pursuing the injunction. I have no idea what went on between them. Sorry, but I don't have anything more to tell you."

Nick stood, stared at the man, tapped his fingers on the edge of the gleaming desk. "There was another accident last night. But I suppose you don't know anything about that either."

Mahoney looked up at him, blue eyes

shifting. "An accident?" His forehead was greasy with sweat.

"Mrs. Wells's tires were slashed. Her truck went off the road."

"That's . . . horrible."

Nick waited a moment, then said, "Oh, just in case you were wondering, she's fine today. But, come to think of it, bet you already knew that." Then he tilted so far forward that his face was in Mahoney's. "If you ever come near Portia Wells or her ranch, if you or anyone ever comes near her again, you'll answer to me, pal."

"You can't threaten me," Mahoney said.

"I think I just did."

Nick sucked in a big lungful of air outside of Mahoney Enterprises. He was shaking with anger. He got like that when his temper flared. Gil was always telling him to stay cool, anger would take years off your life. But he didn't feel cool. Neither inside nor out.

He drove out of Denver too fast, leaving downtown behind, swinging onto the interstate south. A heat mirage wrinkled the highway ahead of him, and even with sunglasses, he had to squint. Just outside Castle Rock he saw the damnedest thing: The sky to the west was gray, the mountains no longer so inviting looking. Was it going to rain?

Mahoney had been lying. Burkhart had been lying. Feeding him just enough truth to sweeten the pot, but basically spooning out bullshit. What he had to do was separate the truth from the crap. He drove, kept glancing at the building storm while he went over his conversations with both men. Christ, it was as if the two of them had gotten together to concoct a story. A story that made them both out to be choirboys, with just enough divergence to avoid being too pat. Yeah, their stories were so close, too close. No way could two people remember so many details from a conversation that took place a year ago. No damn way.

And there it was, at last, the missing piece to the puzzle, staring Nick in the face, as if it had been right there all along, big as life.

The two of them. "Oh, man," he whispered, banging the steering wheel with a palm.

Burkhart and Mahoney, joining forces against Gary Wells, whose intransigence was going to cost Mahoney millions and Burkhart his reputation and his precious NPS. Yeah, they met, all right. They talked; and it wouldn't have taken long for two smart, ambitious guys like that to figure out how to disappear their little problem.

Goddamn, the two of them together. But Nick would bet his life neither had bloodied his own hands. So who did they hire to do the dirty deed? Out-of-owners? Maybe even those nitwits who'd played security before

Nick had let them go. Maybe. But two others had accosted Portia at the Co-op — the same two who'd tried to kill her last night? Guys could have been out of Las Vegas or L.A. Cheap help.

Fine, Nick thought. But there was still that lingering question, same question that bothered Whitefeather. Boys from Vegas or L.A. or where-the-hell-ever wouldn't know squat about sabotaging a ranch, burning barns, cutting the right fences, fouling water tanks. That took local knowledge. Yeah, he mused. The local connection.

"Look, Randy," Portia said.

"What?"

"Clouds. See, over the foothills?"

He stared out the window. "I'll be damned."

"Was there rain in the forecast?"

He shrugged. "The usual. Twenty percent chance. They've been wrong every day for weeks now."

She looked again: yes, there was a definite line of clouds coming from the west, staining the hot, golden hills gray. "Wouldn't it be wonderful . . . ?" she said.

"Probably dry up before it hits the ground."

"Let's hope not."

They'd been sitting in Randy's office, and she'd been writing out checks. The room was too warm and stuffy, and she was glad they were about done.

Lynette had taken their three kids into Colt to run errands, so they'd been left alone to do their work. All those bills, so little in the account. She thought for a heartbeat about the bank account Nick had found, $60,000. She still didn't have the nerve to ask about it, though.

Her brother-in-law was restless, pacing. He never sat down. She knew he hated paperwork. He'd rather be out in the heat or the teeth-chattering cold working at something physical.

She glanced at her watch. Almost four. Damn. When was Nick going to get back? She needed the truck.

"Portia, I gotta talk to you," Randy said.

She finished marking a bill paid and shuffled through the file box to file the invoice. "Sure."

He stopped moving. "Why are you so stubborn about the ranch and the NPS?"

Here we go again, she thought. She said nothing. She'd learned it was better not to say much when Randy was on one of his tirades. What famous man had said you never got in trouble for something you didn't say? She turned back to the checkbook, studiously going over her figures.

"And Mahoney? Who gives a good goddamn if he builds a golf course? If he doesn't, someone else will."

She placed the pen down, thought, *Oh well,* and said quietly, "It isn't just the golf course, Randy. It's Gary's murder. Your *brother's* murder."

"Murder," he scoffed.

"The man has to pay. He can't get away with killing Gary." She drew in a breath. "That's where Nick is right now."

"What?"

"He went to see Mahoney."

"I don't trust your precious cop."

"I do."

"He's sure as hell got you bamboozled."

"He's a good man, Randy."

He cut the air with a hand, his mouth contorted. She was about out of patience, ready to tell him to stay out of her life once and for all, when she heard Lynette's car pull up outside. Then she could hear Lynette and the three boys, car doors slamming, the front door opening, banging shut.

Her anger dissipated. "I've got to get the truck," she said. "Nick was going to give me a ride to pick it up. I've got to get it before five."

"Where's your shadow?"

"Gil? Fishing with the boys. I'll try him."

"You won't reach him."

"Why not? He has his cell phone."

"Can't get a signal down at the pond."

She tried to reach Gil anyway, but as

443

Randy said, there was no reception.

She tried Nick's cell phone. He must be on the way back by now. Again, no reception. He was probably in one of the dead zones between Denver and Castle Rock.

"I guess I could get the truck tomorrow," she said.

Randy stared at her. "I'll give you a ride."

She was a little surprised; he was usually not so accommodating.

"It's just into Colt, right?" He looked out the window then, at the approaching storm.

"Yes, it's at the garage."

"No problem. It's too late to start with the accounts receivable now, anyway." He turned away, digging into his pocket for his keys.

She supposed Nick would be mad, but the truth was, she wasn't going anywhere alone. She was just getting a lift from her brother-in-law. And she'd ask Randy to follow her all the way back to the ranch.

Randy stuck his head in the kitchen, where Lynette was putting away groceries. "I'm giving Portia a ride to get her truck," he said, then before Lynette could reply, he was out the door.

"Hey, Lynette," Portia said, her head still ducked in the door, "if Gil calls or comes back, tell him where I am. Tell him I didn't go off alone. And, God, if Nick gets here, make certain he knows, too."

"Sure thing," Lynette replied. "You drive carefully, hear?"

Portia settled herself in the truck as Randy pulled out of his driveway. He was awfully quiet. He probably felt bad, yelling at her earlier. That was Randy, shooting off his mouth before he thought. She knew he'd never be crazy about her, but they could manage to get along. They had to.

Over the foothills, the gray line of clouds was much closer. Dust devils whirled across the rangeland. "It's definitely going to rain," Portia said.

"Maybe."

"It is, it really is."

At the intersection of the county road and the old frontage highway, Randy turned left instead of right.

"Um, the garage is the other way, isn't it? In Colt, I mean?" she asked carefully.

He didn't answer, just sped up. A blast of wind flung grit against the windshield, and lightning forked in the field beside the road. Thunder rolled a moment later, deafening.

He drove faster.

"Randy," she said. Something was wrong. "Randy?" she said again.

He stared straight ahead, and she could feel the truck surge forward as the first swollen raindrops spattered on the windshield.

TWENTY-FIVE

Nick was figuring all the angles as he drove toward Colt. How to nail Burkhart and Mahoney — maybe one would rat the other out, turn state's evidence in exchange for leniency. But he needed hard evidence, not just his cop's instinct. And he still couldn't picture Mr. Perfect Golf Tan or Mr. Genial Developer getting his hands dirty tossing dead animals in a watering trough. No way. He had to find the thug, the local with ranch know-how; the one Cab Whitefeather was sure existed.

He'd turned his cell phone on when he'd left Mahoney's office, and he tried Portia's number. Couldn't get through. He punched in Gil's cell. Same thing. He was in a dead zone.

He drove, and he noticed that the sunlight had dimmed; the sky was very dark off to his right, the mountains blotted out. Dust whirled across the interstate, and lightning flickered ahead of him. A few raindrops smacked his windshield.

It really was going to rain. Amazing.

His phone finally trilled, and he snatched it up. "Yeah?"

"It's me." Gil.

"I'm on my way. Tell Portia —"

"That's just it," Gil said, and Nick didn't like the tone of his voice.

"Is Portia okay?" he cut in.

"She took off with Randy about ten minutes go. Went to get her truck."

"Shit. She was supposed to wait for me."

"Yeah, I know. I tried her cell phone a couple minutes ago. Nothing."

"Oh, man," Nick said. He knew there was service between the ranch and Colt. Maybe her phone was switched off. Could be the battery . . .

What the hell was she doing, going off with that idiot Randy?

He started to say something to Gil, and then suddenly the hairs on the back of his neck stood up. *Randy.* "Is Lynette there with you?" he got out.

"Yeah."

"Keep her there. I'll be at the ranch in five minutes." *A fucking eternity.*

The windshield wipers swished back and forth, leaving smears of dead insects behind. Rain blew sideways across the road. Precious rain. But what good was it doing her now?

Her phone rang, and her heart leaped in her chest. Nick, it was Nick. He knew she

447

was in trouble. She pulled the handset out of her purse, fumbling with shaking fingers.

But Randy reached across and yanked it out of her hand. He rolled down his window and threw it out, not saying a word. Rolled up the window against the torrent.

"Randy," she said, trying to keep her voice in control. "You don't have to do this. Just turn around and take me home."

Nothing.

She braced herself against the door. He was driving so fast the pickup rocked crazily and hydroplaned, and the rain was so heavy you could hardly see.

"Randy," she tried again.

He stepped on the brakes and swung the wheel. The truck fishtailed on the wet road, then bumped over gravel. He'd turned in somewhere, a parking lot. She tried to see out of the side window, but it was too steamed up.

Randy. She couldn't believe he was the one . . . He'd done all those things. Killed Gary? Killed his own brother? No, he couldn't have, but . . .

He braked hard, drove around a building — she could see it now — the abandoned drive-in theater. The place had been closed for years, sitting on the frontage road, off the main track once the interstate had been built. A low building with bunkerlike windows, mostly broken, a cracked concrete pad around it. The refreshment stand.

Why here? What was he going to do?

He switched off the ignition and opened his door, slid out into the rain, dragging her across the seat with him.

"*Randy!*" she cried. "Please, think about what you're doing. You have children. Oh my God, Randy."

The rain hit her in a deluge, blinding her. Lightning split the sky, thunder shook the ground.

She tried to twist away from him, her skin wet and slippery. She'd run, hide somewhere. Jump in his truck . . . Had he left the keys in it?

She struggled, striking out, but he was strong. He had her arm in an iron grip, and he hauled her along like a calf ready for branding. She slid then on the wet, cracked earth, the soil so dry the rain pooled on top of it, and she went to her knees, but he dragged her up. She couldn't get away, not in this storm; she couldn't run on the slick ground, couldn't even see. . . .

Nick. Nick would find her. He knew . . . Lynette would tell him . . . but he wouldn't know where.

Randy kicked open the back door of the building and thrust her inside so hard she fell. Then he stood there panting, his hair dripping water, his shirt plastered to his torso.

She looked frantically around for a place to run, to hide. Nothing but broken countertops, a bare floor, and shattered glass and splotchy cement block walls, lit in stop-action flashes by lightning, rattled by thunder.

"Randy," she gasped desperately, her heart leaping wildly in her chest.

Nick burst in the front door, the sprint from the car soaking him to the skin. He wiped water off his face, saw Lynette sitting stiffly on the couch, Gil rising to meet him.

"I tried her cell again. She still doesn't answer." He looked around. The boys . . . "Where are the kids?"

"Up at Portia's. Todd and Doug are watching them," Gil said. "Don't worry about them."

Lynette looked scared, hugging herself, her normally cheerful face ashen. "I . . . I got home from doing errands, and, and they were here, in the office. Everything was fine . . . normal."

"How did Portia seem?" he demanded.

"Okay. I don't know. . . . Randy, he said he was taking her to pick up the truck."

"Damn it, I told her to wait," he said under his breath.

"What . . . what's going on?" Lynette asked. "What do you think . . . ?"

The light in the house was oddly dimmed,

rain drumming on the roof, thunder crashing, the trees outside tossing madly.

"Look, Lynette, I just want to find them, okay?" He turned to Gil. "You checked with the garage?"

"Lynette called. Portia and Randy never showed."

He thought furiously, trying not to let fear hamper his reasoning. They'd left fifteen, twenty minutes ago, couldn't be far.

"Gil, get a hold of Whitefeather, have him put an APB out on Randy's truck. Lynette, you know the tag number?"

"Yes." Scared, her voice breaking. "It's 441 DGB, a '94 Ford pickup. White."

"Good girl." He went to her and put a hand on her arm. *Easy, go easy, this is her husband, the father of her children.*

"Please, please, tell me what's wrong," she said. "What . . . ?" Her voice ended in a sob.

"Come on, it'll be okay. That's a girl." He spoke carefully, wanting to swear and race out into this storm to search for Portia. Wanting to do something.

Lightning flashed, a strobe pulse, thunder coming so quickly on its heels he flinched.

He crouched down then and leaned forward, elbows on knees. "I'll tell you what I think's going on, Lynette." *Easy does it,* he reminded himself, while his mind screamed for action. "I think Randy is involved with Patrick Mahoney and Aaron Burkhart. I think they had something to do with Gary's . . . accident."

She gasped and covered her face with her hands. "No, no."

"I don't have proof, but it looks that way. You understand, we have to find them? Fast."

"Randy wouldn't . . . he wouldn't . . ."

"You know him best, Lynette. You can help. But we need to find them before it's too late. Where would he take her?" *Hurry, goddamn it.*

"Oh God, oh God, I don't know." She started crying.

He patted her knee. "Think now. He can't be far. Somewhere around here. Someplace he knows, where he feels safe."

She gulped and took her hands from her face. Her eyes were red, her cheeks mottled now. Outside thunder boomed, rattling windows and china in a dining room breakfront. "Last night, oh God, last night, he was a mess. I didn't know . . . I thought it was just the ranch, money . . . How could I have known?"

Hurry, Lynette. He forced himself to stay calm. "Okay, what did he say?"

"He . . . cried. It was like he just gave up. He said he couldn't take it anymore. I held him. I . . . I tried to comfort him, but he was . . . just . . ." She wiped her nose with the back of her hand, like a child. "He . . . he kept saying he wished it was over and he could go back to the way it was."

He let her talk, wanting to yell at her in frustration, but she had to go at her own pace.

"He was so . . . unhappy. So upset. I was afraid. I've never been afraid of Randy." She looked at Nick. "He cried, and he talked about the craziest things, when we were dating and when he . . . proposed, and . . ." Her voice clicked off.

"Come on, Lynette, you're doing great."

She sniffed, sucked in a rattling breath. "He talked about the old drive-in . . . where we used to go . . . where he asked me to marry him."

"Drive-in?"

"It's been closed for years . . . on the old highway . . ."

But he was no longer listening. He knew the place, had driven by it on his way to see Whitefeather at that fire.

Gil brought her a tissue, and she took it, her hands unsteady. "I got the undersheriff," Gil told him.

Nick stood. "Call him back, tell him to meet me at the old drive-in. He'll know the place. Jesus," he whispered.

"Go on," Gil said, "I'll be here just in case they show up."

But they both knew that wasn't even a remote possibility.

He ran back out into the storm, revved the

engine, spun out of the driveway, keeping the turns he needed to make in his head. Not far, ten minutes maybe, he figured. The windshield wipers stroked a quick rhythm; his world closed in until all he saw was the road in front of him, raindrops splashing from its surface, the streak of lasers splitting the sky.

What if Randy hadn't taken her to the drive-in? What then?

He leaned forward, trying to make out the road, his hands grasping the wheel like claws. The rain slashed at the car, and he could feel his tires lose traction. Thunder still boomed, farther off now, and his body reverberated with its roar.

Ten minutes. Follow the county road to the intersection. Turn left. It'd be on his right on the frontage road. He blinked, trying to see. Everything was gray, drenched, blotted out by the rain.

What if she wasn't there?

A clump of tumbleweed rushed out of nowhere, bounced off his bumper, then flew on across the road. Hurry, hurry.

There . . . the turnoff . . . He yanked at the wheel, lurching onto gravel, rear tires spinning, then catching. A parking lot, a movie screen, a few forlorn speaker posts. A low building, blurred in the rain.

No truck, nobody. An abandoned drive-in. What in hell had made him think she was here?

He pulled around the building, hands slippery with rain and sweat on the steering wheel. Just in case . . . just in case . . .

His heartbeat skipped. The truck. The white pickup.

He slammed on the brakes. No one could have heard him over this storm. Unless Randy had been watching. But why would he?

He took in the scene swiftly, professionally. Poor lighting, intense background noise. Ideal. A low cement block building, a door. Looked ajar. Probably another door around front. He pulled his gun from the glove compartment, checked the clip.

Hurry up, goddamn it. Slid out of the car, not closing the door in case Randy could hear it, crouched, running through the downpour to the pickup, opening the door with one hand, holding his weapon out with the other.

Empty. Okay.

Flattening himself against the building next to the door. Straining his ears. Voices? Nothing. The rain was too loud, masking everything.

He leaned against the wall next to the open door, wiped water from his face, blinked it out of his eyes.

A quick rush, slamming the door open, crouching to one side, sweeping the gun from corner to corner with both ends.

A yell. A shadowed figure leaping at him. He stepped sideways, a reflex move, but the figure closed with him. Grunting, frantic, holding him so he couldn't use his weapon.

Randy was strong, wrestling, trying to grab the gun. Nick stepped back, lowered his guard for a split second. Randy lurched forward. Timing, get it right. A quick move, his arm free, the gun crashing down on Randy's head, the body going limp, dropping like a stone.

Panting, Nick stood over the man for a moment; then he heard her voice.

"Nick, oh Nick!"

And she was there, falling into his arms, wet and cold and shaking, crying out his name over and over. He held her so tightly he was afraid he might hurt her. An endless embrace, there in the sad, forgotten building, the rain thundering on the tin roof.

Finally, he had to let her go. Had to get things taken care of.

"You're all right?" he asked, searching her face.

"Yes. Scared to death." Her eyes were wet with tears, her hair soaked. Her clothes soaked. "How did you find me?"

"Lynette."

"Oh my God, Lynette. Oh, poor Lynette. What is she going to do?"

He called Gil. Got hold of Cab, who was

five minutes out. Kept his weapon on Randy, who was beginning to groan.

Portia was still pale, trembling. "I can't believe it was Randy. I can't —"

"Believe it," Nick said.

TWENTY-SIX

She hugged Lynette hard. "I'm going to miss you so much."

"Me, too." Lynette's voice was raspy.

"You know I'll be back to visit. Whenever I can."

"I know. And I'm coming to New York. Next month. Mom's going to watch the kids. It's all set."

"You're going to be fine," Portia said. "You'll see, everything will work out."

Lynette drew back and looked at her miserably. "A new life, right?"

"Right."

Nick checked his watch. "We have to get going."

She wiped her eyes. "Okay, in a minute."

"This is so hard," Lynette said. "Everything is . . . different now."

"You'll do great. You'll be overrun with men waiting to date you."

Lynette tried to smile. "I'm not so sure I'm ready for that yet."

"You have time."

"Portia . . ." Nick said.

"I'm coming." She squeezed Lynette's hands and said, "Take care of those boys."

"I will."

"I'll call. We'll talk every day."

"Every day," Lynnette echoed. "And I'll see you in a few weeks."

Portia couldn't believe she was driving away, leaving the ranch behind, starting a new life.

But while she was moving back to the city with the man she loved, Lynette was moving into Castle Rock to stay with her parents for a while until Randy's fate was decided, until she knew where to go from there.

"That was awful." Portia sighed.

"Yeah."

"She'll be okay, though. Lynette's a survivor. Her family —" She had to stop.

She looked out her window as Nick drove down the ranch road. The fields stretched away to the foothills, greener now that the drought had broken. Cattle dotted the far pastures. It was September, the summer heat dulled, and in the field next to the road bales of hay lay in neat rows like dominos, curing, awaiting storage for winter feed. The fall crop wasn't spectacular, but the monsoon rains had helped enormously. She'd miss the ranch, oh how she'd miss the land. But it was better this way.

She and Lynette had arranged for an executor to oversee the ranch until Lynette's sons and Todd came of age. Juan and Hernando were moving in with their families as soon as Lynette vacated her house, and they'd manage the spread. They were good people.

Things would work out. She believed that.

"Sad?" Nick asked, driving under the Wellspring Ranch sign, turning onto the county road.

"Yes, I'm sad. But I'm happy, too."

"That's good." He reached over and squeezed her hand. "I want you to be happy."

She smiled. "I am."

"I hope the painters are done," he said.

"We'll stay in your old place if they aren't."

He flinched. "Bad idea."

"So, it's a bachelor pad. I can handle it."

She felt as if she could handle anything now. The weeks since Randy's arrest had flown by. Nick had gone back to New York to return to work in August, and she'd been to the city a few weeks ago to help him look for a new apartment.

She had asked Todd what he wanted to do, and he'd opted for New York. He'd been disappointed when the best option for the time being was for him to live with Judith and Anna, to start the school year in New Rochelle. Remarkably, the situation was working out better than anyone expected.

"He's so noisy," Judith had complained on the phone.

"Kids are," Portia had replied.

"And he eats so much. Anna and I just can't keep food in the house."

"He's a growing boy."

"He does like my marble cake, though."

The board of directors of the Nature Preservation Society had ratified Portia as the new president on September first, and she'd been desperately busy learning the ropes of her position, arranging for the executor of the ranch, going over everything with Lynette and Juan and Hernando, packing and moving and looking for an apartment with Nick.

Busy and exquisitely happy.

Nick had been in close contact with the Douglas County district attorney regarding the capital murder case against Aaron Burkhart, Patrick Mahoney, and Randy Wells. All three were awaiting separate trials. Burkhart and Mahoney had hired high-priced legal counsel, dream teams, but Randy was singing like a bird on the advice of his public defender. The only comforting news Portia had heard was that Randy claimed all he'd done was give Burkhart and Mahoney information as to Gary's whereabouts the night of his murder. Randy had not been the one who'd forced his brother off the road. He'd sworn to Lynette it was the men who'd confronted Portia at the Co-op. Nor had Randy been behind the arson. If Randy wasn't lying to Lynette, the security men — who were *not* security at all — had torched the barn. But Randy had cut the fences and made the phone calls and even shot the animal and dumped it in the water tank. He'd admitted that much. Portia still couldn't quite fit her mind around Randy sabotaging his beloved ranch, but she supposed you never really knew what horrible acts a desperate person was capable of committing.

Nick had assured her there was enough evidence to convict Mahoney and Burkhart and their hired help for murder. Randy would probably do jail time for a lesser degree of complicity in the death of his brother. No charges could be brought against him for the sabotage at the ranch, however; couldn't charge someone for defacing his own property. And she and Nick would have to testify at the trial. But that was a year down the road.

"I love you, you know," she said as Nick steered onto the interstate.

"Yeah, I know."

"Don't get too cocky."

"Who, me?"

"You're supposed to say, 'I love you, too.' "

"I love you, too."

"I know," she said smugly.

"We should get married pretty soon," he ventured.

"Okay, when?"

"Oh, lady, you are too easy."

"No fuss. My mother and Anna. Your folks. Your brother and his family. Todd. Lynette."

"Don't forget Gil and Gladys."

"Right."

"Somehow I can't see my mom and pop clinking glasses with Judith," he said, shaking his head. "So maybe we could do it at the courthouse?"

"Whatever you want."

"Really?" he said. "I thought you'd —"

"It would be nice to go out with everyone for dinner afterward."

"Mom's gonna want to cook," he warned her.

"Uh-uh, no one is cooking."

"You tell her."

"I will, no problem." She put a hand on his knee. "What do you think about children?" Her heart beat too fast.

He shot her a look.

"It's just that . . ." She took a breath. "I've been to a specialist in Denver."

"You didn't tell me?"

"I wanted to hear what he had to say first."

"So, what'd he say?"

"Well, it's kind of complicated. Hormones and that sort of thing."

"And?"

"I have a low progesterone level. That's why I could never carry a baby to term. If I take progesterone, well, it might make a difference."

"You still want kids, don't you?"

"I want *your* children."

"Then take that stuff. We'll give it a try."

"I'm so glad we found each other," she whispered, resting her head on his shoulder.

"Think it was fate?"

"No, actually, I think it was the *Star Gazer*," she said.

He groaned. "You gonna remind me of that every day?"

"Well, not every day. Maybe only every other day."

"For the rest of my life?"

"Oh yes, for the rest of your life."